April Showers

D1526467

A
Trey Branson
NOVEL

The characters in this book are fictitious. Any similarity to real persons,
living or dead, is coincidental and not intended by the author.

Get. Up. And. Go. Get. It.

You're the prettiest girl on your block.
Brains and Beauty.
You have your entire life ahead of you.
Take it slow.
The fast life will eat you alive.
You don't *love* the hustler.
You *love* the lifestyle.

But, the streets…
Don't love *nobody*.

PRELUDE

Listen, I'm not even gonna lie to you, I'm a selfish little bitch. Everything is *always* about *me*, because in *my* world I'm the only one who exists. Not that I'm necessarily proud of that, but it's a fact that I won't deny. After all, I'm only fourteen, so at this stage in my life the only thing that matters to me, is *me* and doing the things that I like to do!

On May 14, 1987 somewhere in Brooklyn, New York my mother pushed me out her womb and named me April. Wait, I know what you're probably thinking, if this girl was born in *May*, why would her mother name her *April*? Well, if you were ever to meet my Mom and witness her corny sense of humor first hand, then you would definitely understand. See, the last name is Showers. Do you get it now?

April *Showers*.

I guess the old saying goes, 'April showers, brings May flowers.' Mommy said that was her own special way of calling me her *flower*. Personally, I think it's very corny. But then again, I'm just happy that she didn't lose her damn mind completely and name me *Flower*! Can you imagine that?

Flower Showers? Yikes!

Hell, she would've been better off naming me *Snow Showers*, I think it has a better ring to it. Not that it even matters anymore because the damage is already done, the name is already on my birth certificate and now I'm stuck with it!

Anyway, let me get on with the story. I'm my Daddy's second daughter, *but* I'm Mommy's firstborn child. Before my parents got married, my Daddy had my older sister, Tiffany. My Mom told me that Tiffany was a mistake, I'm not really sure what that means, but I'm damn sure that she'd never repeat that shit in front of my Daddy. Mistake or not, I'm glad it happened, because Tiffany is like my tour guide through these confusing years as a teenager.

Five years after Tiffany was born, once my parents were together and finally tied the knot, that's when I arrived. Next came my little sister La Reina, or 'La La' for short. La La is twelve, but she *thinks* she a grown ass woman and I'm almost positive that one of these days, I'm gonna end up in prison for killing her little ass. She's too smart for her own good. She's nosy, and she has a smart-ass mouth amongst other things, *please* don't get me started.

Now, I'll give you the two reasons why my Momma lost her sexy, slim hourglass frame. Their names are Cory and Carlito, Cory is seven and Carlito is six. Daddy wasn't happy with three girls, well I shouldn't say he wasn't happy, so I'll just say he wasn't content with only daughters. Let my Mom tell it, Daddy literally chased her around the bedroom until she finally popped out a boy, and then he kept pounding away until she popped out another son soon after.

Up until the time Mommy had my two little brothers, she wore a size 4, and was super-sexy. Olivia Showers is half Venezuelan, half Italian and her curves had been the type to stop traffic. Now at the age of thirty-six, and four children later, she wears a size ten. If you ask me, she still looks fabulous, she's thick in all the right places, but she's self- conscious because she's not the size she was before the boys were born. Mommy's has this bad habit of walking into my room without knocking, and there's been times when she's seen me naked and I peeped the jealousy in her eyes. She probably remembers when her own body was as young and as tender as mine, and it was obvious that she envied my perfect shape. But she couldn't blame anyone but herself, nobody told her to let Daddy keep shooting sperm in her direction like she was his own personal baby-making machine.

These days, Mommy has her tubes tied, but in my opinion it's too late, because the damage had already been done. I guess if she woulda just got her tubes tied right after she birthed *me*, we would both be much happier. I'd be the only child, spoiled rotten, and she'd still be shaped like Roselyn Sanchez. But I guess hindsight is 20/20, huh?

Last, but not least is Daddy. My Daddy's name is Stacey. Stacey Showers. And he's Fine! And I don't see anything wrong with me acknowledging how handsome my Daddy is. He sorta looks like Terrance Howard the actor, except Daddy is cuter. He's light skinned, black and Dominican, with short black wavy hair, a medium build and light grey eyes. Daddy used to be the man back in the days, one of my aunts told me that he was once known for being one of the biggest hustlers in Brooklyn. My Aunt Tracey, who's my Daddy's twin sister also told me that my sister Tiffany's mother used to be one of my Dad's 'mules' back in those days. I don't know exactly what that means, but it doesn't sound too flattering. And while we're on the subject, my aunt talks too damn much, she's the last bitch I'd tell any of my business to.

From what I've heard, my father and uncles had one hell of a cocaine empire back in the good days. But, some how things went sour. Some people got killed, some people went to prison, and for some reason my family had to flee Brooklyn and migrated upstate to Buffalo. Right now, Daddy is a chef at the Adam's Mark Hotel. I guess the coke game is dead, 'cause he'd traded in his Benz for a Dodge minivan and now all the lavish gifts have slowed up. Mommy's a nursing student at the community college, and she doesn't work, so we're living off one modest income. Long story made short, money is tight.

Don't get me wrong, shit isn't *bad*, like *poverty* bad. I mean, we don't sleep in our minivan or nothing like that. We actually live in a nice big house in Buffalo's University District, we definitely not broke or living in the slums. When I say that money is tight, I just mean that there's not enough being pushed in my direction anymore. And that's where the problem comes in.

See, I'm a fly bitch! I deserve top of the line everything. My closet should be overflowing with top shelf designer label clothing. I should have *every* pair of Jordan 23's, Air Forces and Air Max's that are released, covering my pretty feet. But as of right now, I'm a long way from the top of my game. But that's soon to change, because I do plan to reach my maximum potential *very* soon.

My Daddy is the problem. All the way around the board he's hindering my progress. Long gone are the days when he brought in enough money to keep us all laced. Pardon me for sounding ungrateful, because he do pay the mortgage and keep the lights and heat on in the house. But shit, don't have all these damn kids if there isn't enough money to have us all living comfortably.

I'm just saying.

On top of that, the main reason I'm not on the level I should be, is because he won't let me date. That's my biggest problem with Daddy. I'm gonna be honest, these niggas can't wait to spend their dope money on me. They damn near break their necks to get a peak at my plump young ass when I'm out with my Mom. They blow their foreign car horns at me and stop traffic trying to get my number when I'm on the way home from school. Niggas definitely be checking for me! But it's too hard to mingle and make progress, when I have to sneak around behind Daddy's back. Don't get me wrong, I do get my hustle on. I've got a few young ballers who sponsor me. Sneakers, accessories, an outfit here and there, cash even. But, there's only so many gifts I can accept before Daddy becomes suspicious. Daddy's the obstacle I need to hurdle in order to live the glamorous life, and I'm growing more and more impatient as I creep towards the ripe age of fifteen.

My mission is to reach Diva status. I want the finer things in life.   *Why*?

'Cause like I told you, I *deserve it*! What do I mean by finer things? Shit, whatever that means to you.

I want it *all*!

Don't judge me. This is my life. This is my story. I keep it very simple and I simply keep it real. So pay attention, 'cause I'm only gonna tell you this story one time...

CHAPTER ONE

The knock on the door woke me from my beauty sleep. I opened my almond shaped eyes and checked my alarm clock, realizing that it was only 7:05 am. I don't know why this woman even bothered to buy me an alarm clock in the first place. Every night I set the alarm to wake me up in the morning, and every morning she makes it her business to wake me up before the alarm goes off.

I ignored the knock at the door and rolled over onto my stomach instead. I could hear the knob twist and then the soft footsteps walking across my carpet. With the door now open, I could hear the normal sounds of a weekday morning. Cory and Carlito were chasing each other up and down the hallway, and La La was blasting her stereo system as usual, she was listening to the new Nelly CD.

My mattress dipped as my Mom climbed onto the bed next to me. "April, stop acting like you're sleep, it's time to get up for school." She said softly. I didn't respond, instead I began to lightly fake like I was snoring. Mommy started to laugh and her hands immediately grabbed my waist.

"Mommy!" I blurted while laughing as she began to tickle me non-stop. When I rolled over and tried to swat her hands away, all I did was expose my stomach and made it worst, now she had more of a target and it became unbearable. "Okay! Okay!" I tried to surrender while crawling to the edge of my queen-sized bed. "I'm up! Mommy stop!" I pleaded with an involuntary smile on my face. This was how the majority of my mornings started, and I kinda enjoyed it. No matter how fast I tried to grow up, I was still a little girl at heart.

I squinted and covered my eyes as she turned on the big lamp on my nightstand, then stretched across my bed. "If you want a ride to school, you'll have to hurry. If not, you'll have to take the bus. We're leaving at 7:50 on the dot." Mommy said.

I shrugged it off because it made no difference to me. I was too old for the family carpool. Being dropped off in front of the high school with my whole family inside the family minivan wasn't exactly my idea of a diva-style arrival.

"I'm good," I told her. "I'll take the bus." I replied as I stretched and yawned.

Mommy smiled and rolled her eyes. "Let me find out," she crawled over to where I sat on the edge of the mattress and wrapped her arms around my shoulders. "You think you're too grown to get dropped off at school?" she asked playfully.

I lay my head against her body as she held me. "Not too grown to get dropped off," I replied. "I'm just too grown to get dropped off by the Daycare Van." I broke into laughter as she began to tickle me again for using my derogatory nickname for her Dodge Caravan.

"Oh I see, you wanna get dropped of by some baller, huh?" she asked me and I giggled. "A baller with a big chain, a nice car with some big rims, and his music blasting from the trunk!" Now we were both giggling.

"Yup." I answered shyly. Even though she was partly joking, my answer was dead serious. She must have been able to read my mind, but I had to remember that Mommy had been my age once, she knew what was going on inside my head.

She hugged me tighter. "Be careful around these boys, April. You're beautiful, and these young fools are going to be lined up around the corner to steal your heart. You have to be careful who you let inside your world, because the wrong man can ruin you." My Mom whispered softly. "You don't want to end up like your cousin, Winter." She warned me for the gazillionth time.

Legend has it, my big cousin Winter is in prison doing time because of her boyfriend. She's my cousin on my Dad's side of the family and I haven't seen her since I was a toddler growing up in Brooklyn. I listened and took heed to what Mommy was saying, but that shit really went into one ear and came out the other, she really knew how to rain on a parade.

"I hear you, Ma." I replied because I had to. I had to say something or else she would just keep going on and on, getting deeper and deeper.

She kissed my forehead. "Who knows, maybe Calvin will get a car soon, and then he can take you to school." She said this just to get a rise out of me, and then giggled while checking my expression as I rolled my eyes at her. She was definitely playing.

Calvin was our neighbor from across the street. He's three years older than me, but has a mean crush on a bitch. And why wouldn't he? I was everything that he could dream of having. I was every young boys type, but Calvin wasn't mine. He didn't have a thuggish bone in his body, and I was looking for a real man.

"*If* Calvin get's a car, then he can take me to the mall and I'll let him spend his McDonald's check on me." That was my response to my Mom's little joke. She knew that I wasn't interested in that boy, and she found my reply hilarious. Her face lit up, and to her it was just comical.

"Little girl, you are too much! Tiffany's been giving you some game?" She was laughing, "I know you better not let your Daddy hear you talking like that. He'll lock you in this room forever!" she winked at me. She was joking, but I could read the warning between the lines. If it was up to my Dad, I'd be going to an all girl's school and I knew better than to even mention a boy's name in front of his crazy ass.

"I'm just kidding." I lied as I lifted my head and then stood up from the bed. She looked at me with both eyebrows raised, and a wide grin on her face, she saw right thru me. "Okay, I'm serious." I admitted with a sly smile, and we both started to laugh again. "I'll let him take me shopping, but I won't let him touch my peaches, I promise!" I shot her a naughty look and quickly tried to slide past her on the way to the bathroom. Peaches is our code word for 'vagina'.

Mommy smacked me hard on the butt as I tried to slip by. "You'd better not give *anyone* your peaches!" she snapped at me violently, as her smile quickly faded and turned into a scowl. She grabbed my arm just as I reached for my bedroom door, "*April?*" Mommy stood up and was now leaned over me with a three-inch height advantage.

I exhaled loudly and rolled my eyes. Every time our conversation drifted into this direction, I gave her as much attitude as possible. "No Mommy, I'm not having sex!" I blurted in a semi-hushed, but forceful tone. I gave her my answer before she could even ask her question, but tried to keep my voice down just in case my Daddy was lurking in the hallway like he sometimes does. She looked at me with her eyes narrowed, as if that would allow her to determine if I was lying or not. She searched my face for the slightest sign of deceit. I showed none. My poker face was in full effect. When she was satisfied, she let go of my arm and placed a kiss on the bridge of my nose.

"I love you." She proclaimed.

"I love you too." I said before heading out my bedroom door and down the hall. La La's door was closed, and the music was thumping from inside. That Nelly CD was starting to get on my fucking nerves, she'd been playing it for at least two weeks straight. The bathroom was at the end of the hall, just to the right of it was my little brothers room. Just as I was about to go inside for my shower, Carlito darted out the boy's bedroom, running right into me with Cory right behind him.

"Slow down!" I yelled at the two of them as Lito ran behind my leg, using me as a shield from his big brother.

"Help, April!" Lito began laughing as his brother stopped in front of me, pausing in his pursuit. It was too early for this wrestling shit. When they weren't wrestling with each other, they were watching wrestling on TV. If they were too tired to wrestle with each other and wrestling wasn't on TV, they would just play the wrestling game on the PlayStation.

Lito had a firm grip on me, with his little arms wrapped around my thigh. "Carlito, I'm about to get in the shower and I don't have time to play wit' ya'll right now." I tried to speak calmly, but by now Cory had lost his patience and had begun trying to pry Lito's grasp from my thigh. I turned to look back down the hall towards my room, and Mommy was obviously still inside. Probably in my closet, but she needed to come get these badass kids before I hurt one of them.

"Tell him to leave me alone," Lito begged me. He was tired and out of breath, he needed a timeout but Cory wasn't hearing it. They had the typical big brother, little brother relationship. Lito was the punching bag.

I usually don't, but I decided to save him. "Cory!" I grabbed the older of the two boys by his shirt to get his attention. More than likely, Mommy had already fed them both breakfast. Their favorite was Frosted Flakes, and they were always sure to add a bunch of extra sugar, it was no wonder why they could never sit still. Cory stared back at me with our father's grey eyes, "Chill! He's tired, so give him a break." I ordered in my serious voice, while seeing a relieved look on the baby's face. Lito was grateful that I'd stepped in.

Cory stopped immediately. "Okay." He turned and went back into their bedroom. See, Cory is very intelligent for his age. He knew damn well I'd slap him silly if he didn't listen. But, he also had enough sense to know that I was about to disappear into the bathroom, and then he could go back to terrorizing his little brother.

When Cory was out of sight, Lito let go of my thigh. I winked at him, blew him a kiss, and he caught it with a smile. He ran off and I went into the bathroom to get ready. As soon as I closed the door, I heard him scream at the top of his lungs, and then the sounds of two sets of feet pattering down the hall. I had to laugh because it had been expected, those two were like Tom & Jerry.

Immediately I turned on the shower to let the water warm up. In the mean time, I grabbed my toothbrush and went to work on my Colgate smile. One thing I learned was that it didn't matter how pretty a bitch is, if you open your mouth and your grill is twisted, that's not cute. A beautiful smile can get you far in life.

Next, I stood in front of the full-length mirror to admire what the good lord had blessed me with. I removed my pink tank top and let my 34c's spring from underneath. The mere sight of my own titties aroused me. This time last year, I could only pray for a chest, back then all I had was nipples. Boy was I glad to have these puppies! I admired them for a couple minutes before finally sliding out of my pajama pants, then my panties and stuffing everything into the laundry chute.

I turned my back to the mirror and looked over my shoulder. My butt was poking out lovely. In the past eighteen months, not only had I managed to sprout breasts, but a nice ass to match. I was perfectly proportioned. I was feeling myself and you couldn't tell me nothing. My skin was flawless and beautiful, the color of butter. I was yellow and proud. No pimples or blemishes on my skin like the majority of the freshman girls at my school. Luckily, I didn't have those problems.

I also owned a full, thick head of hair that fell down to the middle of my back. It was jet black and shiny, courtesy of Mommy's South American genes. I'd also inherited her slanted almond shaped eyes and her nose. Although I'm a mixture of Black, Dominican, Italian and Venezuelan, people say I look more Middle Eastern than anything. When I go into the corner stores, the dudes behind the register start talking to me in Arabic. It used to piss me off, but now I just take it as a compliment. They probably be thinking that I'm Princess Jasmine from Aladdin.

Barefoot, I stand 5'2" and weigh 115 lbs. I have a twenty-two inch waist, and I measure a mean thirty-seven inches around my hips and ass. At the age of fourteen I've got more curves than any roller-coaster ride at Six Flags. On any given day I could easily pass for eighteen, but lately most dudes don't even care how old I am, which is flattering sometimes, but scary at other times.

When the steam from the shower started to fog up the mirror, that's when I knew it was time to get inside. I tied my hair up into a knot on top of my head, grabbed two wash clothes and got into the shower. The hot water felt soothing as it rushed over my naked skin and my temperature started to rise as I lathered the Oil of Olay soap across my chest. My nipples were hardening by the second, it was too easy to turn myself on.

My life hadn't been the same since I'd discovered the secret button that was hidden in the middle of my body. I'd found it about eight months ago. It was right above my Peaches and I never knew it was there, until my fingers just happened to stumble across it one day. And let me tell you, the electricity that shot through my body when I touched that soft spot was a feeling that I'll never forget. A feeling that couldn't be duplicated, and a feeling that I craved and longed for daily and I couldn't resist. This morning was no different, and my legs trembled as the pleasure passed through each one of my limbs when I was finished playing with it.

Four months ago, I let this clown named Riccardo talk me into believing that he could match that tingling sensation. I met him on our annual family vacation in Myrtle Beach, SC. He was cute, and he talked a good game, so I let him be the first to try my Peaches. As it turns out, he was a liar. It wasn't anything like he made me believe it would be. Not even close. It was quick and painful, the exact opposite of what he'd promised. I swear to God, I wish I could've sued that boy for falsely advertising his dick. Afterwards, Tiffany let me in on a secret. She said, as far as female enjoyment goes, sex is overrated. She said that for men, sex is about pleasure. But for women, sex should be about power. Those were words of wisdom that I'd never forget.

Long story short, my first sexual encounter wasn't as memorable as I would have liked it to be, but it was a learning experience. Now I knew what to expect. So now, anytime a dude used that line, 'I'll rock your world...' I just laughed to myself. Shit, the next time a dick came anywhere close to my treasure chest, it would require a very large down payment. Sort of like a security deposit. That way, even if it were whack, I'd still get a consolation prize for my troubles. And in case you're wondering, technically I hadn't lied to Mommy. I wasn't *having* sex, as in the *present* tense. I'd *had* sex, pretense. It was one whack-ass occasion, and honestly, I'd been so utterly disappointed that it would be a very long time before I went down that road again.

I took my time underneath the hot water. I wasn't in a rush, 'cause hell, the school wasn't going anywhere. When I was done, I wrapped up in a large towel and walked barefoot down the hall and back to my room. This trip, there was no music blasting and nobody's kids were running up and down the hall. Either the Daycare Van had departed early or everyone was downstairs. My alarm clock said, 7:40, so they'd probably already left. I walked over to my window and peeked out the blinds, the white Dodge Caravan wasn't in the driveway and I immediately relaxed. At least I'd have a few minutes of peace and quiet before I finally left for school.

Quickly I started to get dressed, Mommy had ironed some clothes and hung them on the back of my door while I'd been in the shower. Black denim Old Navy jeans, with a tan colored Aeropostale cardigan sweater. I threw on some wheat Timberland boots, slicked my hair into a ponytail, put on my jewelry and went downstairs. I found my short length leather jacket, earmuffs, gloves, then grabbed my purse and book bag. I didn't have enough time for breakfast, but I was sure that one of the boys at school wouldn't mind sharing something to eat with me. Just as I was about to leave out the back door, the phone rang. I skipped across the kitchen to check the caller ID.

"Yes, *Bitch*?" I answered the phone, with my voice full of swagger and sass as I emulated a Brooklyn dialect. It was my best friend, Asia.

"*Bitch*," She sounded sleepy. "Are we going to school today? Or do we have anything else better to do on a Monday morning?" My girl asked sarcastically, but very seriously. Asia was my road dawg, and she was always down for whatever. All I had to do was say the word, and today would be a skip day for the both of us. Honestly, I didn't really have any money to do anything else and it didn't make sense for us to skip school just to hang out at my house. Been there, done that! Plus, Thursdays and Fridays are the best days to skip, so I decided against it, even though I was very tempted.

"Nah, Asia, let's just go. Maybe we'll skip on Friday." I suggested to her, and I knew that she wouldn't really care either way.

"Cool. I'll see you first period." She replied before hanging up the phone. I smiled, zipped up my leather jacket and headed for the door.

CHAPTER TWO

Before I opened the door, I checked the window. I looked directly across our driveway and over to Mrs. Shannon's house. Mrs. Shannon was mad cool, she's been our neighbor for years and her and Mommy had been friends for a long time. The only problem was, she had two stalker-ass sons. Calvin was seventeen and Shad was my age. Calvin sniffed after my scent like a lost puppy, and Shad had an even creepier fascination wit La La. They were both cute, but they were *super* lame, just like all the boys in this neighborhood were. I lived damn near in the suburbs, and these boys weren't my type. I needed a dark-skinned thug in my life, a nigga that wore baggy jeans and rocked Timberland boots. Preferably, one who resembled Allen Iverson or Memphis Bleek.

As soon as I slung my book bag over my shoulder and opened the door, a cold gust of wind slapped me across the face. The weather was typical. There had been a modest snowfall overnight, but it had been light, not the type that stuck to the ground. I guess it wasn't bad for a December in Buffalo, and I couldn't complain because at least there wasn't two feet of snow on the ground. I locked the door behind myself, and then began to switch my hips down the driveway. After months of practice with my new body, I'd perfected rolling my hips with ease. When I walked, I purposely made my ass swing from side to side like a donkey and it drove all the young boys crazy! One time, Daddy caught me walking like that and promised to break both my legs if he ever caught me again.

Lucky for me, Daddy was at work.

I didn't have to look, I knew that Calvin was watching me walk down the driveway, because it was the same routine every morning if I didn't get a ride. This particular morning, I made it seven houses past his before I heard him call my name. Then just like always, I turned and waited for him to catch up. I poked out my hip like Tiffany taught me, shifting my body weight and making my tight denim jeans expand to hug my curves.

One of the reasons that Calvin got on my nerves is because he's so predictable, and every morning it was the same bullshit. Instead of just being a man and ringing my doorbell like, "April, let me walk you to the bus stop..." he would rather sit in his window like a coward watching me walk by his house. Then, he'll let me get halfway down the street and call my name like he hadn't been watching me the entire time. I needed a *man*, because this space between my legs was no place for a lost puppy. No boys allowed, only a man could make me feel like a woman!

Calvin was always on his pretty boy, preppy look. Charcoal grey wool coat, Khaki's with some Clark's on his feet. He looked nice, but shit, it was 2001 and I was sure that niggas stopped wearing Clarks a couple years ago. Even Nas stopped wearing Wallabee's in 1999.

I was cold and I was tired of standing still, so I turned and started walking slowly. I knew that his eyes were glued to the back pockets of my jeans, so I gave him the show that he was looking for. Halfway down the street, he finally walked up beside me and smiled.

"What's up? You act like you were gonna leave me this morning." His smile was pretty, and he was definitely cute. He was about my complexion with big brown eyes and a low Caesar cut. His only physical flaw was that he wasn't that tall, he only stood at about 5'10". That's not necessarily short, but I like my men six feet and better.

I looked at his face to see if he was serious. "Calvin, it's almost eight o'clock. I thought you were probably gone already." I lied to his face. Since he wanted to play stupid, I decided to play even stupider. How could I possibly leave him? Every morning he watched my front door like he was on a police steak-out, just to see me when I left. I'm not making this up! His Mom actually caught him on several occasions, and she'd told my Mom. Our mothers, they think it's cute that Calvin has these stalker-like tendencies. Almost like some twisted fatal attraction type of puppy love. But I bet you my Daddy wouldn't think it was cute.

"I would've left already, but I had to finish some English homework." That was Calvin's answer and he'd probably stick to it. I guess part of me was flattered, although his shyness was a complete turn-off. Why couldn't he just tell me that he waited for me every morning because he was feeling me and wanted to be my man? He was a senior, and I know this whole shy routine couldn't possibly be working with the older girls. And it sure wouldn't get him any buns in college next year. But then again, he was cute, he played basketball, and he was actually nice on the court. So maybe he was just used to all the girls throwing themselves at him. He was probably waiting for me to come to my senses, invite him over one morning and jump all over him. Hopefully that wasn't his plan, because it would be a cold day in hell.

I didn't respond, and we just kept walking until we finally made it to Main Street. I went to Buffalo Traditional and Calvin went to City Honors, so we both took the No. 8 bus towards downtown.

"I heard you did your thing on Friday, one of my home girls was at your game." I started up a conversation while we waited at the bus stop in the cold. My book bag was starting to get heavy, so I switched shoulders.

"C'mon, April. You know I get busy." He said confidently and I looked at him out the corner of my eye. It seemed like the only time he put some swag in his voice was when he talked basketball. "We play Traditional in three weeks, you gonna come watch the game?" He asked me. I was just about to answer, when surprisingly he reached out to lift my book bag strap from my shoulders and held it for me.

"Thank you..." I smiled at him for being such a gentleman. "Umm, I guess so, but only if the game is at my school-"

"It is, and it's a three o'clock game, right after dismissal." He informed me. I went to most of my schools home basketball games, not because I really cared much about sports, but because my friend Darrell was the star on the team. Not to mention the fact that lots of young cuties showed up for the games. My school had the best b-ball team in the city, we were always undefeated, and so the gym was always packed with spectators.

"Good luck." I laughed at him. He knew what I meant but he just smiled. It was a crying shame that he didn't have this much confidence in his game *off* the court.

"I don't need luck. I'm the best point guard in the city. Last year I dropped 32-points on your home court-"

"I wasn't in high school last year," I reminded him. "But I know that my school has been undefeated for the last *six* seasons." I challenged him. I didn't know shit about basketball, but I knew this to be a fact. The entire city knew.

"Not this year." He grinned at me, and then looked me dead in my face. "You gonna cheer for me, April?" He wanted to know.

I bit my bottom lip and put a hand on my hip, almost posing for him. "You trying to get me jumped?" I grinned back at him. "I hope you play good and everything, and *maybe* I'll even smile when you score a basket. But I'm not about to be jumping up and down screaming your name." I started laughing just imagining the thought, and he laughed too. I was glad to see that he hadn't taken it the wrong way.

"That's fair," Calvin looked me up and down, his big brown eyes lingering on my thighs. "So after I score, I'm gonna look at you and you *better* flash me a smile." He told me as our bus rolled up to the corner. I was a little taken back by his words, it seemed as though he had a rare boost of cockiness. I paused before I responded, because I was scared that if I flat out told him yes, that he'd score 100 points just to see my Kool-Aid smile.

"Hmmm. First let's see *if* you can *score.*" I teased in a very seductive manner, but I didn't think he'd catch my sly response. I couldn't believe that I was flirting with corny-ass Calvin from across the street and it turned out that he wasn't as slow as I thought. He grinned, then took my hand to help me step up onto the bus.

"I *always* score, April." He answered, with a slick sexual undertone of his own. It was completely unexpected, and I almost fainted when this little boy licked his lips at me like he was LL or something. "I hope you ready," he added. "Because I'ma have you doing a whole lot of smiling."

I couldn't stop myself. Instantly, a huge smile spread across my face. I wondered what had gotten into this boy for him to lick his lips at me like he was some type of playa or something.

"I guess we'll see." That was all I managed to say in return as we walked down the aisle of the crowded Metro bus and found a pair of empty seats. One thing was for sure, Calvin had better keep his tongue in his mouth. If not, I definitely had some place where he could put it.

CHAPTER THREE

I was sitting in fifth period Algebra. I paid attention and took my notes. I wouldn't say that I enjoyed school, but I definitely knew the importance of it. Being dumb wasn't sexy. Well, unless you're a white girl with blonde hair, which I wasn't. My Daddy is three quarters black, which made *me* black. So, with that being said, I was already born with one strike against me. On top of that, I'm a woman and I know that me being a dumb, black woman wouldn't get me too far in life. So, I made it my business to make learning a priority, maybe not my number one priority, but very close to the top.

So far, high school had been fairly easy. I was a B student. If I tried harder, I could get all A's, but I had other shit to worry about. Algebra was simple, but it was obvious that my opinion didn't apply to everyone. I looked around the classroom in awe. The students who were actually awake, they were scratching their heads looking puzzled like this class was called Chinese Arithmetic 101. The rest of these niggas were either sleep or doing some other shit.

I was scribbling down the formula for one of problems on the board when I felt the metal leg of my chair get kicked. I already knew it was Brandon, because everyday he always made sure to sit right behind me. At first, I tried to ignore him, but he kept kicking my chair and it was beginning to distract me.

"Pssss....April." He whispered my name from behind me, trying to grab my attention as if kicking my chair hadn't been enough. Mr. Lanzo, our math teacher had his back to the class, so I turned slightly, but I didn't open my mouth to respond. I raised my eyebrows to let him know he had my attention and he smiled, finally getting what he wanted.

Brandon leaned forward, "Guess what I put on my Christmas list this year?" He asked me.

"What?" I whispered with a shrug, not caring.

His grin widened. "*You!*"

I rolled my eyes and quickly turned back around in my seat, and then I put my head down and started to giggle. Everyday this boy had a different line for me. One thing I can honestly say, is that he always made me smile, he was always funny and never disrespectful. When I finally lifted my head, out the corner of my eye I caught some nobody bitch looking at me sideways. She was just a random girl, I didn't even know her name and she'd been in this class for the past three months, but I bet you she knew *my* name. Whatever the case, she obviously had a problem with the way Brandon felt about me, but that wasn't my problem. Out of pure spite, I stroked my long, thick, silky ponytail. I ran my fingers through my long mane just to remind her that she didn't have shit on me, and she'd never be on my level. Then I turned my attention back to the blackboard. I hoped that the girl wouldn't lose any sleep behind this, if so, she could surely relax. I didn't want Brandon, she could have him.

When the bell rang, everyone jumped out their seats and rushed for the door similar to firefighters responding to a 911 call. I grabbed my Algebra textbook and three-ring binder, then dipped out the door and into traffic. Brandon wasn't too far behind. When I pulled up to my locker, which was halfway down the hall, he posted up and watched me put my books away.

Out the corner of my eye, I sized him up. Brandon was light brown skin with short curly hair. Noticeably, he was always fly. Today he was wearing yet another pair of spanking new of Air Force 1's, and they were exclusive because I'd never seen those colors before, he must have got them this weekend. I slammed my locker shut, slid my Roc-a-wear purse onto my arm, poked out my hip and stared at this cute sophomore who was sweating me. The poor boy was looking at me like he was trying to put together a 3,000-piece puzzle. Suddenly, he didn't have a clue what to say to me, and when he did finally make up his mind to speak, that's when Asia walked up.

"C'mon, Bitch. Lunch time." Asia grabbed my arm and pulled me away from Brandon, she probably thought she was saving me.

"Damn, Asia." Brandon cut his eyes at my best friend. "Don't you see me and April talking?" He said it like Asia was interrupting our conversation or something. This made Asia stop, she looked at me, checked my blank expression and then turned to Brandon.

"Boy, I just watched you stand there for a whole two minutes and not say *anything*! This bitch doesn't understand sign language!" Asia grinned at me, then continued to pull me towards the stairs. I took one last look at Brandon as I slid off, he was screw facing her like she was the cock-blocker of the year. He wanted to say some slick shit to her, but he knew it might ruin his chances with me 'cause she was my best friend. "Next time," she added sarcastically. "Just write her a note and slide it into her locker, that way you don't gotta be standing here, wasting her time looking all stupid!" She rolled her eyes at my admirer.

I looked over my shoulder and flashed Brandon a sympathetic smile as he watched us walk away. "Bye, B. See you tomorrow." I waved at him, and he smiled before throwing up the peace sign. Then I punched Asia on the arm and we both laughed. "That's my friend, why you put him on the spot like that?"

She rolled her eyes, "That fool was tongue tied. We would have fucked around and missed lunch waiting for his courage to arrive. He got a girl anyway!" She informed me. Now this was new information to me, but then again, Asia is like a walking Newspaper, she knows everything that goes on in these halls.

"I didn't know he had a girl-"

"Girl please, everybody knows that!" She interrupted me. "Oh, and guess what?" She asked as we walked. I didn't answer because it was a waste of my breath, she was going to keep talking anyway. "I heard they caught that nasty hooker Talina inside the boys locker room sucking-"

I immediately burst out in laughter. "Girl, you lying!" But I knew better than to question my girls information, she was like the Wendy Williams of this high school. If she repeated it, it was true.

"Hmmm!" Asia shot me a look. "And guess who it was? *Your* friend, Darrell from the ball team!" My heart dropped as she leaned over to whisper in my ear. "Coach Ryan caught them this morning after the early practice. But you know he isn't gonna tell, 'cause if he do, Darrell gonna get kicked out of school and he won't be able to play basketball." As she broke this news to me, we had just walked into the cafeteria for 6th period lunch.

"That's *crazy*." I couldn't think of anything else to say. These broads were out of control around here, Talina was a freshman too, but she was as fast as a college senior. I tried not to show my disappointment, but it was hard. Darrell isn't my boyfriend, but everybody knows that we talk, so it still makes me look stupid that he got caught in the locker room wit' a slut.

"No," She blurted. "What's crazy is these nasty girls runnin' around here turning tricks, but still wearing dusty ass Reebok Classics!" We both laughed at her logic. "I respect sluts. Shit, my sister is a whore, but at least she gets paid for her services. Back in the day, my sis would've fucked the whole basketball team. But she would've been the flyest bitch in the school, wit' a bankroll in her purse!" I knew Asia's sister, and trust me, she wasn't joking at all.

My homie Asia had a chocolate complexion with shoulder length hair, she wasn't exotic or nothin', but she had a pretty face. Her curves weren't anything like mines, but she had bumps in the right places. Not that it was a competition between us, but in the looks department I had her by a long shot. But honestly, when it came to fashion, that's where she had the edge. Her big sister Tionna was an exotic dancer, and when I say that, I'm being modest. Tionna made tons of money and kept Asia dipped in all the latest shit. I'm talking designer shit that even most grown women couldn't afford. For that reason alone, a lot of girls didn't like her, but they respected her. Asia could fight her ass off, she had a big mouth but could back up everything that came out of it. And the entire school knew that to be a fact.

Me on the other hand, I was known to sometimes have a smart-ass mouth, but for the most part, I tried to keep it in check. Not that I'm soft, because I definitely got heart. But to keep it real with you, I can't fight. I'm not lying, seriously I couldn't fight my way out of a wet paper bag! Laugh if you want, but at least I'm being honest. With that being said, I try to stay neutral and out of confrontations, because I'm way too pretty to have bitches swinging at my face. Scars aren't sexy, and I don't need any on my beautiful skin.

The cafeteria was hectic as always. Everybody was everywhere. Teachers were trying their best to direct traffic, but it never worked. Inside this particular open area, the noise tended to echo and magnify and it was loud enough to burst an eardrum. Adding to the experience was the ghastly aroma that was wafting through the air, there's nothing like the smell of cafeteria food to ruin your appetite. On the way to our table, I glanced at some girl's tray as she walked in the opposite direction. The food was unrecognizable, but if I had to guess, I'd say goulash, although it closely resembled cat food. I *definitely* wasn't about to put *that* food, in *this* mouth!

Asia and me took seats at our table, next to a window that looked out into the big courtyard. In this Cafeteria, technically you could sit wherever you wanted to. But there were levels, ranks, and pecking orders around here. And it wasn't uncommon for someone to sit in the wrong seat, or the wrong table and get their ass whooped.

The sections were segregated. Seniors sat with seniors. Sophomores sat with sophomores etc. My table was cool, we were like the Hollywood A-listers of the freshman class. No weirdo's sat at this particular table, and that was by design. When Asia and I finally sat down, we were the last ones to arrive, but I couldn't help but notice that nobody was eating. It was obvious that I wasn't the only one who felt some kind of way about the menu for today.

I waved, and greeted everybody at our table like the freshman celebrity that I am as I took a seat next to my brother, Cam. "What's up, boo?" I ran my fingers through his long cornrows, and he looked over and smiled.

"What's up wit' you?" He asked real cool and calm. Cam was my homie, and we were like family. He was one of the most certified young boys in the school, and that's saying a lot. Everything about him was official, he was a sweetheart, but at the same time, he was half crazy. He was fourteen too, same age as me, but he was already heavy in the streets. Outside of school, he only hung around dudes much older than himself, and he'd already earned the reputation for playing wit' guns and making money.

I shrugged. "Nothing." That was my reply as I watched him shoot Asia a menacing look. She just rolled her eyes at him, and I tried hard to stifle my laughter. Cam was my brother because of Asia, they've had this real intense 'Love & Hate' relationship going on since elementary school, and it was so cute. One day the girl would be telling me how she wasn't gonna mess wit' him no more, for one reason or the other. Then the next day, she'd be leaving school wit' him so she could get her lil' tunnel dug out.

"What ya'll beefing about this time?" I asked the both of them, because I was lost. Just this morning they'd been all cuddled up at her locker, now they weren't speaking.

Cam waved off my question, he was busy looking through the XXL Hip Hop magazine. "She *stupid*." He mumbled under his breath, and that was all he needed to say to set her off.

"Kiss my *black* ass." She immediately responded while flipping him the finger. All I could do was shake my head, this was a dead topic. I'd tried to help, but I needed to mind my damn business. I gave my best friend a silent look of apology, and in return, she sucked her teeth. "Fuck *him*."

She added. It irritated her that Cam hadn't paid her outburst any attention, he'd went back to his magazine already.

After an awkward silence between us, we were finally able to get into our routine lunchtime conversation. Our regular topics were music, clothes, and high school politics. After a few minutes of debating about things that only matter in the worlds of teenagers, I peeped this girl named Karma walking towards our table.

Now trust me, I'm not gay or nothing, but *damn*! Karma is *fine*. And *if* I *was* gay, or had any plans to be gay in the future, I'd be all over her sexy ass! Karma was the Queen Bitch. I'm not insecure, and I'm not a hater, I pay homage where it's due and there wasn't a broad in this school who could compare to her. *Me* included! Not to toot my own horn, but I'm definitely a dime in the face. *And* I look exotic. But Karma was also a dime in the face, plus she had something that I lacked. She had that grown woman sex appeal.

Karma was a senior. All her outfits were fly. Her hair stayed laced and her nails stayed manicured. She didn't wear sneakers or Timberlands like the other girls our age did, she only wore heels. Like me she was a high yellow complexion, with long hair and a bangin' body. Her titties were slightly bigger than mines, but my butt was definitely fatter. Everyday she was dropped off and picked up by a silver Lexus ES300, and the dude behind the wheel definitely wasn't her father. But *shit*, he was probably old enough to be. This girl was living the life that I deserved, and honestly, I needed to take notes.

I checked her outfit. She was rocking some expensive tight blue denim jeans, and a cashmere sweater, matching a killer pair of five-inch knee high boots. Everything looked exclusive. Her jewelry game was sick, and she put the little trinkets that Daddy bought me to shame. Her bamboo earrings were three times the size of mines, and I doubted that they were hollow like the ones I was wearing. Not to mention that her handbag looked as if it was more expensive than my entire outfit. I think I'm love wit' this bitch.

As she approached our section, the room got quiet. All the dudes had stopped talking so they could glue their eyes to her ass as she walked over to the freshman and sophomore end of the cafeteria. Karma seemed to glide up to the table as if she was walking on air, and she stopped at our table right in front of me. Asia was talking to me, she was in the middle of saying something about Allen Iverson, but I was no longer paying attention, and finally she looked up to see what I was looking at.

Karma was standing there looking down at us. "Sorry, excuse me for interrupting, Asia." Karma was polite and smiled at the both of us, and Asia just shrugged. "Hi, April. How are you?" She asked me.

I flashed her a smile. Karma and me are cool. We aren't exactly friends, but we're cool. Most of the upperclassmen girls didn't even speak to me, but Karma was always nice. Supposedly, there's some type of unspoken beef between Senior and freshman girls.

My sister said it's because the senior girls feel threatened when new girls step into the school. It's a territory thing, especially when one of the new girls in the building looks like *me*. And they definitely don't like it when the older boys start sniffing around the freshman girls, but Karma had never shown me that type of hate and I respected her for that. I don't even know how she learned my name, but she always smiled and spoke when she saw me around. The only thing I could think of was that she was smart enough to realize that I was next in line for the Queen Bitch throne. Because after she graduated, this would be *my* school and the rest of these broads would have to bow down.

Finally I spoke. "I'm fine, just chillin' wit my girl." I nodded at Asia, but just that quick she'd turned her back to me, and now her and Cam were going back and forth whispering in each other's ear.

Karma looked at Asia again and then nodded. "Yeah, I saw you over here, so I came to say hello," That set off my curiosity, because she's never come over to my table any other day just to say 'hello'. "Listen, my locker is on the first floor next to Mrs. Collins Biology lab. If you're not busy, meet me there at dismissal, I wanna talk to you about something important." The fact that Karma was smiling let me know that it wasn't some drama that she wanted to talk about, but just in case, I'd bring Asia wit' me. I wasn't about to walk into no senior bitch ambush and get beat down. Trust me, it *has* happened. And that science wing hallway where her locker was, that shit was dangerous over there. Shit, that corridor is like the south side of Chicago.

"Alright," I answered her. "But you'll have to wait a couple minutes because my locker is all the way upstairs and on the opposite side of the building, but I'll be there." The whole time, I was wondering what she wanted to holler at me about. Maybe she was bi-sexual and she was feeling me. Just the mere thought of it almost made me burst into laughter, but I held myself together.

Karma shrugged as if it didn't make any difference to her, "I'll wait for you. When you get there, then we'll talk." She replied. "Cool?" She asked just to make sure.

"Cool." I assured her.

"Alright, I'll see you later." Karma waved and I waved back, then I watched her as she walked away. I was envious. I thought *my* walk was *tough*, but *her* walk was *mean*! That's when I realized that I needed to talk to Mommy about buying me some heels.

I didn't realize it, but my best friend was staring in my face the entire time. "Damn, Bitch!" she was giggling. "You staring at Karma's ass like you wanna hit that!" Now she was outright laughing at me. "You got something you wanna tell me?" She asked sarcastically.

Instantly my face got hot. I was starting to blush. That was the only problem with being so yellow, my cheeks always gave me away. "Get outta here!" I punched her arm, I was extremely embarrassed but tried not to show it.

"You still my girl, but at least let me know so I can stop getting naked in front of you." She kept joking, and I rolled my eyes as she continued to laugh at me. I hated being the butt of jokes, but this time I'd earned it. Just for the record though, ain't *nothing* gay about me. And I don't see anything wrong with admiring another woman's body. After all, it's not like I was fantasizing about doing some nasty shit.

Lucky for me, that's' when the bell rang. Lunch was over. I stood up quickly, ready to take flight in order to get away from Asia. She was my girl, but she had a way of running a joke into the ground and I didn't wanna hear anything else about this shit. I waved at her and then dipped off into the crowd to get to my next class.

"See you at 2:30! Wait for me!" That was all I said as I disappeared in the direction of the stairs.

CHAPTER FOUR

School was over, and I was at my locker getting ready to go. My cute little leather jacket was on and zipped up, and I was checking my face in the small mirror that was hanging up on the inside of my locker door. I don't wear make-up because I don't need it, but I'm infatuated with lip-gloss and I hastily applied some before I headed off. There's nothing cute about chapped lips, please don't let anyone tell you different.

With my book bag on my shoulder and my purse on my arm, I weaved in and out of the foot traffic that cluttered the hallways. I was almost at Asia's locker when I felt two big hands grab my waist from behind. Immediately, I threw an elbow backwards and it was meant to do damage to whomever was behind me. My blow connected as I turned around with an attitude.

"Damn shorty, you hit kinda hard." Darrell was looking down at me with a confused look on his face. This fool was like 6'5" and he was hovering over me while rubbing his thigh where my elbow had connected. I didn't smile because I wasn't happy to see him, instead, I folded my arms across my chest and gave him attitude.

"If you want to get my attention, all you gotta do is call my name. Don't touch my clothes unless you paid for them!" I snapped at him. He looked at me like I was crazy, like I couldn't have been talking to him. See, Darrell is the star of the varsity basketball team. All these girls treated him like he was the next Kobe Bryant, so he was used to just having his way and that wasn't going to fly with me. We had been talking for a few months here and there, nothing serious, mostly late night phone calls.

Darrell looked surprised that I was flipping on him, and he put his hands in the air as a sign of surrender. "My bad, A. You okay, you having a bad day or something?" He wanted to know. The fact that he acted like he didn't know why I was upset with him made me even more upset with him. So, I rolled my eyes and walked away without saying another word. I was definitely vexed about him and Talina being caught in the locker room together, the whole school was talking about it. I left him standing there, and stepped off towards Asia's locker where she always waited for me after school.

When I got there she was holding her books in her arms, Asia didn't believe in carrying a book bag. "Can you walk with me to the science wing real fast before we go?" I asked her. She nodded but she wasn't making eye contact, instead she was looking over my head. When I turned to see what she was staring at, I wasn't too shocked to see Darrell's tall ass standing right behind me.

He looked at my friend, "Asia can you give us a minute?" he asked her, and she screwed up her face at his request. She could tell by the look on my face that I didn't want to be bothered.

"Give you a minute?" Asia gave him nothing but attitude with her voice. "Look at her face..." She pointed at me. "Do she look like she want to talk to you right now?" She asked him. Out the corner of my eye, I could see that Darrell was wearing the stupid face. That's why I loved Asia, because she had the courage to say whatever she wanted. And most times, she said the shit that I was thinking, but I wouldn't dare say myself.

He ignored her. "April, look at me." I tried not to, but I couldn't help myself. I looked up at him. He had that confidence in his voice that I liked. "I know you not trippin' about the rumor that's going around," Then he shot my friend a quick look. "Don't believe everything that you *hear*."

Asia looked disgusted, and she was about to light his ass up. I recognized the fire in her eyes and quickly spoke up to cut her off. "Don't flatter yourself, D. You not even my man, so I'm not trippin'. But we've been kicking it for a while now, and I'm always telling my girls how cool you are and how much I like you. But now you got me looking stupid-"

"April, it's not true. People don't know what they talking about." He was trying his best to sound sincere and I looked into his eyes as he lied to me. For whatever reason, I was hurt. But I quickly put my feelings in check. The only reason I was mad is because, I was under the impression that he was only chasing me, and it burst my bubble to find out that I wasn't the only female on his mind.

I grabbed Asia and tugged her arm so we could leave. I was done with this situation. "You don't have to explain yourself to me, Darrell. We're cool." I told him as I started to walk off wit' my friend.

"So you not mad at me?" He wanted to know.

I frowned up my face. "I didn't say all that nigga, you still a dog!" I crushed his subtle attempt at smoothing things over so quickly. I would give him another chance, but right now was too soon. Darrell was my type. He was a tall, brown skin, handsome, hood dude. Plus he could play ball, and he was one of the best in the city. I'm not fool enough to just completely diss him, 'cause shit, one day he might be headed to the NBA. I told you I'm *selfish*, but that's a long way from being *stupid*.

"C'mon, April! You know how I feel about you, don't do me like that." Darrell was literally following behind us as we walked to the stairs, and it was somewhat pathetic. I decided that I needed to say something to get him away before Asia snapped on him, because if he kept following us that was bound to happen.

I stopped on the landing and turned around to face him. I poked out my hip, and then watched as his eyes traveled down my body. I licked my lips before I spoke, "Darrell, I'm really not in the mood. You made me think that I was special, now I find out that your chasing Talina too. I thought you were different, so now I'm disappointed and I feel like I've been wasting my time."

"Listen-"

"*No.* I'm done listening." I stopped him from interrupting me with more lies about how I shouldn't believe the rumors. "If I'm special, then treat me like I'm special. You know the type of shit that I like. And you know what sizes I wear, so do something to make me feel better. *Then* we can talk." I laid it down flat just like that, and I had one hand on my hip as I spit my game. Thanks to that slut Talina, I was about to get something new to put inside my closet.

Even though Darrell was wearing a blank expression on his face, I knew that he got the point and that he understood. And I knew that I was dead wrong for making him feel bad about getting some head in the locker room, but hey, I was in the position to capitalize, so why not? There wasn't anything wrong with him spending a couple dollars to keep me happy.

I got my point across, and this time when I walked away, he didn't follow. When we arrived in the science wing hallway, Karma was chilling next to her locker with another senior girl named, Sally. Sally was pretty. I didn't know her personally, but I just knew who she was because a bunch of the freshman boys were always in class talking about how fine she was. She was one of the upperclassmen girls who never spoke to me for whatever reason, but I never took it personal.

I looked at Asia and she waved me off. "Go ahead, I'll wait for you over there." She pointed towards some dude with a cute Sean John jacket on and walked off. Before I could answer, she was all up in the dudes face batting her eyelashes at him. She amazed me. Asia could go from being a pit bull, to being a poodle in a matter of Moments.

I walked down to where Karma was waiting for me and she was wearing a huge smile. She had one of those contagious smiles, the type where you couldn't help but to give her a smile back.

"Hi." I said as I walked up to the two older girls. I didn't really know what else to say, my curiosity was killing me and I wanted to know what she wanted to talk to me about.

"Hi!" she greeted me, and then she turned to Sally. "This is, April, the girl that I've been telling you about." Now she definitely had my attention, because it was obvious that these two broads had been discussing me. I guess my thoughts must have flashed across my face like a billboard, because Karma quickly added, "Don't worry, everything I told her was good." She cleared up her statement. But I was still wondering what could she possibly have good to say about me? She didn't even *know* me. But I just nodded and waited for these girls to get to the point.

"Nice to meet you, I'm Sally." The other girl finally spoke up. She didn't seem like she had an attitude or nothin', so I decided that I should be polite.

"Hi, I'm April." I gave her a smile, and then we both looked back at Karma who was smiling like she'd just brokered a million dollar deal or something.

"Okay, we've been watching you," Karma started talking. "You're pretty, all the freshman seem to like you and I checked with your teachers, and they all say that you're a good student..." This bitch was sounding like the CIA or something. Had she been doing *surveillance*? What the fuck was she doing talking to my teachers about me? Is that even *legal*?

"...Have you ever heard of Kappa Lambda Theta?" Karma was searching my face as she stopped smiling for the first time and turned very serious all of a sudden. I knew what she was talking about, and now I understood what this was about. They were trying to recruit me for their sorority.

"I know what you're talking about, but I really don't know much about it. The Lambda's is a sorority, right?"

"*Junior* sorority!" Sally blurted out just to clarify things. Karma nodded in agreement and then dug into the knapsack that she had dangling from her shoulder. She pulled out a few pages that were stapled together and then handed them to me.

"We're not trying to force you into anything," Karma said as I took the papers. "Just read over this when you get a chance. Kappa Lambda Theta is a sisterhood. We do lots of volunteer community service, lots of college prep programs, *and* we have a lot of fun in the process." Karma was clearly trying to sell me on the idea.

Then Sally chimed in. "Yeah, and don't let *anyone* try to discourage you..." As it came out her mouth, I could've swore she glanced off in Asia's direction. "A lot of girls don't like us. Most of them are just jealous because Lambda girls are the prettiest and the smartest. Not just *anyone* gets picked to be a part of *our* family." She let those words sink into my head. I looked at the two chicks in front of me, and then at the packet of papers. I folded them very neatly and put them into my purse. Apparently, I'd just been chosen and invited into some kind of inner sanctum for bourgeois bitches only.

Unbelievable.

I didn't necessarily dismiss the idea right away, but I was skeptical, because I've never been the type to hang with a clique. The two girls exchanged looks of concern, as if they could sense my hesitation.

Karma spoke up. "You got anything planned for Friday evening?" she asked me as her smile returned.

I shook my head. I was only fourteen years old, and my Dad watched me like a hawk, where could I possibly have plans on going? "Nope, not really." I answered, what else could I say?

Let me check my schedule?

Please, my weekend life was *not* really poppin' like that!

They both smiled at each other. "Good." Karma looked excited. "My phone number is on the last page of the packet I gave you. Tell your parents to call my Moms, then I'll pick you up on Friday and we'll show you how the Lambda's get down!" Now they both were glowing, *shit*, they even had *me* excited. I could use something to shake up my boring life, that's all they had to say in the first place. All that talk about volunteer community service and college prep programs had went in one ear and out the other!

"Okay, I'll tell my Mom to call your Mom tonight." I told her. Then we said bye, and I dipped off to grab Asia. By this time she was chillin' next to the back exit cuddled up wit' Cam.

The first words out her mouth were, "Okay, *Bitch*! You better not start actin' all *uppity* now!" She was trying to sound like she was joking, but she was dead serious.

I responded by putting my arm around her neck, "Bitch, *we* all *we* got." I reassured her.

CHAPTER FIVE

Cam was walking us up the block so we could get to the Metro rail station to catch our buses. The whole hood around our school was considered Cedar Springs, this was Cam's hood and his block was right down the street. He was trying to convince Asia to come over to his crib, but she was frontin' on him. She was still a little upset about whatever they'd been beefing about earlier at lunch. They obviously couldn't come to a compromise, because as we passed the intersection of Cam's street, he just walked off on us. She had him pissed.

It was a crowd of niggas standing on the corner of Cam's block, and they all watched us as we crossed the street and walked by. "Oh girl, that's Cam's brother right there. His name's Xavier." Asia looked like she was getting excited.

"Which one?" I was curious, and I wondering if he was anything like Cam. I was trying to look into the crowd of dudes, but I didn't want to stare and seem too obvious. Trying to be discreet wasn't working because they were all looking in our direction anyway. Most of them were much older than us, some of them looked fly, and some of them just looked plain terrible.

"The light-skinned one with the cornrows, standing next to the tree." She whispered to me and it didn't take long for me to spot him. He was a light skin older looking version of Cam and his hair as even longer.

"*Oh*, I see him." I said softly. And he definitely saw me too, he was watching me like a hawk. He was cute, and when our eyes locked, it seemed like an instant connection. If he was anything like Cam, he was definitely the type of nigga I'd like to meet. I usually don't go for light skin dudes, but I'd definitely make an exception for *him*. I'm not gonna even lie to you, we would make a cute couple. I had to force my eyes to unlock from his as we walked, any longer and it would've just went from magical to awkward.

I had every intention on turning my head straight and focusing my attention in the direction I was walking in, because lord knows I didn't want to trip on the curb and embarrass the hell out of myself. But my eyes just happened to land on the dude standing right next to Xavier. I can't explain what it was, but there was something strikingly different about him.

"He sexy, right?" Asia grinned at me referring to Xavier. I nodded, but my eyes were now on his friend. There had to be close to twenty dudes on the block, and this particular dude was the only one who wasn't paying Asia and me any attention. This nigga *had* to be gay if he wasn't interested in catching a glimpse of *me*!

"C'mere, yellow bone!" On of the dudes shouted and I knew he had to be talking to me, because my friend wasn't anywhere close to being yellow. I looked over, hoping that it was either Xavier or the boy standing next to him who was trying to get my attention. But it was neither. In fact, the dude who was calling me looked like he was damn near thirty, ugly as hell and busted. I definitely wasn't about to stop walking for *him*!

"Oh, *God*! That nigga is *so* dusty!" Asia exclaimed, and we both started cracking up as we began to walk faster. I noticed Cam say something to the dude, and he immediately stopped trying to flag me down. I didn't look back again until we reached the next corner, but when I did, Xavier was *still* watching me. But the boy next to him, he still hadn't even looked my way.

"Who's the boy standing next to Xavier?" I asked her. "The one wit' the leather varsity jacket." I tried not to sound like I was too interested, but Asia was *way* too sharp. She knew me too well, and she knew my type.

"Oh, that's Phee, Xavier's best friend. He from around here too, they all grew up together." She informed me, but that wasn't enough info, so I kept pressing.

"*Phee*?" That was such a unique name, and I'd never heard it before. But just as the boy's name rolled off my tongue, Asia started grinning.

"That's what they call him." She said as we continued to walk in silence. "Why, you want me to hook you up?" She asked. "He definitely official. Him and Cam are like brothers, he always talking about him, I can probably get you his number."

I thought about it, but I didn't want Asia to go opening her big mouth and put me on the spot. "That's okay, I'm good. If he was feeling me, he woulda stepped to his business." I shot her a look. "And you better not tell Cam that I asked." I added seriously.

"Bitch, we don't sit around talking about *you*!" She punched me on the shoulder. "And I know you seen how Xavier was looking at you." I had to smile, because of course I seen him watching. "Like he wanted to eat you alive!" She started cracking up.

I laughed. "It's a long waiting list for *these* Peaches." We slapped each other five.

"So who you gonna give them to..." She grinned at me. "...Xavier or Phee?" She asked jokingly.

I shrugged with a real mischievous grin on my face. "Why can't I have them *both*?" I joked and we both continued laughing as we approached the train station.

My playful response triggered one of Asia's infamous smirks, "Slow down, Bitch. We don't smash homies-"

"I'm *joking*!" I slapped her on the arm playfully as we reached our destination, and prepared to split up. We both took different buses. I was headed north, and my girl was headed west. We hugged, said our goodbyes, and parted ways.

At that Moment, I could've never known the significance of that walk home, and it wouldn't dawn on me for years to come. I would have been better off skipping school today, because this turned out to be the day that potentially changed my life forever. They say that you can *speak* things into existence, and I'm living proof that this is true. Be careful what you say, *even* in jest.

CHAPTER SIX

When I walked into the kitchen, the small TV sitting on the counter was on. Mommy was sitting at the island style countertop with her school books spread out, and La La was sitting next to her eating some pop tarts. By now, my stomach was growling and I should've been concentrating on food, but the first thing I noticed was La La wearing my purple long sleeved Chaps Polo shirt. I'd saved up baby-sitting money for two whole weeks just to buy that shirt. And I'd only had the chance to wear it once.

Two things stopped me from slapping the shit outta her. My Moms sitting right there, and secondly, starvation. I dropped my bag onto the floor, tossed my purse onto the countertop and went straight for the refrigerator.

"Hey, baby." Mommy looked up from her homework. She was about to say something else, probably tell me to get my bag off the floor. But I was already halfway across the kitchen on a hunger mission before she could get any extra words out.

"I didn't eat all day, I'm hungry." Those were the only words that came out my mouth as I snatched open the refrigerator door, and then my heart dropped once I witnessed my options. I slammed it shut and went for the cupboard, which was even worst. I couldn't believe that we were living like this. "Mom!" I was irritated. "This doesn't make any sense!"

La La chimed in. "I just told her the *same* thing." This came from the girl who was talking with her mouth full, she'd just eaten one of the last of the pop tarts. I cut my eyes at her, and she knew not to say anything else. I wasn't a skilled boxer, and I can barely fight at all. But if there was only *one* person in this world that I know I can whoop, it was her. And this had been proven repeatedly. She had no business speaking right now, and she knew she was out of line.

Mom shrugged her shoulders as if there was nothing that she could do. "I'm going to start dinner shortly. Eat some pop tarts or make a sandwich." At least she looked sympathetic to my situation. "We'll be good in a few days-"

"*A few days!*" La La and me both exclaimed at the same time in disbelief.

Mommy rolled her eyes at both of us. "Well, every time I go shopping, ya'll are the main two who eat up everything in the first couple days!" She snapped, as if it was our fault that humans needed food to survive. "So I don't want to hear either of you complaining until you start pitching in on the cost of groceries."

I took the already open box of pop tarts out the cupboard and sucked my teeth loudly. My back was to both of them, but I heard La La giggle.

"*April*," When Mommy called my name, I turned around. "Don't make me put my hands on you." She was calm, and showed no sign of being angry, this was simply a verbal warning. I took it in stride.

I gathered my bag and my purse. I didn't even bother to microwave the pop tarts, I like them better straight out the box. I headed to the stairs, passing them on the way. It pissed me off that La La was wearing my shirt like she owned it. She must have crept into my room while I was asleep last night and swiped it, and it wouldn't be the first time. If nothing else, that bitch had a bright future ahead of her as either a booster or a cat burglar.

LaReina was a split image of my Daddy. She had his eyes and his nose, so did Tiffany and Cory. Lito and me favored our Moms. La La was a dime too, and her body was already starting to fill out. I wasn't a hater, but sometimes I wished that I'd inherited my Daddy's grey eyes instead of her.

"La La," I called over my shoulder after I was halfway up the stairs, she didn't answer but I know she heard me. "One day, I'm going to catch you red handed stealing out my closet, and I'm going to beat you senseless. This the last time I'm going to tell you." I gave her a very calm verbal warning.

As I continued up the stairs, I heard the loud smack. And I know Mommy popped her good, because I heard LaReina mutter 'ouch!' Then my Mom's voice, "What did I tell you about that? Stay out of that girls closet before she hurts you!"

I held my giggle in until I got all the way upstairs, where I found Cory and Carlito playing their wrestling video game inside the family room. "Hi, babies." I stuck my head inside the playroom. Cory didn't pay me any attention, his eyes remained glued to the screen. Carlito on the other hand, puckered his lips at me and made a kissing sound, but he didn't bother moving to give me a hug. They were obviously busy, so I left them alone.

Within minutes, I was busting down the cold pop tarts while sitting on my bed. They didn't last long, before I knew it they were gone and I was still hungry. Thursday was the fifteenth of December, so Mommy would get her food stamps. Keep in mind that we're not *technically* supposed to be even receiving any government assistance. It's a long story. I said, we lived far from the hood, but I never said that we didn't do hood shit! And just so you know, we *not* poor, but we do dabble in some poor people shit. My Daddy is from Brooklyn, what do you expect?

I took off my clothes and threw on a sweat suit, then closed my door and climbed into the bed. I figured I'd just sleep my hunger away until my Moms came to get me up for dinner. Daddy should be home by then, and I wanted to talk to him about a couple of things. My eyes closed and I drifted off, before long I was out cold.

CHAPTER SEVEN

Friday rolled around slowly and it was just my luck that my period had rolled around with it. Okay, let me explain something to you, when I'm on my menstrual and I get these cramps, my mood is shitty. My mouth gets very loose and my temper is quick to flare. And at the same time, a bitch gets super horny. Boys have it easy. They don't have to suffer like this. And God was definitely a *man*; I say that because if God were a *woman*, she'd know better than to design our bodies to ooze blood at the horniest time of the month. That's ridiculous, and it just didn't make any sense at all.

I came home from school with a headache, and an attitude. I needed to take a bath because I felt dirty. I hated everything about my period, besides the fact that it was supposed to clean me out. I hadn't brought home my book bag because I didn't have any homework. Plus, today was the start of the winter break, and school was done until January.

Dropping my keys and purse onto the table, I kicked off my Air Max's and went to go find Mommy. Her and Daddy's room was on the third floor, our attic had been remodeled into one huge bedroom, and I walked towards the steps so I could go and find her.

"April..." I stopped in my tracks when I heard my Daddy's voice calling me from the living room. I was surprised that he was even home this early. I skipped back down the stairs, through the kitchen and down the hall to find him. He was sitting on the sofa watching ESPN, I sat down next to him and wrapped my arms around his neck.

"Hey, Daddy."

"How was your day, Princess?" Daddy was holding me close. He smelled like the Brut deodorant that he wore, mixed with a splash of his favorite cologne. I took a Moment to inhale his scent before I answered. His smell was one of a kind, and was just one of those smells that you could never forget. I immediately noticed that he'd just gotten his haircut, he had a fresh fade and was looking extra handsome.

"It was fine, but I don't feel good." I was sure that Mommy had already told him what time of the month it was, and because our cycles were aligned, I'm sure he got the hint. He stroked my hair and I felt like I could melt in his arms.

"It won't kill you, April. It's part of being a woman, and the pain will go away soon, just like it always does." Although he didn't have a damn clue what he was talking about, his voice made me feel better. It was easy for him to say, only because he wasn't the one with blood dripping from between his thighs. I rolled my eyes. He was my Daddy and I loved him dearly, but he was also a man, which made him numb to my pain.

"I know." I answered quietly.

"So what's this I hear about you wanting to join a sorority?" He just came out and asked me unexpectedly. Sometimes, I wondered what exactly Mommy said to him behind closed doors, and who's side she was actually on. Every time I needed permission for something, I asked my Mommy. She's like my liaison. It was her job to convince my Daddy to let me do what I wanted. Sometimes it worked, plenty times it didn't, but that never stopped me from trying. The thing is, sometimes Mommy would rearrange the facts so that Daddy would say yes, and that wasn't a problem. The problem comes in when Mommy forgets to tell *me* exactly what she told *him*, so that we could make sure our stories were the same.

"*Junior* sorority..." I corrected him using Sally's words. "And I never *said* that I was joining, Daddy. I'm just *thinking* about it. I just asked Mommy what she thought about it, that's all." I needed to get my point across, so that he wouldn't be running around stressin', talking about I'm trying to grow up too fast.

"Hmmm." I guess he was letting this sink in because he got quiet all of a sudden. "So where are you going tonight?" He asked me a trick question.

Let me explain, sometimes when it comes to me and Mommy, Dad will ask a question that he already knows the answer to. That's his way of seeing if things add up. He knew that if he didn't stay on point, my Mom and me would run circles around him. He wanted to see if our stories would match, or if we were trying to run game on him.

"Well, the girls really want me to join and they offered to take me to one of their meetings. Afterwards, they go to a different girls house each weekend and have a sleepover." I gave him the basics because Mommy said that's *all* he needed to know. I didn't lie at all. I misled him, but I didn't *lie*.

"So you're going to a sleepover?"

I shook my head. "I'm not going *anywhere*, unless *you* say it's okay." Mommy taught me how to stroke my Dad's ego. A man was a man, regardless of the relation. They wanted to be in charge, and always had to feel like they were runnin' the show. Mommy had already given me permission to go out with Karma tonight, this part was just for Daddy to feel important.

"Where's the meeting at?"

"Buff State."

"On *campus*?" The way he responded let me know that this was definitely new information to him.

"Daddy, the junior sorority, is sponsored by a real college sorority. The college girls are like mentors and tutors. They're supposed to help us and be role models." I hoped I wasn't sounding too manipulative. "Didn't you read the papers that I gave Mom?" I knew damn well he didn't. And the only thing he cared about right now, was whether there would be college boys anywhere around his fourteen year-old daughter.

"Will there be boys there?" That was the next question.

Bingo!

"Daddy!" I lifted my head off his chest and looked into his grey eyes. "It's a college campus, not a convent. I'm sure that there will be boys around there, *somewhere*." I rolled my eyes at him. "It's not like I go to an all girls school right now, I see boys everyday!" I said it with an attitude, and after it came out I wasn't sure whether I was hurting or helping my argument. My tone was borderline disrespectful, but Daddy put up with my smart mouth because I was his soft spot. If I would've talked to Mommy like this, she would've slapped off my eyebrows.

He didn't say nothing so I kept going in. "If you want to, you can come with me and make sure that no college boys come close to me," I was on a roll. "And while you're at it, maybe you should come to school with me so you can keep all the boys away from my locker! Because they're *always* sniffing around my locker!" I told you, my mouth gets loose around this time of the month. Daddy still didn't respond and that alone was just irritating.

I stood up from the sofa and sucked my teeth. "Like it's not bad enough that I'm the only freshman girl in the state of New York that can't even talk to boys on the phone!" This statement wasn't entirely true. Mommy let me talk to boys on the phone, but they weren't allowed to call the house because Daddy would have a heart attack. My headache was starting to get worst and I needed to find my Mom to get some medicine.

I was just about to walk off on him when he burst into laughter. Right in my face, he started cracking up! I couldn't believe it. My teenage crisis was a joke to him. I quickly dipped off before I said something that would possibly get me grounded for the weekend, and found my Mom upstairs studying on the third floor.

"You just getting home?" She asked me as I crawled onto the bed next to her. I frowned up my face, but didn't answer. "What's wrong?" She asked, able to sense my attitude.

"Your husband gets on my nerves." I half whispered, careful not to speak too loud just in case Daddy was coming up the stairs behind me. Mommy smiled sympathetically. "Plus, my head *and* my tummy hurts." I added.

Mommy put her book down and went to the mini refrigerator that they kept upstairs. She opened up a jar of Mott's applesauce and scooped some into a bowl for me. Then she got two Motrin pills and put them into a plastic sandwich bag. She crushed up the pain medication, then sprinkled the powdery substance into the applesauce and stirred it up for me.

"Thank you." I said as she handed me the bowl.

"You're welcome, baby."

I know what you're wondering, so let me explain. I have a mental deficiency that won't allow me to swallow medication. I can't swallow pills. Any kind. Any size. Any shape. I just can't do it, because my gag reflex is crazy. If I try, I'll throw up. Mommy says that I'm just a drama queen. She's probably right, but to the best of my knowledge, that don't have shit to do wit' the reason I'm unable to swallow pills, tablets or capsules like a normal person. I ate the applesauce and then stood up to leave, I wanted to get in the tub 'cause I still felt dirty.

"What happened?" Mommy asked me before I could make it to the steps. "What did your Dad say to you?"

I shrugged. Now that I think about it, he hadn't said anything out of the ordinary. I'm the one who spaced out and took things too personal. I was lucky to still have all my teeth.

"Nothing really," I told her. "I'm just irritated. I'm bout to go take a bath and then take a nap."

She nodded and then got back to her books, and I got ghost before my Dad came upstairs. On the second floor, LaReina was in the family room on the computer and my brothers were in their room playing with some wrestling action figures. I snatched the cordless phone out of my sister's room and vanished into the bathroom.

While I was soaking in the tub I decided to call Asia's house, but her Mom said she was at the mall with Tionna. That made me think about my sister, so I called Tiffany. Tiff didn't answer, and I guessed that she was probably at work. I missed my big sis, and we hadn't talked much since she'd moved out the house last year when she turned eighteen. I couldn't blame her though, I'm gonna move too when I'm old enough, because no matter how old you get, my Daddy still going to treat you like your twelve. He had another three and a half years to get on my damn nerves, after that, I was gone with the wind.

Next, I dialed my cousin Nica's number as I got comfortable inside the bathtub. "Hello?" My aunt Tracey answered the phone.

"Hey, Aunty."

"April, what's up, Sweetie?" My aunt was usually in a good mood for one reason or another.

"Nothing, I'm good, how are you?"

"I can't complain," She answered. "You looking for Nica?" She asked me, and I rolled my eyes. It was one of those stupid ass questions that old people ask you. A question that I really shouldn't have to answer, because she knew damn well I hadn't called to talk to *her*.

"Yeah, is she home?"

"Umm Hmm, she here. But I'm going to tell you right now, April. I don't have any money to give that girl. Not for the movies. Not for the mall. Not for *shit*!" I started cracking up laughing, my aunt Tracey was a trip. "You laughing? I'm *dead* serious. I don't know what ya'll little fast asses got planned for tonight, but it better not have *nothing* to do with spending any of *my* money. So tell Nica don't even ask me. I don't mind if you come over to keep her company, but ya'll not gonna drive me crazy!" I was still laughing. "You got it?"

"I got it." I was able to stop laughing long enough to respond.

Suddenly I could hear some music in the background and Aunty was calling Nica's name. "April's on the phone for you." I heard her say.

A Moment later, my cousin was on the line. "You read my mind, I was just about to call you. What's up?" She sounded really enthusiastic.

Nica was two years older than me, and she was my favorite cousin. We were joined at the hip, and we chilled together a lot. She only lived a couple blocks down from me, but we lived on the same street. Her Moms is mad cool and lets her have boy company, so whenever I wanted to meet up with a dude, I had to go over Aunt Tracey's house.

"Nothing's up, it's applesauce week." We both laughed because she already knew what I was talking about. "What you doing?"

"I'm on Blackplanet.com trying to find me a man." She was giggling. My cousin is crazy, between her and La La, I don't know which one spent more time on the Internet. "My Mom gonna be leaving soon, you want to come spend the night?"

I would have definitely gone, but I already had plans. That's when I told her about being recruited by the Lambda's and going out with them tonight.

"Since when you start trying to make friends wit' *random* bitches?" Nica sounded shocked and her response came across a bit harsh. I didn't answer right away; first, I took a second and thought about it. I knew my cousin well enough to know that she wasn't hating, she was just asking because she knows I'm not the type to hang with a clique.

"I don't know, Nica. It's not like I'm tagging along, on some, 'just wanna be down' type shit. They *asked* me to come." Now I was unsure, and she'd made me start to second-guess myself. I really needed to talk to my sister. "Why you ask me that?"

"It's no big deal, A. You my lil' cousin, and I don't want you to think that I'm trying to hold you back-"

"I don't think that."

"This all I'm saying..." She paused for a Moment. "Don't never let your friends choose you. Always choose your friends. Feel me?" I was listening intently and I heard every word she said. It was simple. But at the same time, it was deep and it made me think. "But go out and have fun.

See what it's about, and if you like it, then join it." She encouraged me.

I took her words for what they were worth because I knew that she was just trying to look out for me. I was young and I'd just started high school, Tiffany would have probably given me the same advice.

"Okay." That was the only response I gave her, I didn't wanna talk about that subject anymore. "You think aunty will let me spend the night tomorrow, or do you have something to do?" I asked her.

"Bitch, now you know my Mom don't care if you come over here," Nica snapped at me. "And what we need to do tomorrow, is find some cute niggas to take us to the movies or something! We too pretty to be having so much free time on our hands." We both started cracking up.

"That's true." I was inclined to agree. "I'm down for whatever. I'll call you tomorrow afternoon." I promised her right before we both hung up. I soaked in the tub for another 15 minutes and then took a long shower to rinse the dirt off. I was tired and I just wanted to go to sleep. Sitting in school always seemed to drain a lot of energy from me, and plus the medication mixed with the hot water had me drowsy.

I wrapped up in a towel and walked to my room. When I got there, my Daddy was sitting on my bed waiting for me. "So you talk to me like your *crazy*, and then you have the nerve to go and use up all *my* hot water? You had that water running for at least 30 minutes, are you nuts?" He didn't look mad, but then again he wasn't smiling either. Daddy was cheap. Every winter, all he complained about is we using either too much heat, or too much hot water.

"Sorry, Daddy."

"You always sorry about something." He teased, but then smiled a little to let me know he wasn't angry. "Come sit down." He patted the bed, signaling me to sit next to him.

"Oh, I'm *not* sorry about taking a long shower..." I grinned at him. "But I am sorry about talking to you like I was crazy earlier."

"Don't be sorry, I needed a good laugh." He smirked, and I twisted up my face at him. One thing he did well was push my buttons. But I couldn't even get mad because I had that one coming. "You just like your Mommy. You can joke all day, unless the joke is on you, then you can't take it." He said while reading my facial expression.

I just shrugged. He was definitely right about that, but I didn't respond. Instead, I sat there playing with my fingernails. I could really use a trip to the nail salon as soon as possible.

He cleared his throat to get my attention. "I'm going to let you go out with your new friends tonight. But don't play with me, April. If I call that number, you'd better be there at the house you're supposed to be sleeping at. Don't make me come looking for you." He was staring me dead in the face, and there was no hint that he was joking at all.

"You can call me, I'll be there." I assured him. Mommy had already talked to both Karma and Sally's parents. Karma was driving me, but the actual sleepover was being held at Sally's house this weekend.

He rubbed my cheek. "You're getting older, and I gotta be able to trust you. If I cant, I'm not going to let you out of my sight." He gave me a stern look before standing up and walking towards the door. "I left something for you inside your closet," he called over his shoulder. "You can thank me later." Then he walked out, pulling my door closed behind him.

I jumped up and scrambled to my closet to see what he'd bought me. I grabbed the Macy's bag that was on the floor and pulled out the gold shoebox. Inside of it was a pair of five-inch leather ankle boots, and they were *so* cute. They were like an ox blood color that matched a new leather jacket and a purse that I already had.

I smiled. They were the same boots that I'd begged my Mom for yesterday while we were at the mall. Daddy was amazing. I'd needed some heels to go out in tonight because most of the Lambda girls didn't wear sneakers, and I didn't want to be the outcast.

It was 4:30. Karma would be here at 7:00. I put on some panties, a tank top and slid under the covers. Then I reached over, set my alarm clock for 6:15 and dozed off.

CHAPTER EIGHT

I was riding shotgun as Karma whipped the silver Lexus ES300 out of Buff States parking lot. The grey leather bucket seats were heated and so soft that it was like sitting on a cloud. The wood grain was shiny and the entire interior was immaculate. There was no lint on the carpets, no paper, candy or blunt wrappers, cigar guts or anything else lying around. There weren't even any ashes in the ashtray.

The clock said 8:45 pm. The Lambda meeting had went from 7:30 until 8:30, and now we were heading to Hamburg to party at the Roxbury. Hamburg is a suburb on the outskirts of Buffalo, and the Roxbury is teen nightclub that I'd never been to, but I'd heard crazy stories about.

Karma had that Usher 8701 blasting thru the stereo system. The trunk was beating bass through my chest and I was so in love with this car. We were riding dolo, but all together we were four cars deep and there were about 14 of us headed to the club. We were all smart, sexy, and beautiful and oddly enough, we all were a light-skin complexion and most of us were bi-racial. I'm not the smartest bitch in the world, but something told me that our physical similarities weren't a coincidence. I'm almost certain that the Lambda girls only recruited females that fit certain physical criteria. I'm not sure if that's wrong, but it did make me feel a bit weird to be surrounded by girls who all resembled each other.

The meeting had been impressive and I'd been feelin' the vibe that *most* of the girls were giving off. And I do emphasize the word *most*. The college girls were all very nice to me, and it turned out that they were just there to chaperone us. Karma was actually the one who ran the show, and she only answered to a woman named Ms. Debbie who was the founder of the Kappa Lambda Theta *junior* sorority. But she didn't talk much; she was just there for adult supervision. All together, it seemed to be about 50-60 high school girls who were actually members. Then, another 12 girls there were pledging to become members. But today, I was the only girl there who was 'shadowing' as they call it.

I paid attention to what was going on, and realized that there were cliques inside the clique. It was obvious that some of the girls had tension with each other, and you could feel it in the air. But it was understandable, I mean, when you've got seventy of the city's prettiest girls in the same room, you *have* to expect a cat fight or two. There were ranks amongst the sorority, sort of like how my school's cafeteria was set up. Karma's clique was at the top of the food chain; they kept the other girls in check and had this whole organization on lock.

The only thing that I really wasn't feeling is how the pledges were treated until they became sisters. One of the pledges was telling me about this shit called 'hell week'. Hell week is supposedly a week of torture that all pledges go thru. From what I understand, during that week pledges have to wear the same clothes to school everyday, you couldn't take a shower and you weren't allowed to speak during that week unless you were talking to an adult. Plus a bunch of other stuff that I just didn't know if I was willing to do.

You can say what you want, but wearing the same outfit five days in a row is just plain nasty! *And*, these broads will actually smell you just to make sure you haven't showered. But even after you go through all of that, you still had to be voted in, and that didn't make any sense to me.

I had some thinking to do, because there was just some shit that I wasn't going to tolerate. My own mother never even hit me wit' no stick, so I damn sure wasn't about to let no bitch a couple years older than me, smack my ass with no giant wooden paddle. That shit was out of the question.

Karma turned down the volume on the stereo. "So, what did you think?" She wanted to know how I felt about the sorority meeting.

"It was cool." I answered and she nodded. I studied her face for a Moment while she drove. It was dark outside, but the streetlights shined through the lightly tinted windows just enough for me to see her face. Karma is *beautiful*, I know I already told you that, but I can't emphasize it enough. Not to sound like a groupie, but I really admire her style. "I'm sayin' tho..." she looked over at me as I began to speak. "I wouldn't have to wear the same *panties* all week would I?" I really wanted to know. "I mean, the same pants and shirt is one thing, but *panties*..."

Karma burst out in laughter. I was smiling, but I was dead ass serious. That whole 'hell week' situation was on my mind heavy. I needed clarification. I had to know.

"I doubt anyone will check," She was still laughing. "I know I'm definitely not gonna check your panties. You cute and all, but I'm not trying to get to know you like that!" Now we were both laughing.

"And what about that big ass wooden paddle?" I asked her. "What's that for?"

Karma quickly stopped laughing. "What wooden paddle? I don't know anything about a wooden paddle." She answered quickly, then instantly changed the subject. "The next pledge line is in January, so you'll have a couple weeks to let me know if this is something you want to do."

"I'll think about it, and let you know soon." I didn't want to give her an answer just yet, because I needed to think. And I'm not stupid, this bitch thought she was being slick by ducking my question about that giant paddle I saw with the Greek writing on it. I watched enough TV to know what those paddle were used for, I'm not dumb.

"Take your time, it's a big step." She looked over at me. "And once you're in it, you're in it for life. We're like a *gang*," she flashed me that smile again. "A gang of pretty bitches trying to take over the world." I had no choice but to smile, because hers was contagious, so I couldn't help it.

Just then, a loud beeping sound caught both our attention. Karma's eyes left the road Momentarily as she dug into her purse while driving, and I immediately started praying that this bitch wouldn't crash. I wasn't trying to go out like Princess Diana. I was thrilled when she finally found what she was looking for and focused her eyes back on the road. It was a pager, a Motorola two-way, one of the expensive joints that all the rappers were using.

"It's my Boo," she told me. "His name is Vance." When she said the name, it definitely rang a bell. I've never met the dude, but I'd heard his name a lot, because he was definitely a *very* well known hustler around the city's Midtown section. I peeped certain things about being in high school. High school girls always go out of their way to tell you who their man is. She made sure that I knew Vance was her dude, that way if he and I ever met, I couldn't say that I didn't know. "He probably just paged me so he can check on his baby-"

"*Awwwe...*" I cooed with a smile. "That's cute. How long have you two been together?" I asked just to be nosy.

"Two years," She giggled. "But I'm not the *baby* that he called to check on," she looked at me and laughed. "I'm *wifey*, his *baby* is this damn car! Every time he lets me drive it, he pages me a million times just to make sure it's okay. Like I'm going to run off and sell it or something."

"Oh." I laughed along with her, but at the same time, I was a little jealous. I couldn't wait to have a relationship of my own, and be able to share things about my man and me.

"What about *you*?" Karma must have been reading my thoughts. "I happen to know for a fact that there's *tons* of boys at school who like you, why haven't I heard about you having a boyfriend? I know you have to have one." Now it was her turn to be nosy.

"Nope. I'ma be single until I'm at least *thirty*." I just flat out told her the truth, wasn't any sense in frontin'.

At first, she started to laugh, but when she saw that I wasn't joking, she gave me a real sympathetic look. "*Oooh girl*, you don't even gotta tell me. *Trust me*, I already know." Then she started shaking her head like she was reminiscing. "My parents kept me locked in the house until halfway through my sophomore year. If it didn't have anything to do with church, I couldn't go!" Then she winked at me. "It'll get better though. I talked to your Moms on the phone, she's really cool-"

"It's not *her*, it's my Daddy."

Karma shrugged. "Like I said, you don't gotta tell me. I already know what you're going through. Trust me, I've been there and my Daddy is a *Preacher*, so you can just about imagine." Karma reached over and rubbed my knee just to show me that she felt my pain. Then she cranked the volume back up just as we merged into traffic on the expressway heading towards the club. We didn't speak anymore for the rest of the ride, we both just zoned out to the sounds of Usher. Both of us deep in our own thoughts.

CHAPTER NINE

I'd be lying if I said that my head wasn't gassed up. We pulled up to the club like rock stars. We were riding clean. A Lexus, a Lincoln Navigator, a Land Rover, *and* an Audi A8, *and* we were all dress to kill. I had on my new heels, some skin-tight jeans and a cute matching turtleneck. The little leather biker jacket I was wearing, only covered half of my butt and my ass were poking out like crazy!

The Roxbury was like a real nightclub; it was a long line outside and everything. But to my surprise, the line didn't apply to us. We strutted right up to the entrance behind Karma, past the line and right up to the security rope. Some big ass dude who looked like a NFL player moved the rope and opened the door right up for us. It was freezing outside, and all the kids in line who were on the verge of catching frostbite, didn't look too happy to see us cutting the line. But hey, there are levels to life. Everybody can't be VIP status, and it's better they learned now while they were young.

"Lambda's don't *wait* in lines." A girl named Shannon leaned over and whispered that into my ear as we walked inside the club. In the hallway, the music was blaring, and there was another short line where everyone was lined up waiting to pay the cover charge. I pulled my Baby Phat purse off my shoulder, but before I could open it, Shannon grabbed my hand. "*We don't pay either!*" She leaned in once again and made that very clear. She pulled my arm as we followed the rest of our crew straight past the pay booth *and* the security checkpoint. Now, this was the type of shit that I deserved, and I could definitely get used to the VIP lifestyle.

Shannon put her arm around my shoulder. "They let us in for free, because we bring them business. Many people come here on the weekends just to see *us*. Plus, the fact that *we* come here, makes this the place to be." She filled me in as we entered the actual nightclub. I was looking around in every direction trying to take it all in, I was looking like a tourist. After all these years of being sheltered, this was my first official nightlife experience. The club was about the size of two high school gymnasiums, and it was almost packed. I kept scanning the scene as Shannon pulled my arm leading me through the crowd.

The party was a mixed mob of teenagers. White, Black, Hispanic, and everything in between. The music was also a mixture, and the DJ was playing any and every genre of music, as long as you could dance to it. We didn't stop walking until we came upon a little section in the corner that was roped off and obviously reserved for us. There were a bunch of tables and a few sofas there, but nobody had any plans on sitting and immediately began to dance. So, there wasn't anything to do but get my party on! At first, I was a tad bit self-conscious because I've only danced in public on a few occasions when I've gone to a couple house parties with Nica. Other than that, I've only danced in front of the mirror in my bedroom, but I definitely knew how to move these hips.

The strobe lights were flashing and reflecting off the mirrors that were attached to the walls. I was really hype and feeling really grown. Mad cute dudes were coming to our section checking for the girls I was with. I was introduced a few times, and had a few dances with a couple of them. You have to remember, it's applesauce week, and so I wasn't trying to do too much grinding. And after a couple hours of niggas rubbing up against me, touching my stomach and thighs a bitch was extra horny and decided I was done dancing.

I dipped off to the juice bar and ordered something to drink. Daddy had given me fifty dollars, but I didn't want to spend too much because I was going to Nica's house tomorrow and I might need some money. I stood at the counter waiting for the girl to bring me my juice, and when she finally got around to me, I dug into my purse to give her the money. I was just about to pass the cashier a five-dollar bill when a big arm wrapped around my waist and stomach, then some dude pressed himself against my butt. A hand extended, and whoever was behind me gave the cashier a fifty-dollar bill to pay for my drink. I was about to spin around to see who was all up on me, but then I heard Darrell's voice in my ear.

"I know you told me to keep my hands to myself, but I'm hard-headed." Then he subtly rubbed his crotch against my ass just to get his point across. The only reason that I didn't spaz on him is because I was horny and in a good mood. Instead, I put my money away and let him buy my drink. The girl behind the counter gave him forty-eight dollars change, and Darrell slid the money into my back pocket making sure to cuff my ass along the way. I rolled my eyes, but I didn't stop him from getting his feels off.

I had a better idea.

"You still mad at me, baby?" Darrell had his lips pressed against my ear, and he was speaking just loud enough that I could hear him over the music. His hands were groping me, as I answered his question by shaking my head while I sipped my juice. In my head I was wondering if a nigga giving me $48, and then feeling like that made it okay to grope me, was something that I should take disrespectfully. "You smell good too." I took the compliment for what it was worth. I *always* smell good. I didn't answer, but I did have a smile on my face.

I finished my drink and finally turned around to face him. Damn. Darrell was looking good, and he was towering over me making me feel like a midget even in my heels. I noticed that the entire basketball team surrounded him and they all had their varsity jackets on. It wasn't until that Moment that I remembered they'd had a game this afternoon.

Darrell took a seat on the nearest bar stool and pulled me towards him until I was positioned between his legs. He was sitting and I was standing, now we were face to face.

The music was blaring so he leaned in extra close. "I miss you. Why haven't you been calling me?" He wanted to know. I hadn't spoken to Darrell since Monday, and I'd been dodging him all week. But it wasn't because I was still mad; the reason was that he still hadn't bought me a present. Maybe he thought I wasn't serious, if that was the case, he'd really underestimated me.

"I haven't been calling you, because you still haven't done anything to make me feel special yet."

"I didn't forget, April. Don't worry, I got you." I dramatically rolled my eyes at his response. I'd heard that line way too many times, and I wasn't buying it. I needed to see it to believe it.

"Well, you're taking too long and I'm not about to be sweatin' you if you're not treating me right."

"Tell me what you want."

I didn't waste any time because I already knew. "I want you to take me to the movies tomorrow night, but you have to bring somebody for my cousin NIca." I didn't want much, but if he wanted to keep rubbing his hands on me, he was gonna do what I asked.

"Aight." He quickly agreed.

"And you better not even think about asking us to pay for *any*thing." I looked him straight in the eye. It had to be said, because some of these high school boys were out of control. Some of them think it's okay to ask a girl out and then make it a 'dutch' date.

He looked offended. "C'mon, April. You don't have to tell me that. Just call me tomorrow and tell me where you want me to pick you up." He thought he was getting off that easy, but I wasn't finished.

I kissed him on the cheek. "And you better bring me something to make me smile. I didn't forget about that dumb shit you did on Monday at school." I tried to end our conversation right there by walking off on him, but he grabbed my waist and held me there.

"What you want me to bring you?" He asked and it caught me off guard. I really just wanted him too use his imagination. His family had money, so I didn't want to cheat myself by bidding too low, but at the same time, I didn't want to ask for too much.

I stepped back a little so he could get a good look at me. "Darrell, look at my body. You know what sizes I wear, right?"

He nodded as his eyes roamed my curves.

"Then just get me something that'll look good on me."

"*Everything* looks good on you." He made me blush, and I could feel my face turning pink. Darrell got on my nerves sometimes, but for the most part, he was a sweetheart.

"Then just get me *everything*." I leaned over and kissed his cheek one last time. "Congratulations on your game. I heard we're still undefeated." Then I broke out of his grasp and walked away. There were two things that I knew for sure; the first was that Darrell wouldn't disappoint me tomorrow. The second was that my cousin Nica would be thrilled.

I was on my way back to the corner section where all the Lambda girls were, when suddenly out of nowhere Sally was in my face looking all crazy, and waving her hands.

"*April*, stay the fuck away from him!" She was yelling at me above the sound of the music.

Hold up! I know this bitch *couldn't* have been talking to *me* like that. I'm not going to lie; it took a second for me to react, but only because I was so shocked. But when I did come around to my senses, the first thing I did was slap that bitch's hand out my face. And I slapped it *hard*! And the next time she raised it, I was gonna try her mouth.

"Bitch get out my face before I hurt you!" I barked at her. Shit, I don't even know whether or not I would be able to fulfill that promise, but I bet you I'd try. My blood was starting to boil, I hadn't been this mad in a long time. The only *him* she could've been referring to was Darrell, and if that was *her* man, I definitely hadn't known.

Karma came out of nowhere and got between us, she put her arm around me and dragged me off to where the bathrooms were. By now, everyone was looking, and Sally had just created a huge scene in the middle of the nightclub. I'm not really used to being in the middle of conflict, so my heart was beating fast and my adrenaline was rushing.

"April," Karma had pulled me into one of the bathroom stalls. "I don't know if you knew, and you probably didn't since you just got to high school a few months ago, but Darrell is Sally's ex-boyfriend. And obviously, in case you couldn't tell, she's still stuck on him, and that's why she's trippin'."

"So why didn't she just pull me to the side like you're doing right now, and tell me that. I thought Lambda's were supposed to be classier than that, Karma. She just made a *huge* scene over a *boy*? That's not classy at all." Karma listened and didn't interrupt me. "I don't have a problem with her, but I'm not going to let *anyone* talk to me like that, and *especially* not put they hands in my face."

"I feel where you coming from. I like you, April. And whether or not you become one of my sisters or not, you still cool wit me. And you're right; she should've handled things differently. But understand this, Sally is the vice president. And next year when I'm off to college, Sally will be in charge. So you two are going to have to smooth this over or else there will be tension, and trust me, it's in *your* best interest because all the girls like her so she has numbers on her side. Plus you're new, and you're not even a sister yet." Karma was right, I wasn't a part of the clique, and I was an outsider. And at first, it was looking as if I'd fit in, but now I wasn't so sure. Just my luck, I'd made an enemy my first night.

And the more I thought about it, the more I realized that this just wouldn't work. I wasn't about to go through this sucka shit every time a boy started trying to get next to me. It was seventy girls in that meeting today. I don't have time to keep track of who's dating whom, and who is whose ex-boyfriend. Buffalo isn't that big to begin with, and the selection of real niggas is slim, so I was bound to step on somebody's toes again. Or vise versa, and it wasn't worth the trouble.

"You're right, Karma. And I appreciate you inviting me out tonight. I was having a great time up until a few minutes ago, but I'm gonna call my Moms and have her come get me-"

"No. You don't gotta do that boo. I told your mother that I'd bring you home safe and I'm going to do that. I usually don't go to the sleepovers anyway," she grinned at me. "You'd be surprised at some of the shit that goes on there." She winked at me. "Wait here for a second, I'm bout to go curse Sally out and tell everyone that we're leaving." Karma dipped off and left me standing outside the bathroom.

A couple minutes later, all the girls were surrounding me. Everyone had given me a hug, including Sally. "Sorry, April." She apologized to me. "I got emotional, and I was out of line. Everyone was having a good time, sorry that I went and ruined it." Sally actually looked sincere, but probably only because the other girls had told her how wrong she was for coming at me like that.

"It's okay," I smiled at her. "We're cool." I said it and I meant it. I forgave her, but that didn't mean that I trusted her or her apology. Karma on the other hand, she was pissed. I could tell by the way she was screw-facing Sally from a few feet away.

Shannon wrapped her arm around my neck. "See, everything's cool. Let's finish partying and then we can go back to Sally's and chill." She was doing her best to lighten up the tense mood, but it was a little too late.

That's when Karma jumped in. "She already called her Mom and told her she was coming home, we're about to leave." She lied for me; she knew damn well that I wasn't about to spend the night at Sally's house after she'd just flipped on me.

Then Karma turned to Sally, "And, that's a twenty-five dollar fine! As Lambda's, we *always* show respect, and exhibit self-control at *all* times. Don't we ladies?" I watched as all the girls nodded in. "Don't we, *Sally*?"

"Yes." Sally didn't hesitate to answer.

"So make sure you pay that fine by next Friday at our meeting," Karma was staring her down, but Sally was looking at the floor. "Unless you like splinters in your ass!" She added angrily. When she said that, all the girls grimaced and exchanged looks, and that's when I knew the myths about the wooden paddle was true.

Ouch!

Karma and me left the club and dipped off in the Lexus. For whatever reason we didn't speak for the majority of the ride, we just listened to Usher. About thirty minutes later, she pulled into my driveway behind the Dodge Caravan Daycare Van.

"What are you going to tell your Mom?" she asked me.

I shrugged. Honestly, I really hadn't bothered to think that far ahead. "The truth I guess, or at least something close to it." I looked at the clock and it was almost midnight. I hoped that I ran into Mommy first, that way I wouldn't have to explain anything to my Dad.

She nodded. "Well, you've got my number, you can call me anytime. It doesn't matter what you want to talk about, I'll listen." She hit me with that smile again.

"Okay." I reached into the backseat and grabbed my overnight bag, and I was just about to get out the car when Karma grabbed my arm.

"I saw you working your magic on Darrell. He was drooling all over you. That's why Sally got so mad, because he never used to look at her like that." I listened, but I was wondering where this conversation was leading to and why she was telling me this. "I know you heard the phrase, 'pussy is power', right?"

I nodded. I'd heard it plenty times from my sister.

Karma was looking at me with eyes like lasers. "Well, it's true. But try not to use your power the wrong way.

That's how people get hurt. And most times, it ends up backfiring on you, especially when you use it for selfish reasons. And you know when it'll come back to haunt you, right?" I shook my head, because I didn't know the answer. Tiffany hadn't put me up on the other half of the game. This was the second time in one day that another bitch had to pull my coat to something she'd forgotten to mention.

"No. *When*?" I was curious as hell, and hanging onto her every word, eager to soak up game.

She patted my shoulder. "When you finally fall in love for real, that's when your past and all your dirt will come back to haunt you. If you use your power to manipulate and mislead people, one day the person you least expect, will use that same power to hurt *you*."

This shit was too deep, and I was lost. "How can they use my power against me? It's mine." I hoped I didn't sound too naïve, but I needed to get an understanding.

Karma smiled. "Because when we *really* fall in love. I mean, when we fall in love for real, we give our heart to him. And once you give a nigga your heart, your power is gone. Now he's got it-"

"Can you get it back?"

Karma frowned. "Let me ask you something. Did you ever leave a dollar bill inside your pocket and accidentally it gets washed and dried along with your clothes?" I looked at her like she was crazy. What the *fuck* did that have to do with what we were talking about?

"Yeah." I answered reluctantly.

"And when you get the dollar bill back, it's still money. But it don't look the same no more. It's faded and worn out, and it doesn't feel the same anymore either. And that's how you're heart gonna be when you finally get it back. Washed up, dried out and ruined. That's *if* you ever get it back. Sally still hasn't gotten hers back yet. Think about it."

Now I understood perfectly.

We said goodbye and I climbed out the Lexus. I'd made up my mind not to be a Lambda, but at least I'd experienced what it was like to be popular for one night.

It was a lesson well learned.

CHAPTER TEN

I couldn't believe I was sitting inside the movie theater watching 'Harry Potter and the Sorcerer's Stone'. On any other date, this would've been very unacceptable. I was in a good mood so didn't make a big deal about the movie selection, but trust me; I'd be picking the movie from now on. Darrell had brought his boy Bean to keep Nica company for the night. Bean was cute, he was tall and played basketball for Seneca high school. Needless to say, Nica was thrilled.

Only problem was our dates were acting immature. These two fools were being mad loud inside the theater. Every time Harry Potter did some crazy shit, Darrell and Bean would get real hype. They were jumping around, slapping each other high fives 'n shit. Shit, had I known I would be babysitting tonight I would've brought Cory and Lito with me too. The only reason I wasn't irritated was because Darrell had done what I'd asked, so I gave him a pass on his stupidity. He'd brought me three bags full of clothes from the Galleria Mall. Two outfits, two pairs of kicks, and two purses. *And*, he'd given me a crisp hundred-dollar bill, so I was a happy camper. Sally would just have to be pissed at me because I was really close to making Darrell my boyfriend.

So far Nica hadn't seemed to mind their behavior either, she was laughing and having a good time and I can't front, the movie wasn't that bad. It was actually good, just not the romantic comedy that I'd had in mind. I could've whined and pouted my way into seeing another flick, but I figured he deserved to see what he wanted since he'd done such a good job picking out my presents. I didn't even have to curse him out for bringing me the wrong sizes, because everything had fit perfectly.

Darrell just needed a little training. He needed to work on his manners a little bit, because this nigga be actin' like his hand is broke when it come to opening doors for a bitch. Minus a few other minor flaws, but I could definitely train him to be obedient, he did have some hubby potential.

I started shifting in my seat. I wanted him to touch me. He could at least put his arm around me or somethin'. But he was so into the movie and interacting with bean that it made me feel like I was on an island by myself. I was in my own thoughts when the entire theater erupted into loud gasps of 'oohs and aahs!' Then Darrell turned around and slapped Bean five for the gazillionth time, and that's when I had enough.

"Yo, you see that shit?" Darrell was amped, he was beaming like a five-year old. I was starting to find it a bit strange that these two seventeen year olds, was so extra hyper over this lil' white boy magician with glasses. It was beginning to be disturbing. I turned to look at Nica, they was sitting in the row behind us. She was giggling, and when she saw my irritation, she just looked at me and shrugged. Its bad to say, but my cousin was just so happy to get out the house that she didn't care what was going on.

I turned back around and decided it was up to me; I'd have to take matters into my own hands. Literally. My leather jacket was on the seat next to me, I grabbed it and spread it across Darrell's lap. He gave me a weird look because at the minute he didn't understand. I laid my head on his shoulder, reached under my jacket, slid my hand down his pants and started squeezing him. I'd finally gotten his undivided attention. That's when he finally put his arm around me, and he didn't move or make another sound for the rest of the movie. There were no more high-fives or loud outburst, and finally that problem had been solved.

*   *   *   *   *

When the movie finally let out, it was almost 10pm and afterwards Nica and I went to the bathroom while the boys waited outside for us. I went straight for the sink, and the first thing I did was wash my hands

"You nasty!" Nica was laughing at me while she began fixing her hair in the mirror.

"What are you talking about?" I asked her innocently. I dried both my hands, and then went into the stall to handle my business.

"Bitch you *know* what I'm talking about." She snickered. "Now I know how you got him to go shopping for you." My cousin was cracking up. We played like that though, and she didn't mean anything by it, she was just joking.

"Tuh! I know damn well Aunt Tracey didn't raise no *hater*! Are you jealous Tanica?" I flushed the toilet and fixed my clothes before coming out the stall, and then we stood face to face grinning at one another.

"What you do to him?" She asked, ignoring my sarcasm. I didn't respond, I just gave her a blank expression as I washed my hands again. "Ya'll was doing something, April. It was way too quiet up there the second half of the movie." Nica was being nosy.

"Oh," I shrugged. "I told him to shut the fuck up, and stop embarrassing me. And that's exactly what he did." We both cracked up and stepped out the bathroom.

"What's so funny?" Darrell grabbed me as soon as I came out the restroom and took me by the hand.

I wiped the smile off my face. *"Nothing."* I looked up at him. He had his GUAGGI skullcap cocked to the side exposing part of his tapered wave cut, and he looked so handsome. We walked hand in hand, but his legs were so long that I couldn't keep up and he was damn near pulling me to the exit. "I'm hungry." I told him as we hit the parking lot.

"I'll take you to Applebee's. Is that okay wit' you?" It was a good sign that he was asking permission. He was a quick learner. I nodded, and then turned around to look at my cousin. Bean had his arm around her as they walked behind us.

"Nica, you cool wit' Applebee's?"

She nodded wearing a grin. "Yeah."

When we reached Darrell's Jeep Grand Cherokee, he hit the alarm to open the doors and then let go of my hand to walk towards the driver's side door. He was about to get behind the wheel without walking me to the passenger side and opening the door for me, but I wasn't going for it.

I followed him and grabbed him by the coat. "Come here!" I pulled him around to the other side of his truck, and waited for Bean and Nice to get inside before I checked him. "D, I know your mother taught you how to act. It's nothing cute about being ignorant. I'm a lady, open the door for me!" I snapped at him loudly.

For a second he just stared at me without moving, he wasn't used to a female talking to him like this, and I could tell that he wanted to say something slick. Maybe I'd been expecting too much from him too soon. So I decided to give him a way out to protect his ego, I flipped my body language and put my tone in check.

"*Please*, D. Can you open the door for me like a gentleman?" I asked very soft and submissively.

For the most part, I feel like I carry myself like a woman, so I think I deserve to be treated like one. At this Moment, I lost *all* respect for Sally. She'd obviously hadn't even trained this boy to do the simple things, so now I would have to start from scratch. Now I was wondering what else I'd have to teach this nigga.

Darrell scratched his head and cracked a smile. "You too much, April. You're really going to drive me crazy." He said while finally opening the door for me.

"I promise, I'll be worth all your trouble." I smiled at him and slid into his truck. Maybe *he* didn't know the value of a bad bitch such as myself, but *I* knew *exactly* what I was worth. And I refuse to accept anything less than what my hand calls for, and I'll keep checking his ass until he gets it right.

April Showers should *never* be confused with his ex.

CHAPTER ELEVEN

Applebee's was crowded with tons of people eating out on a Saturday night. We were all chilling' in the front lobby waiting for the host to find us a table. Darrell and Bean were being annoying on some hood shit. I know I said I wanted a thug, but I need one who at least knows how to act in public. To make things worst, even Nica was starting to get irritated.

My cousin and me had to huddle up to evaluate the situation. "Damn, bitch! Where'd you find these niggas? The *circus*?" Nica had her hand on her hip and clearly had lost her patience with the situation. A couple feet away from us, D and Bean were talking shit to each other about who was winning the battle between Jay-Z and Nas. Each of them had a different opinion, and that was cool, but they were wild loud reciting rhymes and nobody else in this restaurant gave a fuck about Ether or Takeover!

"...I'm glad I don't go to public school." Nica added disgustedly, and I tried my best to ignore her ignorant ass comment. Nica went to private school in the suburbs, and she was used to being around a bunch of shy and quiet type dudes.

"Listen," I had to think rationally because Nica was talking about calling a cab and leaving. "We'll just separate them, I'll make Darrell get us a separate table, and you go eat with Bean." That was some real kindergarten shit, but it was the best I could come up with.

Nica rolled her eyes. "*No, bitch*. How about *we* get our own table, and those two clowns can finish they freestyle battle." I didn't wanna laugh but I couldn't help but giggle. Not because of what she said, but how she said it. I just wish you could've seen her face.

"Tanica, I see you all the time. I'm not trying to be all in *your* face, I'm trying to be in *his* face!" I nodded towards Darrell.

Again, she rolled her eyes. "*Fine*, April. But if these fools yell across this restaurant *one* time, I'm leaving." She looked serious. Nica wasn't about to keep getting embarrassed in public. It was one thing for them to be loud in a dark movie theater where nobody could see our faces, but a restaurant setting was something totally different and I respected where she was coming from.

"Bet." We broke our huddle and I strutted over to Darrell. I put my hands inside the pockets of his navy blue and gold varsity jacket and pulled him off to the side. "D, can we get our own table? I wanna be alone with you." I said it as sweetly as I could. I was wearing my hair down today, I'd ditched the ponytail and rocked it the way he liked it. I used my fingers to comb the long strands of hair over my shoulder and looked at him intensely with my almond shaped eyes.

"April, I already told the hostess-"

"Darrell!" I was starting to lose patience. "Go tell the lady that we want a separate table." I folded my arms across my chest. I couldn't believe that I was out on a date with a 6'5" ten year old, and it made me wonder how he'd act in front of my parents. The thought scared me.

I stood still and watched him walk off, but before he went to the hostess he stopped and said something to Bean. Bean looked over at me, and then back at Darrell, he smiled and shrugged his shoulders like he didn't mind the change of plans. Why should he? My cousin was a dime. She looked just like the girl Kelly from Destiny's Child. If he didn't want to be alone wit' Nica, he had to be gay. The two of them walked over to the hostess together, and a smile spread across her face. She was probably thrilled that these two morons wouldn't be sitting at the same table, and I wouldn't be surprised if she seated us on two opposite sides of the restaurant.

Bless her heart.

Eventually, my date and I ended up seated side by side in a cozy booth in the corner of the restaurant. Darrell couldn't keep his hands off me; his palm was rubbing my thigh the entire time. I wasn't trippin' though, at least he was behaving himself. Bean and Nica were about four tables away and he hadn't even glanced in that direction.

"You want desert?" He asked me after we'd finished our dinner.

Who was he kidding? Of course I did. "Please." My Mom always taught me to use my manners. *Please* and *thank you* were mandatory in my house. He passed me the small desert menu so that I could flip through it. "I want some cheesecake." It was a real sweet and subtle demand.

To make me happy he flagged down the server and ordered two slices for us. "What were you doing up at the Roxbury last night?" he asked me after she'd taken our dirty dinner plates and walked off.

I just shrugged and flipped the question back on him. "What were *you* doing up at the Roxbury last night?"

He smiled. "I'm *every*where, you *never* there!" He quoted Jay-Z. "Me and my team at The Roxbury every weekend, we regulars, but I *never* seen you there before. Who you came wit'? My boy said he peeped you leavin' wit Karma, is that true?" He was looking at me real funny.

"Yeah, that's true. Why? You don't want me hanging with her or something?" I asked just to see what he would say, because I could sense that he had a problem. Not that I cared how he felt, after all, he wasn't my man.

"Nah, it's not that. Karma cool, I just don't fuck wit' them east side Midtown dudes, and Vance is her man." Darrell's explanation was credible, but confusing, unless you understand how the hoods work in Buffalo. See, Darrell's from the Cedar Springs section and his friends had beef wit' Vance's side of town. And when I say *beef*, I mean *beef*. Like niggas is *dying* type of drama.

"Oh, well me and Karma is cool, but we not road dawgs or anything like that."

He looked at me suspiciously. "It's just not a good idea for you to be riding in *that* Lexus. The windows are tinted and niggas will never know who's inside. I don't want you to end up in the wrong place at the wrong time." His words gave me a chill in my spine, I'd never thought about that.

He seemed genuinely concerned and at that point I felt obligated to tell him about the Lambda situation, I figured he should know because I didn't want him to think I was just on both sides of the fence. Darrell is in the streets real heavy, I don't know what he's capable of *personally*, but I've heard stories about some of his friends, Bean included. If I was gonna deal wit' Darrell I needed to be careful how close I got to Karma, it could be a potential disaster, and that could've been a factor in his break-up with Sally. He shrugged it off and threw his arm around me. The subject changed and we chilled until our desert arrived.

I was halfway done with my cheesecake when Bean stormed over to our table looking furious. "Yo, we gotta *go*." He tapped Darrell's shoulder. I didn't know Bean that well, but I knew he was mad about something. Immediately, I turned to see if Nica was okay. She was staring back at me with a confused look on her face, but she didn't look mad or upset.

"What up?" D asked him.

Bean cut his eyes towards me, making it obvious that he wasn't gonna talk about it while I was sitting there. "C'mon man, I'll tell you on the way." Bean said before walking off.

Darrell looked at my half eaten cheesecake, then at my face. "Put your coat on and grab your purse." He instructed as he stood up, pulled out a wad of money and tossed some bills on the table to pay for our meal. At first, I thought about protesting, but I'm not an idiot, I know when it's time to do as I'm told. I followed instructions as he walked off to catch Bean, and then I went to talk to Nica.

"Why Bean look like he a ghost?" I grabbed her hand and we hurried to catch our dates before we fucked around and got stranded. "What you do? You must have shown him your ugly ass feet!" I threw a joke at my cousin and we both cracked up as she punched me in the arm. "Seriously, what happened?" I wanted to know.

Nica shrugged. "Somebody paged him. He went to the pay phone and came back looking crazy, talkin' bout it's time to go." She told me. "Probably some baby mama drama-"

"Bean got kids?" My jaw dropped.

"He has a daughter, she's one." Nica gave me one of her looks. "I just found out during dinner. And this the last time I let you hook me up with anybody! I cant believe you got me sitting in Applebee's wit' some bitches baby Daddy!" I was laughing my ass off. "You a trifling' little hooker, April. You probably knew-"

"I promise I didn't." I was still laughing as we walked towards the parking lot. "I wouldn't do that to you girl. And I'ma curse Darrell out for even bringing him, he need to be at home with his daughter." I knew it wasn't funny, for some reason, I couldn't stop snickering.

CHAPTER TWELVE

By the time Nica and I were dropped off, it was after midnight. It was long after our curfews, but aunt Tracey was out getting her groove on, she wasn't coming home tonight. Darrell had begged me to come by later after him and Bean got finished doing whatever they had to do. When I asked him exactly where he was going, he gave me some bullshit excuse and changed the subject. I didn't mind him coming back later to watch a movie or something, but this wasn't my house and Nica wanted to go to bed, so I told him no and I'd see him later. He walked me to the door and gave me a long kiss that almost made me change my mind, but not quite.

Nica and me fell asleep while laughing and joking about our night on the town. It was definitely a night to remember, I doubt we'd forget it anytime soon. We were laid under her covers asleep when the phone rang, I nudged her and then stuffed my head underneath the pillow. It must have rung a gazillion times before Nica finally stumbled to her desk to grab it. I just happened to peek out at her clock and it was after four in the morning, the first thing I thought was that Darrell still wanted to come over. I rolled over, stuffed my head back under the pillow and closed my eyes. If it was who I thought it was, Nica was about to cuss his ass out.

"*Oh, my God!*" Nica screamed at the top of her lungs and it jolted through my entire body. "April, wake up!" I heard the phone hit the floor and before I could sit up, Nica had jumped on top of me. "April, it's Darrell! He got shot."

"*Huh*?" I was so sleepy that I just knew I'd heard her wrong.

"He's *dead*, April! Darrell just died at the hospital."

Slowly tears started to run down my cheeks and began soaking into the pillow. Nica just held me as I cried myself back to sleep. I can't say that I believed it was true, because it really seemed like a nightmare. All I could do was pray that the next time I opened my eyes, everything was okay, and this turned out to be just a bad dream.

CHAPTER THIRTEEN

The next morning I woke up with an excruciating headache and it became worst after I realized that the bad dream I was hoping for had turned into reality. I was laid across Nica's bed in my pajama's listening as she shared with me everything that Bean told her about what happened last night.

The daze that I was in made it impossible for me to process everything that she was saying. Something about Bean being paged because, somebody got robbed. Then an hour later, somebody was shot. Then I guess Darrell and Bean was coming out a corner store in their neighborhood when a car pulled up and started shooting at him, now *he* was dead. None of it made any sense to me, and Nica had very little details.

It was just like it always happened in the movies. Darrell had become the latest 'Ricky' from 'Boyz in the Hood'. Out of all the dudes outside that corner store, why did D have to be the one who got shot and die? And it's so ironic because out of all his friends, he definitely had the brightest future by far.   I'm not saying that he was completely innocent or a saint, I'm just saying that it's fucked up what happened to him.

"Did you *love* him?" Nica asked me as we lay there.

I thought about the question and I honestly didn't know.   As far as I knew, I've never been in love.   So, I wouldn't know what it felt like or have anything to compare it to.

"I'm not sure." I admitted to her.   "I *liked* him and I feel terrible about what happened, but I don't know if I'd call it *love*."   That was all I knew for sure, I wasn't too familiar with that particular four letter word.

We laid in silence, and I started crying again as I replayed our double date over in my mind.   It just was so unreal that a person could be here one day and gone the next.   Darrell was just with me, he'd just held me yesterday and I'd kissed his lips just hours ago.   His face was so vivid in my memory that I just couldn't close my eyes without seeing his smile.   I still remembered how he smelled, and the way that he could piss me off and then turn right around and make me laugh.   This was too tough for my young heart to take.

"Maybe I should've told him he could come back to see me, if he would've been here with me, he'd still alive." I said quietly, but it was more a case of me thinking aloud.

Nica wiped the tears from my face.   "April, Darrell seemed okay.   A little immature, but I know he really liked you.   But no matter how you look at it, he didn't have any business on that corner at four in the morning.   And trust me, even *if* he had come back to see you, I would've kicked his ass out of here *long before* 4am.   So you really shouldn't feel responsible."

"You not making me feel any better, Tanica."   In fact, she wasn't helping much at all.   Hopefully this bitch would never get a job as a suicide prevention counselor. Not that I'm contemplating suicide, I'm just saying.

"Sorry, but all I meant was that, it happened because that was God's plan. It's not your fault. So all that, *maybe I should've done,* you shouldn't even be thinking like that."

I wasn't so sure that Nica knew what the fuck she was talking about, but I wasn't in the mood to debate, so I just remained quiet.

But my silence didn't deter her from opening her mouth again. "Shit, even if you *would've* told him to come back, he might've stood your yellow ass up. Him and Bean might've got into one of they heated rap discussions and he might've forgot all about your ugly ass!" Now *that* made me laugh and her joke was exactly what I needed.

I gave her a hug for putting a smile on my face. "Thank you."

Nica pulled away from me. "April, get off of me! Get your dirty ass in the shower." She pulled the covers back and started to giggle while she checked the sheets. "And you better not have leaked all over sheets." I rolled my eyes at her and hopped up to get in the shower, I always felt dirty this time of the month.

But more than anything, I needed to wash Darrell off my mind.

CHAPTER FOURTEEN

The next few days went by fast and now it was Wednesday, you know time always flies during vacation. Christmas was this upcoming Sunday and I stayed busy by helping Mommy around the house. I kept her company while she ran errands back and forth to the grocery stores and the malls to shop and pick up toys for the boys.

Mommy was a nervous wreck. Every time Abuela came to town, she had to work overtime to make sure that everything was perfect. Abuela was my Mom's mother, our grandmother and a professional critic. Well, at least that's what Mommy said when Abuela wasn't around. My grandma is 100% Venezuelan, she grew up in South America and always had a gazillion stories about how it was back home in the old days.

Abuela's money was *super* long. She'd married some rich man from D.C. and when he retired, they'd moved to Myrtle Beach, SC. She kept trying to get Mommy to move down south closer to her, but Daddy wasn't having it. All his family is from New York so he wanted to stay here. Plus, he wasn't really feeling Abuela like that anyway. Whenever *she* was around, he *wasn't*! Especially, if my Aunty Leah was around too.

My Mommy, Abuela and Aunt Leah had a bad habit of speaking Spanish to each other and laughing a lot. If you didn't understand Spanish and you were in the vicinity, you would swear up and down that they were talking about *you*. And you'd probably be right. That shit pissed Daddy off. My Dad is part Dominican, but he doesn't speak a lick of Spanish and I think that's what makes him even angrier. I can't speak it at all either, but I can understand it a little bit, but only if they speak slowly, which they never do.

I remember one time Abuela criticized a meal that my Daddy had cooked. Now mind you, my Daddy is a professional chef, that's what he does for a living. I've never seen him so mad. To top it off, Abuela said something to Mommy in Spanish and they both laughed. Daddy left the house and didn't come back until Abuela was gone. You probably don't think it's that serious, right? But get *this*, it was a two-week visit, and we didn't see my Dad for a full thirteen days. Just keep that in mind, because things tend to get live around the holidays. Trust me, its good entertainment.

I already knew some sparks was gonna fly this year, so I was prepared. My little sister and me had been studying the Spanish-English dictionary for the past couple of days trying to memorize some key words that we thought we might need to know. Because if any shots started being thrown, I wanted to be on point, feel me?

Right now, I was with Mommy at the grocery store and she was looking disgusted. She said none of the supermarkets carried the right brands to make her dishes properly. Me, I was just plain bored and ready to start some shit.

"Ma?" I got her attention while she scanned a whole section looking for a specific brand of canned milk.

"Huh?" She answered but didn't look.

"You and Abuela not gonna run Daddy out the house this year, are you? Because I kind of want him to be around for Christmas." I was fighting myself in order to keep a straight face, and it took everything I had not to laugh.

Now she looked at me, and that's when I suddenly realized that maybe this hadn't been the best time to play. "April?"

"Yes, Mommy?"

"When's the last time I put my hands on you?" She asked a simple question and then quickly refocused her attention on the shelves.

I shrugged.

I *definitely* remembered, and I'm pretty sure that she remembered the last time that she'd slapped me too. So there wasn't any point in me responding and us reminiscing about domestic violence. But this was one of those trick questions that grown ups ask sometimes, and she wasn't expecting an answer, this was designed as a scare tactic.

But sometimes, *sometimes* when I'm bored I don't heed the warnings. Sometimes, I drive right through the stop sign without looking left or right. "Mommy, I wasn't trying to be-"

"I wasn't being funny either." She found what she was looking for and dropped it into the cart, then shot me a look. But it wasn't enough to deter me.

"Well can you at least teach me Spanish so I can laugh at all the jokes too?" This time I couldn't help it, and I cracked a smile.

"Girl, I told you before, me and Abuela do not crack jokes on people." She answered, but I wasn't buying it.

"So why ya'll be laughing so much?" I asked as she started walking up the aisle and I followed close behind her pushing the cart.

"The same reason why you and Jaime are always laughing. Because the two of you don't see each other often, so when you do see each other, there's a lot to catch up on, right?" This was the best she could come up with. Jaime is my cousin; she's my Aunt Leah's daughter.

"Nope." I shook my head. "Me and Jaime be laughing at ya'll!"

"About what?" She stopped and turned around.

"Because ya'll dysfunctional."

Mommy started laughing. "April, shut up." She turned around wearing a smile and kept walking.

After following her around the market for another hour or so, I was ready to go. I was restless and hungry. It's *impossible* to spend 90 minutes inside a grocery store and *not* get hungry. And there was only so much that I could *sneak* and eat without security runnin' up on me; I wasn't trying to go to jail over no grapes and peppermints. C'mon, don't act like you never stole a snack from the produce or bulk food section!

We were in the frozen food aisle, and I was secretly finishing off the last of the jellybeans that I'd stolen when she was finally done. "C'mon, baby, we can go home now." She started walking towards the checkout lines.

"It's *about time*." I mumbled under my breath. I didn't think she'd heard me but I was wrong.

"What you say?" Mommy turned and took a step towards me.

"Nothing. I didn't say *any*thing." I copped a plea quickly, and she turned back around. My Mom needed some kind of counseling, she's *way* too violent.

She started surveying all the lines trying to figure out which one would be the quickest. All them joints were long as hell; this was the worst part of shopping during holiday season.   It was close to Christmas, these people had gazillion things to buy and everybody had attitudes. As I looked around, I saw a boy that I used to go to elementary school with working one of the registers.   I couldn't remember his name, because the nigga just wasn't that memorable. All I remembered was that he was two years older than me, because he'd been in the same grade as Nica. He wasn't cute *then*, and Lord knows he wasn't cute *now*. But I was bored and looking for something to do.

"Over here Mommy."   I started pushing our cart towards his line.

"No April, that line is *too* long!" She grabbed my arm.

I gave her a look. "Ma, I know him." I nodded at the ugly cashier. She looked, immediately wrinkled up her nose and gave me a look that said, *'who cares!'* "I might be able to get you a discount." I was now speaking her language, and I knew this would make her reconsider.

Just like I thought, she let go of my arm and rolled her eyes. "Who you think you are?" she asked me sarcastically. I took it as a challenge that she was skeptical of my mack skills, so I decided to show her.

"Ma, c'mon. All the lines are long anyway." I kept pushing and reluctantly she followed me up to register number 5.

See, I stay looking sexy just for times like these. I had on a crisp pair of Timberlands, snug fitting blue denim jeans and a tan thermal shirt covered by a tight matching Timberland bubble vest. The vest was obstructing a great view, so I unzipped it so that the outline of my titties would be visible for our cashier.

There were three customers ahead of us, and each of them had full carts of food. I stared the boy down trying to catch his attention, but it was hard because he was so focused. This nigga was a *professional* cashier. Like, *this* was his calling in life. His hands were moving at the speed of lightning, and he was really into it. I was too far away to read the name on his tag, but I could surely see all the gold stars. This nigga was probably the reigning MVP, or employee of the month. Something like the LeBron James of cashiers. And by the look on his face, he took his job extra serious.

I started to have second thoughts and re-think my strategy. This nigga might have me arrested on cashier bribery charges if I tried to get Mommy a discount. That's how serious he looked about this job, you should've seen him.

Finally, he looked back to where I was standing. Quickly, I made my eyes light up and flashed him a huge smile. He looked shocked but he definitely smiled back, today was his lucky day. After I had his attention, I waved at him. Now he was cheesing and *he* waved back. If *I* remembered *him*, I know he *had* to remember *me*. I wasn't this thick in elementary school, but my face was always a dime and he definitely couldn't forget this smile. The other people in line began turning around to see why he was smiling so hard all of a sudden and that's when Mommy pinched my butt.

I jumped.

"April, do *not* embarrass me in this store!" I couldn't believe this woman just pinched *my* butt in public, and then had the nerve to tell *me* not to embarrass *her*.

I started digging through my replica Gucci purse looking for my lip-gloss. "I'm not going to embarrass you," I found what I was looking for and pulled it out. "Just listen. Whatever I say when we get up there, just agree with me."

Her head began to shake. She looked at the lip-gloss in my hand, and then at my face. "Don't say anything *stupid*!" She warned me.

I turned back around and waited, while staring at him with intensity while he worked. He couldn't help but sneak peaks in my direction every few seconds or so, and every time he did, I'd hold his gaze by biting my lip, playing with my ponytail or doing something seductive.

Finally, it was only one customer in front of us. I waited until he looked again, then I turned to my Mom and pretended to whisper something to her while I maintained eye contact with him.

"Mommy, look at him and smile." I whispered, and reluctantly she played along. Then I strained to peep his nametag, his name was Tony. When the woman in front us were almost done, I started to apply the lip-gloss real slow and sensual and Mommy almost went crazy.

"*April!*" She pinched me even harder this time. That shit hurt, but I ignored her. Tony gave the woman her receipt and change, and then she left. I stepped around the cart and Mommy began loading our groceries onto the conveyer belt.

"*Hi*, Tony!" I walked up to him.

"What's up, April!"? I knew he would remember me. He called my name right out and I didn't even have a nametag on. Truth be told, he probably wasn't the only 8th grade boy fantasizing about my young ass when I was in 6th grade.

"Nothin'." I started playing in my hair, because for some reason dudes just take that as a sign that you like them. We both looked each other up and down, and I knew that he liked what he was seeing. On the other hand, Tony wasn't *ugly*, but he wasn't cute either. Okay, he *was* ugly! But, I will say this, his teeth were white and straight, he was tall, he had deep waves in his hair, and his face was free of acne. So I guess all of those things were a plus.

He was examining me like a physician, staring at me so hard that Mommy had to clear her throat to remind him that she was standing there. I didn't pay her any attention, but Tony immediately snapped out his daze and got to work on our groceries.

"I didn't know you worked here." I stepped closer to him, there was only a thin partition that separated us.

"Yeah, almost a year now." He answered proudly, chest poked out.

"My mother usually goes to the other Wegman's across town," I bit my lip. "But, I'm gonna tell her to start coming to this one from now on." I smiled as I lied him. Nervously he eyed my Moms, but still returned my smile. "Mom," I turned to her. "This is Tony. Tony, this is my Mom, Mrs. Showers." I introduced them.

"Hi, Tony." Mom smiled.

"Nice to meet you, Ma'am." He loosened up a bit.

Then I *really* started lying. "This is the same Tony that I used to tell you about," I looked at Mommy and she looked puzzled. "The one who used to ignore me at school everyday." I gave her a look and she caught on.

"*Oh*," her face said it all. "*That* Tony."

He was scanning and bagging up our groceries, not quite knowing what to say. He was probably trying to figure out how it was possible that I'd noticed him back then and he'd not known about it.

"What school you go to now?" He tried to make conversation.

"Traditional. Where you go?"

"Hutch Tech." He told me.

Then I started to fidget like I was nervous. "So is this the only time I can talk to you, if I come grocery shopping?" When I asked this, he looked past me, probably to see if Mommy was paying attention. I didn't have to turn around; I already knew she was listening.

"Tell me your number," he whispered to me. "I'll remember it."

I gave him a look that said I was tempted. "I have to ask permission first, and this isn't really a good time right now. My Mom gets in a cranky mood any time she has to spend a lot of money." I hinted by glancing at the screen on his register, it was already at $126.98 and we still had *lots* of items left on the conveyor belt.

He winked at me. "Don't worry, I'll make sure that she's in a good mood." He told me as he continued to ring up and bag our stuff.

Five minutes later he was done, he hit some keys on the register and the total balance decreased by two hundred dollars. "$43.78, Mrs. Showers." He smiled at us.

Mommy was shocked. She gave him a fifty-dollar bill and put the rest of her money away. While he began putting the bags in our cart, I stepped to Mommy. "I told him that I'd ask if it was okay for him to call me." I whispered to her. "Can I give him the number?"

She looked at Tony and then back to me. "Your Daddy will flip out, April. You already know that." She warned me.

"Tell Daddy I saved him two-hundred bucks." I reasoned with her.

She thought for a second. "Fine. But tell him *not* to call until *after* the holidays." She instructed me.

I pulled a pen and paper from my purse and wrote down our house phone number. Worst-case scenario, Tony would call, Daddy would curse him out, and I'd deny ever giving him my number. After Mommy got her change, I handed him the paper, gave him a smile and told him not to call until after the holiday.

"Don't call until after Christmas, because it's really hectic at my house right now." I explained to him as he put the paper in his pocket then hit a switch on the register. When he hit the switch, the light on top of his register began to blink.

He nodded. "That's cool." He smiled. "C'mon, let me help you and your Mom with all these bags. It's time for my break anyway." He stepped away from his register.

Let me tell you, the customers in line behind us were *furious*. They started moaning, groaning, complaining and talkin' shit. It was really about to get ugly until some white boy rushed over to take Tony's spot behind the cash register. He followed us outside to the Dodge Caravan and loaded up the back of it with our groceries, the whole time Mommy was staring at me in amazement.

When he was done, he looked at her. "I work Monday thru Friday after school, Mrs. Showers. Just come through my line and I'll take care of you."

"Thank you so much, Tony. You are such a sweetheart." She was smiling form ear to ear, that two hundred dollars had her looking like she'd won the lottery.

"You're welcome, Merry Christmas." He waved at us.

"Call me." I said before getting inside the van.

Mommy started the Caravan up and put the heat on. "April," she looked at me. "I don't know where you learned that from, but you'd better be careful playing with these little boy's emotions like that." She had a very serious look on her face.

I was listening, but to me it wasn't that big of a deal. "*All I did* was smile at him and give him my number. It's not like I told him that I was *in love* and wanted to have his baby." I responded innocently.

"You know what I mean, April." She put the vehicle in reverse and backed out the parking spot.

"I know." I admitted quietly.

I'll be honest with you; this day was one of the biggest turning points in my young life. I learned a valuable, but dangerous and deadly lesson. Pussy *is* power. I already knew that. But *what I didn't know* was that, giving off the *presumption* that you want to share your pussy with someone, is even *more* power. I didn't even have to sleep with boys to get what I wanted from them, all I had to do was *pretend* that I wanted to sleep with them. This was just the tip of the iceberg. The point when I began to realize the power I had over the opposite sex. Me, being young and naïve, this *seemed* like a good thing at the time, but *eventually* it would contribute to my life spiraling out of control.

CHAPTER FIFTEEN

I slept in on Friday morning; I didn't get out the bed until almost 12:30. I'd been up late on the phone with Tiffany talking about almost everything under the sun. The main thing I needed help deciding, was whether or not to attend Darrell's funeral this morning. I had a few reasons that I didn't want to go, and they all seemed good enough to stay home.

Darrell had been good to me and I'd never forget him. But, being in a church with a gazillion other teenage broads, and we're all crying over the same boy, now that was out of the question. Darrell was popular to say the least; the whole city knew him for being a local basketball star, so all the chicks would be out like it was a fashion show. It's sad, but you know it's true. Had we been an official couple, of course I would've been there, that would be a very different story. But we *weren't*, and *that* made all the difference in the world. Plus, I was pretty sure that Sally would be there blowing snot and boogers all over his casket and making a ratchet scene. The last thing I needed was for her to see me there and go into an emotional rage like she did that night at the Roxbury, this time she may take a swing at me. There was no telling who Darrell and Bean told about our double date, and for all I knew the entire church could know about it. I could just imagine walking in and everyone pointing at me, '*there she goes. That's April, the girl he was with right before he got killed!*' Then, I'd get stomped out by a mob of jealous bitches.

Nope. Wasn't gonna happen. That's why I stayed my yellow ass in the bed this morning. I lay on my back, staring at the ceiling while my thoughts ran ramped. Life was some tricky shit; you just never know what can happen, and to me that am scary. Death is tough pill to swallow and digest, it never seems fair.

There was a soft knock at my door. Before I could say anything, it opened and Mommy was walking in. Some things I would never understand. If you ask me, it's even *ruder* to knock, but open a door before a person has the chance to invite you inside. Personally, I'd rather she just bust right in without knocking at all. That shit is irritating, and one day I'm gonna get the courage to tell her about herself.

"You going to lay here all day?" She closed the door and climbed into the bed next to me.

"No, I'm just thinking."

"About your friend?" She asked softly and I assumed that she was referring to, D."

I nodded. "Mostly."

She exhaled slowly and gave me a sympathetic look. "I don't think you should just lay around thinking about it, it'll just make you sad. I'll be leaving soon, do you want to ride to the mall with me?"

I didn't really feel like moving just yet, but if there was anything that could lift my spirits, it was a trip to the

Galleria. "I'll go with you," I decided. "But *only* if it's gonna be the two of us, I don't feel like dealing with your three foster kids." We both giggled at my joke, but I was serious and she knew it.

"That wasn't nice. I gave birth to all four of you, I've got the scars to prove it." She was smiling. "But cool, just the two of us then. Maybe I'll get you something nice with the money you saved us the other day." She gently slapped my thigh.

"You didn't give Daddy his money back?" I tried to sound surprised but I really wasn't.

"Do I look like a fool to you?" I scrunched up my face and fought the urge to say something slick. Mommy read my mind, and before I could weave, she popped me on the forehead. "Here, take this phone. Nica called a few minutes ago, and she said to call her back." She put the cordless phone on the bed next to me.

I was busy rubbing my forehead, because that shit stung. "Ma, you gotta stop being so violent, I didn't even say nothing."

"You was about to," she laughed and stood up. "Make your phone call, then get up and get cute so we can go." She disappeared out my sight closing the door behind her.

When she was gone, I stretched, yawned and dialed Nica's number. Thankfully, Aunt Stacey didn't answer the phone, because I wasn't really in the mood right now.

"Yo, what's up?" Nica answered.

"Nothin'. Tired. What's up with you?"

"Ummm. Bean called here looking for you. He wanted your number, but you know I wasn't 'bout to give it to him." She told me.

"What does he want?" I asked curiously.

"Don't know. He wouldn't say, but he left a number for you to call, and he said it's important." Nica gave me the number and I wrote it down on a piece of paper on my nightstand.

"So what you doing today?" I asked her.

"Nate home from college. He supposed to take me somewhere, but you know how that goes. He'll probably get tied up with that bitch and stand me up." Nica sounded somewhat sour. Nate was her big brother, and he went to school in Connecticut but he was home for the holidays. Every time he came back to town he let the females distract him and Nica was fed up.

"Oh. Well if you get bored later, come over. I'm about o go to the mall with my mother, but we shouldn't be gone that long." I told her, and we agreed to get together later before hanging up. Then, before I forgot, I dialed Beans number but pressed *67 to block my number.

"Hello?" Bean answered the phone immediately, and there was lots of noise and commotion in the background.

"Hi, Bean. This is, April."

He didn't respond right away, but I could tell that he was moving away from the noise because it got quiet. "I was looking for you, but you wasn't there. That's fucked up that you didn't come to my man's funeral." Bean didn't sound mad, but he sounded *really* hurt.

I took a deep breath. "I would've felt very uncomfortable, I don't really like funerals, Bean. But I did call his mother a few days ago, and I told her I wasn't sure if I'd make it." That's all I told him, because I didn't think I owed him some long, deep explanation.

"You didn't have to stay long, but you should've at least showed up to say goodbye to him. That nigga was in love wit' you!" Bean caught me off guard with that one, and now he was beginning to sound more aggressive like he was getting angry. His words also sounded a little slurred and it was apparent that his underage ass had probably been drinking.

"Bean listen, I hope I didn't call just so you can try to make me feel even worst about not coming this morning. I said goodbye to Darrell that night before he left with you, and that's the *only* way I want to remember him. He gave me a long kiss and smiled at me, that's the *only* image of him that I want in my memory. I never want to think about him, and remember seeing him laying in a box, *okay*?" Now I was starting to get emotional. I couldn't believe that this boy was about to get me worked up again, and I didn't feel like crying anymore.

"*Whatever*, April!" He completely dismissed my feelings. "We need you to do something for us," I could hear the resentment beginning to build in his voice. "You cool with that bitch Karma, right?"

My eyes closed. I didn't like where this conversation was headed, and I wished I'd never called. "I know her, but we not friends or anything." I told him.

"*Shit*, it looked like ya'll were friends when I seen you leaving the club together last weekend!" Now he was raising his voice.

My face turned pink. "She gave me a ride home, *so what*? What's that gotta do with anything?" I matched his intensity.

"Where she live at?"

I caught a chill. "I don't know where she live!"

"Find out, then call me back."

This nigga was out his mind! "Listen, Bean-"

"No bitch, *you* listen! That nigga Vance killed my best friend! We been looking for him, but can't find him. You know what *that* means?" He asked me, but my intelligence wouldn't let me answer.

"...That means, until we can catch *him*, we gonna kill the next thing closest to him, *Karma*! So you find out where she lives and then call me back!"

"Bean," I tried to calm down. Maybe if I lowered my voice, he would too. "I *can't* get involved in this. I'm sorry about what happened to Darrell, but I *can't* help you." I whispered softly.

There was a pause.

"Shit about to get real crazy, April. You better choose a side real fast, because if you *don't*, you gonna end up on the *wrong* side!" He breathed angrily.

Then the line went dead.

I was sitting Indian-style on my bed, shocked and staring at my wall in disbelief. *Did this nigga just threaten me?* Was he insinuating that if I didn't help him get Karma's address that it somehow meant I was down with the enemy?

See, this is why they should have a mandatory age requirement to listen to rap music. Because, you got young dudes like beaning, who listen to DMX and then starting thinking that they Tommy Buns from the movie 'Belly'. This is crazy. This is real life, *not* a movie! You can't just go around killing females, just because you *think* their boyfriend did something sour.

I was shaking. *Literally*, my body was shaking. I'd envied Karma before, but *now*, I began to see the other side of the game. When you dealing with dudes who are *deep* in the streets, this is the type of shit that happens. All the shoes, all the purses and the money don't mean anything when people want you dead! This is when I should've learned my lesson, but you know how it is when you're young and stupid. You *think* bad things only happen to *other* people, and I could *never* see myself in Karma's position. But that just goes to show you...

I put the phone on my nightstand and slid back under the covers. Fuck the mall, I was going back to sleep. I'm *only* fourteen. There's no way that I should have to deal with this type of shit!

CHAPTER SIXTEEN

On Christmas Eve, my house was packed. A whole bunch of people came over to freeload and eat up all our food, or at least that's what my Dad said. Tonight, he was on his grumpy swag shit. A mixture of Scrooge McDuck and the Grinch.

Daddy doesn't like a whole bunch of people in his house, because he said something always ends up missing. He wasn't lying either, and I could definitely attest to that. Last year, after everybody left, we couldn't find Cory and Lito's brand new Madden 2001 video game. The year before, a whole present disappeared from under the damn tree. It was fully wrapped! We didn't find out until Christmas morning that it was missing, and guess what? The present was *mine*. A brand new jewelry set, can you believe that shit? Well I didn't! I made Daddy show me the receipt, because I swore that he was trying to run game. Turns out he wasn't bluffing.

Anyway, fast forward to this year. Daddy was on the move like Border Patrol! He was watching everyone real suspicious-like. He told me last night that he was gonna catch the muthafucka red-handed this year. *His* words, not mine! Daddy is crazy, this nigga set up booby traps and everything! He told me he even might search people on the way out this year. He had me cracking up.

Peep the funniest shit. Usually our presents are under the tree already on Christmas Eve. But *this* year, Daddy hid and locked up all the *real* gifts. All the gifts under the tree this year were decoys! He replaced the real gifts with dummy boxes, that's what he called them, '*dummies*'. But Mommy told me, that *he* was the only *dummy* around here. And ya'll know me; I had to go tell Daddy *exactly* what she said about him.

That's when he told me that *Mommy* was a *suspect* too!

Awe man! He had me in stitches, I was laughing so hard that I almost peed. Dad said that it was *her* side of the family that was doing all the stealing, and that Mommy might be down with it! Now, that part didn't make any sense at all, but it was just funny to hear it come out of his mouth and know that he probably believed it.

See, Mommy had two twin brothers named Stevie and Sammy. Daddy called them Heckle and Jeckle and said that they were two of the sneakiest muthafuckas he'd ever met in his life. He told me that if I wasn't careful, that they'd steal the hair off my head. That they'd package it and sell it, before I even knew it was gone. So, *I* told Daddy, that it would be *impossible* because I'm always playing in my hair, so they wouldn't be able to steal it. Daddy said, '*Trust me baby girl. If they want it, they'll steal it. One of them will distract you, and the other one will sneak up behind you with the scissors and your ponytail off!*'

So now, I was sitting here in the living room with everyone who was under the age of 18. Me and my cousin Jaime had our eyes peeled for signs of any funny shit, but so far nothing had caught our attention. Cory and Carlito were running around with some of my other little cousins doing what little boys do, and I knew that before the night was over, one of them would get their ass kicked. I just hoped that I wouldn't miss it.

La La and her best friend Amber was sitting across from us on the other sofa whispering back and forth, they were definitely up to no good and probably plotting. But as long as it didn't have anything to do with my closet, I could care less.

Later, after everybody ate dinner, my Aunt Tracey came by with my cousin Nica and the two of us disappeared upstairs to my room. Jaime said she'd be up in a few minutes after she finished off another plate of food.

While we were alone I decided to fill her in. "Girl, you know this boy Bean done lost his damn mind!" I couldn't wait to tell her about the phone call.

"What? What happened?" Nica asked me.

I told her what happened when I called him yesterday, and her eyes got wide. *For real?* Ooh, I hope he don't call my house anymore." She looked worried. "*Damn,* he knows where I live!" She blurted after she'd thought about it.

I rolled my eyes at her. "Nica, that boy not gonna do nothing to you. The funeral was yesterday and he was just emotional. He'll get over it just like everyone else." I assured her.

"*Well,* I'm still not talking to him anymore, I'm trying to forget that I ever met him." She was dead serious.

I shrugged and changed the subject. "What's up with my cousin, Nate?"

Now it was her turn to roll her eyes. "We haven't seen him since yesterday. Some girl came to pick him up last night and he hasn't been back since. My Mom is so pissed!" She filled me in.

"Did he take you somewhere yesterday?"

She looked at me in disgust. "Girl, do you know this nigga tried to take me to the Science Museum." I started dying laughing, my cousin Nate was *too* funny.

"Get outta here." I was holding my stomach.

"And when I told him I didn't want to go, he took me back home! Then he gonna say *'That's your problem, you never wanna do anything educational, all you wanna do is things that will warp your mind'.*" Nica did a great imitation of her brother's voice.

"He's so funny." I was almost in tears.

"There's nothing funny about that, April. He went off to college and came home acting like Shereef from 'Menace to Society'. He had the nerve to tell my Mom that we shouldn't celebrate Christmas anymore-"

"Yeah, right! And what did Aunt Tracey say?"

"She said that was the smartest thing that *ever* came out his dumb ass mouth! Then we went to the mall and returned all his shit!" Now she was laughing with me. "My Mom said since he don't wanna celebrate Jesus birthday, he don't need any presents."

We chilled and laughed for another 20 minutes, and then I checked the clock. "Where's Jaime at?" It was a dumb question since Nica had been here with me the whole time. She shrugged her shoulders, and then I jumped up. "C'mon, we might be missing something funny!" I grabbed her and we went to see what my cousin Jaime was doing.

When we came down the back stairs and landed in the kitchen, Jaime was standing in the corner looking real cozy with Calvin from across the street.

"Ooh, that bitch *stole* your man." Nica was in my ear, and I gave her a soft elbow to the ribs. Mommy was at the counter talking to Mrs. Shannon about something, but she was looking at me to see my expression as I watched Calvin. I wouldn't say that I was *jealous*, but I will say that they didn't have to be all up in each other's face in my kitchen.

"Hey, gorgeous!" Mrs. Shannon said when she spotted me. "Merry Christmas."

I went to give her a hug. "Merry Christmas."

"Hey, Tanica."

"Hi, Mrs. Shannon."

I looked back over to the corner. "What's up, Calvin?" I gave him a smile, but then turned beet red when this boy gave me a dry, half-ass wave. It was the equivalent of him throwing me the peace sign, and he didn't even speak, he just continued his conversation with Jaime.

My Mom and Nica didn't miss a beat; they both caught the look on my face as I headed back for the stairs. "I *know* he didn't just play you like that!" Nica was in my ear again, this time she was giggling and trying to instigate some shit.

When we were back inside my room and sitting on the bed, she turned to me. "You always swear you don't like Calvin, so why you look so stupid in the face when you seen him talking to Jaime?" She wanted to know, not wasting any time.

Nica had touched a sensitive nerve and she knew it. "I don't care *who* he talks to. He's not *my* man, and he's *not* my type." I said defensively.

"Keep telling yourself that, April. You two are going to get married one day, watch and see." The way she was looking at me, Nica had me convinced that she really believed that.

I knew what my problem was, but I wasn't going to admit it to Nica. It's like this, when a dude shows interest in me, I wanna be the only female on his mind. He shouldn't be sniffing behind me one day, then all in another chicks face the next day. The truth was, seeing him talking to my cousin really fucked with my ego. I guess you could say, that even though I really didn't want Calvin, I didn't want to see him with anyone else either. Does that make any sense? Shit, well I told you that I was selfish, didn't I?"

"You know what your problem is?" Nica wasn't going to let it go, and very soon I was gonna have to kick her ass out of my room.

"No, Tanica. What's my problem?" This bitch was starting too sound like a damn therapist.

"Number one, you're in denial! Number two, you think you want a thug, but you really don't! You see what happened to Darrell? If you want to keep going through shit like *that* for the rest of your life, then keep fallin' for the 'bad boys'. Calvin is cute, smart and he can play ball. But you don't like him because he don't wear Timberlands or sag his pants? That's *stupid*!" Nica was looking in my eyes like a gypsy, almost like she was trying to see inside my soul.

My face screwed up instantly. "If *he's* so great, then why don't *you* marry him, *and* have his babies?" I rolled my eyes at her. I was tired of talking about this. Nica was sixteen, only two years older than me and she didn't even *have* a man. The school she went to, was full of dudes just like Calvin, so how she gonna tell me something and she don't even follow her own advice?

"*Because*," she cracked a smile. "He's not my type." We both started laughing.

CHAPTER SEVENTEEN

As all our guests began to leave the house, Daddy was on high alert. He was posted up in the kitchen watching everybody leave, and Mommy was watching him and shaking her head. When everyone who was leaving was gone, he still hadn't captured the Christmas Eve bandit. Nica and Jaime were spending the night, and I was pretty sure that neither of them were going to steal anything.

Mommy looked at him with a grin on her face. "Well, I guess all the *dummies* are still here." She started laughing.

Daddy shrugged. "Next year is another year. They'll be back, and I'll be waiting." He looked at me and smiled. "Right, baby girl?"

"Yup." I blew him a kiss. "So what if we didn't catch the thief, Daddy. At least we still have all our gifts this year, and there's nothing missing this time." Then I laughed. "And I still got all my hair!" Daddy and me cracked up laughing; everyone was looking at us like we were crazy because they didn't understand the joke.

As me and my cousins headed back upstairs, my Mom called my name and I had to come back to the kitchen. "Here, take this across the street to Mrs. Shannon." She handed me a brown paper bag with a pan of Apple Pie inside. I didn't mind doing it, but La Reina was sitting right there at the counter.

"Mommy, I got company. You can't send La La-"

Smack!

Mommy popped me square on the forehead. All I heard was mad hushed giggles and cackling, but nobody wanted to laugh too hard and risk being next.

"Take *that*," she pointed to the bag. "Across the street to Mrs. Shannon, *right now*."

I hit the closet, grabbed my North Face snorkel and threw on some boots. Everyone else vanished and Mommy blew me a kiss on her way up the stairs. I scrunched up my face at her and then hurried out the door, one of these days I was gonna end up hitting her ass back.

Outside, I crossed the street and walked up Mrs. Shannon's driveway. It was almost midnight and it looked like all the lights were off. It was late and I was a little skeptical about ringing the doorbell because I didn't want to wake anybody up. That would be kind of rude, so I hoped she was waiting on me.

When I got to the side door, it was already open, the hallway light was on and Calvin was standing right there. When I got close, enough he opened up the screen door.

"Here, this is for your mother." I basically shoved the bag into his chest and then turned on my heels. I still wasn't feeling how he'd tried to play me earlier.

I didn't know that this niggas arms were so long, he grabbed the sleeve of my North Face before I could get two good feet away. "Come here, April." I turned and looked at this fool like he was crazy, because he *was* for grabbing me like he owned me. But my look didn't deter him; he kept a firm grip on my jacket.

Now listen. I've known this boy for at least six or seven years since my family moved on this street. His Mom and my Mom are friends. His Dad and my Dad are cool. With that being said, I didn't just wanna spaz and curse his ass out for grabbing me. Mainly because I didn't know If Mrs. Shannon was anywhere, close enough to hear me use the colorful language that I had in mind.

"Calvin," I spoke very calmly. "If you wanna get my attention, all you have to do is say my name. *Please* don't grab me, you didn't pay for this coat I have on and I *know* your Mom didn't raise you like that." He quickly let go of me. "Thank you, now what's up?"

"Can you come inside for a minute?" He was holding the door open, but I hesitated for a minute. This was still the same dude who be watching me out the window every morning before school, so I was a little skeptical. And, Calvin isn't some scrawny dude, he works out regularly. I stepped into the hallway reluctantly, but only because I was sure that this nigga wasn't crazy enough to rape me in his Momma's house. But when he put down the paper bag and closed the door, I almost panicked.

Oh God, was anyone else even home?

"I came over to your house to see you earlier, because I wanted to give you something-"

"You did see me earlier, Calvin. You didn't give me anything, and you didn't even say hi." Automatically, like it was second nature, my hand went to my hip. I don't know why I do that; I guess it's just a habit.

Calvin started laughing. "Yeah, I'm sorry about that. Your Mom said the best way to get your attention is to make you jealous and ignore you." He had this big stupid smile on his face. "I guess she was right."

I couldn't believe Mommy did that, and Jaime had been apart of it. I wasn't mad though, I was more relieved. Because for a minute there I'd thought that, I'd possibly lost my touch. I took a long look at him and realized that Nica was right, Calvin was definitely fine, but that's something I already knew.

I returned his smile. "Don't keep listening to my Mom, she's gonna get you in trouble." That's when he dug into his pocket and pulled out one of those long jewelry boxes.

"Here, I got this for you." He offered the box to me. I looked at it, and then looked at him with the same smile still on my face. I accepted it and admired the nice velvet box, which wasn't gift-wrapped or anything.
"It's not really a Christmas present, I was thinking about you, so I bought it." He said while I examined it. The box said Reed's Jewelers so I figured that whatever was inside had to be acceptable.

When I opened it up, I saw that it was a gold teddy bear linked bracelet. It was beautiful, I loved it, and it absolutely showed across my face. "Thank you, Calvin! I love it!" I smiled at him.

"I'm glad, because I love to see you smile." This boy had my cheeks turning red, and I had to drop my eyes from his because I was blushing. This was something new to me, this was the first time that Calvin had ever given me butterflies or made me nervous. "Do you mind if I put it on for you?" he asked permission, but it was written across my face that he had the green light.

He stepped in close and I wondered if he could feel the extra heat coming from my body. I held out my right wrist so that he could fasten the bracelet around it, and tried not to make eye contact. But when he was done, something came over me. I grabbed his shirt, stood up on my tippy toes and pressed my lips to his. I kissed him until

I felt something hard poking my stomach, then I stepped back and looked down at it. Whatever he had inside his sweatpants was about to burst through the seams, and he was looking at me like he was ready to get naked right here in the hallway. That's when I reached for the doorknob.

"That's what you get for ignoring me earlier." I gave him one last smile, then left him standing in his hallway with a thirsty ass look on his face.

When I got back into the house, Mommy was waiting in the kitchen for me wearing a silly ass grin. "Let me see it! Let me see it!" She was so excited.

"See *what?*" I gave her a weird look.

"April, stop playing with me! Let me see what he got you." Mommy was all over me, so I showed it to her just to get her away. "Awe, that's *so* cute!" She was beaming. "Do you like it?"

I nodded, not able to contain my smirk. "Yeah, Mommy. I like it." She wrapped me up in a hug like I was being engaged or something. Mommy liked Calvin, and she really wanted me to like him too. But it wasn't up to her, and luckily, for me, this wasn't the Middle East where parents arrange marriages. Because if it was, Mommy would've already sold me to Calvin for two goats and a lamb.

Daddy came speed walking into the kitchen and caught us smiling. "Baby girl," he was looking directly at me. "You not gonna believe this shit." He looked so frustrated that I couldn't imagine.

"What Daddy?"

"They got us *again!*" He exclaimed.

I had no clue what he meant. "Daddy what you talking about?"

He was shaking his head. "Heckle and Jeckle! Them sneaky muthafuckas robbed us *again!*" I couldn't help it, I cracked up!

CHAPTER EIGHTEEN

The holidays came and went, and now that the excitement was over, things were back to normal. It was now 2002, and it was back to business as usual, today was the first day back to school.

Mommy poked her head inside my room. "Baby we're leaving, and Calvin's outside waiting for you so hurry up!" She smiled and then disappeared. Hmmm, now this was something new for a change. Calvin was actually downstairs waiting to walk me to the bus stop, instead of hiding out in the window waiting for me to leave. I hurried because I knew it was cold outside, and though I wasn't in love with him, I liked him enough not to wanna see him freeze to death.

When I got outside, he was leaning against the railing on the stairs. He was wearing some khaki, Eastland loafers and his burgundy and grey Hutch-Tech varsity jacket. I could see that he was wearing a necktie as well, so I figured he had a basketball game today.

"What's up?" he asked casually.

"Hi." I gave him an encouraging smile. He had been coming along at a snail's pace, and at the speed he was going; he'd probably ask me out on a date sometime around the time I graduated from college. Not that it made me any difference, I'm just saying.

We started walking in silence, and he didn't even bother to ask me whether I was wearing his bracelet. Which I certainly was. Also, as we walked, I couldn't help but imagine how many times he'd replayed our kiss in his dreams as he lay in bed at night. I certainly had done it a few times.

"You going to the game this afternoon, right?" He asked me.

Damn, I'd forgotten that today was the day that our teams played each other.

"Calvin, I forgot to let my Mom know that I'd be staying after school today, but I'll try to be there though."

"My Dad can bring you home." He told me. I figured it shouldn't be a problem as long as I called Mommy and at least left a message to let her know.

I nodded. "I'll be there."

*   *   *   *   *

A half an hour later, I got off the bus at the bus station and said goodbye to Calvin. Asia was waiting for me and we took the 15-minute walk to our school.

"You good?" She asked me as we walked, probably because we'd both been extra quiet this morning.

"Yeah, I'm good. *You?*" I looked at her.

She nodded. "Yup, it's just a shame that our vacation is over." Asia looked sad.

I exhaled slowly, "Tell me about it." I definitely had to agree with that. We'd just stepped into the school building, we said goodbye and went our separate ways. I'd see her at lunch.

At the top of the stairs, as I headed to my locker, I saw Brandon walking with some other dude. "Damn, what happened, B?" I walked up behind him. "I thought I was on your Christmas list. You must've been naughty, huh?" I started laughing when he turned around with a big smile on his face.

"What's up, baby? I know you missed me, didn't you?"

"Of course I did. Two whole weeks without you kicking my chair, I almost cried." I teased as I walked off.

The hallways were buzzing and everybody was rocking the new shit they got for Christmas. And of course, many people were still talking about what happened to Darrell, but I stayed out of those conversations. I just wanted to get past it, I'm a naturally happy person and I wanted to continue being able to smile, laugh and joke around. Being depressed isn't how I like to spend my days, so I didn't even want to think about it.

After fifth period Algebra, Brandon was walking me to my locker when I bumped into Sally. Surprisingly, she threw her arms around my neck and gave me a hug.

"How are you?" She asked me.

"Cool. How about you?" I asked, while Brandon stood there.

"Good. I was gonna call you, but I couldn't find your number, and Karma wouldn't give it to me." She rolled her eyes.

I started to think that maybe I'd misjudged Sally off that one bad incident. Maybe she wasn't so bad. I gave her my house number and my new pager number. The pager was a Christmas present. I was now *officially* allowed to talk to boys on the phone, but they still couldn't call the house, they had to page me and I'd call them back. Sally gave me another hug and disappeared into the crowded hallway.

"April," Brandon was looking at me grinning. "It really turns me on, to see you hug another pretty girl."

"Brandon, get lost!" That's when I dipped on him so I could go find Asia for lunch.

We met up on the first floor and slid into the cafeteria. The smell wasn't so bad today, so whatever it was that they were serving could *possibly* be edible. It turned out to be grilled cheese sandwiches and we both decided it was worth a try. I'd never met anyone who could ruin a grilled cheese, and luckily I wasn't disappointed, it turned out to be good.

At the V.I.P freshman table, we were just chilling' and waiting for the bell to ring. Asia, Cam, Jerrell and myself. Rell is Cam's friend, he also lives in this neighborhood, and he's that one dude who only comes to school once or twice a week. You know the kid that you forget even goes to school with you until he shows up unexpectedly? That's my boy, Jerrell. And *every* time he shows up, he got on some new fly shit, smells like a pound of weed and has a war story to tell. He reminds me of Bishop from the movie 'Juice'. *If* Rell ever makes it to senior year, I'd be surprised, and in the yearbook, he'll probably be voted most likely to have a gun in his locker.

I'm just saying

Cam and Asia seemed to be on good terms today, but probably only since they'd had a two-week break. They were cuddled up making googly eyes at one another, and I had a good feeling that she was going to stand me up after school to go get her back dug out.

"Rell, you need to start bringing your ass to school." The two of us were talking how we always do, on some brother-sister shit. The thing I liked most about Jerrell was that I could talk to him about *anything,* and it would *never* come back out his damn mouth. I'd known him since fourth grade and he's always been the same. He's the very serious, tight-lipped, militant type and his eyes are *scary.* You look into that boys fourteen year-old eyes, and see *thirty* years old hard living, his environment had taken ahold of him at an early age and it was hard to watch him self-destruct.

"I be havin' shit to do, April. I'm out here on my own, and I don't have anybody to take care of me. If I don't hustle, I won't survive. I'm gonna get it together though, soon, I promise." He looked sincere. "What about you? I been *hearing* some shit, your name came up a few times and I've *never* heard your name in the streets before. What's happening?" He wanted to know. So, I told him everything that happened during the vacation, starting with the altercation with Sally at the Roxbury.

He listened and didn't say anything until I was finished. "Damn, April." He started shaking his head.

"What was I *supposed* to do, tell him where Karma lives?"

Rell shook his head. "Nah. You did the right thing, and I'm gonna have a talk with Bean because he's out of line for even trying to involve you. I been knowing him for years, our peoples do business together and we all on the same team-"

"But ya'll from different hoods-"

"But we all get money together. It's hard to explain, and you wouldn't understand. Don't worry bout Bean, I'll talk to him."

I nodded.

Just then, the bell rang and everyone jumped out their chairs and started scrambling for the exits. I said goodbye to my friends and dipped off. I was halfway out the cafeteria when somebody put an arm around my shoulders.

"April," Rell was in my ear walking on one side of me, and Cam was right next to him. They were both looking at me wearing weird expressions, causing me to get a strange feeling in my gut. They were definitely up to something, because they both had these shady looks on their faces.

"Huh?" I stopped and faced the two of them.

"When the dismissal bell rings, stay inside the school. Just go straight to the gym for the basketball game and make sure Asia is with you."

"*Why?*" I asked, but neither of them responded. Cam and Rell walked off in the *opposite* direction that they *should've* been headed in, and if I didn't know any better, it looked like they were leaving school early. I just shook my head and went to class, there was no use trying to figure it out.

CHAPTER NINETEEN

My eighth period class was American History. History was okay, I definitely liked it better than Science. Today we were talking about the bombings at Pearl Harbor in 1941 and my teacher Mr. Carpenter started getting very emotional about the topic, because his father was in the military at the time. Mr. C was going in very hard about the Japanese. I mean he was talking *extra* greasy!

When we got to 1945 when America dropped a big ass bomb on Hiroshima, Japan, he started smiling, talking about how the United States will always be the worlds #1 super power. Mr. C had been in the Army for a few years and he struck me as one of those crazy ass war veterans. I saw his pickup truck in the teachers parking lot, and this fool got a gazillion U.S. flags all over the place. Bumper stickers, air fresheners, and even a U.S. flag hood ornament.

Don't get me wrong; I'm as patriotic as any normal person is, I guess. But I don't go overboard, because I know about the other part of American history too. The part where the white people thought it was cool to treat my fathers ancestors like shit. Whips, chains, and all that other stuff. I couldn't wait until we got on *that* subject and see what M.C. had to say about *that*.

He'd probably use some politically correct spin of events to try to cover up the ugly truth. Just like he did a couple months ago around Thanksgiving, when we were talking about the Pilgrims and the Indians. According to Mr. Carpenter, the Pilgrims arrived on the Mayflower in 1620; they encountered the Indians and became friends. He said that the Pilgrims taught the Indians how to survive the winters, and that's when shit got *very* ugly.

This Native American boy in my class jumped out his seat and called Mr. C a *fucking liar*. His name was Semi, and Semi said that Mr. Carpenter had the story fucked up. He said that it was the other way around, that the Native Americans helped the Pilgrims prepare for the long winter. Then Semi told the class that in return for their hospitality, the Pilgrims tricked his people. They got the Indians sloppy drunk and ambushed them. Killed the men and raped their wives.

Mr. Carpenter had turned bright red in the face and kicked Semi out of class. On his way out, Semi told Mr. C that he hoped Osama Bin Laden and Suddam Hussein joined forces to take over America and kill all the white devils. The classroom had erupted into cheers, and Semi ended up being suspended for three days behind that. He was lucky that he hadn't ended up in Guantanamo Bay.

Trust me, when the slavery issue does come up in class, I'm going to speak my mind. But I'm not going to make any terrorist threats! Semi's ass is crazy. I wouldn't be surprised if Homeland Security was now tapping that boys phone, cause I'm sure that Mr. C called somebody to report him.

The bell interrupted our teacher knee deep in his patriotic Moment and niggas started bum rushing the door almost knocking him over. One thing you *don't* do is stand in front of *any* door in my school when that dismissal bell rings. I don't care who you are. Your ass is liable to end up underneath somebody's shoes.

He tried to call out a homework assignment, but it was too late, half the class was already in the hallway. I was the last one out and he just looked at me and shook his head.

"See you tomorrow, Mr. C." I smiled at him.

"Take care, April." He returned my smile.

In my opinion, Mr. Carpenter wasn't a bad person, he was just brainwashed by the military and false politics. It must have been hard for him to come to work every morning and deal with a bunch of inner-city kids who were mostly out of control. He put his life on the line everyday for a bullshit check, because teachers in this school were known to catch a beat down every once in a while. Him and me were cool though. I stayed quiet in his class and did my homework, in return, when test time came around he looked out for me. That was our unspoken understanding and it work out for me.

I peeled off towards my locker to grab my stuff, and on the way upstairs I literally bumped into Karma. "Hey, boo. What's up?" She asked with that bright smile.

"Nothing, about to go watch the game." I told her.

"Oh, okay. Well I'll catch you tomorrow. I gotta go, *bye!*" She already had her coat in her hand and was speeding off.

"Bye." I called over my shoulder.

I made it to my locker and fixed myself up in my small mirror. When I had my coat on, I loaded up my book bag, grabbed my purse and went to find my friend. She was at her locker talking to our friend Kiara, and we all walked to the first floor together and then Kiara left to get on the bus.

"You want to run to the store real quick before the game starts," Asia asked me. "I'm *starving*." She was rubbing her stomach with a pitiful look on her face.

I just shrugged, "Cool." I had a few dollars in my purse to spare. We were headed towards the door when it finally hit me what Rell told me after lunch. "Hold up, Asia." I pulled her arm to stop her from getting any closer to the door. I didn't know what to say to her, but I was gonna have to make up something. But then, right on cue we all paused and listened to a loud rumbling sound that seemed to be coming from outside. At the time, it sounded as if there was thunder in the sky.

"Never mind, it's probably about to rain." Asia said. "You heard that thunder, right?"

I nodded. "Yeah." I was glad she heard it too, because at first I thought it was just me. And, I was glad that I would have a ride home, because I didn't have an umbrella with me and I would *hate* to get rained on.

Suddenly the door that we were near, it *burst* open! Then, it was a wild stampede of kids running back inside the school, and with the door opened we could tell that what we *thought* was thunder, turned out to be the loud echoes of gun shots ringing out! Everybody was scattering and trying to get low to the floor. People were screaming and panicking. Asia, and I got down and huddled up together on the floor in the corner until the gunshots finally stopped. And I'm not over exaggerating when I say the shooting lasted for a full minute.

Once it *seemed* safe again, it was straight confusion inside that hallway. Everybody was talking and trying to figure out just what had happened. When I finally lifted my head, and opened my eyes, I saw Mr. Randy one of the schools security guards rush through the doors carrying Karma in his arms. She was crying hysterically, tears streaming down her face and she was covered in blood. I'll never forget that sight as long as I live, because it truly traumatized me. It was a scene straight out of a horror movie, and all the blood covering Karma made me queasy.

Kiara ran over to us, her eyes were wet and her face was pale. "Ya'll not gonna believe this, somebody just killed Karma's boyfriend, right in front of the school." Kiara's eyes were wide like she'd just seen a ghost.

"*Get out*! The dude in the Lexus?" Asia asked her.

Kiara nodded franticly. "*Yeah*. He was parked out front, Karma had just got inside and some car pulled up and just shot that joint up!" Kiara looked as if she was going to faint.

I heard her, but I was in my own thoughts. *Damn*. I felt bad for Karma as I watched security try to console her. She was literally breaking down, they tried to hold her up, but she slowly slid to the ground and curled up in a ball. People were trying to comfort her but it wasn't working at all. The shit was *sad*, and I've never seen anything so terrible in my young life. Like 'Boyz in the Hood' when they found out that Ricky got killed, except *this* was real life. I couldn't stop watching Karma while thinking to myself that even as bad as things seemed, *at least* she was still alive. Because if Bean had gotten hold of her address, she'd probably be dead. But instead, she'd just watched the love of her life be murdered right in front of her eyes. So, despite how tragic things had just become, she was actually lucky.

That's when Asia snapped me out of my daze by putting her arm around me, "I guess what *goes* around, *comes* around..." she looked at me and shrugged.

CHAPTER TWENTY

The police had blocked off the entire block around the school, and of course, they cancelled the basketball game so that left me to get home the usual way, public transportation. I was on my way to the rail station, and Asia walked with me up the Avenue but her plans were to stop and stay at Cam's house. I'd called and left a message this morning, so Mommy wasn't expecting me until after the game was over, but I didn't have anywhere else to go.

"*Damn*, where everybody at?" Asia asked me.

I shrugged. "I don't know." I mumbled at her stupid question, but I'd been thinking the same thing. Cam's block was like a ghost town, I'd never seen this corner empty, there always seemed to be somebody out here hustling. But not today.

"Maybe they ditched school and went to Cam's house. Let's go see, and then you can get Rell to walk you to the bus stop." Asia suggested, and we slowly began walking in that direction. I followed Asia and stopped as she walked up the front porch and knocked on the door. As she waited, I looked up at the sky and admired the snow flurries that were beginning to fall. Meanwhile, some woman opened the front door, said something to Asia, and then quickly pushed it closed. I'm no rocket scientist but I think it was safe to assume that Cam wasn't home.

"His mother said he's on his way home right now." She reported once she'd came back off his porch, and I hoped that this bitch didn't think I was about to wait out here in the freezing cold, just so *she* could receive an eight minute roller coaster ride. Because it wasn't going to happen.

"Asia, I'm cold." I told her. "I'm not bout to stand out here." I added just so she wouldn't have to read in between the lines.

"Okay, but let's just walk slow." She was wearing this dumb ass grin on her face and the bitch had no shame,

"Fine." I rolled my eyes and agreed. But only because I knew that she'd do the same for me if I ever ended up being this thirsty. It's amazing the things a girl will do just to catch a nut.

We walked as slow as our short legs would allow us, but when we finally reached the corner, there was still no sign of Cam or Rell. Asia stopped in the middle of the intersection and looked at me. "Go ahead and catch your bus," She told me. "I'm gonna wait right here." She must have had no idea how stupid she sounded, but I looked at her like she was crazy just to let her know. 2002 had just started, but she was already the retard of the year.

"*Bitch*, you 'bout to stand on this corner and wait for *him*? It's freezing out here!" I was completely appalled.

There wasn't a nigga alive worth catching frostbite over. This bitch was dizzy. "Shit, you might as well turn a couple tricks out here while you're at it!" I started to walk off on her.

"I'm *not* a *hooker*!" She yelled at me.

I stopped. "Whatever the difference is, I can't tell, because you about to freeze your ass off, standing on the corner waiting for some dick!" I shouted over my shoulder.

"Fuck you, April." Asia was laughing it off. I wasn't. There was nothing funny.

I took a couple more steps before finally turning back around. "Asia, bring your dumb ass on!" I yelled at her, and she looked like she was debating just as a shiny black Q45 Infiniti rolled up beside her.

Damn. Niggas probably do think we out here turning tricks!

When the driver's window slid down, I immediately recognized the boy behind the wheel. It was the dude that had been wearing the leather varsity jacket standing next to Cam's brother. I'm not lying; the inside of my thighs began to tingle when I saw him. I watched him call Asia over to his car and I got jealous as he spoke to her. The conversation was a short one, he said a couple words and she nodded, then he began to pull off. As the Infiniti glided past me, he took a slight glance in my direction and slid the tinted window back into place. I wanted him to stop so badly, but he just accelerated down the block.

Asia was walking towards me quickly. "That was, Phee." She told me, as if I was blind and couldn't see. The huge Kool-Aid smile on her face was designed to piss me off, but I didn't fall for it.

"So what." I tried to sound like I could care less, but I really wanted to ask her a gazillion more questions about him.

"He told me to take my friend and get the fuck off his corner-"

"*His* corner?"

"Girl, that's what he said. And the *way* he said, I *believe* him." Asia was grinning at me, and I didn't know whether to take her serious or not. "He said it's hot in Cedar Springs right now, and that there's probably gonna be a war. This corner isn't safe, and that's why we're the only two assholes out here." Asia cracked up laughing.

I didn't see the humor in it, so I didn't laugh. I know that boy didn't call me no *asshole*! "Asia, you get on my damn nerves! Got me out here looking stupid!" I was heated. I can't even honestly say that I was mad at Asia; I was more frustrated that Phee hadn't noticed me. It was really messing with my ego.

We walked the rest of the way to our bus stops in silence, we said our goodbyes, then we went our separate ways and I took my ass home.

My mind was spinning on the bus ride, mostly about what I'd seen today after school. In the back of my mind, I knew that some kind of way, Rell and Cam knew something about Vance getting killed. It was just too much of a coincidence that they'd warned me not to be outside, and I guess it was only because they didn't want me to get hurt on accident. I was almost a hundred percent certain of that. Knowing this became a burden on my shoulders, and although I hadn't pulled the trigger, I felt like an accessory to murder.

*   *   *   *   *

That same night, I had the hardest time falling asleep. I'd been tossing and turning all night under the covers. It was almost 4am on a school night and things that I had no control over were weighing down my brain.

A few times this afternoon, I'd reached for the telephone to call Karma. The only reason that I didn't go through with it is because I had absolutely no idea what to say. But I still couldn't get her off my mind. I'd never be able to erase the image of how she looked as Mr. Randy carried her into the hallway. How she'd curled up into a ball and cried her eyes out.

I felt so bad for her but at the same time, I was torn, because her boyfriend deserved what he got *if* he had anything to do with D's murder. Excuse me, I know that doesn't make it right, but it's the truth. It had been a long time since I'd prayed, but tonight I said a long prayer for my girl, Karma. I know time heals all wounds, but I prayed to God that he'd speed up the process for her, because she'd done nothing to deserve hurting so bad.

I vividly remembered the conversation that we'd had in my driveway last month, as we sat inside the exact same Lexus that her boyfriend was killed in. I knew that she'd given her heart to Vance, but how would she ever get it back now that he was dead? Would she ever be capable of loving again? I tried to put myself in her shoes, but I just couldn't imagine it and I hoped that I'd never feel that type of pain in this lifetime.

And then I felt stupid. Because I realized that, I was *still* lusting after that exact same lifestyle. I *still* wanted to be *her*. All I could think about was Phee, and riding inside that Q45. Even after losing Darrell, and even after seeing Karma lose Vance, I *still* wanted to be the wife of a hustler. It just seemed *so* exciting.

I didn't *want* to be with a Calvin, I *wanted* to be with a gangster.

CHAPTER TWENTY-ONE

A couple weeks had passed and my life was still as boring as could be. I had a couple dudes blowing up my pager, but none of them gave me that feeling. I decided to call Nica because it was Friday and I needed something to get into, I wasn't about to sit in the house tonight.

"Hello?" I could barely hear my cousin's voice because in the background it sounded like she was using the blow dryer.

"Hi, Tanica. What we gonna do tonight?" I checked the clock, and it was almost 6pm.

"*Well*, April. I'm not sure what *your* gonna do, but *I* have a date tonight." I could tell that she was smiling.

I laughed. "*Yikes*! *Who* the *fuck* asked *you* out on a date? Is he blind? And, it is a *he*, right?" I had to mess with her.

She cracked up. "Somebody sounds jealous!" She joked. "It is a *he*, and *he* is *fine*! Don't hate because *you're* alone for another weekend." She took a jab at my corny social life.

I was still smiling because I was happy for her; it was about time she got out the house. "Where you going?" I asked just to be nosy.

"I don't know, it's supposed to be a surprise." She answered proudly.

"Hmmm, that sounds kinky. What's his name?" I started digging.

"I'll tell you everything later. I'm still trying to get my hair done and finish getting ready-"

"All you need is a mask-" I cracked up as Nica hung up the phone on me.

I guessed that I'd be on my own tonight. I would call Asia, but it is excessively much drama at her house. The problem with her is that we both be looking for somewhere else to go. If *I* go over *there*, then *she's* not happy cause she still stuck in the house. And if *she* comes over *here,* then *I'm* still stuck in the house. That's why me and Nica fit together so well, she's always home alone so most of the time she's just happy for some company.

Now that it was clear that I'd be stuck inside tonight, I went downstairs looking for some action. I was bored and determined to get on somebody's nerves. La La and her friend Amber were in the living room watching Fresh Prince of Bel Air repeats, and the rest of the house was too quiet which *usually* means that Mommy and the boys were gone. But obviously not in this instance because I walked into the kitchen and there was Mommy standing at the sink, and it looked like she was about to make dinner.

"Why's it so quiet around here? Where are all the guys at?" I asked as I climbed onto one of the stools at the counter. I'd been in my room since I'd come home from school hours ago, and I had no idea what was going on around here.

"Daddy's at work, and your brothers are at the barbershop. So when you get the chance I need you to walk down the street and pick them up, they should be done soon." She said while eyeing the clock on the stove.

"What time is Daddy getting off work?" If my Dad was at work, then chances were that he probably had the van.

"At eight-thirty, *why*?" She asked with her back to me.

"When he gets home, can we go to the mall?" My question was actually a suggestion.

"You have some money?" She looked over her shoulder at me.

I shook my head because I was definitely broke. "No, but we can just window shop and people watch." I was smiling as I recited Mrs. Shannon's favorite line.

Mommy laughed. "Not tonight babe. The mall closes at ten, and by the time we get there, it'll be after nine. Maybe we'll go tomorrow night." She gave me a sympathetic look.

I was disappointed and it wasn't hard to see it in my face. We were silent for the next few minutes as I watched Mommy prepare dinner. But I could only remain quiet for so long, especially when I thought about Nica out having fun while I was stuck in the house doing nothing.

"Mom, when can you talk Daddy into letting me go out on a date once in a while?" I was sitting with both my elbows on the counter and my palms propping up my chin.

"April, that's going to take some time. I fought tooth and nail just to get you that pager for Christmas, and for you to be able to call boys on the phone without sneaking-"

"But Mommy, that's not really helping my social life."

"Baby, your birthday is only a couple months away and you'll be fifteen. Wait until then and I'll see what I can do, okay?" I knew that Mommy would do her best to convince my Dad, but I wasn't so sure that he'd budge.

"Okay." I responded because I had no other option. Then I hopped up to go get my North Face and boots, so that I could go down the street and get my brothers. It was freezing outside and the snow was falling hard and at a steady pace. When I came back into the kitchen Mommy gave me the money to pay the barber.

"Be careful, it's dark outside. And hurry up." She told me as I walked out the door. In the back of my mind, I wondered why she would send me if she was *so* worried about my safety, but I decided not to ask. I was tired of getting smacked in my forehead all the damn time.

I hiked two blocks through the snow down to Main Street, where Hair Creations was located. Hair Creations was a huge unisex hair spot that included a barbershop and a beauty salon. And it was packed because today was Friday and everyone was trying to get laced for the weekend. I looked around at all the dudes as I walked in, some were young and some were old, but they all checked me out as I entered. Out of nowhere Lito came running towards me and wrapped his arms around my legs, I looked down at him and noticed that he'd already had his haircut.

"What's up, boo boo? Let me look at you." I squatted down to check him out and admired the job that Emory had done. "You look so handsome." I gave him a quick kiss on the nose.

Cory was sitting in the barber chair at the Moment, and when Emory saw me, he waved me over. "What up, girl?" he was all smiles.

"Hi, Emory." I forced a smile to be polite. Emory was cool, but sometimes he went into borderline stalker mode. He had to be about twenty-two, but that never stopped him from trying to get my number every time he saw me.

"Give me like ten minutes. This lil' nigga got a big ass head." Emory cracked a joke, but I only laughed after I saw that Cory was smiling. I'm not even gonna lie to you, Cory does have a little extra up top.

I went and had a seat in the corner, and sat Carlito on my lap as I watched Emory cut my little brothers hair. I was enjoying myself in the barbershop, and it was cool to listen to the dudes talk shit to each other. I listened and laughed as they told dirty jokes that I had no business hearing, and I was thoroughly entertained. Finally, when Cory was done, I got up, took Lito's hand and walked over to give Emory his money. Right before I could get the money out of my pocket the door swings open and guess who walks into the barbershop.

Phee.

He walked straight up to Emory and gave him a pound. "Hold up one second, April." Emory said as the two of them disappeared into the backroom of the barbershop, and I had no doubt that he would try to get my number again when he returned. That was his usual, he'd wait until it was time for me to pay for their haircuts, then he'd tell me to keep the money and ask me to give him the number. But tonight, I didn't want to be bothered. And I didn't want Phee to see Emory trying to get me, because if they were friends that would ruin my chances.

I gave the twenty-dollar bill to Cory. "Here, give this to Emory when he gets done talking." My little brother took the money and tucked it into his pocket.

When the back door opened, they both came in laughing and I took this opportunity to check Phee out up close. He was rocking a green and yellow Nautica ski jacket, black denim, and some crisp Timberland construction boots. This was the first time that I'd really got a good look at him, and he was cute in his own way. He wasn't Memphis Bleek cute, but he had a different type of appeal. Honestly, it wasn't his face that attracted me to him, I really just liked his style. He looked like a boss, and you could see the confidence in his posture. I'm not bullshitting you, this nigga walked like he owned the world! And even though he didn't, I'll tell you what, he was capable of it. I could smell it.

Cory raced over and gave Emory his money. As he did that, Phee was walking towards me in order to head back out the front door and for a second or eyes locked, but once again he kept it moving on me. It *crushed* me. I was so disappointed and I couldn't stop my face from getting hot, so I knew that I was turning red. I just tried to shake it off as I helped my brothers put their coats on so we could leave.

Outside, I held both their hands as we crossed the busy Main Street intersection, then I let them go once we hit the sidewalk. Cory and Carlito walked ahead of me down our street, pushing and shoving each other the entire way. I just shook my head, they must have inherited their violent behavior from Mommy. When we were two houses away from ours, a car slowly glided up beside me. When I looked, I almost fainted as the tinted out Q45 stopped beside me, and I almost died when the passenger window slid down. Then, the unthinkable happened.

He actually spoke to me.

"When I saw you in the barbershop, I was hoping that you weren't there to cut off all that pretty hair." His voice was just like I'd imagined it would be. Not high-pitched, and not too deep. It was Perfect. He was smiling at me from the drivers seat, and I had on my earmuffs, but I heard every word that he said.

"I'll cut it *all* off if you want me to." I have no idea where it came from, but that's what came out of my mouth.

He laughed, but I was dead ass serious. I'd wear a Mohawk if he wanted me to. "You don't even know me, so why would you do that?" he wanted to know.

I shrugged. "It'll grow back." I answered. I'd stopped walking completely, and my brothers had too. Now they were walking back towards me trying to be nosy and see who was in the car.

"Who is that? April, who's that?" Both of them were asking me in unison. I didn't answer instead I was checking to see if our driveway was still empty, and I was thrilled to see that my Daddy hadn't made it home from work yet. I wasn't worried about my Mommy, she wouldn't mind.

I looked at my brothers. "Don't worry about it, go in the house and show Mommy your new haircuts. Both of you look so handsome." I pointed towards the house. "Go ahead, it's too cold out here for ya'll to be standing around." I needed them to hurry up, and reluctantly they started walking again, so did I and the Infiniti slowly followed.

"It seems like every time I see you, you're out walking in the cold. What's up wit' that?" He asked me, but I didn't respond until I reached the foot of my driveway.

"What's up with you?" I reversed the question on him. "You scared of me or something? You never spoke to me before, so what makes tonight so special." I was curious and I wanted to know.

To my surprise, he put the Q45 in park and hopped out. I kid you not, my heart skipped a beat as he walked right up to me, and I could've sworn that I was dreaming.

"Because now, it's just me and you. There's none of our friends standing around watching." He stepped in real close. "My name's, Pharaoh..." he extended his hand for me to take, and when I did, he kissed the back of it and I started to tingle. "Everybody just calls me, Phee."

"I'm, April."

"Nice to meet you, April. I hope I'm not going to get you into any trouble by being in front of your building like this." When he said that I looked towards the door. I'd forgotten that it was locked and Cory must have rung the doorbell, because right now Mommy was standing in the doorway looking at me.

"No, my Mom is cool."

He nodded and followed my nervous eyes to the door. "Is that her right there?" He asked me and I nodded. Then my jaw dropped as he started walking up my driveway towards the house. I wanted to ask this nigga what he was doing but I was speechless, and all I could do was follow. When she saw us approaching, Mommy opened the screen door and stepped out into the cold.

"How are you this evening, ma'am?" Phee asked Mommy. She didn't answer right away; instead, she looked past him at me with a puzzled look on her face. "My name is, Pharaoh." He introduced himself immediately.

"Hi," she looked him up and down. "You can call me, Mrs. Showers." She tried to be as polite as she could under the circumstances because I could see how confused she was.

"Mrs. Showers, you have a *very* beautiful daughter," He was speaking to Mommy, but making me blush at the same time. "And if it's okay with you, I'd like to borrow a few Moments of her time. Can I please speak with her alone, I promise I won't keep her too long?" He spoke so politely and Mommy seemed so impressed, that she started glowing.

"Sure, I don't see why not." Mommy grinned at me and stepped back inside. "Nice to meet you, Pharaoh." She said over her shoulder as she began closing the door.

"Same here, Mrs. Showers." Phee leaned against the railing on the porch and stared at me. My eyes were on the ground, and I was avoiding his gaze because it was just too intense. I did however manage to catch him peeking at the gold watch on his wrist, and I wondered if he had somewhere to be.

"What do you want out of life, April Showers?" He was still staring at me.

It took me a while to respond. Finally, I shrugged, not really knowing how to answer the question. "Just to be happy."

He nodded as if he accepted my answer, and then looked off into the sky as if he was in deep thought. While he looked away, I snuck a look at his face, he only looked a couple years older than me, and my guess was seventeen. But he seemed extra mature, and I could tell by the question that he'd asked me. This wasn't the typical icebreaker that boys my age use to begin a conversation, and that turned me on.

"So if I make you happy, what are you gonna give me in return?" He was back to looking me in the eyes.

This time my response was automatic. "I shouldn't have to *give* you *anything* in return for you making me happy, either you want to make me smile or you don't. But you shouldn't be looking for something in return." I didn't know if he was asking me a trick question or not, but I just kept it real.

He gave me a curious look. "So I shouldn't expect for *you* to make *me* happy in return?" He wanted to know.

"It depends on what you mean by that." I had to be careful, niggas were getting very clever with their game these days, and Pharaoh looked like the clever type. If I didn't stay on point, he'd probably talk me right out of my panties.

Phee laughed. "We're not on the same page, April." He stepped off the porch and began to slowly walk off. "I'll holler at you some other time, tell your Mom I said goodnight." He said over his shoulder as he headed to his car. My pride wouldn't let me call his name or run after him, so I just stood there with my mouth open looking stupid. I didn't have a clue where things had suddenly went so bad. All I knew was he'd climbed into his whip and pulled off.

Mommy was in the kitchen when I walked inside, but I didn't feel like talking. "That was quick." She said while looking up from the sink.

I didn't stop, I went straight for the stairs. "I'm going to bed."

She gave me a worried look. "Dinner will be ready soon-"

"I'm not hungry, I'm going to sleep." I hurried up the stairs and damn near ran to my bedroom. I couldn't believe that I had him, and then let him slip through my fingers. I went to sleep in a shitty mood because I was so disgusted in myself. I just kept replaying our short conversation in my head, and wondering what I *should've* said different.

What I did was, I made up in my mind that the next time I was in Pharaoh's presence, I wouldn't let him get away.

That was my New Years resolution.

CHAPTER TWENTY-TWO

I'm used to being woken up by my Mom, but this time was different. "April, get up! I have to go somewhere." I lifted my head from the pillow and forced my eyes open, my light was still off and Mommy's silhouette was in my doorway.

"Where you going?" I asked sleepily.

"Don't worry about it, just get up so that you can watch the boys." My Mom flipped on my light switch and walked off. I squinted as the bright light hit my eyes. This woman really knew how to test my nerves. The clock on my nightstand read, 8:42pm. I'd been asleep for the past hour or so since coming back from the barbershop. I was dead tired, but that didn't affect my curiosity, and I wondered how Mommy was going somewhere if Daddy had the mini-van. That's when I heard the back door slam shut, so I jumped out the bed and ran to my window jut in time to see Mommy climbing into the backseat of a taxi. I wondered what was going on because it wasn't like my Mom to just leave the house, especially when Daddy was probably on his way home from work.

I walked out into the hallway and made my rounds around the house to see what was going on. The boys were in their room fooling around, and La La was in the family room on the internet with her friend Amber. I was tired, and all I could think about was going back to sleep, so I decided that's exactly what I was going to do.

I stood in the doorway of my brother's room and motioned for the two of them. "*Both* of you come here." They stopped playing and walked nervously over to where I stood, then I turned and led them down the hall to the family room. "Go inside." I pointed, and both La Reina and Amber looked up. "Either play the video game, or watch television. But you'd *better* be quiet, and *don't* leave this room until Mommy comes home." I instructed the two of them as La La looked at me with an attitude. She was mad and I could tell, but I didn't care.

I gave her a look to let her know that her attitude didn't mean anything to me. "Watch them until Mommy gets back, and if she's not home before 9:30, get them ready for bed." I ordered my younger sister. Before walking away, I stood there for a couple seconds just to see if she was going to have something smart to say. Truthfully, I almost wanted her to because I was definitely in the mood to go upside her damn head. But she kept her mouth closed and just nodded, so I walked back down the hall to my room and closed the door.

You see, part of being a great leader, is knowing how to delegate responsibility to those beneath you. Mr. C, my history teacher had taught me that and it proved to be a lesson well learned. I climbed back into my bed, slid under the covers and instantly fell back asleep.

The next time I opened my eyes; it was because loud yelling had interrupted my sleep. It was exactly 11:27pm, and I sat up straight in my bed and tried to listen. My Mom was going crazy, she was screaming and cursing at somebody. I knew it was bad when I heard a couple loud thuds, and it became apparent that she was throwing shit too.

Damn!

The first thing that came across my mind was that La Reina must have gotten herself into trouble just that fast, because Mommy definitely wouldn't be using that kind of language with the boys. Then I realized that the commotion was coming from upstairs in the attic, so something must have happened between my parents. Whatever it was, Mommy was steaming mad and that was confirmed when she went on 2-minute verbal tirade in Spanish. The whole time, I didn't hear Daddy say anything at all, but then again he was never the type to raise his voice.

Her tantrum lasted another thirty minutes or so, then it just stopped altogether. After that, there was no words being spoken, just lots of movement, someone was doing lots of walking back and forth. Their floor was carpeted, but my room was directly underneath the most commonly used area of their bedroom and it sounded as if things were being moved around and dragged across the floor. My eyes widened and got real big. I hoped that this crazy woman hadn't killed my Daddy.

I listened and tried to distinguish the sounds all the way, up until I heard the back door open and then close. I didn't get out the bed and run to my window, because I didn't have to look at the driveway to know who was leaving. My heart cracked wide open, shattering into a gazillion pieces. All I could do was put my head underneath my pillow and worry myself back to sleep.

It wasn't until the next morning that I found out what happened. Apparently, Mommy had been suspicious about Daddy working so many Friday evenings, she called his job and it turned out that he wasn't even on the schedule. That's when she took the taxi downtown to his job at the hotel. My Mom was telling me the story, and as I listened, all I do was shake my head. Mommy had gotten on some real undercover, Inspector Gadget type shit. Almost like on that TV show 'Cheaters'.

She'd spotted our mini-van in the hotel parking lot, so she knew that he was there, he just wasn't working. Well, he *was* putting in some work, just not in the kitchen. Mommy went into the hotel and waited inside the restaurant near the lobby, until she spotted Daddy getting off the elevator with some young Mexican bitch.

"So what did you do then?" I asked Mommy. I was laying under the covers as Mommy sat on the edge of my bed. It was early the next morning and she was giving me *all* the details, not the sugar coated version that she'd give someone else.

"I followed behind them until they got outside, then I whipped that little bitch's ass all over that parking garage!" Mommy answered me with a satisfied smirk on her face. In my mind, I could definitely envision my Mom beating up some young, pretty, Mexican chica as they screamed curse words at each other in Spanish.

I frowned. "Oooh Mommy, that definitely wasn't classy at all." She shot me a look, and I discreetly used that time to check her face for bruises or scratches, but I didn't see any. "Nah, Mom..." I decided to clean up my statement.

"I'm just saying, that girl probably didn't even know that Daddy was married-"

"So what? She got her ass whooped, and if she *still* wants him, *now* she can have him!" The way she said that last part scared me, honestly, it really hurt me bad. I loved both of my parents, a lot. But I've always been a Daddy's girl, and it rubbed me the wrong way to hear Mommy talk like this about him.

"Did you hit my Daddy too?"

She raised her eyebrows at me. "What have I always told you about putting your hands on a man?" She asked the question as if it was a pop quiz or something.

"Don't do it, unless I'm prepared to catch a beat down." It was one of those lessons that I'll never forget. Mom expressed this to me one day after Tiffany learned the hard way and came home with a black eye and a busted lip.

Mommy waved her index finger at me. "And don't you *ever* forget that. Your father has *never* put his hands on me, so I show him the same respect." She looked real serious.

I wanted to tell her, that the hot tamale chica never put her hands on her either, and probably didn't deserve to get spanked. But I decided that it probably wouldn't be wise to speak my opinion, I didn't want to be her second victim in a twelve-hour period. Me personally, I'm not fighting over a man. *Period.* Boyfriend, Fiancé, or husband, it doesn't matter. It's just not my style, and men are too easy to replace. But on the other hand, I put myself in Mommy's shoes. 36-years old with four kids, maybe she didn't have the luxury of finding a new husband so easily. Not that I wanted her to, that's definitely not what I meant, I'm just saying.

"So now what?" I asked softly. I usually don't ask questions that I'm scared to know the answer to, but I couldn't help it. I just prayed that they'd fix it and move on. The last thing I wanted to hear was the word 'divorce'.

"April," she looked at me sadly. "I'm done this time. This is the third strike." Mommy rubbed my cheek and I closed my eyes to make it easier to fight my tears. I understood where she was coming from, nobody wants to be lied to and deceived. But c'mon, Daddy messed up three times in eighteen years. That's a good average, especially considering how handsome Daddy was. I'm not saying it's okay, but lets face it, men are dogs! *All* of them, with *no* exceptions. In my opinion, leaving a man who treats you good, just because he cheats won't solve your problems. *Why*? Because, then you're just gonna meet another dog, fall in love, and that nigga gonna cheat on you too. Then what? You gonna go your whole life playing musical chairs, searching for the perfect, faithful man. Chasing a ghost that doesn't exist!

Any woman who *thinks* her man *is*, always has been, or always will be faithful, is a God damned fool! The happily married women in this world are the ones who've never *caught* his ass, or the ones who understand what I'm saying and just accept it. When I get married, I'm never even gonna try to catch my husband cheating. As long as he keeps it out of my face, I'm good. When you go looking for something, chances are that you'll find it. Mommy should've stayed her ass home last night and we wouldn't be having this conversation. Daddy *loves* us, he takes care of us, and he'd *die* for each one of us. What else do you expect? But of course, I didn't express this to my mother.

"Your Dad moved out." She said quietly, still rubbing the side of my face. I didn't mean to cry, but the tears started to seep through my eyelids and Mommy's fingers caught them as they fell.

"Is he coming back?"

"I don't know, April. But you know how much he loves you-"

"Mommy!" I interrupted her. "I didn't ask you if my Daddy loves me. I *know* he loves me, and I don't need *you* to tell me that! I *asked you* if he was coming back." I was starting to get angry, and at this point, I didn't care about being hit. There was a slight pause before she answered. I don't think that she was debating her answer, because it was something she already knew. I think it took her so long to respond because she was afraid to tell me.

"No, April." She whispered. "Your Dad's not coming back." Even though I was already expecting this response, the words cut me so deep and hurt so bad that I became numb. I started to feel something towards my mother that I'd never felt before. I wanted to scratch her eyes out. I wanted to kill her for ruining our perfect family. Instead, I just cried.

I turned over on my side so that she couldn't touch my face and so that I wouldn't have to look at her. "I can't believe that you ran Daddy away from us." I said it loud and clear, I didn't mumble or whisper it and I didn't care if she slapped me or beat me up.

"April-" She reached out to touch me and I jerk away from her.

"Please don't touch me." I scooted all the way to the opposite edge of my bed. "I wish you'd just get out my room, I don't wanna talk to you." My heart was in so much pain that I blurted these words out in total disregard for my safety. I braced myself for a blow to the head, but it never came. My mattress shifted as she got up, then a second later, my door opened and closed.

I didn't care if I'd hurt her feelings. This bitch had just up and ruined my whole life. And I thought *I* was selfish. Did she even think about her children before she chased their Dad away? What were we supposed to do now? Spend the weekends with him, twice a month or some dumb shit like that? Who was going to protect us? Who was going to teach my little brothers how to be men? Did she think about that? Better yet, how the fuck were we supposed to survive? This bitch didn't even have a damn job! Aren't these the things that a smart woman would consider, *before* kicking her husband to the curb?

I could see us now, living inside the mini van, and all of us eating dinner out of the same plastic bag! The police would arrest Mommy for child endangerment, then La Reina, the boys, and me would all end up in foster care. Mommy would end up strung out on drugs. La La and me would end up turning tricks for some sleazy pimp named Chico, and my little brothers would end up like Heckle and Jeckle.

And, as if these thoughts weren't bad enough, my mind shifted to my Dad. Where would he go? What would he do? I know one of these young broads was gonna snatch his handsome ass up real quick. Then he'd get whipped and sprung on some fly bitch in her 20's and forget all about us. He'd get her pregnant, move out of town and start a completely separate family. At the thought of that, I began crying so hard that I got a huge migraine, and the headache knocked me out cold.

CHAPTER TWENTY-THREE

For the next few days, I avoided my Mom, and the sight of her face made me sick to my stomach. I stayed barricaded inside my room. I didn't feel like being bothered and no one bothered me. Monday and Tuesday, I didn't even get up to go to school and Mommy didn't try to make me. Every night, she sent Carlito up to my room to bring me dinner. She knew he was my soft spot and I wouldn't take my anger out on him like I would the other two. My pager was blowing up, but I wasn't making any calls.

My Daddy still hadn't come home. I was losing my mind, and now I was even beginning to get angry with *him*. I was starting to take it personally. If he didn't wanna be bothered with Mommy, cool. But what about *me*? He knows how much I need him, so he had to know how much I was hurting right now. So why wouldn't he come check on me? At least come make sure that I wasn't suicidal, and thinking about fucking killing myself!

That's when it hit me.

What if Daddy was suicidal, right now? What if he'd hurt himself? What if he missed us so much that he got really depressed and didn't want to live anymore? The thought made my stomach ache. He couldn't have called, because Carlito would've brought me the phone. I wondered if my Aunt Tracey had heard from him. But the last person I was gonna call was her, she talked too damn much.

By Wednesday, I was tired of lying around feeling like shit. I got up early and got ready for school because I needed something to take my mind off everything else. I waited until I heard the Daycare Van leave and then dipped out the house. At first, my plan was to go downtown to my Daddy's job so that I could see him, but I decided to go to school first. His normal shift was 8:30-5pm, so I'd just go after school and hopefully catch him later.

When I got to the bus stop Calvin was already there. When he saw me, his eyes got very big like he'd just seen Lazarus come back from the dead. I could tell that I was the last person that he'd been expecting to see. I had no doubt that Mrs. Shannon knew what was going on in our house, and if she knew, Calvin knew. At first, he looked like he didn't know what to say, and knowing him; he'd just stand there looking stupid if I didn't speak first.

"Hi, Calvin." I stopped on the corner, and stood next to him right in front of the barbershop.

"What's up, April? My bad, I should've come to see if you were going to school today." He apologized.

"It's okay. I'm a big girl, I can walk by myself." I shot him a smile so that he knew I was only joking. I tried to lighten up the mood but he still didn't say much, so I left it alone. Trying to get a good conversation out of this boy was like trying to squeeze wine from a damn rock. If it didn't have anything to do with basketball, this fool was a social retard.

The bus came and we got on. I found a window seat and glued my eyes to the glass. Calvin sat next to me, but by this time, I was through with him. It was obvious that he was incapable of making me smile and taking my mind off the latest tragedy in my life. Mrs. Shannon should be so proud to know that her son had such a promising future as a Mime, or perhaps one of those idiots who sit puppets on their laps and make them talk. How could he ever hope to be my man if he was too scared to speak up, talks to me and try to console me, when he obviously knew something was wrong?

What a moron.

I got off the bus at my stop, and didn't even bother saying goodbye. This whole shy and bashful routine Calvin had going on was beginning to get old. One day, he'd show a little confidence, and the next he'd display *none*. He was hot and cold. Talk about bi-polar? That boy had issues.

I wasn't even surprised to see Asia hanging out alone at the bus station. That was my bitch. Ride or die. Rain, sleet, or snow! "I missed you. Are you okay?" Asia gave me a big hug. I wondered how much this girl knew. When it came to breaking news, this girl was like Barbara Walters! She had her own confidential sources and everything.

"Yeah," I said with a smile. "I'm good."

She looked at me skeptically like she wasn't buying it. "I called you a million times. Your Mom said that you weren't feeling good, but I called the next day and Lito answered," Asia started smiling. I immediately started to laugh, Carlito was my baby, but I know he can't hold water and plus he has a crush on Asia.

"And what did he say?" I asked grinning as we walked towards the school.

"He said you locked yourself in your room and wouldn't come out," She looked at me. "He said, he missed you." When she told me what my baby brother told her, it made me feel rotten because I hadn't stopped to think about how my behavior had affected anyone else.

"Everything's cool. I was just in one of my moods, I'm good." I told her while praying that the subject would change. Asia's my best friend, but I don't tell bitches my business. In high school all your *current* friends, are *potential* enemies. I'll never let a bitch know what makes me cry, my weaknesses aren't for anyone else to know.

"Well you could've at least called me." Asia rolled her eyes.

"Sorry, it won't happen again." I said sarcastically and we both laughed.

I was just happy to be out the house and back at school. Spending the last four days cooped up in my room had been hell, and it was good therapy for me to get back to living my life. The rest of the day went by pretty quick. People were saying hi to me, like I'd been gone forever. And I did notice that Karma still hadn't come back to school yet.

According to Asia, Darrell was related to some people in this neighborhood and Vance was killed in retaliation. She said that's what Phee meant when he said that there was about to be a war. I just hoped that nobody else would get hurt, especially nobody that I knew. I didn't need anymore bad news.

The day was almost over and I couldn't be more thrilled. I walked into my eighth period History class and Mr. C called me over to his desk.
"April, take your things and go down to the main office." He handed me a hall pass.

I scrunched up my face. "Why?" I asked him and he gave me one of those looks that said, he was a teacher and I was a student and I shouldn't be questioning him. Then, I gave him a look of my own.

"I was told to send you to the main office. You should get going." It was clear that he wasn't going to say anything else, so I grabbed my stuff and headed downstairs. I was shaking my head the entire way, hoping that the Principle wasn't tripping about two measly ass absences. My homeroom teacher had asked me this morning if I had a note from home or from a doctor for the two days I missed, but I didn't. If Mommy 'd known that I was coming to school this morning, she would've given me a note.

I walked into the office prepared to answer their questions about my attendance, but almost fainted when I saw my Daddy standing there waiting for me. He was holding a big bouquet of flowers and a huge Teddy bear in his hands.

"Hey, baby girl!" He had a huge smile on his face as I walked to him and he hugged me. He held me for so long that I could've melted in his arms. I inhaled his scent and he smelled just the way I remembered.

"I missed you." I said into his chest.

"I missed you too," He said as he let me go.

All the ladies who worked in the office were being nosy and minding our business. They were smiling like this was a scene from a movie or something. And most of them were probably just lusting over my handsome Daddy. "Go get your coat, April."

He didn't have to tell me twice. I shot out the office and up the stairs to my locker, I grabbed my coat and them slipped to the second floor. Asia was in her Algebra class; I walked by and looked inside. This bitch was damn near unconscious at her desk, sleeping like a baby. I got the girls attention that was sitting next to her and Asia finally looked up. I held up my coat and gave her the signal that I was leaving, I'd call her later, and then I bounced.

Daddy was waiting for me at the door. He gave me a kiss and then handed me the flowers and the teddy bear. "I'm sorry, baby girl." He was staring at me with those grey eyes.

I just nodded. I didn't really know how to respond, but I had a Kool-Aid smile on my face though. We walked outside together and he opened the passenger side of a brand new Ford Taurus, I got in and he closed the door for me.

When he got behind the wheel, I looked at him. "Daddy, you're not about to steal me, are you?" I couldn't help but ask. I'd heard stories about parents kidnapping their own kids during custody disputes.

My Dad cracked up laughing. "April, where do you get this shit? Why do you always just say the first thing that comes to your mind?" He was wrong about that, because there's a lot of stuff that I keep to myself.

I shrugged. "I don't always."

He was amused. "No, I didn't come here to steal you. I came to take you out on a date, just the two of us, is that okay with you?" He didn't even have to ask, I was smiling from ear to ear.

"I thought you forgot about me, Daddy." I told him honestly.

His smile faded and he shook his head. "I could *never* do that."

*   *   *   *   *

Daddy took me to the movies to see 'Meet The Parents', and then we went to eat at TGI Fridays and had a long talk at the restaurant. I told him everything that was on my mind. *Everything.* He didn't get mad at me for putting my emotions on the table, and the things that came out my mouth; he took on the chin like a man. With my Dad, I never had to worry about being popped upside the head unless I was blatantly disrespectful, and with Daddy, I never was.

He even told me the truth about what happened, and I respected him for that because most Dads wouldn't feel the need to explain themselves to their fourteen-year old daughter. Daddy asked me for my forgiveness. I gave it to him. Then I asked him when he was coming home, and he told me he wasn't. This time I didn't cry. I was all cried out. I'd been shedding tears for the past four days and I couldn't do it anymore.

We drove to Niagara Falls, Ontario and spent the rest of the evening taking in the sights. Aquarium, wax museum, go carting and then we went to the Hard Rock Café for a late dinner. When Daddy finally pulled up the driveway behind the mini van it was after eleven.

"You know I love you, April. No matter what happens between me and your Mom, you're still my baby girl, right?"

I nodded.

"Do me a favor," he said as we sat quietly in the rental car.

"Okay." I didn't hesitate.

He looked me in the eyes. "Please stop giving your Momma a hard time over this. She's going through enough, and she doesn't deserve that from you. If you wanna be mad at someone, be mad at me. Your mother is a good woman, and she stood by me through a lot of shit that you have no idea about. So stop treating her bad like it's her fault, okay?"

I nodded. "Okay, Daddy."

"You promise?"

I smiled at him. "I promise."

He winked at me. "I should have my own place by this weekend, and as soon as I do I'll give you a key. I'll be here on Saturday to pick up the boys, and Sunday I'll come get you and La Reina. So let them know."

"Okay."

"And if you want to talk, just call the hotel and ask for me. I love you." He leaned over and kissed my cheek.

"I love you too." I opened my door and stepped out into the cold. I walked up the driveway, clenching my flowers and teddy bear as I hurried to the door. Daddy waited until I was safely inside before he hit the horn and pulled off. It was dark in the kitchen so I turned on the lights, and just like I thought, Mommy was sitting at the table waiting for me.

CHAPTER TWENTY-FOUR

I put my Biology book down and rubbed my temples, this science shit was frying my brain. How is knowing the difference between Meiosis and Mitosis gonna get me thru life? I was more of a numbers person. Math was easy to me. I wanted to be an accountant, or work at a bank. I wouldn't even mind being a math teacher or professor, but this biology thing wasn't really for me.

I needed a break so I flipped on the television. 106 &Park was on and they were playing a new Cam'ron video, so I stopped and started bobbing to it. Just then, my door cracked open and Mommy poked her head inside my room.

"Come here, April." She said before turning and walking off.

I got off my bed followed her down the hall, she went down the back stairs and I was right behind her. When I stepped into the kitchen, I was beyond shocked to see this boy Phee in my house. He had his shoes off and he was leaned against the counter drinking a glass of orange juice like he lived here.

"What's up, April?" He was cool like he'd been here a hundred times before. My heart began to beat out my chest, I just got so nervous by being in his presence.

"Hi." It was the best I could do, I was still in shock that he was actually here. I looked him over and he was fly as usual, and my Mom stood there enjoying my reaction.

"Your friend happened to be riding by and he was nice enough to help me carry the groceries inside," Mommy winked at me. "The bags were kind of heavy. And I invited him inside to offer him something to drink." Then she turned to him. "Thank you so much, Pharaoh. I appreciate it."

"Anytime, Mrs. Showers." He said politely right before Mommy walked off and left us alone.

I noticed that he'd finished his juice, and he was staring at me. "You want something else to drink?" I stepped towards him.

"No thank you. I'm good." I walked over and took the glass from him, rinsed it out and put it in the dishwasher. The pink velour sweatpants that I was wearing were so tight that you see a v-shaped print between my thighs. I caught him looking as I walked back across the kitchen and leaned against the wall.

"I'm ready to make you happy now." I went on the offensive and caught him off guard; I could tell that I'd surprised him. I remembered my resolution, and I vowed not to let him walk out my kitchen without leaving a lasting impression in his mind. "Whatever you give me, I'll give it back to you in return." I stared at him intently.

"Why couldn't you say that last week?" He wanted to know.

"Last week, I didn't *need* anyone to make me happy. I was *already* happy. But this week, things are a whole lot different." My Daddy moving out had left me feeling empty.

I had a void that I needed to be filled. I needed someone to make me feel safe and make me laugh the way Daddy did.

Pharaoh walked over and sat down on the steps next to where I stood. "Sit down, talk to me." The staircase was barely wide enough for the two of us, but I squeezed onto the step next to him, and my heart began pumping faster from us being so close.

I exhaled slowly. "The last time I saw you, you were talking like you could make me happy. So, I wanna see if you can. We don't know each other, but I wanna get to know you," I looked at him. "I want to be everything that you need. I'm a good girl, and you won't have to worry about me." I was wearing my most innocent face as I spit my game. I had to bag him, because I needed a man right now, more than ever. "*And*, I'm loyal, I *promise* I'll *never* make you look bad." He looked like he was thinking about my words, and then he threw a curveball at me.

"I got my life together. So, what do *you* bring to the table? You look good, but so do millions of other girls. What makes *you different?*"

My mind started speeding as I searched my brain for the right answer. This boy stay asking some clever ass questions! Last time, I'd messed up and he'd kept it moving on me. This time, I decided to just be honest and say what's real. If he couldn't respect *that*, then we had nothing else to talk about.

"I don't have *anything* to bring to the table. I need *you* to teach me how to be *your* girl. I've never had a boyfriend before, so you've gotta show me what to do. I'm a quick learner." I looked at him out the corner of my eye. "I read somewhere, that a woman is a reflection of her man. Do you believe that?" I flipped it around and hit him with a question; he wasn't the only one who could come up with some clever shit.

He started laughing. "Oh really? You read that somewhere, huh?" He was smiling at me, and I nodded to answer his question. "Yeah, I believe that it can be true. Not *all* the time, but *most* of the time."

And just like that, he fell right into my lap. "So I guess the question should be, what makes *you* so different? Because the things that *you* teach *me*, that's gonna be what will separate me from all the other girls. Right, Pharaoh?"

He was shaking his head. "That was real slick. I like the way you tried to spin my question, who taught you that?"

I was giggling. "I learned it on my own."

"Well, I'll be honest with you. There's another female who I'm in love with," My heart dropped, and my eyes went to the floor. "I've got mean crush on your Moms!" Phee started laughing. "She's the real reason why I came by." He was cracking up.

I punched him in the arm, probably a little harder than I'd intended to. "Get out my house!" I got up from the steps, pouted and crossed my arms across my chest.

"Can I at least say bye to your Mom, before you kick me out?" Now we were both laughing as he stood up from the stairs and walked to me. I back peddled away from him until my back was against the kitchen counter and I was pinned against it. Phee had to be about 6'3", and he was towering over me. I looked up at him as he pressed his body against mine, my flesh began to heat up and I was moistening by the seconds.

"We'll take it slow, alright?" It was a question, but he said it like a statement. I just nodded. We could do it however he liked. "Remember this number..." Phee gave me seven digits, and I locked them into my memory like the numbers wiz that I am. "Call me tonight before you go to sleep," he instructed before scooping me up into his arms and I wrapped my arms around his neck. I inhaled his scent and closed my arms as he held me. His arms stayed around my waist, he didn't attempt to run his hands across my butt and get some cheap feels. Not that I would've minded, but I was happy that I was dealing with a gentleman.

When he let go, I was still clinging to his neck. "I gotta go, April. I'll talk to you tonight." I finally let go slowly, but was very reluctant to do so. I didn't want to let him go, but I didn't want him to think that I was some young, crazy, fatal attraction.

"Alright." I sighed, watching him put on his Nike boots and zip up his black leather jacket. When he was ready, I opened the door for him.

"Come here." He turned at the last minute and I got butterflies in my stomach thinking that I was about to get a kiss. But instead of getting some face action, I got robbed. Phee grabbed me and pulled off the elastic scrunchie that held my ponytail in place, that made my hair come undone and fall into my eyes. I brushed the long strands out my face and watched him stash my scrunchie into is pocket.

"Oh, so you a thief?" I asked with a grin.

"Something like that." He turned back towards the door. "Now I've got something to remember you by." He walked out my back door and I watched him climb into that black Infiniti, then back down our driveway. I stood there and watched until his car was out my line of sight and then I slowly closed the door.

"He's nice." I jumped at the sound of Mommy's voice. She'd snuck up behind me, and I had no idea that she was standing right behind me wit a huge grin. "He's a little bit older than you though." We both sat down at the counter and got comfortable. I didn't even know how old he was; neither of us had asked ages, it hadn't seemed important. "But I guess four years isn't such a big deal, your Dad is *five* years older than me. And he's *very* polite; I can tell that his Mom taught him manners.

My guess was that Mommy approved of Pharaoh, so I tried my luck. "So do you mind if he takes me out?" I hadn't even been invited out on a date yet, but I figured that it had to be coming soon.

She smiled. "Gotta ask your Dad." She answered and I started to frown. Maybe she hadn't gotten the memo, but Daddy was gone. If I wanted to continue living by all of *his* rules, then I would just go live with *him*!

I decided to keep trying. "Mom, if Daddy was still here, you would've *never* invited Pharaoh inside this house. You didn't call and ask permission to let him in, so why do we need permission for me to go out to the movies or something? You met him, it's not like he's a stranger." I tried my best to reason with her.

She looked like she was considering it, but I didn't really expect her to crack. Even though she was mad at Daddy, she probably still wasn't willing to do anything to make him curse her out. And if he found out that she let me out on a date, she was sure to get cursed out.

"I'll think about it. But from now on, he's welcome to come over anytime, just as long as I'm home. And he can call too." My face lit up. Hey, this was better than nothing.

"But *only* him!" She quickly clarified. Mommy knew she'd better be specific, or I'd have dudes pulling up here like this was the McDonalds drive thru.

"Okay." I kissed her cheek in appreciation then headed towards the stairs to finish my Biology homework before it got too late.

She called behind me. "Dinner at 6:30. And I saw Tony today at the grocery store, he said to call him." She gave me a look as I rolled my eyes and she laughed. I sprang up the stairs to handle my business, I'd call Tony later, but only so that we could keep our shopping discount. It was wrong, but it needed to be done. I looked at it as my contribution to the household. My beauty was helping to put food on our table. All Tony wanted to do was hear my voice occasionally, I flirted and talked sexy to him and in return, he was nice to Mommy when she went shopping. Fair exchange wasn't considered robbery, because like Mr. C says, this *is* America.

Later on, after the boys were asleep and Mom and La Reina were in their rooms, I went to take a long hot bath. Afterwards, I moisturized my body, put on a fresh pair of panties and a tank top, and then grabbed the cordless phone. I climbed into the bed and dialed the phone number that Pharaoh had given me, from the first three digits it looked like a cell phone.

"What's up, baby?" He answered on the second ring. I was taken back by the greeting and I hoped that it was meant for me.

"Do you even know *who* this is?" I asked quickly.

"This a brand new phone, and I only gave my baby the number." That was his reply and it had me open. The smile on my face was so wide that I was afraid my jaws would start hurting.

"You'd better not be lying-"

"Never. What you doing?" He asked me.

"Laying down, I just got out the tub." I wanted to paint a picture for him, but I wished he was under the covers with me and we were talking face to face.

"You sleepy?"

"A little." I answered truthfully. I'd been up since seven this morning, Mommy was back on her alarm clock shit and I hadn't had the chance for a nap this afternoon.

"We can talk later then-"

"No, I'm up. I wanna talk to you now." I hoped I didn't sound too thirsty, but I'd been waiting for this for weeks now, every since I'd seen him outside that first day.

"Okay, calm down, sweetheart." He brought a smile to my face. "You've got my undivided attention. Ladies first, tonight is all about you. Tell me everything that I need to know about, April. I'll be quiet, let you talk and ask questions later. Then tomorrow night we'll switch, okay?"

"Okay." I answered. I was cool with that, *shit*, I can talk my ass off. I hope he had a few hours to spare, because I was about to break down fourteen years worth of fabulousness.

"I'm ready." He let me know I had his attention.

I sighed. "Okay, first I'll tell you all my favorite things, just so you'll know."

"Alright."

"And, I'm only gonna tell you my favorites one time. If you don't remember them after tonight, we're going to have a problem. Two years from now, if you don't remember what my favorite movie is, I'm gonna curse you out! Got it?" I was dead serious, so he should consider himself warned.

"I got it, baby." He answered quietly. He spoke soft but confident, just like my Daddy. And the way he called me *baby*, it turned me on tremendously.

For the next two and a half hours, we talked. Well, I talked and he listened. Once every couple of minutes, I'd check to make sure this boy hadn't dozed off on me, but every time I asked him a question, he was wide-awake and paying attention. So I talked. I talked and I talked. I told him about the little girl in my first grade class who was jealous of me and stuck gum in my hair. I told him about my family and how I was born in Brooklyn, NY. Bed-Sty to be exact, and then we moved to Buffalo when I was three because my Daddy went to prison. I told him my fears. I told him about my insecurities, and the things that I was ashamed of. I told him things that even Asia didn't know, things that only Nica had known up until now. I hoped he appreciated my honesty, because the things that I'd shared left me vulnerable to be hurt. I told him things that he could possibly use against me in an argument, things that I'd never tell another man as long as I lived. I was giving him the opportunity to know me completely and accept me. And he'd be the only man to have this chance. If Pharaoh hurt me, every other man after him would pay the price for him doing me wrong.

If I was lucky, this would be my first official relationship and one that possibly would blossom into that type of love that lasted forever. Lastly, I explained to him my parent's situation and what I'd meant when I told him in the kitchen that things were different this week. He was sympathetic and told me what I needed to hear in order to feel better about it; he didn't freeze up like Calvin.

"I didn't bore you, did I?" I yawned, and then checked the clock, and it was after midnight already. Another six and a half hours and Mommy would be coming to wake me up for school.

"Not at all."

"You think there's something wrong with me? Did I scare you away?" I hoped he'd be honest. Phee didn't say anything for a minute and I got a little worried. Damn, maybe I'd told him too much. He probably thought that I was an emotional wreck. I cursed myself for being so honest, I should've just sugar coated everything.

"I'll be there at 8:00 on the dot." He finally said. "Be ready, I'll drop you off at school before I go to work." Then the line went dead.

Did this nigga just hang up on me?

That was so rude, but even so, I fell asleep with a huge smile on my face.

CHAPTER TWENTY-FIVE

When Mommy poked her head inside my room the next morning, I was already up and trying on outfits. She took one look at me and narrowed her eyes, because naturally she'd become suspicious.

"April," her hand went to her hip and now I realized exactly where I got it from. "Why are you up so early?" She was looking around at all the clothes scattered around my room.

"I'm getting ready for school." I told her, but the look she gave me let me no that she was no fool.

She waved her finger at me. "If I call up to your school today, and you're not there, I promise that you'll be the only freshman girl that needs dentures. Are we clear?"

I started to crack a joke, but I didn't think she was in the mood. "I'll be there all day long." I told her with a grin, and she turned to leave. "Mommy, wait!" She stepped back, turned back around and looked at me like a priest waiting to hear a confession. I figured I should just come clean with her, because if I didn't, it would hurt my chances in the long run. All it would take is for Mrs. Shannon or anyone in her house to see me leave in Phee's car and I'd be busted.

"Yes?" she waited impatiently.

"Mom, Pharaoh-"

"April," She cut me off. "If Pharaoh wants to drop you off at school, it's fine with me. But your ass better be at school on time. And if he picks you up, you'd better be home before 2:45. Got it?" Mommy went out her way to let me know that she was a damn psychic. I stopped to think, was it that obvious what was going on? Or had she been eavesdropping on the phone last night?

"Yes, Mom."

"And, what's his phone number?" Mom wanted to know, so I gave it to her. He'd be thrilled if she called him. "April, I was fourteen before, *and* fifteen, *and* sixteen. I was pretty too, and I had boys chasing me also. I know what you're thinking before you even think it. Don't ever think that you can pull the wool over my eyes, I've been in your shoes and I'm *always* two steps ahead of you. So don't even try it, because I'll break your neck." She threatened me like it was nothing, then walked out and closed my door. I didn't sweat it; I brushed it off and went back to my wardrobe crisis.

I decided to put on the outfit that I'd worn almost a month ago to the Roxbury. I'd never worn heels to school before, but I figured that today was as good a day as any. But I prepared for the worst. I tucked a pair of Air Max's into my bag just in case Phee kicked me out his whip or something. I wasn't planning on giving up any butt, so there was no telling what was liable to happen.

The mini van pulled off at 7:45 and Calvin rang my doorbell at 7:50. I told him that I was getting a ride to school this morning and that I'd see him later. I tried to rush him off, but he'd picked today of all days to become talkative. He was saying *something* about *something*, but I wasn't really paying attention.

Who knows?

I was just trying to get him away from my house before Pharaoh pulled up. *But,* my luck isn't that good. The Q45 glided up my driveway just as Calvin was walking off the porch, and he was taking his sweet time, as if he'd been waiting to see who my ride was. I could tell he was straining to see who was in the luxury car, but Phee's windows were pitch black and intended for privacy.

I started getting nervous as I stepped outside and slowly locked the door behind me. It's not like I had something serious going on wit' Calvin, but it just seemed weird and awkward for them to both be in my driveway at the same time. I knew he had a terrible crush on me and I didn't wan to hurt his feelings, but right now, it seemed inevitable, especially when Pharaoh opened the door and stepped out his car looking like a professional ball player. To make things worst, I was wearing the bracelet that Calvin had given me on Christmas. That's the part that made me feel bad, and I can't explain it, but I just felt trifling.

When Calvin saw him, he almost broke his neck hurrying down the driveway, it was the fastest that he'd moved all morning, and he didn't bother to look back. I knew that his feelings were crushed, but what could I do?

Phee just acted as if he never saw him, I guess he wasn't the least intimidated by Calvin's presence. "Good morning." He greeted me while gently taking my hand. He was looking me up and down like he wanted to put me on a plate, and the attention he was showing made me want to smile, but I had to hide my satisfaction until *after* I checked him.

"Don't you ever, *ever* in life, hang up the phone on me without saying goodbye, goodnight or see you later! That was *so* rude of you." I didn't waste any time saying what was on my mind. I figured it was better to get it out the way now, instead of voicing my displeasure once I was halfway to school and Phee could easily throw me out onto the side of the road.

He didn't respond right away and he didn't even seemed fazed at all. "Do you feel better now that you've got that out of your system?" He helped me down the stairs and took my book bag.

I stopped and gave him some attitude. "Do *you* think I'm joking?" I asked while narrowing my eyes and working my neck at the same time.

He left me standing there and walked around to the passenger side of his car, he opened the door and stood next to it. "You're going to be late." He completely ignored my question and tossed my bag into the back seat.

I rolled my eyes at him, but decided to let it go. I strutted around the car in my heels, got inside and he closed the door behind me. The interior of the Infiniti was plush. Crisp black leather, shiny wood grain, spotless black carpeting and it had that new car smell. I crossed my legs and got comfortable.

"Thank you." I told him once he was inside.

"For what?"

"For being a gentleman." He'd actually opened the door for me without me giving him a hint.

He shrugged. "If you act like a lady, I'll treat you like one." He put the car into reverse and backed out my driveway. "You look nice." He added, checking me out from the corner of his eye.

"Thank you." I answered softly, suddenly becoming shy. That's all I wanted, a man who was paid, handsome, respectful and showered me with compliments. I'd spent the entire morning trying to look my best for him, thank God he noticed.

"I've never seen you wear heels before," he looked down at my feet. "You wore those for me, didn't you?" He smirked.

I started blushing. "*No.*" I lied. Of course, I did, but why would he ask me that. I was so embarrassed.

"Yes you did, stop lying." Now he was laughing.

"You're an *ass*hole." I mumbled with a smile.

"I'm just teasing you, but I like you in the heels though." This boy was supposed to be watching the road but he kept looking down at my shoes, like he had a foot fetish or something. I made a mental note to buy some more heels when I got the chance to.

After a fifteen-minute ride, he finally pulled up to my school. He parked the car, reclined the seat back and got comfortable because I still had a few Moments before I needed to be in homeroom.

"Where you work at?" I asked him curiously. "Last night you said you'd drop me off before work, what do you do?" I was curious because he didn't have on a uniform or nothing. Honestly, I'd just jumped to the conclusion that he was a hustler, I'd never thought that maybe he had a job.

"Tonight on the phone I'll tell you everything that you need to know about me, just hold your questions until then, okay?"

"Fine. I'll be looking forward to it." I turned my back to the door so that I could get a good look at him. Phee had that smooth light brown complexion; he was clean cut, and wore his hair in a low Caesar with the waves. He had no hair on his face besides a light mustache, and if I didn't know any, better I would've mistaken him for a college boy, except he had a street hustlers swag.

"Good. I'm gonna keep you up all night, just like you did me." He smiled. "I'm surprised you're not tired."

"I am." I admitted as we stared at each other.

After about 20 seconds of mild awkwardness, he broke our gaze and concentrated on the Baby Phat purse in my lap. "Let me see." He pointed at it and I looked at him like he was crazy. Everything in my purse is private, and I've never given any male permission to look inside.

"*No!*"

"You hiding something from me?" He reached for it slowly.

"*Pharaoh!*" I gripped my purse like it contained the keys to my soul. "You're not supposed to look in a woman's purse."

"I can look inside *my* woman's purse any time I get ready to." The way he said it, led me to believe that *I* was now *his* woman. My face began to turn pink, and my brain became flustered. "Give it to me." He said in a low whisper that made the inside of my thighs heat up. I gave him my purse. Don't ask me why, but I did.

He took it, unzipped it and turned it upside down so that the contents fell onto his lap. "Who was that dude coming out of your house this morning?" He wanted to know as he began looking through my precious belongings.

"That's just Calvin, he lives across the street. And he didn't come out of my house, he was waiting outside for me because we usually walk to the bus stop together." I explained and clarified the situation.

Pharaoh just kind of nodded and gave me a look that said he understood. "That kid can play ball, I've seen him on the court quite a few times," he complimented Calvin's game. "But let him know that you won't be needing an escort to the bus stop anymore. *Ever.*" That made me smile like I'd won the lottery.

But my smile didn't last too long. It began to fade as my face turned fire engine red when he held up the small zip lock bag that contained my spare panties. He was about to make a comment, but when he saw my expression, he put the bag down. Everything else he examined thoroughly, my pager, address book, lip-gloss, nail polish, and any and everything you'd expect a teenage girl to be carrying in her bag. I turned my head for a split second and when turned back, he'd picked up the zip lock bag again.

"*Pharaoh!*" I reached for it but I was too slow and he gently slapped my hand away.

"Chill. I want to see something." I watched in horror as he pulled my spare underwear out of the plastic bag. I didn't know whether his intentions were to smell them, or check for skid marks. Either way, I was just plain embarrassed.

"April, what are *Eundies*?" He was examining the tag of my cheap generic brand of underwear. Okay listen, my panties weren't raggedy. They were actually brand new, but they were those cheap joints you'd find at Wal-Mart. I was staring at him in disbelief and I didn't know whether to continue being embarrassed, or to be angry. "I'm gonna have to take you shopping this weekend. Ask your Moms if I can take you to the Galleria on Sunday, okay?" I wanted to crawl under the seat and die, but instead I just nodded as he put the panties back into the bag and then reached for my wallet.

Next, I watched him flip through my pictures. "Oh shit, that's your Dad?" He showed me the picture that he was talking about and it made me cringe. I immediately got this funny feeling in my gut once I realized that he recognized Daddy.

"*Why*, how you know my Dad?" My eyes were squinted and I was waiting for his response. Not that it was unthinkable that the two of them could've crossed paths before; it's highly likely because the city is so small. But the look on Phee's face is what made me so interested in his response. It was almost like he'd seen a ghost, and his body tensed up like he'd become nervous or something.

He shrugged his shoulders. "I've seen him around," he looked away. "Mostly at the barbershop because my boy Emory cuts both our hair. His name's Stacey, right?"

"Yeah." I nodded.

Listen, I'm *not* stupid! And I know how to read a nigga's body language just as good as the next bitch, and it was obvious to me that somehow, someway, Phee and Daddy knew each other. Or maybe Phee had just heard some old stories about how 'gangster' my Daddy used to be back in the *old days.* I didn't know what it was, but I made a mental note to find out why Phee began sweating when he seen Daddy's picture.

"He knows who I am, we're not *cool,* like friends or anything. But we've spoken a few times over the years. I like your Dad, he's a cool dude." Pharaoh tried to clean it up, but I was already onto him and realized that something wasn't right. "This all the money you have?" He switched the subject as he thumbed through the billfold of my wallet. I probably had about twelve or thirteen bucks to my name, fifteen at the max.

"Yes." I nodded and automatically Phee started digging into his pocket. His hand almost got stuck, but when it emerged, I was looking at the biggest wad of money I'd ever seen in my young life. I'm talking about some rap video shit, *all* hundreds. He peeled off three bills from the top, and then he looked at me for a split second and peeled off two more. He put the money into my wallet and stuck it back into my purse.

"Thank you." Honestly, I'd never had five hundred dollars before. Not five hundred of my own, that I could do whatever I wanted with.

"You're welcome." He started putting my things back where they belonged, then put my purse back on my lap.

"Don't ever let me catch you with less than a hundred dollars in your purse again. If you need money, let me know. I'll make sure you're *never* broke, but you're also gonna have to learn how to *save* money too."

"Okay." I was trying to camouflage how excited I was, but trust me, I was *thrilled*.

"*And*," he reached over and grabbed my chin. "You not going to just spend up all my bread without bringing *something* to the table. I don't have a problem giving you anything you ask me for, as long as you're on your job. But if you wanna be *my* girl, *my* reflection, then you gonna have to be a hustler too and learn how to make your own money." I guess when he figured he'd gotten his point across he let go of my chin.

"How am I supposed to do *that*?" Now he really had my attention, I was too young to get a job until my birthday, and I know this boy wasn't talking about no crazy shit! I wasn't about to be sitting inside no crack house serving fiends out the window, or riding the Greyhound bus wit' my coochie stuffed full of cocaine. I like Phee a lot, but I wasn't about to end up in prison for no dude.

"I've got something planned for you. I'll let you know soon so that you can talk to your Mom about it, I'm sure she won't mind." I was relieved that whatever he was talking about wouldn't require high heels, a short mini-skirt, and standing on a corner.

"I'll do anything to help, just as long as it's not something that'll get me in trouble-"

"I would never put you in that position, that's not even something you've got to worry about. What I'm saying is that you need a hustle, you need to be able to earn money. I don't want you to have to depend on me or anybody else for the things that you need. Walking around with thirteen dollars in your purse is *disgusting*; you're better than that. But you in good hands now though, I got you." He leaned over to kiss me on the cheek.

I couldn't contain my smile; he was starting to make me happy already. "Phee, I have to go." I checked the time on his dashboard.

"Go head, I'll be out here at 2:20 to pick you up." He reached into the back seat and handed me my bag. "I'll see you later."

"Bye." I opened his door. "Thank you for the ride and everything, I appreciate it." I said as I stepped out.

"It's not a big deal. I'll give you whatever you want, and do whatever I can to make you smile." His words made me moist as I emerged from the Infiniti with a huge smile on my face. I closed his door gently and switched my hips as I walked towards the entrance of my school. I turned and waved before I went inside, I couldn't see him through the tinted windows, but I knew he was watching. He tapped the horn twice and pulled off.

CHAPTER TWENTY-SIX

It was hard for me to think about anything but Phee for the entire school day, every period I had to stop my mind from wandering off. Each time he crossed my mind a big smile hit my face, and I felt like I was on top of the world, like I no longer had any worries at all. It's funny how one person can come into your life and change it completely, and I couldn't help but wonder what the future had in store for the two of us.

Seventh period biology class really killed my buzz. I was scribbling down notes as fast as I could, but my teacher Mrs. Robards had a fucking motor mouth and it was hard to keep up. On top of that, she wrote too fast. She also had this bad habit of writing one definition or explanation at a time on the blackboard, and she talked as she wrote. Here's the problem, half the time this bitch would be blocking the blackboard with her body, *then* she'd erase the definition too fast and start on the next one before I had the chance to finish. I wanted so bad to snatch that chalk eraser and go upside her damn head with it. I guess this lady figured that since there were only two students awake in her class that she could just do a half ass job of teaching. Well I was getting sick of it!

"*Wait!*" I shouted at her for the gazillionth time. "Mrs. Robards, I'm not finished yet." My eyes were rolling.

"Come on, Ms. Showers, let's *focus*." She had the nerve to be
looking at me like *I* was the problem.

"Umm, Mrs. Robards, I'm not done yet either." Elizabeth Crowley spoke up in my defense, and she was the only other person in this room who was even paying attention.

Mrs. Robards turned to face the two of us. "Ladies, June will be here before you know it and these are must-know Biology terms for the NYS Regents exam. I'll slow down a tad bit, but we can't afford to stall out. We still have a lot of work to do." She gave us a half smile that made Elizabeth and I exchange frustrated looks.

The sad thing is, there are twenty-three kids in this class and Mrs. Robards doesn't pay the other twenty-one of them any attention at all. I looked around the room at my classmates and felt very *un*inspired. They were reading magazines, and whispering back and forth. One fool was listening to his Walkman, and four niggas even had a spades card game going on in the corner. Mrs. Robards had three children, and two of them were in high school. Neither of them attended a Buffalo Public School. I wonder why? I wonder if Mrs. Robards would approve of the teachers in *her* kids classrooms letting this type of shit happen around *her* children while *they* were trying to learn. It was hard to concentrate on learning while sitting in the middle of a zoo, but what were my options?

I refocused on the chalkboard. The problem at hand was the word Eukaryote. I was definitely gonna have to make some flashcards for the upcoming quiz. I somehow managed to scribble down the entire definition before Mrs. Quick Draw McGraw made it disappear. I wanted to celebrate, but instead I got my pen ready for the next one.

By eighth period, I was fighting myself just to stay woke. Mr. C's class wasn't too bad because at least there was *some* class participation. But little do you know how elated I was when the dismissal bell rang. I've learned to delay my reaction, but Mr. C hadn't, and today he almost got himself stampeded over as everyone bum rushed the door. I waited until everyone jetted 'cause I hate being pushed and shoved from behind. And since it was Friday, *and* I had heels on, dismissal bell rush hour would be an adventure. I looked both ways before easing out of Mr. C's room and merging into high-speed traffic. I took the back stairs near the library because hardly anyone ever used them, for obvious reasons. I made it to my locker, fixed my hair, abused my tube of lip-gloss, and made use of some tic-tacs. When I had everything I needed, I peeled off towards the exit, because my man was waiting for me.

Asia was at her locker. "Hey, what you doing tonight?" She asked me as we walked to the door.

I shrugged. "Don't know, but hopefully I can get out the house. What you doing?" I boomeranged the question.

"I'm 'bout to chill around the corner with Cam for a while," she gave me a stupid-ass grin. "Then, Tionna's gonna pick me up later, but after that, who knows?"

"Well, I 'll call you either tonight or tomorrow, aight?" We walked outside into the cold.

"Okay, be good." She smiled and we hugged.

"No bitch, *you* be good." We both laughed.

The Infiniti was parked at the curb in the boyfriend section. Pharaoh had the driver's window down and Cam was leaned against the roof, they were talking about something. Asia walked up to Cam, and I walked around to the passenger side and got in. I placed my bag on the backseat, crossed my legs, and got comfortable waiting for Phee to be done talking. I could tell that whatever they were talking about was none of my business 'cause they started whispering once Asia and I were within earshot.

Finally, they gave each other a pound. "Bye, sis." Cam winked at me through the window and I waved bye to him.

"See you Monday." I replied as Phee hit the button to send the window sliding back into position, then he leaned over and kissed my cheek.

"How was your day?" He asked me.

"It was okay, I'm tired though." I laid my head back against the leather headrest. "How was yours?" I asked him.

"Cool. So far anyway." He pulled off from the curb and pushed the Q45 towards my side of town.

We were almost at my house when pulled over in front of Hair Creations. He cut the engine off and looked at me. "I'm about to introduce you to somebody. Be polite, she's family." Then he jumped out and came around to open my door. "We gotta hurry before your Mom thinks I kidnapped you." He joked.

He led the way into the beauty salon half of the hair spot. I'd only been inside once or twice with Nica, this is where she gets her hair done. There were quite a few stylists working, and each of their stations was occupied with a customer. All the dryers were full and there were women everywhere. It was Friday afternoon and everyone was trying to get fly. A few of the stylists waved at Phee and smiled, he greeted them back but he didn't overdo it. Not really knowing if I should follow him, I stood in the doorway as he walked up to a pretty brown skin lady who looked about my Mom's age.

"Come here, April..." Pharaoh called me. When I was a couple feet
away he introduced me. "Ms. Natalie, this is my girl. Her name's, April."

The woman gave me a big smile. "Hey, cutie. How are you?" She was in the middle of using a pair of scissors on some girl's hair.

I returned a genuine smile. "Fine, and you?" I asked politely. Ms. Natalie seemed really nice, and her smile had been real. It wasn't one of those fake joints that people give you when they could care less about an introduction.

She winked at me. "I can't really complain, even though I've been on my feet all day. But I guess if I didn't have any customers to stand up for, *then* it would be a bad day." She chuckled.

"Ms. Natalie," Phee interjected. "I'm about to go holler at Emory, I'll be back in a minute." He gave me a look and then dipped off towards the barbershop. I looked at him like he was crazy, but he didn't stop, he just left me standing there with a complete stranger.

There was an awkward period of about thirty seconds before Ms. Natalie spoke up. "That boy didn't tell you why he brought you here, did he?"

"No." I shook my head, and continued to stand there looking stupid.

"I didn't think so," she looked at me apologetically. "Well first off, Pharaoh and my son Jeremy are friends. I've known Phee for a very long time, since he was a baby. Did he tell you that?" She asked me. I shook my head again, and she laughed. "That boy is something else! Listen, he wants me to teach you how to do hair so that you can make some money. I told the boy that he should *at least* ask you first, to make sure that it was something that you would want to learn." She stopped working long enough to look at me and see my reaction. Shit, I was thrilled. I used to do my Barbie dolls hair all the time.

I was smiling. "I'd love for you to teach me." I told her. "I mean, if you don't mind. I don't want to inconvenience you."

"It's no problem, I do lessons from time to time. I used to teach girls on the regular basis, but it got to be a headache 'cause a lot of you kids these days can't listen too well-"

"Ms. Natalie, I listen and follow directions very well. I wont give you a headache at all." I let her know.

She nodded. "Well if you're serious, be here Monday after school and I'll start showing you the basic things. You're welcome to stay here as long as you'd like everyday and watch me work. You'll pick up things quick, you seem like a very bright young lady." She smiled "Tell Pharaoh that he needs to buy you some practice mannequins. Oh, here he comes now." She nodded towards the door and I looked up just as he was walking towards us.

He looked at me. "So what's up? You gonna let Ms. Natalie teach you?"

"I want to, but I have to ask my Mom first." I told the both of them.

"Alright," he took my hand. "Thanks, Ms. Natalie. I have to take her home, I'll talk to you later."

"Okay, sweetie. Bye, April, hopefully I'll see you on Monday." She waved goodbye.

"Nice meeting you," I waved back. "I'm sure I'll be here." I added confidently. I knew that Mommy wouldn't have a problem with me coming here after school, especially since the shop was right down the street.

Phee was pulling me by the hand out of the salon. He opened the door so I could get inside the Infiniti, then he got behind the wheel and drove me home. When he pulled into the driveway, it was 2:42. I had three minutes to get my ass in the house. He went into the center armrest console and pulled out a cell phone, it was brand new in the box.

"Here, take this. If you go somewhere, take the phone with you. I need to know where you're at." He handed the box to me. "The only dudes who call that phone, better be blood relatives! No step-brothers, distant cousins, *neighbors*, none of that!"

"Okay." I examined the box before stuffing it inside my purse.

"Don't forget to ask your Mom about Ms. Natalie. Oh, and see if it's okay for me to come get you on Sunday, so I can take you to the mall."

"Sunday isn't a good day. My Dad's coming to get me and my sister on Sunday." I reminded him.

He exhaled slowly, like he was gonna have to rearrange his schedule or something. "Then I'll take you tomorrow. You want me to ask your mother, or you gonna do it?" He looked at me.

"I'll ask her." I reached over and ran my fingers across his waves for the first time ever. "Come inside for a while. You don't have to stay long, just a couple hours." I didn't want him to leave just yet.

"I can't." He shook his head. "I've got some things that I've gotta do, sorry. If you miss me, just call me." He leaned over. "Give me a hug."

We grabbed each other, I squeezed his neck tight and kissed his cheek. "I'll see you tomorrow." He told me when I finally let go.

"Alright." I said quietly. I was kind of upset, because I'd hoped he would come inside and spend some time with me. What good was it that Mommy said I could have boy company, if I didn't have anyone to chill with.

He spotted the disappointment on my face. "Baby, why you frowning? Didn't I make you happy today?" He asked while trying to read my face.

"Yes, but I get bored just sitting in the house all the time, I told you that already." I kept my frown in place, hoping that it would make him reconsider.

He didn't reconsider; instead, he dug into his pocket and pulled out *another* knot of money. This time it was a wad of fifties; he counted off ten of them and held the bills out for me to take. "Call Nica or Asia. Go to the mall, the movies, dinner, bowling, whatever. Just stop looking at me like that, you're making me feel bad."

I stared at the bills in his hand. "Pharaoh, this isn't going to work every time." I was *lying* through my pretty white teeth! Five hundred dollars would work *every* single time! Shit, I wondered how much he would give me if I shed an actual tear. One day I'd definitely have to find that out, I made a mental note of it.

"I'll make it up to you tomorrow, that's my word." He sounded sincere. I looked at his eyes and then back to the cash. I extended my hand and he placed the money in my palm. "You mad?" He asked me as I tucked the money inside my purse along with my new phone.

"No. Go handle your business. I'll call you if I decide to leave the house." I opened the car door, but kept my eyes on him. "Thank you, I'll see you tomorrow." He didn't answer; he just smiled and blew me a kiss. I blew one back, then stepped out and closed the door. My heels clicked against the pavement as I walked around the car and up the stairs. I stuck my key in the door, opened it, and turned to wave at him. He tapped the horn twice and began backing down the driveway.

I would've been thoroughly surprised had Mommy *not* been in the kitchen waiting for me to walk through the door. She was. She had her nursing books spread across the island counter top and she was studying. I put my things down and took a seat on the stool next to her.

"Hey baby, how'd it go today?" She asked me, but didn't bother to look up. Her face was buried deep inside her thick college textbook.

"Fine." I smiled still thinking about him. "Just fine," I exhaled loudly to let her know that I had something on my mind. "But I've got a couple things I need to talk to you about, if you're not too busy right now."

Mommy put her bookmarker on her page, and closed the textbook. "What's up?" She gave me her full attention.

First, I told her about the opportunity to train under Ms. Natalie at the beauty salon. I explained everything and made perfectly sure that she understood that it wouldn't cost her any money.

"Oh, I think that's a wonderful idea. That's a good skill to have. Wow, Pharaoh is very thoughtful, huh?" She grinned at me.

I nodded, then pulled out the cell phone and put it on the counter so she could see it. "He gave me this." I told her. "He didn't say anything about a bill, so I'm assuming that he's gonna pay for all the costs." Mommy picked up the phone and cut her eyes at me. "If you don't want me to have it, I'll give it back." I told her quickly.

After she examined it, she set it back down on the countertop. "What else?" She asked knowingly.

I cringed, knowing that I was about to press my luck. "He wants me to ask you for permission to take me to the mall. He wants to take me shopping tomorrow." I tried to keep a straight face, but I felt a huge smile coming.

She didn't respond right away, and it seemed like an eternity before she said anything. "You can keep the phone. *He* gave it to you, so *he* pays the monthly bill. Don't ask *me* for a *dime*." She made that very clear and her eyes asked me if I understood.

"Okay."

"And you already know that your Dad is coming by tomorrow to pick up your brothers. If Pharaoh wants to take you shopping, he can pick you up *after* your Dad leaves, and he'd better have you home *before* 9pm. Alright?"

"Thank you, Mommy!" I gushed into a cheesy smile, wrapped my arms around her neck and she hugged me back. When she let me go, I dug into my purse and pulled out my wallet. I placed a hundred dollar bill on the countertop. "I just wanna help out." Mommy looked at me like she had a gazillion questions floating around her mind. I rushed off to the stairs before she could either start asking me shit, or before she could try to give me the money back.

"April!" Mommy's voice caught me halfway up the stairs.

I cursed under my breath. "Yes?"

"Come here..."

I came back into the kitchen and stared at her with the most innocent face that I could muster. "Huh?"

"...Let Pharaoh know that he won't need to pick you up for school on Monday morning-"

"*Why*, Mommy?" I scrunched up my face.

"Because I scheduled a doctor's appointment for you at 9am." She removed her bookmark and put her nose back into her textbook. "I'm putting you on birth control. I'm too young to be a grandmother." She said it like it was no big deal, but to me, it was a *huge* deal. My jaw had dropped so far that it was in danger of being dislocated, and I just looked at her like she'd lost her damn mind!

Maybe, Mommy *was* always two steps ahead.

CHAPTER TWENTY-SEVEN

As soon as Daddy turned the corner the next morning, I called my Boo and let him know that I was ready. Last night during our phone conversation, Phee promised that he'd spend the entire day with me, just the two of us. He pulled up my driveway at 9:45, and I damn near fell down the stairs running to the car. That's how excited I was to see him. I was wearing a brand new outfit that I'd bought last night, an outfit that I'd purchased just for him. Nica and me had went to the Boulevard Mall last evening so I could get a new pair of heels, jeans and a sweater for my date. I looked absolutely fabulous, if I don't say so myself.

"What's up, beautiful? Damn you look good." His eyes twinkled with admiration for my beauty as he looked me over, then he pulled me close and held me tight.

"Thank you. You look nice too." When I finally stepped back I checked him out. He was wearing a brown leather bomber jacket, a tan cashmere sweater, a brown pair of corduroy's and some Timberland boots. He always seemed to dress nice, so this was no surprise, but after our conversation from last night, I was looking at him in a completely different light.

As we headed to the IHOP for breakfast, I briefly replayed our talk in my head. It hadn't taken him long to admit that he didn't *technically* have a job. He said that he uses the word 'work' as a metaphor and that one day when the time is right, he'll talk to me about how he earns his money. He was trying to be real secretive about it, but I knew one thing for sure, this boy didn't work for the CIA and he wasn't no James Bond! But whatever he was doing he was obviously good at it, because he was eighteen, driving around in a sixty thousand dollar automobile. You know I had to go online and check the blue book value. The Q45 wasn't brand new, but it was still worth way more than what he *should* be able to afford.

He told me about his family, and I learned that we come from similar backgrounds. We both grew up in a two-parent household and both of our father's were major hustlers back in the days. Well, Phee's Dad *still is* a big-time hustler in the city. His name's Sylvester "Iceberg" Green and he's like the black John Gotti of Buffalo. I've never seen him, but I've heard his name enough to feel like I've met him before. And Pharaoh is his son, so *obviously* he's following in his Dad's footsteps. Although he admits that the street life was never meant for him, and he just got sucked into it. He claims that he's addicted to the cash and the lifestyle, and he can't stop chasing the street dream. He said that his life would probably never have a fairy tale ending, so he's just trying to enjoy it as much as he can until it was over. The way he spoke, it brought tears to my eyes, because it's as if he's predicting that something awful will happen to him. It was sad, but it made me feel closer to him because he'd shared some of his deepest thoughts. I wanted to be with him and help make him better, the same way he was trying to make me better.

"Phee, did you think about what I said last night?" We were almost at the restaurant and my eyes were glued to him.

"Not yet. I will though." He sounded like he was just trying to appease me with his response, and it didn't seem sincere at all. I told him that I wanted him to at least consider enrolling into the community college in the fall. He hadn't seemed enthusiastic or the least bit interested, but I was gonna keep pushing.

"I'd be *really* proud of you."

"I told you, I'll think about it." He looked towards where my eyes were trained on him. "I promise." He added, and I figured it would have to be good enough for now, so I decided to drop it. The last thing I wanted to do was irritate him *before* we went to the mall. That wouldn't be smart.

Over breakfast, we talked about many different things. I liked the fact that I could be silly with him and he didn't get mad when I made jokes or got sarcastic with him, he had a great sense of humor.

"I hope your toes don't look like your fingers." At the Moment, the joke was on me. He was laughing at my nails, and he had every right to, I was definitely slipping. Usually, I would've been embarrassed to be out with my fingers looking a mess, but he was new man. He'd already chosen me, now he was stuck with me, but I knew I had to start keeping my shit tight.

"My toes are cute! Thank you very much!" I giggled.

"I hope so. I'ma see for myself *real* soon." He smiled confidently, and the way he said it gave me goose bumps.

"But seriously, you should've used some of the money I gave you to get your nails done, that shit look tacky." He gently reprimanded me.

Now I was embarrassed. "I know. You don't have to tell me that." I spoke calmly. "I just got the money yesterday and I didn't have time. I'll take care of it, and it wont happen again. I promise, I'm gonna keep myself looking good for you, okay? Jesus, give me a break we only been together for three days." I rolled my eyes at him.

He laughed. "If we have time, I'll take you to the nail salon later on and you can get your feet done too. They need to be pedicured, that's the only way your toes are going in my mouth." He gave me a nasty grin.

"Eeew! That's nasty!" I turned pink in the face. I'm not going to lie; I always wanted to get my toes licked, amongst other things. But of course, I had to act like the thought of it was disgusting. It's reverse psychology, a tactic I'd learned along the way.

He must have been reading my mind. "If you think that's nasty, wait til' I show you some of my other tricks." Phee put his hand under my chin. "Come here..." He kissed me on the lips softly. It was our first real kiss, and it happened right here during breakfast at the IHOP. I'd never forget this Moment. I was sitting a good thing, because had I been standing, my legs would have probably given out.

After the initial kiss, we couldn't eat fast enough. We emptied our plates in a hurry and spent about twenty minutes in the Infiniti kissing passionately. Phee kept a grip on my ponytail, his free hand wedged between my thighs as our lips locked. I really, really needed to change my panties at the Moment, because they were becoming uncomfortably moist. I wanted to touch him, rub it and massage it for him, but I didn't want to be a tease. So, I kept my hands to myself. I told him that I'd only been intimate once before, and that I was inexperienced. It was the truth, but I doubt he believed me because all the nasty broads my age say the same shit. He said he'd wait until I was ready and to take my time. I decided that I would make him wait a while, but not *too* long, because he'd already proven himself as far as I was concerned. As of right now, he seemed like he'd be worth the trouble.

When my lips started to get sore, I had to stop him. This boy seemed as though he wanted to kiss me all afternoon. "Okay, okay! That's enough." I said sternly, but playfully as I pushed him back over to his side of the car. He'd been damn near on top of me, making a bed out of the passenger seat. "That's enough." I repeated with a satisfied smirk.

"One more, let me get one more." He laughed and reached for my jacket.

"No! Pharaoh, no!" I was cracking up and fighting him off at the same time, but he was too strong. He grabbed my jacket, pulled me over to him and held me close for another five minutes.

When we finally made it to the mall he took me straight to Victoria Secret's, and we stopped right outside the entrance. He grabbed me by the hips and pulled me close. "Listen, this right here..." He lightly smacked my butt. "That's mine. Those cheap ass panties that you've been covering it with, when you get home throw them all away. *All* of them! Understand?" He whispered in my ear.

"Yes."

"From now on, all your panties and bra's gotta match each other, and they should match your outfit too. If your shirt is red, your panties are red. If your shirt is yellow, your panties should be yellow."

I nodded. "Alright." I couldn't argue with that, it made perfect sense to me. I listened as he schooled me and I soaked it all in. Self-consciously, I wondered how many girls there had been before me that he'd went over this with, but I guessed it didn't matter. It was my turn now!

"C'mon." He took me by the hand and led the way into the expensive lingerie store. I thought I'd already knew my sizes, but Phee made me get measured by one of the sales girls. As it turned out, I was wrong about my bust size, which was why some of my bras fit so uncomfortably. By the time we left the store, he'd spent almost $1,500 just on lingerie for me. He bought me two different sets in each color, plus extra panties. I had enough lingerie to wear a different set everyday for a month straight.

Next, he took me to Macy's and I was like a kid in a candy store. He didn't bother me or nag me at all. He let me shop, kept quiet and gave me his opinion when I asked for it. He waited patiently while I tried on jeans, skirts, blouses, dresses and everything the big department store had to offer. If he liked it he would smile, if he didn't he'd shake his head. He followed me around the mall to damn near every urban clothing store inside the Galleria Mall. When we accumulated too many bags, he would leave me, put the bags in the Infiniti and come right back.

Before I knew it, it was two o'clock. We went to the food court for a quick lunch break and then it was back to the stores. I noticed that he never sweated the price tags. If I saw it and I liked it, he bought it, no questions asked. I decided that he would get my peaches even sooner than expected. Hell, he deserved it! And, I'd give him all he could handle, whenever and however he liked it.

We were inside Bath &Body Works and I was taking my time smelling the fragrances and lotions, when he grabbed me. "Time to go, baby." He wrapped his arm around my waist.

My face went into an automatic pout. "Can I just go to one more store, please?"

Phee looked at his watch. "Alright, but you gotta hurry." He gave in.

I walked in front of him while he followed close behind carrying all of my bags. I switched and rolled my hips for my Boo as I led him through the mall. The Guess jeans that I was wearing, might as well have been painted on my body, that's how tight they were. And I knew for a fact that my booty looked delicious in them. I'd made sure of that before I left the house this morning.

"Where you going, April?" He asked from behind, and he sounded like he was getting impatient.

I turned and looked over my shoulder. "Just come on, it'll only take a minute." I kept walking. I'd never in my life been to the mall by myself, and there was something that I'd wanted to buy for the last few months, but I was too embarrassed. I led Pharaoh into Spencer's Adult Store and showed him what I needed.

His jaw dropped when I picked out a battery operated vibrator. "I'm not buying that for you, are you crazy?" He was laughing, but seemed a little uncomfortable.

"Please," I begged him. "I *need* it." I licked my lips at him. I wasn't old enough to buy it myself, so I really did need him to get it for me.

"What you gonna do with *that*?"

I looked at him like he was retarded. "What do you think, smart ass?" Shit, I was gonna put myself to sleep every night. Every morning, I was gonna use it to start my day off right, and I'd enjoy it anytime in between.

Now he looked hurt. "What about *me*?"

"What about *you*?" I teased him. "You'll get your chance, but until *then*..." I pressed myself against his chest and kissed his lips. "...I need *this*." I held up the toy.

He gave in. "Don't let your mother find it. And if she does, you better not tell her that I had anything to do with it." He looked very serious.

"Don't worry." I kissed his lips again. "I'll keep it hidden inside my *secret* hiding place." I promised seductively.

He blinked twice. "You nasty." He caught my sexual innuendo.

"And I can't wait to show you just how right you are." I placed the box in his hand so he could purchase it for me since I wasn't eighteen. "Make sure you grab some batteries for me too." I added as I followed him towards the cash register.

When we finally left the mall, Phee took me downtown on Allen St. to get my hair done by some Dominican ladies. I have no idea what they put in my hair, but it had never smelled so good, or looked so shiny. They trimmed my edges, washed and shampooed it, and even gave me a facial cleansing. I enjoyed every Moment of it.

"I'll bring you here every Saturday morning. Is that okay?" He asked me when he picked me up from the beauty salon. It sounded like a trick question, because there's no way in hell that I was about to decline this type of princess pampering. I just nodded, because I doubted that he needed me to answer him.

"How come you just don't take me to Ms. Natalie and let her do my hair?" I asked him.

Pharaoh looked at me like I'd lost my damn mind. "I like Ms. Natalie, I've known her my whole life, but she only specialize in *ghetto* hair! All she does is put weave in chick's hair. You got your own hair, and I don't want you fucking it up putting glue in it."

I just laughed. "I don't want any weave in my hair anyway, I was just asking."

"You don't have to ask, just let me take care of everything, that way things will go smooth." He winked at me.

I rolled my eyes at him. "We'll see." I responded as we rode down the street to a nail salon, so I could get a manicure and a pedicure. He sat in the corner patiently as I got worked on, but I could tell that he was bored out of his mind, and I even caught him dozing off a few times.

I was almost finished when two pretty girls walked inside the nail salon; both of them looked a couple years older than me. "*Hi*, Phee!" The prettier of the two exclaimed, and she seemed *really* excited to see *my* man. I kept my mouth shut, but my ears and eyes were wide open.

"Whassup." He responded. I checked his face. He smiled, but he didn't over do it. Lucky for him.

"Nothin'. Just came to get a fill..." She stopped short and started looking around the shop, like it had just entered her brain that Phee must have been here with a girl. "What *you* doing here? She asked nosily.

"I'm waiting for my wife." He answered quickly. Just then, the girl and me locked eyes. Neither of us had any hostility in our glare, but she was sizing me up. She was too late; I'd already sized her up when she walked through the door. She was pretty, and her body was okay. But she couldn't fuck with me on her best day, and the look on her face let me know that she knew it. I have no idea what they *used* to have goin' on, but he'd moved on and he'd found something *better* and *wetter*!

"Oh..." her jubilant look deflated. "...Okay, well it was nice to see you again." She walked over to where her friend had taken a seat and sat next to her.

"Yup." He responded.

I don't know what he meant by *yup*, but I would definitely find out later. The two girls immediately started whispering to one another, but I didn't even bother to look in their direction. I was secure, and the last thing I wanted to do was start a face fight on some tacky and immature shit. I didn't want Pharaoh to think I'm on some childish shit. I sat there, got my nails done and played my position.

When the Korean lady was done working on me, I inspected her work and then called for Phee. "Baby, I'm done." And I said it loud enough for the two whispering bitches to hear it too. He came to check on me, I showed him my fingers and my beautiful toes. His smile gave me his stamp of approval and it was time to go.

"Alright, that's good." He pulled out his very resilient bankroll of hundred dollar bills that hadn't seemed to be affected by my shopping. He paid the Korean woman as I put my five-inch DKNY booties back on my feet, and I dreaded it. These shoes were killing my feet, I felt like I'd walked a mile in them already today. He took my hand and we walked out the shop together, he didn't bother looking in the direction of the girl as we left.

"Who was she?" I couldn't wait to ask him once we were safely inside the Q45.

"Old friend."

"So, what's your old friends name?" I asked him. I wasn't about to make a big deal out of nothing, but I did wanna know the bitch's name just for future reference. I told you, I'm not with the Inspector Gadget shit. I'm not gonna be spying on this boy, hiding behind trees and parked cars trying to catch him cheating with his 'old friend'. *But*, it wouldn't hurt for him to *think* that I would!

"Royce." He mumbled, and seemed a little reluctant to say her name.

"Oh. That's all I wanted to know." I dropped the subject.

He reached over, and used his hand to rub the inside of my thigh. "Now what, where you wanna go?" He asked me as we both checked the time, noticing that we still had an hour before it would be 9 o'clock.

"I'm sleepy, can you take me home?" I was exhausted. For the last three nights, I'd been up super late, plus I needed to take off these shoes. "My feet hurt, I can't walk anymore." I giggled.

He laughed. "Okay." He pushed his ride in the direction of my house.

When we arrived, he pulled up into the driveway behind Mommy's minivan. He jumped out and carried my bags into the house, then gave me a long kiss before he left. He said he had some business to take care of, but if you ask me, he probably doubled back to the nail salon to see his *old friend* Royce. But I wasn't gonna worry about it. I'm a smart bitch, and I take the game for what it's worth. I don't have to be the *only* girl in Pharaoh's life, just as long as I'm the *number one* girl in his life! I'm not gonna moan, groan and complain about him being faithful, because niggas are gonna cheat regardless. I'd rather just reap the benefits of being with a baller. I'd rather be cheated on by a nigga who spends money on me, than get my heart broken by a broke nigga with nothing to offer. I'm trying to teach you something, so all you dizzy bitches better pay attention. As far as I'm concerned, Royce could have him for the rest of the night, *I'm* the one with a brand new $8,000 wardrobe. I'm wifey! As long as my competition understands that, and doesn't step on my toes, things should go smooth.

But then again, things never go smoothly in this life. Do they?

CHAPTER TWENTY-EIGHT

"You know what tomorrow is, right Boo? I shot Phee a smile as he pulled up in front of Hair Creations. He'd just picked me up from school, and now I was about to meet up with Ms. Natalie for my beautician lessons.

"You think I don't?" He smirked at me.

"What is it?" I teased.

"*Peach* day." He looked excited and thirsty at the same time; I rolled my eyes and laughed at his expression.

"No, it's Valentines Day."

"No, it's Phee gets the peaches day!" We both laughed as I punched him on the arm.

Tomorrow was the special day that we'd both been waiting for. My baby had hung in there for a little over a month without any type of sexual relief. He'd treated me like a queen even though sex hadn't been a part of the equation. He'd showered me with gifts, taught me so many things about life, and just brightened up my life overall. Now it was time for his reward.

"Yeah, tomorrow you can get the peaches." I leaned over to give him a kiss on the cheek. "Go get some rest, you're gonna need it. Every time it goes up, I'm gonna put it back down." I whispered in his ear. As excited as he seemed, I didn't know who was more thirsty, him or me.

"I can't wait..." he licked his lips.

"I know." I gave him another kiss, grabbed my bag and opened the door. "I'll call you when I get home." I called over my shoulder as I stepped out the Q45.

I waved as I walked into the salon, then he hit the horn twice and pulled off. "Hey ladies! Good Afternoon." I greeted everyone as I strolled inside. There was a chorus of 'hey girl' and 'good afternoons' in return. I'd been coming here for about a month now and all the girls loved me. There were seven regular stylist; Aimee, Lauren, Nicole, Kristen, Alicia, Jennifer, and Ms. Natalie who turned out to be the owner and boss lady in charge. Most of the ladies were in their twenties, with the exception of Ms. Natalie and Alicia, and they all treated me like a little sister. They gave me advice and pointers on different styling techniques, and a few of them even tried to use me as their own personal assistant, but I didn't mind because I was learning the game in the process.

Right now, I was learning basic braiding techniques, which could earn me some money immediately. Cornrows, micro-braids, and extensions are what Ms. Natalie had me focusing on. Anytime a customer came into the shop for anything along those lines, I was right there observing. No matter who the stylist was, I watched, learned and were talked thru the entire process. Phee had bought me a bunch of mannequins from the beauty supply store and I practiced daily. My goal was to be the go-to girl at my school for cornrows and micro-braids. A bunch of dudes at my school had long hair, and lots of girl's rock micro's, especially the girl's basketball team. Pharaoh had created a desire in me to make my own money for the first time, and now I was about to get my hustle on.

I walked to the back employee room and took off my coat and heels, replacing them with a colorful smock and some matching Air Max's. When I was done, I went to check in with Ms. Natalie, she was working on pretty girl who was getting her hair dyed.

"What's up, Ms. Nat?" I looked over her shoulder as she worked.

"Hey cutie, how are you?"

"Fine, how about you?"

"Good. How's my nephew?" She was talking about Phee.

"He's good. He's *such* a gentleman."

"Hmm. Just let me know if he gets out of line." We both laughed.

"I will. Trust me, I'll let you know."

She nodded. "You keeping him out of trouble?" She looked at me for the first time.

I shrugged. "I'm trying to, Ms. Nat. But you know he's hardheaded. Plus, I've must go to school, and then I come here. I can't keep my eye on him all day." That was the only answer that I could give her.

"April, you know it's a lot going on over on that side of town and knowing Pharaoh, he's probably right in the middle of it. Young boys have been getting shot and killed, robbed and going to jail everyday since that boy Vance got gunned down outside of your school." She gave me a look.

"I know."

"He's your man, and he's your responsibility. Do what you can to keep him out of trouble." She told me.

"I'll talk to him." That's what I told her, but I was really just going to mind my damn business, because I already got cursed out once for being too nosy.

The beef was heating up between Pharaoh's team and those Midtown dudes for the past month or so. One time, I asked Phee about the war and he told me that the Midtown dudes had their facts wrong. He swore that his boys had nothing to do with Vance being murdered outside my school, and I believed him. But Asia was giving me a very different scoop, and she had no reason to lie. According to her, Pharaoh and his Dad had some money invested in Darrell's future as a basketball player, and when he was killed, it fucked up their plans. Asia said that the word on the street is that Phee paid Cam and Rell to kill Vance in retaliation. Asia very rarely has her facts mixed up, but this time I prayed that she was wrong. But either way, like Phee told me, it wasn't any of my business.

"You should, because somebody got killed last night in Midtown, then, not even an hour later my son's car got shot up in Cedar Springs. He's just lucky that he wasn't inside of it; the car had twenty-seven bullet holes in it! I keep telling Jeremy about those streets but he's hardheaded..." Ms. Natalie talked while she continued to apply dye to her customer's hair. In my mind, I'm wondering exactly what she wanted me to do about the situation. If *she* can't stop her own son from acting a damn fool, what makes her think I can control Phee's actions?

"...Well anyway, Lauren is over there doing some crazy-ass micro-braid design, go check her out." I was glad when Ms. Natalie finally changed the subject, because she was talking a little too loud anyway and I didn't need the entire salon all in my man's business.

"Okay." I dipped off across the salon to where my girl Lauren's station was. Lauren was my favorite, I admired her, and her style was crazy! She's 23, pretty with a smooth dark bronze complexion. Her parents are Panamanian and she was born and raised in New York City. She'd just graduated from the University at Buffalo with a Psychology degree, and she'd used to have dreams of being a social worker until she began making tons of money doing hair.

"Whassup, Lauren?" I was all smiles.

"Hey, Ms. Thang. You came to hang out with me today?" She grinned at me.

"Yeah, I came to learn from the best." I giggled as I gassed her up.

"Damn right, and don't forget it. But don't say it too loud, you know it's a lot of hating going on in this joint." She laughed.

I'd never known how competitive it is working inside a beauty salon. In just a short time here, I'd witnessed quite a few catfights, and they mostly involved Lauren. Lauren doesn't have a problem with stealing clients from the other girls. But the way I see it, it's a free country and the clients have a right to get their hair done by whomever they choose. I didn't respond to her comment though, because I wasn't trying to keep the conversation going and risk the other stylist overhearing us. I needed to be cordial with everyone so that I could learn, and I didn't need any secret enemies because of my relationship with Lauren.

"This is my girl, Toccara. Toccara, this is my lil' homie April, she's studying to be a hair stylist." Lauren introduced me to her customer and the first thing that caught my attention was her hair.

"Hey, April."

"Hi, Toccara." We smiled politely and greeted each other.

"Okay A, listen..." Lauren stopped and turned towards me. "...Don't ask me why this girl got me hooking her hair up like some tacky ass video ho-"

"Bitch, watch your mouth." Tocarra interrupted.

"But my job is to give my clients exactly what they want, even if I don't agree. Because I'm a beautician, and not a damn therapist!" Lauren gave Toccara a crazy look.

"Whatever, just hurry up and get done! I've been here for three hours already, I've got shit to do!" Her customer rolled her eyes.

"Shit, you gonna need a new man after Keith see's your hair looking like *this*! I don't know why you're making me do this shit to you." Lauren continued to joke at Toccara's expense. Toccara wasn't laughing anymore and it looked like she'd had enough of the comedy.

I watched as Lauren braided pink and red strands of synthetic weave into Toccara's hair. Lauren was official! She'd made three heart designs, one above each of Toccara's ears and a slightly larger one at the crown of her head. Me personally, I wouldn't rock it, but it looked cute on her.

"Ummm, Toccara." I interrupted. "I'm not trying to be funny or nothin', but I like it. Lauren's doing a good job on you." Lauren gave me a roll of her eyes as I complimented her work.

Toccara kept her head tilted down, but fixed her eyes on me. "Thank you, girl. At least *somebody* has taste around here! It's just something special for Valentine's Day, something special for my man, you know?"

I nodded. "I bet you've got a cute outfit to rock with it, right?" I started to get hyped up.

"Oh girl, you already know! I got this red and pink Donna Karen skirt, blouse and matching heels. Plus, matching lingerie."

"Awwwe." I started gushing. "His eyes are gonna light up when he sees you." I wished I'd thought about doing something crazy with my hair to surprise Phee, maybe not *that* crazy, but something different.

"Well, I hope he appreciates it..." She exhaled loudly. "...You know how niggas are, all they care about is getting you naked. They don't care about all the work you put into looking good, or making it special." We all nodded in agreement. "What about you, you got a man to spend Valentine's Day with?" She asked me.

I smiled and started to think about him. "Yeah, but I don't know where we're going, it's supposed to be a surprise." I answered truthfully.

"I hope you have a good time." Toccara smiled at me. "Now, this bitter Bitch behind me, she's *never* gonna have a man because she's an asshole!" She threw a jab at Lauren.

Lauren cracked up laughing. "Toccara, don't make me send you out of here baldheaded!" She joked. "April, come here and look at this." I moved around to position myself so I could see where she was pointing. "Whenever you run into a problem like this, you have to stop and redo the whole braid. Don't just keep going because it'll get worst. It won't look right, and it'll come apart very easily. We wouldn't want it to fall apart tomorrow night while Keith is tugging on it." Lauren giggled.

I watched her take the braid apart, she rolled her eyes obviously annoyed that she had to start over. "Have you been practicing at home?" She asked me.

"Yes."

"Has that happened to you yet?"

I shook my head. "No."

"When it does, just remember what I told you. It's frustrating to start the braid over, but it's better than losing a client. Keep it tight, because once one piece starts to unravel, it wont be long before it all starts to unravel."

"I got it." I kept watching. Both girls were silent, both of them probably irritated by now. Lauren's fingers were probably cramped and her feet sore. Toccara's neck was probably cramped and her scalp sore. I   jumped when my phone began to vibrate inside the pocket of my smock. "Hello?" I answered quickly.

"I miss you."

When I heard his voice, a huge smile spread across my face. "I miss you too."

"I just wanted to tell you that."

Click.

The line went dead, and just that fast he was gone. It was so rude, but so sweet, and I was just too happy to be mad. Every since I'd given him a hard time about hanging up on me, he went out of his way to do it purposely. It got on my nerves, but I knew he didn't mean anything by it.

Lauren was smirking at me, and Toccara was staring at me too. "April, wipe that stupid ass smile off your face! You look like you just won the lottery or something." Lauren snapped at me.

"*Awwwe*! That must have been the guy who's gonna surprise you tomorrow, huh?" Toccara chimed in.

I was blushing like crazy, even if I wanted to lie, my face had already given me away. "Yeah, that was him." I confessed.

"That's little Pharaoh's wifey." Lauren opened her big mouth and told her customer my business. I really didn't appreciate it but I kept my mouth shut. One thing about the beauty salon, there are no secrets here.

"Get outta here! *Really*?" Toccara suddenly seemed surprised, and the mention of Phee's name made her neck snap. "Hold up, L. Let me get a good look at Ms. April." Lauren stopped braiding so that she could take a good look at me. Toccara started scoping me out from top to bottom and I felt like I was inside of a fish tank. "Okay, Okay! Ya'll definitely make a cute couple, and girl you got yourself a *winner* too! Don't let him go girl, you'd better hold on *real* tight to that one!"

"What?" I scrunched up my face at her. I didn't mean to, but it was my natural reaction. I didn't like the way she said I should hold on *real* tight to him, like somebody was gonna take him from me.

Lauren burst out laughing when she saw my face, and Toccara shot her a look that made her wipe the grin off her face. "April, I'm 27. Phee is a little boy to me and I watched him grow up, running around in a diaper. I meant that a compliment, I didn't mean to offend you sweetie."

"No it's fine." I cleared the air quickly. "I just didn't know what you meant by 'hold on tight', like you were being funny or something."

"Girl please, I've got my own headache to deal with." Toccara settled back into the chair and tilted her neck back down so Lauren could finish.

It took another twenty minutes, before Lauren was finally done. "You learn anything?" Ms. Natalie asked me after Toccara was gone.

"Yup."

"Good, you can leave after you do me a favor."

"Okay."

"This young lady right here..."Ms. Natalie nodded at an older lady in her chair who looked to be at least sixty. "I need you to wash and shampoo her for me. Then you can leave if you want to, okay?"

"Alright."

"Oh, and on Wednesday I'll have a live client for you. I want to see how far along you've come with your micro braiding. The client, she doesn't want anything exotic, it's just a basic job."

"I'm ready." I smiled at her. I was excited to show the rest of the girls in the shop that I'd truly been learning something over the past weeks. I looked at Ms. Natalie's customer, "Hi. I'm April, you don't mind if I wash your hair do you?" I smiled at her.

"Of course not." She smiled as I took her hand, helped her out the chair and over to the row of sinks against the wall. This lady didn't stop talking the entire time I washed her hair. Whew! Lord only knows I thought about drowning her. I thought my Aunt Tracey had a motor mouth, but this old lady, she told me all of her kids and grandkids business in less than 20 minutes. I knew so much about their drama that I felt like I'd just been to their family reunion. I didn't answer any of her questions when she asked me about my life, because I knew if I did, I'd be the topic of conversation the next time she got in someone's ear.

When I was done, I said my goodbyes and headed to the back room to change and soon I was headed out the front door. As I walked towards the intersection, I passed the separate entrance used for the barbershop. Emory and Xavier were standing outside talking, but stopped their conversation as I passed by.

"Whassup, April?" Emory spoke to me, but I didn't respond, I just waved at them and kept it moving. They were both looking at me in a way that I knew they wouldn't dare had Pharaoh been anywhere around. But I didn't sweat it; I just crossed the street and headed home. It was cold out, so I moved fast. Phee wanted to take me home every evening, but I didn't want to inconvenience him just so he could drive me two blocks.

Calvin was outside shoveling snow and as I passed his driveway, I waved at him. "Hi, Calvin."

"Hey." His tone was *really* dry, and I could tell that he didn't really wanna talk to me. I'd probably broken his heart by getting into a relationship, but that was something he'd have to deal with. I hadn't worn his bracelet since the first day Phee picked me up from school, and now it just sat in my jewelry box collecting dust. Speaking of jewelry, Pharaoh had better get me something nice for Valentine's

Day tomorrow. I'd been dropping him hints for the last two weeks and he's not stupid or slow, so I know he caught on.

I walked up our driveway past the Daycare van and I could feel Calvin's eyes glued to my butt. I turned quickly and of course, I caught him staring at me from a distance. Poor child, he was never going to get any sex acting so damn shy. When our eyes locked, he dropped his head and looked at the ground. I just turned, shrugged and went into the house where Mommy was waiting for me in the kitchen.

"Hi, baby." She kissed my cheek.

"Hey, Mommy." She was at the stove cooking dinner and I reached over her to grab the cordless phone and dial Phee's number.

"Hello." He answered on the first ring; he was probably waiting for my call.

"I'm home, Boo." Mommy turned to look at me as I dropped my bag on the counter next to her books.

"Aight. Do your homework, and call me later. You need anything?" He asked me.

"Nope."

"You sure? I'll bring it to you."

"I'm good, thanks anyway."

"Where's Mommy at?" He wanted to know.

I looked at Mommy, not surprised that she was still watching me and trying to listen to my conversation. "She right here, we're in the kitchen."

"Tell her I said *hi*, and ask her if she needs anything."

"Ma, Phee said *hi*. He wants to know if you need anything."

Mommy looked like she was thinking. She really liked Phee, and trust me, if she needed anything she had no problem letting him know.
"No, tell him thank you."

"I heard her." Phee said in my ear. "Handle your business and call me back later." He was rushing me off the phone, and I hate it when he does that. It makes me suspicious.

"You busy or something?" I asked him.

"Actually, yeah." That was his response.

"Doing *what*?" I asked with an attitude.

"Handling my business, now handle yours. Go upstairs and put your face in the books, then practice braiding. Make me proud."

I immediately calmed down and took the attitude out of my voice. "Okay."

"Talk to you later."

"Bye." I put the phone back onto the charger. I loved when he told me what to do, that shit turned me on. "Mom, I'm going upstairs to do my homework. Call me for dinner."

"Okay."

*   *   *   *   *

Later, after everything had wound down, I started to get ready for bed. I had butterflies in my stomach thinking about tomorrow, and they weren't going anywhere. I stripped down to my Vicki's and ran a bathtub full of hot water, then added some strawberry scent bubble bath. I admired my body in the full-length mirror and smiled, tomorrow Phee was in for a treat. I was gonna let him explore every inch of me. Every crack and crevice, and every nook and cranny. I wanted him to use his tongue to hunt for hidden treasures. I needed it slow, fast, deep and hard. I needed to get it good and I hoped I wouldn't be disappointed, because I'd been waiting too long.

I climbed inside the hot bubble bath and soaked for a few minutes before returning Nica's call. "Hello?"

"What's up, Tanica? You busy?" It was almost ten o'clock.

"Nope, just getting some stuff ready for tomorrow, what you doing?"

"Bubble bath."

She laughed. "Uh oh! Gotta get that thang ready for a good pounding, huh?" We both cracked up laughing.

"There won't be any *pounding* going on. We're gonna make love." I corrected her.

"Bitch please. He's been waiting over thirty days, so all that built up frustration he's got, he's gonna pound that tiny little coochie to death! Wait, you'll see." We were still laughing.

"He better not."

"Or what? You gonna make him stop? Please, you're gonna love every minute of it. Shit, all *five minutes* of it!" Nica joked.

"Whatever! I smell you hatin' over there. Don't be mad 'cause it's me about to get a roller coaster ride for a change! Lord only knows, you've had enough for the both of us!" I almost died laughing.

"Oh, *very* funny, April! *That* was a good one!" She replied sarcastically, and even though she was trying not to, she couldn't help but laugh too.

Now, don't misinterpret the joke, my cousin isn't a ho or anything, not in the least. Trust me, I know some bitches her age that are ho's, and she's not one of them. At sixteen, Nica only had four boys in her bed. Now, I say *only* because let's face it, this is the 2000's! There was a time when women went their entire life without touching four penises, but nowadays there are girls my age who are already in the double digits. Personally, I wish I could take back my virginity and give in to Phee. But it's too late.

"Just kidding."

"I know." She was still snickering. "So, did you shave it like I told you?"

I frowned. "I did, but Nica are you sure that dudes like it bald like that?" I asked skeptically. I'd let my cousin talk me into shaving off all the hair between my legs, and it felt weird. I looked like a little ass girl down there and now I was a little self conscious about it.

"Yes! Trust me bitch, no man wanna put his face down there if it looks like you wearing a nappy afro!" She started giggling. "And, that's nasty, April. Hair traps odor and all types of other stuff, trust me, I wouldn't lie to you." She reassured me. "Are you gonna suck it?"

"Hell no!" I blurted quickly, and I tried to sound super offended by this line of questioning. But secretly, I was thinking about it and I really wanted to. I just might suck Phee's dick, but I wasn't gonna tell Nica that! I told my cousin everything. But the one thing that I'd never admit to thinking about, or actually doing, is putting *any* dick anywhere near my face.

"Liar!"

"Fuck you, Nica!"

"Shit, don't get mad at me 'cause you won't keep it real! But let me tell you this, if you're gonna do it, you'd better practice first. Get a carrot, or a small cucumber or something and learn to do it without scraping your teeth across it. Because if you make a mistake and bite that boy, he's gonna slap the shit outta you! And *that*, is not sexy at all-"

"Sounds like you've experienced this first hand! You have a story you wanna share with me, Tanica?" We burst into laughter.

"Hooker, are you crazy? Tracey's daughter isn't sucking on anything that isn't sold in the supermarket!" Nica said quickly, but I didn't believe her. But hey, certain things were nobody's business. I definitely wouldn't tell her if I did it, so I'm sure she felt the same way.

"I heard that!" I agreed, and then changed the subject. "What you doing tomorrow?" I asked.

"There's a dance after school, I'm going with my friend Tyree. Then I'm coming home, unless he can get his Dad's car. If he can get the car, then we'll probably go to the movies."

"Oh, okay. Then I'll just call you tomorrow night."

"Alright, have fun, Tramp."

"*Skeezer!*" We hung up.

I finished my bath and then took a ten-minute shower to get the dirt off. After I lotioned up, I climbed into the bed and crawled under the covers. I pulled out the toy that Phee bought me from underneath my pillow, and turned it on as I dialed his number. I wanted him to tell me goodnight as I rocked myself to sleep.

CHAPTER TWENTY-NINE

The slumber that I'd fallen into was close to a coma. When I finally opened my eyes Mommy was sitting on the edge of my bed. I didn't have to ask or check, I knew it had to be 7 o'clock on the dot.

"Time to get up."

I stretched and yawned. "I'm up." I whispered.

She stared at me for a few seconds before speaking. "So, I guess I won't be seeing you until later on tonight?" She asked. Phee had spoken to Mommy about taking me out today after school. I have no idea *what* he told her, or *where* he told her he was taking me, but whatever he said, she agreed.

"11 o'clock, right?" I double-checked my curfew.

She nodded. "Yup, and you'd better not be late."

"Ma, where'd he tell you that we're going?" I asked with a grin.

Mommy laughed. "You're asking me to ruin his surprise? I can't do that, April." We were both smiling. I don't know why *she* was smiling, but *I* was smiling because I'd finally outsmarted her. I knew where we were going, to a hotel to get our freak on! Which hotel? I had neither a clue nor a care. I'm quite sure Phee had a surprise for me, but the destination wasn't it.

"Give me hint."

"*Nope.*" She stood up and walked towards the door. "But have a good time, okay?"

"Okay."

"And you'd better be at school all day." She added.

I rolled my eyes. "He'd never let me miss a day of school, even if I wanted to."

"That's good to hear." She gave me a look that said she didn't believe a word I'd just said. "I left something on your nightstand, use it!" She walked out and closed the door behind her.

I looked at me nightstand and my jaw dropped as I saw the birth control patch that she'd left me. This woman must have super powers! Now, I was just plain creeped out. Last month, at my doctors appointment she'd gotten me a prescription for the birth contraception and she told me to let her know when I was ready to have sex so she could get the prescription filled. But I'd never mentioned it again, so how did she know that *today* was the day? After I thought about it, it really didn't matter, so I grabbed the patch and stuck it to the back of my shoulder. Then I got ready for my day.

As always, my Boo was right on time. I stepped outside with another new outfit on. Phee, had bought me this cute Anne Klein charcoal grey wool skirt, matching vest, and a colorful low dipping blouse underneath. I killed the ensemble with a badass pair of Nicole Miller ankle boots and Grey wool Burberry Pea Coat.

He stepped out the Q45 and took my hand. "Look at *my* girl!" He smiled happily as he helped me down the porch steps. "Damn baby, turn around so I can look at you." I was cheesing, he definitely knew how to make me smile. I turned around slowly to model for him, and he grabbed my book bag from my arm. "How'd I get so lucky to have you?" As he pulled me into his arms, my cheeks became red from all the attention.

I didn't know how to answer his question, so I just kissed him; I knew he'd appreciate that even more. "Baby, it's *freezing* out here." I whined as he held me hostage in the frigid morning air. I didn't mind being hugged up, but we could do that in the car.

"Happy Valentine's Day." He let me out of his grasp.

"Happy Valentine's Day to you too!" I said quickly as I tried to break for the car, but he grabbed my coat. I didn't give him a crazy look, or say anything smarts because not only did he buy this coat, he'd purchased *everything* I was wearing. As far as I was concerned, he could grab me anytime he wanted to.

"Hold up." He went into the pocket of his coat and pulled out a nice sized jewelry box. It was gift wrapped and had a bow on top. "Here, open it." He handed the gift to me.

I wasted no time snatching the box from his hands and ripping open the red wrapping. Inside the paper was a green box with a gold emblem, "Oh, shit baby!" I lifted the lid and gushed over the watch. "Baby, a *Rolex*?" It was a brand new Lady Rolex Datejust, a yellow gold joint with a diamond bezel, and it was beautiful! Phee took the watch out the case and fastened it to my left wrist. As soon as it was clamped on securely, I threw my arms around his neck.

"Thank you!" I was too happy. Mommy would die when she saw this present.

"You're welcome. I'll give you only the best, that's what you deserve." He whispered in my ear. All I could think, was that it was about time someone recognized that I was worth my weight in gold!

"I've got something for you too." Not to be outdone, I wanted to give Pharaoh the present that I'd bought him. "It's in my bag." I let go of his neck.

He waved me off. "Just wait and give it to me later when I give you yours." He winked at me.

"Huh?" I didn't understand. I must have missed something.

"That's not the real present. I had a good week, so that's just to show you how much you mean to me. The watch was just something to make you smile for me, I've got something *better* for you later." He hurried around to open the passenger side door for me. Wow, this boy had my head in the clouds. The entire ride to school I toyed with my new watch, I couldn't keep my eyes off it. When he pulled up to the entrance, I gave him the biggest kiss I could because I didn't really want to leave his side.

*   *   *   *   *

Right before sixth period, my name was announced over the loud speaker. "April Showers, please report to the main office! April Showers, to the main office!" I was sitting in study hall when I heard the announcement, and suddenly all eyes were on me and everybody was giving me that look. The look where everyone is trying to figure out how much trouble you were in. I knew I hadn't done anything to be in trouble, but I still had butterflies in my stomach. I hoped that Daddy hadn't come here to surprise me again, that would ruin my entire day!

"Ms. Showers, I have a pass ready for you." Mr. Jenkins yelled and his voice startled me. This dude had one of those real loud voices like Samuel L. Jackson. He couldn't whisper to save his life. I got up and grabbed my books, took the pass and broke out. The whole walk to the main office all I could do is pray that Daddy hadn't shown up. I even took off my new Rolex and stashed it inside my purse just in case.

When I walked into the office, all the ladies seemed to be waiting for me to show up. I looked around but didn't see Daddy. "April..." Mrs. Anderson walked up to the counter.

"Huh?"

"Do I look like your personal assistant?" This bitch asked sarcastically, like she had an attitude or something.

"*What?*" I gave her a crazy look, and threw her attitude right back at her.

She rolled her eyes. "Listen, tell whoever sent you these, that this is not an office building, this is a high school." She went behind the counter and pulled out a long white box with a red bow, plus a heart shaped box of chocolates. The *expensive* chocolates. "These were just delivered here for you, April. Put them in your locker, *please.*" Mrs. Anderson still had the attitude in her voice, but she was trying to be somewhat professional.

I just gave her a look, snatched my gifts off the counter and bounced! I didn't smile until I was out of sight, and I didn't open the box until I was at my locker. There were a dozen fresh red roses inside with a note, and of course, they were from Pharaoh. The smile on my face was wide enough to last forever!

The rest of the day sped by, and at dismissal, I damn near broke my neck running towards the exit. I'd left my bag in the car, so all I was carrying was my purse and my presents. I didn't even bother to look for Asia; I had a feeling that she was going around the corner with Cam anyway.

I got inside the Infiniti wearing the same smile from earlier, and it hadn't faded yet. "Thank you!" Those were the first words out my mouth and he just shrugged. "The ladies in the office were hating on me." I told him proudly. He didn't reply, he just put the car in drive and pulled off. I sat back and looked him over, he wasn't dressed up like I thought he'd be, but he looked cute. He was wearing a wool Mitchell &Ness varsity jacket, blue jeans and some matching Jordan's.

"*Pharaoh*!" I said loudly to get his attention after I'd gotten tired of being ignored. He looked at me as I sat there, staring him down with my arms folded across my chest. "Say *something*! You didn't even say hi to me, and where's my kiss?" I could tell that his mind was somewhere else, and it was obvious that something was wrong. Compared to his mood this morning, there was a big difference in his attitude.

"Whassup, baby? Why you so upset?" He wanted to know.

I just looked at him like he was nuts. "I'm *not* upset, *I'm* fine. What about *you*, why you acting funny? What's wrong?" I checked his facial expression.

"Nothin', I'm chillin'." He tried to sound like everything was normal, but I knew better.

"What you do while I was at school?" I asked him so that maybe I could piece together what the problem was.

"Nothing. I've been waiting for you since I dropped you off. I missed you." He looked at me and grinned, but it wasn't genuine. It was one of those joints that he does when he wants to throw me off the scent. I hadn't known him for years, but I've been studying him long enough to know when he wasn't in a good mood or something was bothering him. Nine times out of ten, if he was in a sour mood, it had something to do with money. Shit, today was our big day and he hadn't mentioned my peaches at all. Something was *definitely* wrong.

"So you ain't do *nothing*?" I asked again.

He shrugged. "I went to look at a new whip, that's all."

"What kind? What's wrong with this one?"

Phee started fidgeting like I was getting on his nerves. "It's time for me to get something new. The whole city knows what car I drive, so I'm about to switch up. I went to look at a Navigator." He kept his eyes on the road as he spoke. I decided not to ask any more questions because I could tell by his body language that he was almost at his patience limit. One more question and he'd probably say something stupid that would ruin our day, so I left it alone.

I reached over and rubbed the side of his face, and then I ran my fingernails across the back of his neck. "Take me somewhere so I can make you feel better. I know what you need to relieve your stress." I told him softly. He smiled, and this time it was genuine but there was still some worry behind it.

"Let me stop by and give my Mom her gift first." He said.

"Awe, you got your Mom something for Valentine's Day? That's so sweet, baby." It made me smile to know that. I've always heard that a man, who treats his mother special, will always take care of his woman. We pulled onto his Mom's block and he parked behind his mother's Ford Explorer.

"Come inside for a second, she's always asking me why I don't bring you around more often." He told me.

"Okay." I'd only met his Mom four or five times, but she was a nice woman. I don't know if she actually liked me, but she was always polite.

We walked up to the front door and Phee unlocked it. "Hold up for a second." He left me in the foyer and ran upstairs, when he came back, he was carrying a white box identical to the one he'd sent me and a teddy bear. "Come on." He whispered to me as he led me to the back of the big house.

His Mom was chilling in the kitchen reading a magazine when we walked in. "Happy Valentine's Day!" Phee said to her, she looked up and smiled when she saw the two of us, then stood up.

"Oh, Thank you!" She gave Phee a big hug. "Hi, April! How are you?" She gave me a hug too.

"Fine, Mrs. Green. How are *you*?" I gave her a huge smile. I wanted her to like me, because if she didn't it would cause tension in my relationship with her son because they were extremely close. Sort of like how Daddy and Cita's beef had affected my parents relationship somewhat.

"I'm good, sweetheart." Mrs. Green sat back down and began to open the box and smiled at the dozen roses that her son had bought for her. "Ooooh!" She looked excited. "I'm going to put these in some water right now. Thank you!"

He shrugged. "You're welcome, Ma."

Next she opened the card, it was stuffed with cash and some gift certificates. She paid the money no attention, she focused on the words on the card and when she was done reading, she stood up and gave him another hug.

"So what are you two about to get into?" She looked back and forth between us. I didn't answer; I just waited for Phee to respond. That's when I saw the look of irritation resurface on his face, and Mrs. Green saw it too. "What's wrong with you?"

"Nothing." He said quickly. Now his Mom was looking at me for answers, she must have assumed that I'd know why he was in such a shitty mood.

"He's tired, I kept him up all night on the phone again." I spoke up for him. "He's taking me somewhere nice, but it's supposed to be a surprise, he doesn't want me to know where we're going." I smiled at her, but she wasn't smiling. Her eyes were stuck on Phee who was looking like he was ready to go.

"Then he should've just said that it was a surprise, instead of looking at me like he's lost his *damn* mind!" I think she was speaking to me, even though she was looking at him. "Boy, don't make me-"

"Ma, I gotta go. I'll talk to you later." Phee cut her off by giving her a hug before she could finish her threat. "I love you." He added just to smooth things over.

Then he grabbed me and pulled me towards the door. "Bye, Mrs. Green..." I shrugged and gave her a silent apology with my eyes for her son's rude behavior.

"Nice seeing you, April." She didn't bother following us out the kitchen, she sat back down and got back to her magazine. I waited for him to lock the door and we went back to the car.

We rode through the city streets in silence as we headed towards the suburb of Amherst with Jagged Edge playing through his sound system. Once every couple of minutes, I'd look at him hoping that he'd say something, anything. But he kept quiet. Maybe it was something I'd said or did to make him angry with me. I had no idea, but I decided to stay on mute and wait for him to speak.

We were heading up Niagara Falls Boulevard, and I narrowed it down to a few places where he could be taking me. All of the possibilities were fine with me, just as long as a hotel suite was the final destination. I needed to be dug out! And the stupid look on his face let me know that he needed some butt to make him relax, we could both use some loving.

The right hand turn onto Sheridan Drive threw me off, now we were heading into the residential part of Amherst away from the shopping area. A couple minutes later we pulled up a long driveway next to a brick duplex on Carmen Road, he cut the engine off and opened his door without saying a word. I rolled my eyes, *now* he was starting to get on my nerves.

He walked around and opened my door, making the brick cold air smack me in the face. "C'mon, get out." He held the door open for me and I was obedient, I followed him to the side door of the duplex. I wanted to ask him a gazillion and one questions, but I somehow managed to contain my curiosity. Well, for the Moment anyway, because if I didn't get answers soon, I would let the questions start flying.

Instead of ringing the doorbell, Phee pulled out a key and opened the doors. He pulled me inside and closed the doors behind us. "Baby, whose house is this?" I asked him.

I looked around at the beautifully decorated duplex in awe, but he didn't answer me. He wrapped his arms around me from behind and kissed the back of my neck, then slowly walked behind me towards the kitchen area. I looked around taking everything in, the kitchen was nice, clean, and all the appliances were new and state of the art. He directed me to a door, opened it and led me downstairs to plush carpeted basement. There were a few leather sofas, a giant television, a pool table and a mini bar. What caught my attention was the corner of the basement. There was an area with mirrors, a chair and hairstyling equipment.

"When you get some clients, you can do hair down here..." he whispered to me. "...But *nobody* is allowed upstairs in *our* house, bring all your company to the basement."

Now I was so excited that I could hardly contain it. "Baby, this is *our* place?"

He started laughing. "Mine, *ours*..." he winked at me. "What's the difference?"

CHAPTER THIRTY

I reached for his belt, "Where's the bedroom?" I grinned at him while pulling him by the jeans all the way to the staircase. I was ready and anxious to handle my business. The whole way upstairs, our palms were all over each other. His hands were all the way up my wool skirt and he was rubbing me down. I know he could tell how wet I was once his fingers slid inside my tights and underneath my satin thong.

At the top of the stairs, I made the wrong turn. "This way." He pulled me to the left and into what appeared to be the master bedroom. It looked like some shit straight out a magazine, it was decorated basic but beautiful and expensively. I didn't have time to admire my surroundings because Phee was undressing me so quickly. He tossed my coat and purse onto the floor, then sat on the edge of the bed and pulled me to him. I stood between his legs while he unbuttoned my skirt and let it fall to the carpet, next he peeled off my vest and blouse, followed by my heels and stockings.

No words were spoken as I stood in from him wearing nothing but a matching platinum colored bra and panty set, and a filthy grin. I straddled him on the edge of the bed, then pushed my warm tongue between his lips and kissed him passionately. His hands roamed all over my bare skin exploring my curves, before long he'd unsnapped my bra, freed my titties and began to tease them with his lips and tongue. A gasp escaped my lips as he took his time and pleasured my nipples. I closed my eyes and placed kisses on his forehead while he concentrated on my breast. The middle of my body was tingling and I was sure that I was leaking a puddle of liquid passion on his jeans as I grinded on his lap. I slid my hand down and massaged my secret button at the same until I began to shake in his arms.

Suddenly, Phee stood up, lifting me into the air. He turned around so that he was facing the bed and gently lay me down onto my back. He took his time pulling the platinum colored thong off my hips and down my thighs. Now that I was completely naked, he tossed my panties to the side and admired my body as I lay in front of him. I smiled, I loved the look that was on his face, he couldn't wait to feel me and I knew it. I spread my legs wide, so that he could get a good look at my swollen, clean-shaven peach. At the same time, I massaged my nipples in anticipation for his touch. Pharaoh looked overwhelmed, like he couldn't figure out what he wanted to do to me first. I really didn't care, just as long as he did something quickly!

He read my mind. The next thing I knew, his hands were underneath my butt and his face was buried between my young tender thighs. I don't know how he found it, but he'd taken my secret button hostage. The first time his tongue grazed over it, I jumped and arched my back. I thrust my hips off the bed and grabbed his head to keep him focused on that exact spot. Pharaoh's lips and tongue felt well than my fingers could ever feel. It felt better than the showerhead, and even better than the toy vibrator that I keep underneath my pillow. My legs locked as I trembled, he had a firm grip on me and he wouldn't stop even as I begged him to. I tried to push him away, but he wouldn't let go. He kept assaulting me with his tongue until I finally submitted, my body stiffened as I climaxed repeatedly. I bust a nut so violent; that I could have swore I was having a seizure. The boy licked me so good that I almost died! Swear to God!

I wasn't even done cumming when he grabbed my ankles and pulled me to the other side of the bed. He dropped his jeans and his boxer briefs, and my jaw dropped when I got a good look at it. This boy was gonna stretch my tight little peach like a rubber band. I laid back, closed my eyes and took a deep breath, because it was about to go down! Just as Phee spread my thighs and prepared to get on top, my phone rang and he hesitated.

"C'mon baby, put it in..." I begged for it. I needed that feeling. I craved it. I was open, sprung, turned out already and I hadn't even been penetrated yet. That damn phone just wouldn't stop ringing, and it was ruining the mood. Pharaoh continued to glance at my purse as it sat on the floor, then he looked back at me lying in front of him. My hair was partly covering my face, I was completely naked, and my legs were spread wide waiting to lock around his waist.

I rolled my eyes at him as he made a move to grab my purse off the floor. "It's probably your Moms, and you know she's just gonna keep calling until you answer." He tried to reason with me but I wasn't trying to hear it.

"So *what!*" I snapped.

Phee handed me the phone. "Just answer it."

"No, she can wait!" I snatched the phone and tossed it to the other side of the bed. "Come on..." I reached out and pulled him towards me. "...I *need* you, and I *really* wanna thank you." I pulled him down on top of me and kissed him just as the phone stopped ringing. I swear to you, the kiss didn't last long because as soon as we got into it, the phone started ringing again. I sucked my teeth loudly as he reached for it again, but that didn't stop him.

"Phee!" I pouted. "I swear, if you answer that phone, I'm getting dressed and you can wait another *long* month for *this*!" I looked up at him. I tried my best to sound convincing, but it didn't work.

"Hello?" Phee answered my phone while I was pinned underneath is body. Even if I *wanted* to throw a tantrum and get up, I couldn't because all his weight was on top of me. I had no choice but to lay there and listen to him talk on the phone. "Hi, Mom." He said, and I knew he had to be talking to Mommy. I watched his face as he listened to her talk, and I don't know what she said to him, but all of a sudden, his eyes got *really* big. He rolled off me and jumped out the bed like the police were coming, and he walked over to the window and started whispering into the phone. In my head, I was wondering what kind of secret would Mommy be telling Phee that I wasn't supposed to know about. "Don't worry, I'll tell her." He tried to whisper, but I managed to catch those last words before he hung up.

"Tell me *what*?" I was out the bed and tiptoeing towards him. "What you gotta tell me?" I wanted to know.

Just as I reached him, he turned around wearing a blank expression. "Boo, something *bad* happened to your Dad. He's in the hospital, and he's not doing too good." He whispered softly.

"*Huh*?" Suddenly, I felt a sharp pain in my chest and I became light-headed to the point where the room began spinning. I just remember my legs getting weak, and collapsing. Had Phee not been there to catch me, I would've hit the floor!

CHAPTER THIRTY-ONE

Six hours later, I was sitting inside room 229 at the Erie County Medical Center. My Daddy had just come out of surgery a couple hours ago, and he was listed in critical condition. He needed to have another surgery soon, but he wasn't stable enough yet. He'd been involved in a terrible car accident on the Route 33 expressway, and he'd been ejected from the windshield of his rental car. The State Troopers said that the car in front of him had lost control, and Daddy had swerved trying to avoid the collision, but instead he ended up crashing into a cement barricade at almost 60mph.

Mommy was a *wreck*! I hadn't witnessed her take a break from crying since I arrived at the hospital. Daddy's mother, Grandma Pearl was here too, along with my aunts, uncles and a few cousins. Mommy and Grandma Pearl was sitting next to Daddy's hospital bed as he lay unconscious, while me and La La sat in the corner. Carlito was on my lap, and Cory had his arms wrapped around La Reina's neck.

My Mom had this really painful expression on her face. She's been in love with my Dad for almost twenty years, so I couldn't imagine how she felt inside. One thing I knew for sure is that she was blaming herself for what happened to him. She just kept rocking back and forth in her seat with this pitiful look on her face, while Grandma Pearl tried to console her. The whole vibe in this room was way too depressing for me to handle. My Daddy wasn't the type of nigga to have people sitting around feeling sorry for him, and I'm sure that he'd be *very* disappointed at this scene if he could see it. Especially, Mommies crying and carrying on after she'd kicked him out of her life just recently. If he could see her right now, he'd probably laugh and say some very dry, sarcastic, slick shit.

It was 9:30 pm when I decided I couldn't take anymore; I'd had enough of sitting here mourning. It was time to go. I was all cried out, and every time I looked at my Daddy and saw tubes coming out his body it made my skin crawl. Visiting hours would be over at ten, but the nursing staff would be in for a brawl if they thought Mommy and Grandma Pearl where going anywhere, anytime soon. Don't get me wrong, I like to see a good fight just as much as anyone else, but I didn't wanna see or be apart of this one.

Lito was sleeping in my lap and it was a tough job to stand up and gently place him on the chair without waking him up. I sat him down on the chair and headed to the door. Both Mommy and grandma Pearl were still awake, La La and Cory were sleep. All the other family members had trickled off one by one. I opened the door and walked into the hall, the bright light temporarily hurt my eyes. I let the door close softly so I wouldn't wake my brothers and sister.

I was shocked to see Pharaoh still sitting inside the second floor waiting room. I smiled looking at my Boo. He had his fitted cap pulled low over his eyes while he snoozed lightly. There were only a few people inside the room, no one that I recognized. I took the seat next to him and lay my head on his chest. A second later his arm wrapped around me and his hand stroked my hair.

"You okay, baby?" he asked me.

"No." I answered being honest. There wasn't any need to pretend like everything was okay, when it wasn't.

"Your pops gonna be okay, April. Try not to stress too much, it won't do any good. All you can do is pray," he held me tight. His response made me feel a little better. We sat in silence for a couple minutes.

"Bay, you been here this whole time?" I finally asked him.

"Yeah."

"You can go. You don't gotta stay, everybody else left already." I said to him with my cheek against his chest.

"I gotta make sure you get home safe." Phee said, stroking the back of my neck. His touch felt so good that I wanted to climb onto his lap and fall asleep there. "What's up with your Moms?" he asked me.

"Still crying." I responded

"What she gonna do at 10 o'clock?"

"They gonna have to call the U.S. Marshalls to get her and grandma out that room." Phee chuckled, "I'm serious, baby." I added. I could see it now, Mommy and grandma fighting the whole police department. La La too. Cory and Carlito biting knee caps and kicking the police in the balls. All this while Daddy lay in the bed unconscious.

"Go tell Mom that if she want, I'll take you, La and the boys home. And I'll make sure everybody get to school tomorrow." Phee said to me.

I let out a deep breath. "Alright... but I'm not going to school tomorrow."

"You gonna do whatever I tell you to do..." Phee corrected me quietly. I didn't argue, cause I knew he was right. "Go tell your Moms what I said." He repeated. This time I got up and went to do as I was told. When I looked back at Phee, he was watching me walk away. No doubt, he had the same thing on his mind as I did. I felt kind of guilty cause Daddy was unconscious and I still was thinking about getting bent over and pounded. Quietly I pushed open the door to room 229, I waved for my Mom to come outside.

"What's wrong?" She asked when she stepped into the hallway.

"It's almost 10 o'clock Mommy." I told her something that I was sure she was aware of already.

"I know, Grandma Pearl is gonna drop y'all off at home, then she's coming back here." Mommy said.

"Mom, Pharaoh is still here. He's in the waiting area. He told me to let you know he'll drop us off and take everybody to school in the morning too."

"He's *still* here?" Mommy looked really surprised and impressed at the same time. She started walking down the hallway towards the waiting room. Phee was sitting where I left him a second ago. He stood up when he saw us walking over to him.

Mommy gave him a hug. I just watched. "Thank you for sticking around Pharaoh." Mommy said.

"No Problem, I didn't wanna leave until I told you how sorry I am about your husband. I hope everything is okay." Phee told my Mom.

"Well thank you, again." She smiled at him.

"If you need anything just let me know. I know you probably gonna be spending some time here at the hospital until Mr. Showers recovers, so I'll help April take care of the house if you need me to." Phee volunteered.

Mommy looked at me shocked, obviously, at how polite my boyfriend was. I just smiled sheepishly. I was thrilled that he was making such a fan out of my Mom because I was gonna need permission to spend time with Phee at our new apartment.

"You are such a gentleman..." Mommy blurted out, Phee smiled at the compliment. "If you don't mind, I'd like to take you up on your offer to drop my kids off at home. They don't have to go to school tomorrow unless they want to. So you probably won't have to worry about that." She said. Pharaoh nodded, then Mommy looked at me. "It's late, but April your gonna have to make dinner. I know everyone is probably hungry..." She looked at Phee then back to me." Pharaoh is welcome to stay for dinner, too." She added.

"Okay." I quickly responded before she could change her mind.

"I'll go pull the car around to the front door, April." Phee pulled out his keys. "Mrs. Showers, I'll see you later." He said to Mommy.

"You sure will." Mommy gave him another hug. "Thank you so much." She thanked him again. Phee dipped off towards the elevator, then Mommy and I walked to the door of Daddy's room. She stopped before we went inside. "April..." she looked at me, "That little boy is perfect for you. Don't let him get away!" She said sternly.

I giggled. "Oh really? I thought you wanted me to marry Calvin, so you and Mrs. Stephanie could be related." I joked trying to lighten the mood.

Mommy chuckled. "Calvin's nice but he's got a lot of growing up to do. I cant wait for your Dad to meet Pharaoh, he's gonna like him a lot." She said seemingly convinced. I didn't bother to tell her that Phee already knew who Daddy was and that they'd met before. We were about to walk inside when she stopped again, "I don't mind him being inside the house while I'm here at the hospital. Just please be responsible." She added.

"Okay." I responded, while straining to keep a straight face. I went to get my siblings so we could leave. Twenty minutes later, I opened up the back door and let everyone inside the kitchen. Pharaoh followed behind me with the big bags from McDonalds, and La La carried the sodas. We had decided in the car that it would be better to eat take-out tonight. The boys were exhausted and by the time I prepared a meal, they'd probably be knocked out in the bed already. So, hamburgers and french fries was the best remedy for our hunger pains. We sat in the kitchen and bust down all the food. No one really did any talking at all. I don't know if it was because everyone was sleepy, because of my Dad's accident or because they weren't used to being around Phee. But whatever it was, the kitchen was mad quiet. Even Cory and Carlito weren't screwing around as they usually did.

"La, can you help them get into bed while I clean up the kitchen, please?" I asked my little sister after everyone was done eating. I half expected her to say something stupid, but she didn't. She took the boys upstairs with her. I got up and started to clean up the mess that they'd left behind once they were gone.

"Phee, go wait for me in the living room. I'll be done soon." I told him while I loaded up the dishwasher. " I have to sweep and mop, your gonna be in the way."

"Aight." He left.

A second later I heard the television come to life in the next room. I finished up the kitchen then went up the back stairs to my room. The boys were already in the bed, and La La's door was closed. Inside my room, I quickly undressed and went to the bathroom to jump into the shower real quick. I washed up in record time. I threw on a pair of red silk panties and a white tank top, put my hair in a ponytail and went downstairs to get Phee. The boys were knocked out and La La was in her room for the night. I needed to release some stress.

My ass jiggled in the panties as I walked into the living room. Phee sat on the sofa watching some basketball game. I walked straight to the television and turned it off. Then I turned around to face him. Lustfully he couldn't even look me in the face, his eyes traveled up and down my body. My nipples were hard as pebbles and poked through the thin cotton fabric of the tank top.

"Come upstairs with me." I said softly walking over to where he sat. I reached out to take his hand, and then he stood and followed me upstairs. As soon as we reached my room, I gently closed the door and started to undress him down to his boxers. He sat on my bed while I neatly hung up his clothes and put them inside my closet. Afterwards, I hit the light, crawled onto my bed and slid under the covers. I didn't have to say anything, he was right behind me.

Within seconds, we were both completely naked under the sheet and blanket. My man had me pinned to the mattress and he was deep inside my love. He felt at home between my soft thighs, like there was no other place that he'd rather be. I held onto him tight, Mommy told me not to let him get away and I wouldn't. I wrapped my legs around him to hold him right there, right where I needed him most.

It was almost 4 o'clock in the morning when we stopped trying to hurt each other. Both of us were completely drained. Our bodies stuck together from all the sweet fluids that we shared with each other over the past few hours. I collapsed on top of my lover. My slick titties rested against his chest, our heartbeats both beating up-tempo rhythms, and slowly he eased himself from between my thighs. When it wasn't there anymore I felt empty, but I knew it wouldn't be too long before I got another dose.

We just laid there for a while listening to each other breathe. He held me with his hands massaging my bubble, he broke the silence first.

"I love you, April." He whispered to me in the darkness.

I closed my eyes and smiled. "I love you too."

I had him open. I knew there was nothing this boy wouldn't do for me. I wasn't sure if I was truly in love, but I did know that this was either love or the closest that I'd ever been. Another couple of Moments of silence went by before I spoke again. "Baby?" I whispered.

"Huh?" Phee sounded like he was bout to fall asleep underneath me.

"Earlier today, you seemed kinda mad about something. Was it something that I did?" I finally got the nerve to ask him again. This was something I'd been thinking about all day.

"No, it wasn't you." Phee yawned. He slid his body from under mine and lay on his side next to me.

"Then what was it?" I asked him. I positioned myself on my side so that we were face to face in the darkness.

He took a deep breath, and then spoke after a couple seconds. "Somebody stole some money from me, that's all. It had me tight at first, but I'm over it. Sorry I took it out on you." He said sleepily.

I kissed his lips. I could still taste the flavor of my syrup on his tongue. "It's okay, I was just worried that I might have did something wrong." I said quietly. His explanation lingered in my head and I couldn't resist the urge to ask more questions "How much did you lose, was it a lot?"

"A few thousand." He responded, and I wondered what a few was.

"Who stole it?" I knew I was probably pushing my luck, but what can I say, I'm nosy!

"Somebody that I call my friend." He answered quickly. Now I was confused. Phee didn't have too many friends. He had dudes that he chilled with from his hood but he only had a handful of close dudes he called friends. He wrapped his arms around me and hugged me.

"I don't understand, Babe. Why would one of your friends take something from you? If they asked, you'd give it to them, right?" After it left my mouth, I realized how naïve it sounded.

"Baby, the type of life I live loyalty and trust don't come very easy. Just cause a nigga is my friend doesn't mean he won't get jealous and try to take what's mine." He said.

"Soooo… what you gonna do about it?" I asked

"Nothing. Keep him close to me. Cause now he's not just my friend, but he's my enemy too." Phee said to me. This shit puzzled the hell out of me so I decided to drop it. Maybe it was one of those things that I just wouldn't understand. "April, one thing you should know is that I'm not gonna be around forever. I'm eighteen years old playing a grown man's game. The money is good, and everybody knows my name. But eventually, I'm going to end up like Vance. *Dead*."

I gasped. "Why would you say something like that, Pharaoh," I sat up in the bed, I was pissed off that he would even try to predict some shit like that.

"Because, it's the life I live. Everybody in the city think one of my homies took a contract to murder Vance. Nobody from Cedar Springs killed Vance; his best friend killed him for that money. Outta all the enemies he got, one of his friends pulled the trigger. Now we at war with the same nigga who killed him, cause he tryna cover up the role he played by pointing the finger at me and my team. And if that's not enough, now I got a jealous nigga in my circle stealing money from me. So what do I do, April? Kill my friends or my enemies? If I focus on my enemies, who's gonna protect me from my friends? See baby, when you look at me, you see me in a different light than the niggas in the streets. You can't see the big bulls eye on my back. I'm a moving target, everyone waiting for me to slip up. They waiting for me to get gunned down or go to prison so they can try to live my life." Phee rolled over turning his back to me. I wrapped my arm around him and started running my fingers thru his pubic hairs.

"That's why I want you to go to college. You smarter than you think, Pharaoh..." I kissed the back of his neck.

"I told you I would think about it." He whispered.

"What's there to think about, you got niggas trying to kill you, and friends you can't trust? It seem like you'd be smart enough to make the decision to stop doing whatever it is you into. What about me? What will I do without you?" I asked him trying to make him think.

"You gonna cry for a couple days and move on." Pharaoh answered quickly. I opened my mouth to respond but I couldn't find any words. His response cut me deep, probably cause what he said had already proven to be true by losing Darrell. The difference is, I didn't *love* Darrell, but I love Phee. It hurt me to know that this was how he felt, but I didn't know what to do to change his opinion.

"It won't be as easy as you make it sound." This was all I could say, and I hoped that it would be enough. I wrapped my fingers around his manhood and fell asleep with it in my hand. It was mine, it belonged to me and we both knew it.

CHAPTER THIRTY-TWO

The next morning my alarm clock finally did its job for the first time in months, it woke me up. Unfortunately, today was the one day that I didn't need it to. Pharaoh didn't even budge. I climbed over him to turn it off, that's when I noticed that he was rock hard. I looked at it, then, I looked at him lying there still asleep. A chill hit me as I caught a flashback from last night and instantly my nipples got stiff. I knew what needed to be done so I did my job. I straddled him with my eyes still half closed from exhaustion, and in one swift motion, our bodies came together like a puzzle. Pharaoh woke up with a grin; it turned into a look of pleasure mixed with pain. Eleven minutes later he was back to sleep.

I put some pajamas on and tip toed out my bedroom to see what was going on around the house. La La's door was still closed. I couldn't hear any music, which was a good sign. When I got to the end of the hallway I peeked into Cory and Carlito's room. Both of them were awake. Each lying in their separate bunk bed talking quietly.

"Good morning." I pushed open the door just a little. They stopped whispering and looked over at me standing in the doorway.

"Good morning." Both of them responded quietly, I checked them out. They were both still under the covers. I wondered what they were just talking about.

"Is Daddy better yet?" Cory asked me. They both stared with eyes wide-open waiting for my answer. I wished that I had some good news to share with them but I didn't.

I tried to smile and appear optimistic "I'm sure he's doing a lot better, baby. When Mommy calls me I'll let you know, okay?" I answered his question the best I could. Cory nodded.

"How long is he gonna be in the hospital?" My youngest brother Carlito asked. Lito's eyes were lit up with question marks, and I knew for sure that I didn't have *any* of the answers.

"Don't know Lito. Shouldn't be long though. He'll be better soon." I said trying to believe my own words. I decided to switch the subject. " What do y'all wanna eat? I'm 'bout to go down and make breakfast."

"French Toast!"

"Pancakes!"

They both shouted out their choices, "Aight. French Toast for Lito, and Pancakes for you, Cory." I winked at them and started to pull the door back closed. "I'll be done by about 8 o'clock. Keep the noise down and stay out the hallway cause La is still sleep." I gave them a warning look as I closed the door.

I went into the bathroom to brush my teeth and wash my face real quick. When I was done, I peeled off my pajama's to inspect my body in the big mirror. There were passion marks all over my skin. I'm a high yellow bitch so all the red blemishes really stood out. Phee had marked up both my titties, stomach, inside of my thighs, my butt and the back of my neck. I wasn't worried cause none of them were visible with my clothes on except the back of my neck. But when I let my hair down, even that one was impossible to see. Most importantly, my birth control patch was still in place. Which was a relief, because we hadn't used not one condom all night. And I'm sure at this Moment I had enough sperm inside me to be impregnated with quintuplets, at the least. To be honest, I didn't even feel the same anymore. I felt like a grown ass woman! I had just spent the entire night getting my insides stretched out by a young, fly, hustler who I could call my own. He did my young body good. Somehow, he'd managed to make me cum in every position. Just the thoughts of him lying in my bed right now butt naked, made me want to cream my pajama pants. Now I understood how some good pipe could fuck with a bitch's brain. That Cedar Springs dick was the reason why Asia was always grinning at 2:20 on her way to Cam's house. And willing to wait on the corner in the cold to be dug out. I could finally sympathize with my home girl. A good nut is addictive, and I finally found the one who could duplicate that good feeling between my thighs.

I slid downstairs to the kitchen and prepared to make breakfast for everyone. I could cook my ass off. Mommy started teaching me when I was like six years old. Spanish food, Italian food and soul food I could make it all with no problem. Breakfast food was the easiest. I bust out the frying pans and set up shop. Luckily, we had the right ingredients for me to make what everyone liked.

Thirty-five minutes, later I was pretty much finished. Pancakes, French toast, Waffles, Scrambled eggs, Sausage links and grits. I was in the middle of making some orange juice when the kitchen door swung open, then up and in walks Mommy. If I could see my own reflection in a mirror, I knew I had the look of a deer caught in somebody's headlights. I was expecting a phone call, not a guest appearance.

"Smells good. Looks like I'm right on time." Mommy smiled, she closed the door behind her. She had this real slick smirk on her face.

"Hi, Mommy." I forced a nervous smile. "You hungry?" I searched her face for any sign of aggression. There was none. Either she had a mean poker face or she hadn't seen the Q45 in the driveway. Since I knew damn well she wasn't blind, I braced myself for an ass whooping.

"Starving, I haven't eaten since yesterday." Mommy said taking off her coat. When she walked behind me, I got nervous and flinched a little bit. I was expecting her to slap the shit outta me.

"Did Daddy wake up yet?" I asked quickly. "I've been waiting for you to call me." I looked over my shoulder as she stood behind me with her back leaned against the island counter. I finished stirring up the orange juice and put the top back on the pitcher.

"No. Not yet. He's unconscious still, but they say he's getting more stable. He's gonna be going into another surgery this afternoon. He's in bad shape, April. His back, hip and legs are gonna need a lot of rehab and therapy for him to walk again." Mommy spoke softly probably cause she didn't know if the boys were asleep or not. I didn't know how to respond, so I just nodded so she knew that I understood. My Dad was strong, I was sure that he would be back to normal. At least I hoped he would. I couldn't see him being pushed around in a wheel chair for the rest of his life. The thought of that instantly made me sad. My feelings must have showed on the outside because Mommy stepped over to hug me.

"Try not to worry. Your Dad's been through worst. He's been shot, stabbed, once he almost even drowned. A little car accident won't stop him." Mommy chuckled. It was obvious to me that just like me, she was over the initial shock of the accident. She seemed very different than she had yesterday when she cried for six or seven hour's straight.

She let me go, stepped back against the counter and crossed her arms against her chest. "Pharaoh's car is outside. Where is he?" The way she asked the question I knew it was a set- up. I couldn't believe that I'd been so stupid to let him spend the night. But I honestly didn't think Mommy would come home so early, especially without calling first. She was looking at me waiting for an answer. I don't know if I was more embarrassed or terrified to tell her that he was asleep in my bed. In all actuality, I shouldn't be either because she's the one who put me on birth control. So basically, she gave me the green light to have sex, right?

"When we got back last night, it was late. He fell asleep..."

"On the sofa?" Mommy asked with her eyebrows raised.

I could've lied and said yes, but something told me she wasn't going for it. Plus, it wouldn't be too difficult for her to bust me out in my lie. Then things would get violent real quick and I'd be at the hospital in the room next to Daddy.

"Not exactly on the sofa..." I said softly, almost a whisper. I was looking at the tiles on the floor, cause I couldn't look her in the face. I just hoped that she wouldn't beat me up too bad. I never had a black eye before and it wasn't something that I was looking forward to. I couldn't go to school tomorrow looking like I'd just come off the set of the Jerry Springer Show.

"April..." my Mom looked at me in utter amazement "When I said he could be here when I'm gone, I didn't mean let him spend the night in your bed." Mommy rolled her eyes at me. "Are you at least wearing your birth control patch?"

"Yes." I was relieved that for once I had the right answer to one of her questions. Surprisingly, she didn't look like she was thinking 'bout hitting me. But I was still on my toes, just in case I needed to duck, bob or weave.

Mommy just shook her head. She walked towards the stairs.
"Next time, at least make him park somewhere besides the driveway. You know Mrs. Stephanie is nosy as hell." She said over her shoulder. "I'm gonna take a shower and change before I go back to the hospital. Hurry up and fix the plates so we can eat breakfast." She added as she disappeared upstairs.

She left me in the kitchen without any bumps or bruises. I was shocked; I couldn't wait to tell Nica this shit! First, I quickly fixed Pharaoh a plate and slipped up the front steps to my bedroom. This boy was still asleep. I rolled my eyes. Mommy could've been beating my ass down in the kitchen and he would've been no help at all.

"Baby..." I whispered, sitting on the edge of the bed I held the plate and rubbed his cheek with my other hand.

"Huh?" He answered sleepily opening his eyes.

"Mommy's home."

"Oh, shit!" Phee sat up straight like he was looking for somewhere to hide.

"She already knows you're in here..." I told him. Now he really looked scared. "It's okay, she's not mad. Here..." I handed him the plate, then realized I forgot to bring him some juice. "She 'bout to leave soon, but just stay here until she gone." I kissed his lips before heading to the door." And put some clothes on, just in case she come in here." I closed the door and walked down the hall. La La was in the family room on the computer already at only 8 o'clock in the morning.

"La La, come downstairs and eat." I said from the doorway.

"What did you make?" She asked looking up from the computer screen. She was still wearing her pajamas and a scarf on her head that covered up her long hair.

"Breakfast." I said rolling my eyes with a sarcastic smile.

"Duh! What tho?"

"Come and see." I walked off to get my brothers. La La was right on my heels. One thing about my little sister, she was never one to be late for any meals. At the end of the hall the boys bedroom door was open. The two of them were on the floor playing with their wrestling action figures. "Hey babies. The food's ready." I stopped at the door. They both jumped to their little feet and broke for the door to run past me. This must be how Mr. C felt last period when the student's bum rushed him to get out his class. I caught Carlito by the back of his t-shirt and pulled him into my arms.

"Ahhh!" He yelled while laughing

I planted a kiss on his nose. "Thanks for being quiet for me while I got breakfast ready." I let him go.

"You welcome." He said taking off after Cory to the stairs. I followed behind them to the kitchen. By the time I got there, La La was making her plate already. I fixed both the boys plate then made my own. Upstairs I could hear

Mommy cut on the shower. I wondered what was going on in her mind. She'd been way too calm earlier about the whole Phee spending the night thing. It kinda scared me a little that she didn't even pop me in the forehead one good time. Mommy was getting soft.

When everyone was done eating, as usual they scattered and left me to clean up the mess. I coulda made La La do the dishes, but I was in a sorta good mood. I couldn't wait for Mommy to leave so I could go back up to my room and get another good pounding.

She came down the stairs a few minutes later while I was sweeping the floor. She looked around for a second, then at me. I noticed the duffle bag that she sat on one of the chairs. It looked like she'd be gone for the rest of the day.

"I'm not even gonna ask you if you can run the house while I'm gone, cause I know you can..." Mommy said as she walked over to the stove where I had her plate covered and waiting. She picked it up and went to sit down. "I'm about to make my 9 o'clock class. Afterwards, I'm going back to the hospital. I'll be there for the rest of the night..." She said in between bites of her french toast. I finished sweeping, rinsed my hands and went to the refrigerator to get her some orange juice. "So, you've gotta take care of La La and the boys. You already know what they can and can't do. If they give you a problem, slap them."

"Oh, you know my hand stay ready, Mommy. I got my slappin' skills from you." We both laughed as I put a glass of juice in front of her plate.

"April, don't kill none of my babies." Mommy grinned at me.

"I won't Ma. I'll take care of everything here. You go take care of Daddy." I pulled up the stool next to her and rested my elbows on the island counter top.

Mommy exhaled, "Deal." She dropped her fork and gave me a high five and a wink. I chilled while she finished up her breakfast. When she was done, I cleared away her dishes while she put on her coat to get out the door in time.

"Oh, Mommy." I blurted out. I'd almost forgot.

"Huh?" She turned as she approached the door and dug into her purse.

"I gotta leave La La here with the boys for a couple hours, while I'm at the hair salon. Is that okay?" I asked.

"That's fine." She said pulling out a folded sheet of paper from her purse. She handed me the paper then opened the door to leave out the house. "Tell Pharaoh, if he's going to lay up in my house it's fine with me. But, he's gonna contribute. Ain't no grown man sleeping here for free." Mommy smirked; she walked out and closed the door behind her. I opened the paper, it was a long ass-shopping list full of all types of shit that we needed around the house. I didn't know what to think. Mommy always knew how to get the last laugh. I couldn't help but giggle. This lady was pimping me out to Phee! Using my peach to make him spend for her expenses. Only in America.

I took the list upstairs to my boyfriend. When I opened my bedroom door Pharaoh was sitting on my bed watching TV. "She left already?" He asked me as I closed the door behind me. I nodded at him. "You *sure* she not mad? I don't want ya Moms to stop liking me..." he looked so worried.

"Trust me. She's not mad, Pharaoh." I giggled tossing him her shopping list. As he unfolded the paper, I began to undress down to my birthday suit. As he read the list with a puzzled look, I walked over to him butt naked and climbed on his lap. "Didn't you tell her to let you know if she needed anything?" I whispered in his ear.

"I know. But damn April..."

"Damn what?" I snatched the list from him and tossed it onto my nightstand then pushed him onto his back. He didn't respond, too busy tryna unbuckle his pants. "Damn what?" I repeated leaning over him with my titties in his face.

"Nothing..." he mumbled seemingly distracted. Phee tried to dip into my cookie jar; I raised my hips and moved out his reach. He tried to pull me back down onto him, and I slapped his hands from my waist. "What baby?" he asked desperately. The look on his face let me know how badly he needed me.

"Are you gonna make sure my Mom gets everything on that list?" I asked quietly.

"Yeah." He answered quickly.

"That's all I wanted to know." I lowered myself onto him slowly, and then watched Phee's eyes roll back in his head. The mounting pleasure soon became visible on my baby's face. "It'll be worth it. I promise." I whispered. Then I used my hips to rock us both into frenzy. After he let me have my way, he turned me over onto my stomach and killed it.

Before I knew it, 2 o'clock had slipped up on me. Pharaoh and I were parked on Main Street outside of Hair Creations Salon. As always, he was giving me instructions, the usual. Answer the phone when he calls. Call him before I leave the salon, for any reason. Don't embarrass him. Blah, Blah, Blah. I'd memorized all his rules by heart. So far, I hadn't broke any. Not cause I was scared of him, but out of the respect that I had for him.

"Bae, you don't gotta tell me these things *every*day. I know what I'm supposed to do. I know what I'm not supposed to do. You make me feel like you don't got any faith in me when you repeat yourself." I said starting to get irritated.

He stared at me for a second, then leaned over and kissed my cheek. "Well, I'm glad you know *everything*. So I shouldn't have to worry about any excuses, right?" He smiled at me knowing he was starting to get on my nerves.

"Bye, Pharaoh." I reached for the door handle.

"Call me when you leave. Call me when you get in the house." Phee said as I stepped out the Infiniti and into the cold.

I just rolled my eyes at him, "Yes, *Daddy*." I responded sarcastically before slamming his door shut. He hated when I did that. I couldn't see his face behind the tinted windows. But I got a little satisfaction out of knowing that it pissed him off. Quickly, I switched my ass into the salon before he had a chance to roll down the window and say something stupid. When I was safely inside, I turned and smiled as he pulled off from the curb.

"Hey ladies!" I greeted everyone inside the salon. I got a chorus of hello's hi's and hey's plus some smiles in return. I went to the back room to put away my coat and purse, grabbed my smock and headed out to check in with Natalie. When I tapped my smock pocket and realized I'd left my phone inside my coat pocket, I doubled back to get it. Pharaoh would have a fucking heart attack if he called twice in a row and I didn't answer. I giggled at the thought of him speeding through traffic from across town to get here and make sure I was all right.

"Hi cutie. How did your special day turn out?" Ms. Natalie asked when I finally made it over to her station.

"Not too good." I answered.

Ms. Natalie frowned, "Aww, what happened? Is Pharaoh okay? He just dropped you off didn't he?" Ms. Nat looked concerned; she stopped working on her customer and looked at me.

"Ms. Nat, Phee's fine…" I assured her. "It's my Dad. He got into a car accident yesterday…"

"On the 33 expressway?" She asked looking very sympathetic.

I nodded. "Yeah."

"Oh sweetie, I'm so sorry. I didn't know that was your father. How is he?" She asked sincerely.

I sensed the customer in Ms. Nat's chair straining to listen to our conversation so I kept vague. "He's okay, he's hanging in there for the most part." I answered. Just as I thought, the woman was on some nosy shit and chose this exact time to butt into the conversation.

"Ummm, Natalie I saw that on the news last night. That was one *bad* accident! A couple people got hurt *really* bad. One guy flew through his windshield, they say he may be *paralyzed*." The nosey woman voluntarily blurted out.

I just stared at this bitch. I could feel my entire face catching fire and turning red. Nobody asked her for her input on the topic. I really wanted to put my hands on her, but right now all I could think about was Daddy. For the past sixteen hours, Pharaoh had kept me distracted from the reality of what had happened to my father. Now I was stuck, the word *paralyzed* slapped me in the face like a ton of bricks.

My eyes started to gloss over but I could see Ms. Natalie shoot her customer a real nasty look. "April, baby you shouldn't be here. Call Phee to come get you." Ms. Natalie said quietly. I nodded as my eyes teared up, and then I quickly ran off to the back room.

Behind me, I heard Ms. Natalie go off, "Noreen, *why* would you say some dumb shit like that? Nobody asked you anything, next time I'm talking to one of my girls, don't say *shit*!" I overheard this as I stepped into the employee room and closed the door. I pulled out my phone to call Phee.

"Hello?" He answered on the first ring.

"Boo, I need you to come get me." I was in tears by now.

There was a slight pause. "You where I dropped you off at?" he asked.

"Yes." I was sniffling and wiping back tears.

"Are you safe?" He asked cautiously.

"Yes."

"I'm on my way right now, don't move." Phee hung up. I took off my smock, put back on my coat and grabbed my purse. I knew he'd be here in less than a few minutes. On my way out I bumped into Lauren, literally, as she came in to check on me.

"A, I heard what happened..." she gave me a hug, "I'm sorry, let me know if I can do anything."

"Alright." Was all I said in response? I was ready to get outta there, and soon as she let me go I jetted outside to wait for Phee. Just like I knew he would, he pulled right up.

"What's wrong? Why you crying? Somebody hurt 'chu?" he had jumped out the Infiniti and was towering over me with a serious ass look on his face.

"No." I said answering only the last of the three questions. He was just standing there while the wind whipped across my face. "Bae, I'm cold, can you open the door, please??" I asked with both hands inside the pockets of my new North Face jacket.

He did as I asked. Once I was inside, he told me to sit tight for a minute then dipped off into the hair salon. I shook my head watching him walk off; I hoped he wouldn't do anything to that old ass woman for making me cry.

When he got back into the car a couple minutes later, I had pretty much regained my composure. Not because I wasn't still an emotional wreck, but 'cause I didn't want him to see me break down. He didn't say anything; he just put his hand on the top of my head and ran his fingers through my hair. I hit the button to recline my seat a little, then put my head back against the headrest.

"Bae, can you take me to the hospital? I wanna see my Daddy." I whispered with my eyes closed. I felt like shit, my priorities were fucked up. I needed to be making sure my Dad was okay. For all I knew, Mommy could be trying to sugar coat things so it wouldn't sound so bad. She did say he would need some rehab to walk, but it was that word paralyze that the nosey bitch used that made me shiver.

"Yeah." Phee said putting the car in gear. We drove the entire 15 minutes to ECMC in silence, well besides the sound of my sniffles here and there. I needed to blow my damn nose.

When we pulled up, Phee parked in front of the main entrance and looked over at me. "Do you need me to walk you inside? I cant' stay 'cause I got sumthin' that needs to be done. Plus, I'm gonna go to the store and get the stuff ya Moms need. I'll be back in a few hours, unless you call me before then." He leaned over to kiss me.

I shook my head. " I'm fine. Take care of your business. Don't worry 'bout the shopping list we can do that later." I said between our kisses. "I love you, Pharaoh."

"Love you too." He gave me one last kiss before I got out and headed into the hospital. When I got upstairs to the second floor nurses station, it was the same nurse that had been working last night. She smiled as I approached. I guess she remembered me too.

"Hi there…" she said real enthusiastic like, "You here to see your Dad?" She asked. Fortunately, I was able to refrain from rolling my eyes at this stupid ass question. I even stopped myself from saying something dumb like, *no Bitch, I came to see you!*

"Yes." I forced a smile 'cause I didn't wanna be disrespectful. After all, this was one of the nurses who looked after my Dad. If I gave her an attitude, she may take it out on him.

"Go ahead inside sweetheart." She nodded down the hall towards Daddy's room.

"Thanks." I replied, and then took off in that direction. I pushed open the door to room 229 expecting to see both Mommy and Grandma Pearl. Instead, Daddy was alone. I checked my Rolex; it was almost 2:30. Mommy was probably on her way, so I hurried over to my Dad's bed and sat next to him on one of the chairs. It was hard for me to look at him, and my tears quickly came back. Part of his face was swollen; he had mad scrapes and bruises all over it. A plastic tube went into his nostrils, another one attached to his arm. His eyes were closed, but his breathing was slow but steady.

"Hey Daddy..." I said not knowing if he could hear me or not. I took his hand and held it. I kinda felt stupid. I'd seen way too many movies where this exact scene had played out. I felt like an idiot trying to talk to him, like there was something I could say to make him wake up. So, I just kept it short and simple, "I love you Daddy. We all love you. Mommy still loves you too. I can't wait until you get better." I said quietly and left it like that. If there was a chance that he could hear me, I knew he wouldn't care if I said anything at all. He was just happy that I was here. Same way he'd be here for me.

It wasn't too long before Mommy poked her head into the room; maybe twenty minutes had gone by. I knew she wasn't too far away because I peeped her duffle bag under Daddy's bed.

"Hey baby. What're you doin' here?" She was obviously surprised to see me. She walked over and sat down next to me, she was staring at me real intensely, like she does when she's trying to read my thoughts. Mommy reached over to wipe away one of my tear smudges. It's a good thing I don't wear make-up or I'd look like a hot mess right now.

"I came to check on Dad." I replied, not that it was a question that I feel really deserved an answer. I had the right to be here too.

"That's obvious, April. But *why*? What happened?" She asked. I didn't really know how to take this. Why did she automatically assume that something had happened to make me come here? Then I started to feel even worst, more tears came. 'Cause I realized that if it wasn't for the nosey bitch and her dumb ass comment, I *wouldn't* be here.

I told her 'bout the nosey old bitch at the hair salon, and what she'd said that made me feel bad. Mommy wrapped her arms around me.

"Baby, your Dad isn't gonna be paralyzed. His spine is okay. But he has many broken bones and it's going to take some time for them to heal. He has a serious concussion, and some fractures to his skull. But he doesn't seem to have any brain damage. Like I told you earlier, he's in bad shape right now. But, he's not going to die or anything like that. It's just going to take a long time for him to get back to normal." Mommy said as she held me close. "Okay?"

"Mmm. Hmm."

"Feel better?" She asked.

"Are you just saying this to make me feel better? Or is it the truth, 'cause I'll go ask the nurse myself, Mommy." I was dead serious, "I'm not La La, and you don't have to lie to me." I added.

Mommy paused before answering. "April, I'm sure they have room for another patient in this hospital. Don't make me hurt you in here, you're not too grown to get your ass whooped." Mommy tapped me lightly on the back of the head.

"I wasn't tryna be disrespectful-"

"When I tell you something, don't *ever* question me." She interjected. Mommy had gotten her point across, and that was the end of that. She wasn't the type to dwell on her words, that conversation was over. I got quiet, and then decided to switch the topic.

"Ma, where's Grandma?" I asked. A couple seconds went by before I spoke.

"She left already. She was here this morning while I was at school. She'll be back tomorrow morning. We just ate lunch together, that's where I was when you showed up." Mom explained.

"Oh."

"And you..." Mommy squeezed me. " You can't stay too long, because the longer you're here, the longer La La has to be at home with my babies. And we both know, that'll only go smooth for but so long. Right?"

"Yeah," I giggled. "La La will lock them in the basement and starve them as soon as they get on her nerves!" We both laughed.

I chilled with Mommy up until 4 o'clock then I said goodbye. I kissed Daddy and went down to the lobby to call Phee so he could come get me. He didn't answer cause the call went straight to his voice mail. For some reason his phone was turned off, which was strange. I tried again, and still got voice mail. The battery had to be dead cause Pharaoh never turned off this phone. The only people who had the number was me, his Mom, his sister and well my Mom had it too, only because I'd given it to her. I dug through my purse to find the number for his other phone, the one his boys called him on. Just so happens that the call went straight to his voicemail too.

Now I stood in the lobby of the hospital contemplating my next move. First, I covered my tracks. I called his private number and left a message. Then I called his Mom.

"Hi, Mrs. Green." I said after she'd answered the phone.

"Hey April. What's up?" Mrs. Green sounded like she was in a pretty good mood.

"Nothing much. I'm trying to find your son. Have you spoken to him in the past couple hours?"

"Nope. Sorry, I haven't. Yesterday's the last time I seen him or spoken to him. He got that new apartment, now he don't know how to act." His Mom chuckled. "Is everything okay?" Her voice suddenly began to sound concerned.

"I hope so. I tried to call but couldn't reach him. He's supposed to pick me up from ECMC-"

"April, what you doing at the hospital?" She wanted to know.

"Phee didn't tell you my Dad was in an accident?"

"No."

It didn't surprise me at all that he didn't. He wasn't the type to volunteer information. He probably figured if I wanted his Mom to know, I'd tell her myself. So I did, I told her what happened.

"Oh, April, I'm *so* sorry to hear that."

"It's okay Mrs. Green, he's gonna be fine." I said quickly 'cause I didn't really wanna even think about it right at this Moment. I'd cried enough for one day. "But, if you do talk to him, just please let him know I called." I switched the subject back to Phee.

"Do you need me to come pick you up?"

"No, It's okay. My Mom's here. Thank you anyway." I responded. We both said goodbye and hung up. I started to go back upstairs to tell my Mom she had to take me home. But I didn't want her asking me gazillion questions, so I called a taxi. I didn't call one of the ghetto ass services. I called the airport limousine service that Phee made me promise to use if I ever had an emergency. I was under very strict orders never to ride any public transportation or use a cab that wasn't a black Lincoln Town car.

While I waited for my driver to show up, I kept trying Phee's cellular phone. *Nothing.* Now I was starting to get a little worried. What if something happened to my baby? I should've asked him where he was going before I got out the car. I had no clue where he might be right now. Finally, the car service arrived and I was on my way home. When I got there, I paid the driver, gave him a tip and headed inside. It had already started to get dark outside, although it was only a little after 5 o'clock.

*   *   *   *   *

By 9:30 pm, I was sick. He hadn't called or showed up. I'd already called Mrs. Green back, *twice.* She hadn't seemed too devastated, which really irritated me. I'd already made dinner, everyone had eaten and the boys were in bed. La, as always was on the computer doing whatever it was that she does on there.

When the house phone rang, I didn't move. People had been calling all damn day asking questions about Daddy. I was tired of giving the same answers repeatedly. It rang again, still I didn't move. Three times back to back and I didn't budge. I was lying on my bed reading the new Vibe magazine, my television was on BET but I wasn't paying any attention to it. As far as I was concerned, everyone who I talked to regularly had my cell number. Tonight, I didn't feel like being bothered with anyone else.

My nose was still in the magazine ten minutes later when my cell phone rang. I didn't recognize the number but answered anyway, I hoped it was Pharaoh.

"Hello?" I answered quickly.

"April, this Xavier. Where you at?" Phee's best friend asked.

"*Why*?" I asked him. This nigga was not my man or my Daddy. And he was sounding *way* too aggressive right now.

"Phee looking for you." He said.

Something wasn't right. "Pharaoh knows how to get in touch wit' me." I replied.

"He just called you at home. You not there, so where are you?" Xavier asked again. Damn, I wondered if that was Phee, who just called the house phone but still wasn't about to answer any of Xavier's questions.

"Tell him to call my cell-"

"He *can't*, he's locked up-"

"He's *what*?" My heart skipped a beat, as I sat up and swung my legs over the edge of my bed. Instinctively, my mind flashed to the instructions Phee had given me in case this ever happened.

"Phee got arrested. You got his bail money right?" Xavier asked. Now my head was spinning, I did have some of Phee's money hid away in case he got in trouble. But I wasn't 'bout to tell Xavier shit, cause that wasn't his business.

"I know what to do. Thanks for calling, Xavier." I was about to hang up, but he called out to stop me.

"*Whoa*! April, I'm about to come get you so we can go pay the bail bondsman-"

"Xavier, I'm not going *any*where with you. I already know what I'm supposed to do. But thanks for your help though, I'll talk to you later." I hung up on him.

I knew damned well Phee didn't tell that fool to come pick me up, he must think I'm stupid or something. Niggas be thinking they slick. First, I called downtown to Central Booking to see if Phee was *really* locked up. He was. Next, I called the number for the lawyer that Pharaoh had given me in case this ever happened. It turned out that he wouldn't be arraigned until tomorrow morning, and he couldn't find out the charges 'til then. Then, I called the bail bondsman to make some pre arrangements.

    Now, I was really stressed. The two men I loved were both in bad situations and it was nothing I could do to help either of them. I turned off the television and the light. I curled up under the covers hoping that my boyfriend would call back. Then, I cried myself to sleep while I waited.

CHAPTER THIRTY-THREE

The next morning I was up super early. I had shit to do, and my Boo needed me to take care of business. By 7:20, I had the boys up and dressed. I fed them, then stood outside in the cold while we waited for their bus to show up. They only rode the yellow school bus on special occasions, usually only when Mommy didn't have to go to class and she didn't feel like driving them. Once they were gone, I went back inside to check on my sister.

La La's door was closed and the music was blasting. Even if I knocked, she wouldn't hear me. So I did what Mommy was known for, I walked right in. This fool still wasn't dressed yet, and she was sitting on her bed fidgeting around with some shoelaces. Two pair of Nike's lay on the floor next to her feet. Neither of them had any laces in them. I walked over to turn off her stereo.

"La La, if you not dressed in ten minutes, I'ma kick your ass. Try me." I told her very calmly before leaving out and closing her door behind me. I walked back down the hall to my room and went into my closet. I climbed up the small stepladder that I used to reach the top two shelves and pushed up the corner tile of my ceiling. This was my secret hiding spot. There were three zip lock freezer bags stashed on top of the tiles on my ceiling. Each had $10,000 inside. The money was Pharaoh's, and it was only for emergencies. I took one of the bags down, and then put the tile back in place, I needed five grand to give his lawyer, Andrew Lotempio. The other five grand I'd take to cover the bail bond, although I probably wouldn't need the whole five. Unless, God forbid this boy had fucked around and killed someone. If that turned out to be the case, he could probably forget about a bail all together.

I put the cash inside of my black Coach bag and put on my matching black DKNY leather winter coat. I wore some ash grey denim jeans, grey and black wool turtleneck and matching shoe boots. The driver for the car service should be on his way any minute. I wanted to be gone before Mommy showed up; one thing for sure was I wasn't going to school today.

It was a miracle that La La didn't make me go upside her damn head. She was dressed and ready when I walked past her room. Not long after we got downstairs, the driver blew the horn from the driveway.

"C'mon La La." I said when I looked out the window and saw the black Town car. We walked out into the cold.

"I thought Pharaoh was taking us?" La La asked suspiciously.

"He had something to do." I answered, while I locked the door behind us. The middle aged white man already had the back door open for us when we walked down the stairs.

"Good morning, Ladies." He said cheerfully.

"Good morning." La La and I replied in unison. Once we were seated, the driver closed the door.

"I could get used to this." La La looked at me and smiled.

"I bet you could." We both laughed. The driver got behind the wheel and backed out the driveway, and then I told him where we were going. La had no clue I was going downtown to the County Court building. That girl couldn't keep a secret to save her life. As we pulled off down the street, I saw Calvin stepping outside onto his porch. He watched as the shiny black Lincoln rode by his house, and I could only imagine what was on his mind.

After we dropped La La off at school, I gave the driver the real destination. It was just barely 8 o'clock; the court proceedings didn't start until 9 o'clock so I had him stop at the McDonalds drive-thru first 'cause I was hungry. The lawyer's office was only a block from the court building inside the Statler Towers, the driver pulled up in front and I told him to wait for me.

The foyer of the office building was huge. Businessmen in suites, ties and overcoats were hustling through the lobby towards the elevators carrying their briefcases. I felt out of place as I stepped onto one of the cars and pressed the button for the seventh floor. The small square shaped space was stuffed with people, all looking at me like the only stranger.

I was glad when I got off a found Andrew Lotempio's office. I pulled open one of the double glass doors that led into the suite of the Law Firm. This joint was plush. I mean, it looked like the president of the United States could do business here. Everything was trimmed in gold, everything! There was a pretty receptionist sitting at a long gold desk a couple yards from the doors.

"Hi, can I help you?" She asked with a smile. The lady looked to be in her late twenties, she kinda looked like the daughter from the Soprano's.

"Yes, I'm here to see Mr. Lotempio. He's expecting me." I said, trying to sound as mature as possible.

"Are you a client?" The woman opened up a book that looked like a calendar of appointments.

"No, I'm here for Pharaoh Green."

Her eyes lit up. "Oh my God! Are you Pharaoh's girlfriend?" Suddenly her professional body language went out the window. She spoke as if she knew my baby personally.

"Yes."

"It's so nice to meet you..." she stood up and extended her hand for me to shake. "...I'm Carmelita Lotempio. I'm the lawyer's niece, I've known Phee forever, our family's go back a long way. My Mom and his Mom are friends, and both teachers at the same school. *And*, before Pharaoh got so grown, I used to babysit him for extra money. I remember when he used to wet the bed." Carmelita told me with a grin. We both laughed. Shit, I remember when Phee made *me* wet the bed. But I kept that to myself.

I gave her a smile, "I didn't know that, my name's April. Nice to meet you." I said politely.

"It is. Too bad it's under these circumstances," she walked from behind her desk and down the hall. She motioned for me to follow her, so I did. She stopped at a huge office at the end of the hall. The door was open, but she still knocked. "Uncle Andy, this is April. She's here to see you about Pharaoh."

The short Italian man walked towards the door wearing a blue pinstriped three-piece suit. "Okay, please come in, April." He said with a smile. Carmelita turned and left us in privacy. I stepped into the office and he shook my hand. "Your gorgeous, I see the kid has good taste like his Dad, and uncles." He grinned at me.

"Thank you." I gushed at the compliment. Andrew Lotempio reminded me of one of them slick talking Italian gangsters from the movies. He dressed like them and his hair was slicked back like an old La Costra Nostra Mobster.

"Have a seat, this will be quick." He took a seat behind his desk and motioned for me to sit in one of the big ass leather chairs in front of it. This joint felt like I was sitting on a cloud, I wonder how much a chair like this cost.

"Okay, first things first. I made a couple calls this morning. He's being held on illegal firearm possession charges. He was pulled over during a routine traffic stop. The police smelled marijuana and searched his vehicle, they found a loaded .40 caliber handgun." The lawyer said.

I scrunched up my face. "Pharaoh doesn't even smoke marijuana, at all." I told him. On the other hand, he did ride with the handgun at all times. But I didn't tell him that.

"Well, whether its true or not, it's the officers word against his. But, luckily, this isn't too big a deal. He's not going to prison or anything like that. Don't worry; I'll get him probation. The bail will be low, probably $7,500 or maybe even $5,000. You pay ten percent of that with a bond. Do you know how it works?" The lawyer asked me.

"Yes. I already talked to a bondsman last night." I told him.

"Good. Then you should be able to get him released in a couple hours at the latest." He said standing up and walking around his desk. He sat on the edge of it and faced me. "I don't know if you're aware but I've known your boyfriend for his whole life. I grew up with his father Iceberg, and his Mom and my sister have been friends for years. I tried talking to him the last time I got him outta trouble, last year he was caught with a shit load of cocaine.

He got *very* lucky; I was able to get the case dismissed on a technicality. Did you know that?" He asked me.

"No, I didn't." I wondered why he was telling me this. But I was sure that I'd find out soon enough.

"He's pretty hard headed. Just like his uncle Sly. Sly's in a federal penitentiary right now, serving a life sentence for doing the same thing Pharaoh's doing right now. Did you know that?" The questions continued. Phee had told me about his uncle, but shit, everyone in Buffalo knew about his Dad's family. Sly Green was one of the most notorious drug dealers in the city's history, and he'd been the only one of the brothers to actually be convicted and sentenced to life in prison. Phee's Dad, Sylvester, or "Iceberg" had been the lucky one and been acquitted at trial.

"I know about his uncle." I answered.

"Do you love Pharaoh?"

"Yes." I didn't hesitate.

"Would you like to see him spend the rest of his life behind bars?" He asked me. This had to be a rhetorical question, how many answers could there be for this one.

"Of course not."

Mr. Lotempio looked very sincere. "Then you need to talk to him, maybe he'll listen to you. He's being watched, not *officially* under investigation, but the cops all know who's behind all the cocaine distribution in Cedar Springs. Pharaoh's the boss, and *every*one knows that. Now supposedly, there's some kind of war going on and the police want him off the street. So, they're gonna keep targeting him, and if he doesn't chill out, they'll get him, and lock him away for a *long* time. My advice is that you talk some sense into him."

"I've been trying to. And I'll do what I can, but I can't really make him do anything he doesn't want to." I answered honestly.

"He nodded. " I understand." Mr. Lotempio stood up from the edge of his desk. "Did you bring the retainer fee?"

I kinda figured he wouldn't forget to collect his money. "Yeah, I've got it." I dug into my purse and pulled out a $5,000 stack of hundred dollar bills. I handed the payment to the lawyer. He walked around to write me a receipt for the retainer.

"This is the last time I'm giving him a discount on my fee. If he wants to keep getting into trouble, he'll have to pay $10,000 just like everyone else from now on." He told me this as he gave me the pink copy of the receipt.

"I'll let him know." I said standing up. We shook hands again and we headed to the door.

"Go ahead to the court building, I'll catch up with you there around nine. It'll be real quick, he'll plead not guilty, get his bail set and be out soon after."

"Okay. Thank you Mr. Lotempio." I said leaving his office.

"Sure thing."

*   *   *   *   *

Two hours later, I was sitting inside the back of the Lincoln Town car outside of the Buffalo Holding Center. The arraignment had gone just like Mr. Lotempio said it would. Except for the fact, that Phee's bail had been set at $10,000. I gave the bail bondsman $1,000 to get him out. Now I sat outside waiting for him to be released. My Rolex said 10:40 on the dot. I was still thinking about what the lawyer had said to me in his office. There had to be some way to trick Pharaoh into investing his money and slowing down in the streets. I definitely didn't want him to go to prison. But at the same time, I'd grown accustomed to having certain things. He gave me whatever I asked for. I never had to worry bout anything, he took care of it all. If he quit hustling, would he still be able to keep me laced in all the fly shit that I liked? Or would I just go back to being a regular bitch? It was like a 'Catch 22'. One thing for sure, I deserved to have the best. Only the finer things in life for me from here on out. I was too spoiled to ever settle for anything less than how I was living right now.

My eyes lit up as I watched my baby walk out the front doors of the county jail. I stepped out the back of the luxury car and quickly walked onto the sidewalk to meet him halfway. I flashed him a big smile and jumped up into his arms.

"You did good baby. I knew I could count on you." He said while kissing my face.

"You can *always* count on me." I told him. We walked to the Lincoln hand in hand, smiles on our faces. Just happy to be together again.

CHAPTER THIRTY-FOUR

For the next couple months while Pharaoh was out on bail everything went smooth. My life had pretty much fallen into a very comfortable routine. I went to school during the day, after class Phee dropped me off at the hair salon. La La watched the boys until I came home at 5 o'clock. And everyday I made sure Phee took La La, my brothers and me to the hospital to visit Daddy for an hour or so. Whenever my Mom wasn't at school, she was with Daddy. I was pretty much running the house by myself, with Pharaoh's help.

We were living like a married couple with kids. Pharaoh had pretty much moved into my bedroom. All his things were there, he helped Mommy with the bills and expenses, and he even had his own key to the house. So, you already know how thrilled I was to be getting my insides pounded every night on the regular! The sex was *soooo* good; that it had even changed the way I walked. I strutted like a grown ass woman now. My hips were starting to spread, and my butt was getting even fatter. You couldn't tell me shit!

On the weekends, Grandma Pearl and a couple of my aunts took turns staying with my Dad. That's when my Mom took a break, and that's when I got a chance to get out the house. Mommy had agreed to let me spend the weekends with Phee at our apartment out in Amherst. Since it was already so obvious that we were having sex, Mommy said it wasn't a big deal. She really liked Pharaoh, and she called him her son. As long as I was with him, she didn't care where I went 'cause she knew he'd take care of me.

Nowadays, my hair skills were up to par, as far as micro braiding and weave extensions. I was getting official with my work. I could glue in weave tracks, sew in bundles, or braid extensions that would make a bitch look like Beyoncé. I had even learned how to do facial cleansings. When Phee saw how good I'd gotten, he scouted me some customers. Some of the dudes that he knew, he'd arranged for me to do their girlfriends hair, some sisters and even a couple mothers. I had set up shop in the basement of our apartment. Phee had real strict rules about who was allowed inside our crib, and *nobody* was allowed upstairs. Not even Nica or Asia, that was the way he wanted it.

Whatever Pharaoh was doing, he'd stepped his game up. That meant my shit was getting upgraded. All my Rocawear and Baby Phat apparel had been replaced with D & G, Louis Vuitton, Gucci and Prada. He'd even bought me some shit that I couldn't pronounce correctly; I had no idea how to say the word Hermes. But I knew it cost a lot of money. The Q45 Infiniti had vanished, now he was pushing a jet black Lexus LS430. On the weekends, a jet black Range Rover HSE. My baby was getting money!

But y'all already know. Mo' money, Mo' problems. That was one of Pharaoh's favorite lines. Fortunately, I'd been able to talk him into putting more money away for a rainy day. Since I was good with numbers, Phee let me manage the money. I never stole a dime, never even was tempted. There were times when he'd come home with loads of money that wasn't even counted. He'd have no idea how much was even there, but I never cuffed a cent. He trusted me, and I wouldn't betray him.

This one particular Saturday morning in the middle of April, I woke up with a nasty ass taste rising from the back of my throat. I had a mild headache and my stomach felt queasy. I jumped out the bed and covered my mouth, then hurried to the bathroom. For the third morning in a row, I vomited into the toilet bowl. When it happened the first time, I had dismissed it. But after two days in a row, I'd gotten very nervous. Phee and I had been sexing up a storm. Fact of the matter is, I'm a 14-year-old nympho. I need it *every*day, at least two or three times a day. There were times when Pharaoh became irritated 'cause he'd be out handling business and I'd make him come home. When he'd get here and find out there wasn't really an emergency, except me needing to get my back blown out, sometimes he got mad. But I always made it up to him, one way or another.

I was on my knees, butt naked in front of the toilet when he walked into the bathroom behind me. "It happened again, huh?" Phee pulled my hair back and helped me to my feet.

"Yeah." I answered softly as he guided me over to the bathroom sink. My feet were freezing from the cold marble floor.

"Hurry up and brush your teeth, so I can give you a kiss." Phee joked.

I rolled my eyes then grabbed *his* toothbrush, "This is *your* fault. *You* did this to me, Pharaoh." I watched him stand behind me in the big mirror over the sink. He just smiled. Since he didn't try to stop me, I put the Colgate toothpaste on his toothbrush and started brushing. Now I smiled back and stuck my tongue out at him.

Phee laughed. "That was cute..." he slapped me across my bare ass with his palm.

"Oww!" I yelped with a mouth full of toothpaste, and jumped at the same time.

"When you finished, I got something else for you to put in your mouth." He left me in the bathroom with a stupid grin on his face.

I know what you're thinking. And I know what I said that I'd *never* do. But I have a confession to make. I've been sucking dick for the past 2 1/2 months now. Turns out that I'm a natural, and to my own surprise, I actually *like* doing it! Nica doesn't know, and I'll probably never admit it.

I finished brushing my teeth then slowly sauntered back into our bedroom. Phee was sitting on the end of the mattress in a pair of plaid Nautica boxers waiting for me. The television was on ESPN, pretty much the only station he ever watched.

"Why you looking at me like that?" I asked him playfully. I still had a mildly lingering headache, but a good nut would solve that.

"You know why. Come here, stop playing." He said. Phee pulled it out and I quickly handled my business. I did it just the way he liked, the way he taught me. I didn't even gag when it was time for him to finish. After that, it turned into an all out brawl. In the end, Phee turned out to be the winner, 'cause before I knew what hit me, my legs were shaking and I was asleep under the covers.

When I woke up a couple hours later, he was gone. I checked the clock; it was almost 11 o'clock in the morning. I got up to start my day. I had two hair appointments this afternoon, plus I still had to clean up and have something to eat ready for Phee whenever he decided to show up.

First, I got into the shower. I washed up real good, moisturized my body and got dressed in a tight Nike tracksuit and my slippers. I started in our bedroom. I changed the linen, dusted, wiped down the walls and wood paneling, vacuumed and organized everything in its place. I hit all the rooms saving the two bathrooms for last, once that was taken care of I started cooking. Hopefully, Pharaoh would take me out tonight. I didn't care where, but I wanted to get out the house.

I decided to just make something quick and easy in case he came home hungry. So I put together some Spanish rice Diablo, nothing fancy but enough to keep me from getting cursed out. Pharaoh didn't demand too much. He wanted the house kept clean, I had to cook everyday, keep my grades up in school, and give him sex whenever he wanted it. All his rules were mostly just common sense to any bitch worth a penny. All I had to do is keep my mouth in check and reaped the benefits of being his queen. One thing I'd learned is, pleasing a man is simple. The hard part is not doing shit that gets on his damn nerves! I was still trying to master that aspect. My biggest problem is being so nosy. I ask lots of questions, Phee *hates* that. Yet, it doesn't stop me from asking him about a gazillion of them everyday. Like now for example.

"Hello?" Phee answered on the second ring. I had just finished making the Spanish Rice Diablo meal. Now I had some free time until 2 o'clock when my first hair appointment would show up.

"Bae, where are you?" I asked softly. See, what I forgot to mention is sometimes I even like to get on his nerves on purpose, just for fun.

"What I tell you 'bout asking me that over the phone?" Phee responded. I rolled my eyes. It wasn't that I'd forgotten the rule, but I knew he wouldn't answer me anyway. So what difference did it make?

"Sorry, Bae." I said quickly. Phee is crazy paranoid, he thinks the feds are listening to every conversation that he has, so he really don't do too much talking on the phone. "I called 'cause I miss you. I made you something to eat, too. You gonna come home?" This was the second question.

"Not right now. Soon though." He said vaguely

"Do you miss me too?"

"Of course, Baby. You know I do."

"So why you didn't call me and tell me that you missed me?" I tried my best to sound wounded.

"I'm sorry. I been a little busy-"

"Doing what?" I smirked 'cause I knew he was about to start getting frustrated.

"Working."

"Phee, you still could've called to check in. You know I get worried about you. When I woke up, you were gone. You didn't even leave a note."

"I know baby, I'm sorry." He apologized.

"I should be done with my appointments by 9 o'clock, I want you to take me somewhere later."

"It depends, because I gotta-"

"That wasn't a question, Pharoah." I interrupted him in a really soft, sensual tone. Most of the time he lets me have my way.

"Where you wanna go?"

"Make it a surprise." I said, in the background I could hear a dude calling his name.

"Aight. I'll take you out, but right now I gotta go." Phee said rushing me.

"Bring me two McDonald's apple pies when you come home" I instructed.

"Aight."

"And, a vanilla milkshake too. Don't forget!"

"I wont."

"I love you Phee, you love me?"

"Yeah." He laughed. "I love you."

I started smiling. "What's so funny?"

"*You*, now stop playing around, I gotta go do something." Phee said chuckling.

"What 'chu bout to do?" I started giggling.

"You stupid, April. I'll see you later." Phee was laughing when he hung up.

I sat at the kitchen table for a Moment, then I called him right back. I knew he'd answer the phone, he wouldn't he able to help it. He answered on the first ring as if he'd expected it.

"One more thing."

"What is it?" He asked.

I stared at the pregnancy that I'd taken after my shower; the white part had turned pink. "Hurry up and get home, it's something important we need to talk about. And be careful." I put the phone down.

*   *   *   *   *

My second client arrived at 4 o'clock on the dot. Nia pulled her white BMW 540i into the driveway and tapped the horn once. I peeped her on the surveillance camera that Phee had installed and went to open the door. I punched my code into the keypad of the alarm system and let her inside.

"Hey girl!" Nia said loudly with a bright ass smile.

"Hi Nia." I returned her smile. I closed and locked the door, then reset the alarm before leading her into the basement. Nia was pretty; she had light brown skin, chinky eyes and a short Halle Berry hairstyle. She was about my height, 5'2" or 5'3" but slim with nice curves and I think she's about 19. I'd met her one day when Phee took me out to eat at the Olive Garden. We were waiting for our table when some dude that he knew named Milk came inside with Nia. Long story short, it turned into a double date and Nia and me became cool.

"That purse is cute." I admired her handbag, that shit was fly.

"Oh thank you, it's Fendi. I got it in Toronto. You gotta tell Pharaoh to get you one, before all the broke bitches get they hands on some knock off replicas." Nina joked.

"How much?" I asked.

"Only $1,200. I got mines last weekend and they only had four left so you better hurry." Nia said sitting down on one of the leather sofas.

I'll have to see what I can do. I got some ostrich skin open toe sandals that'll look good wit' one of those." I said taking another look at the bag; I definitely had to get me one. And my birthday was less than a month away, so it would be sooner than later. "Soo… you ready?" I asked her getting down to business.

"Yeah." Nia stood to take off her jacket. I'd scoped her head out the whole time. This was the first time that I'd be working on her. She told me over the phone that she was about to grow her hair back out, she'd been rocking the short cut for almost three years and was tired of it. She decided to start doing the micro-braids for the time being, because it helps your hair grow faster.

"You washed it already, right?" I asked her as I headed over to the big comfortable chair that I used. I stood behind it and motioned for her to sit down, then turned my attention to the counter that Pharaoh had attached to the wall to hold all my beauty supplies.

"Yup. It's ready." She said sitting down in front of me. I took a handful of the 18" human hair that I'd be using for her hair and showed her.

"Nia, this is the hair I picked out. The color is called "Brown Honey," let me know now if you think it's too light." I advised her. She was gonna be shit outta luck if she waited until I was done, before she spoke up. Nia took the hair and examined it closely. The lighting in this area of the basement was more than good enough for her to make a judgment call.

"I like it. What you think?" She handed it back to me, and watched for my response.

"I think its perfect for your skin complexion." I told her honestly.

"Cool. Let's do it." She said happily.

I turned on the radio to 93.7 and went to work; I'd have to hurry to be done with her head by 9 o'clock. It was 4:10; I'd be cutting it close.

I'm not gonna lie, I was starting to get kinda pissed that Phee still hadn't brought his ass home yet. The Spanish rice Diablo was up in the kitchen inside the oven untouched, and I refused to call his phone again. While I worked on Nia's hair, my thoughts were scattered all over the place. How would my family react to me being pregnant? The thought was scary. Mommy would be more disappointed than anything. Daddy on the other hand when he gets better, will try to kill me! I'm *only* going on 15 next month, I wasn't ready for this. It would be too much for me to handle. What about school? I wasn't trying to drop out and get no GED, I wanted to graduate and walk across the stage. This would be a disaster, Mommy had trusted me to be responsible but I wasn't. I'd gotten lazy with my birth control patches; I hadn't been switching them when I was supposed to. There were even times that I'd go two or three days without wearing a patch. I wouldn't even remember unless Pharaoh reminded me. If I couldn't manage the simple responsibility of birth control, how was I gonna be a good mother? Depression was starting to set in, and I felt my mood getting darker by the second. I decided to use Nia to distract myself from drowning in a sea of pessimism.

"So Nia, what's good? How's school?" I asked while I braided. I needed to take my mind off my own problems. The best way to do that was to listen to someone else's.

"Girl, college is kicking my ass!" Nia blurted with her head down at an angle. "It's a lot of work." She added.

"What's your major?"

"I don't have one yet, 'cause I haven't decided. I'ma wait until sophomore year to choose. But I'm thinking about broadcasting & communications. I think I'd make a cute news anchor or reporter."

I smiled, "Okay! I can see you now, doing your thing on the channel seven news at 6 o'clock." I said.

"Yeah, that would be nice, right?"

"Sure would be. I think you should do it. If that's your goal, go for it." I tried to encourage her. I felt like it was the right thing to do, especially since I was on the brink of ruining my own life.

"BEEP! BEEP! BEEP!"

The sounding of the motion sensor alarm from the driveway interrupted our conversation. I peeked at the black and white monitor that was hooked up to the camera system. Phee's Range Rover had pulled up and parked behind Nia's Beemer.

"How's the college life? Is it exciting like everybody makes it seem?" I asked curiously after the sensor stopped beeping.

"Shit, girl honestly, I don't have a clue. You know, bitches like us don't do too much partying. Our hubby's aren't going for it. When I'm not at class or studying, I'm taking care of Milk. You know how the *wifey* life is. But truthfully, I'll take shopping sprees over college nightlife any day! I can live without the excitement on campus, but I can't live without that Fendi, Prada and Gucci!" Nia exclaimed.

We both cracked up, " I know that's right!" I said laughing.

The basement door opened and I could see Pharaoh's feet coming down the stairs. He stopped at the landing and looked over to the corner where my little station was.

"I'm home."

" 'Bout time." I said rolling my eyes at him.

"I brought you what you asked for." He said quickly. He could see that I was a little tight and was trying to make peace. I just gave him a look, like *so what!* He just stood there for a minute looking at me, I kept braiding.

"The food I made you is in the oven. But, I'm pretty sure it's *cold* by now." I said sarcastically not bothering to look at him.

"Boo, you act like I been gone all day. It's only quarter to six, why you trippin'?" When I didn't answer, he got the point. "I'm going upstairs. When you finished, we'll talk." Phee turned around to go back up the steps. "Hi, Nia? Excuse my manners." He said over his shoulder.

"Hey, Phee." Nia answered sounding kinda uncomfortable witnessing this awkward Moment. Pharaohs disappeared and the door closed. "Girl, me and you got a *lot* in common!" Nia started to laugh.

"He gets on my damn nerves." I continued to braid quickly as possible, I was only a quarter way through and already my feet were killing me.

"Trust me, I can relate." Nia said sympathetically. "I go through the same shit."

Honestly speaking, Pharaoh hadn't done anything wrong. I was just having one of my mood swings. I wasn't really mad at him, but I had a lot on my mind. Although, I wished that he would've made more of an effort to get here sooner, when I told him that I'd cooked for him and that we needed to talk. But either way, it wasn't a big deal; I'd over reacted as usual. Mommy was right; sometimes I was a drama queen.

A half hour later Nia had to pee, so we stopped for a break. While she was in the bathroom, I went over to the coffee table to check my phone. I'd forgotten it was set on vibrate; I'd missed a few calls. Nica, Asia, and some other number I didn't recognize had called like four times. I tucked the phone into the pocket of my Nike hoody and decided to call the two of them back later.

After a couple minutes Nia came out the bathroom, "I'm ready." She said plopping back down into the chair. The sofa felt so good that I hated to stand back up. Pharaoh was gonna have to rub my feet later on. I exhaled, stood up and went back to work. Truth be told, this hair stylist shit didn't even out. I had to stand on my feet and play in another bitch's hair for five or six hours, for $150 dollars. I mean, if I was broke that'd be a different story, but I wasn't. At any given time, all I had to do was go into Phee's sock drawer and take two or three hundred dollars if I wanted it. Shit, I had about $900 in my purse right now, and another three thousand tucked away at Mommy's house. I didn't *need* to do hair, but I wanted to show Phee that I wasn't lazy.

I was doing my thing, Nia and me was kickin' it about some people that we both knew, when my phone went off. "Hold on real quick." I told her. I wiped the grease of my hands with a towel and pulled my phone out. I didn't know the number, but it was the same one that called before. I kinda had an idea what was coming up, so I quickly prepared myself mentally.

"Hello."

"Hi, *April*," the familiar female voice greeted me. "I just wanted you to know that your man just left my house. He really fucked me good too! Now, I'm 'bout to take a nap.

He should be home soon, when he gets there tell him said thank you, because I really needed that." The anonymous caller started to snicker on the other end.

I rolled my eyes. "Well, I'm so glad you enjoyed yourself. And, I'll be sure to give him your message when he gets here, okay?" I said politely. I didn't understand what kind of bitch spends her time playing on another bitch's phone. I'd been getting these calls for the past couple weeks now, but I refused to let this broad here me get angry. That's what she wanted. She wanted me to get fed up and break up with Pharaoh, so she could have a shot with him. Every time I spoke to him he told me he was faithful and not to worry. Did I believe him?

Never.

"I really don't know why he even bother wit you, you're a *little* ass *girl*. He told me all *you* do is get on his damn nerves, that's why he's always here with *me*!" She said trying get under my skin.

I rolled my eyes. "Honestly, I don't know why either. You should ask him next time you see him, sweetie. As for you, he only fuck wit you cause he's a *dog*. That's what dogs do. They run the streets, find a tree to piss on, then they come back home." I had to laugh, I just couldn't help myself. Nia turned around to look at me, she was wearing a smile.

"Oh you think you funny, Bitch! You got a smart ass mouth, how 'bout I put my foot in it!?" My prank caller started to get hostile.

"Listen, Boo. I'm *way* too classy for violence. That's the difference between us. That's why he chose *me* for a wife, and *you* for a mistress. And if you *ever* get out of line and put your hands on me, Pharaoh will blow your fucking brains out, and you know it. But, anyway, it was nice talking to you again. Maybe next time you call, you'll have the balls to tell me your name." I said very calmly before hanging up on her.

I put the phone back in my pocket. I was pissed, and I'm sure steam was coming out my ears by now. Immediately she called back, but I ignored the phone. I grabbed the braid I had been twisting up and went back to work. My phone went off again but I ignored it. "Ouch! Damn, April!" Nia jerked her hand. I must've pulled a little too hard.

"Oh, sorry." I apologized.

"Don't take it out on me." Nia said. I didn't respond. My phone continued to ring but I was done with this broad. I had enough shit to deal with, I didn't have time to go on and on wit' this stupid and obviously bored bitch. One thing for sure, Phee was gonna get his ass cursed out 'cause I wasn't in the mood. *Now* I was mad!

"I had one of those when I first started messin' with Milk." Nia said finally. "She didn't stop til' I hit her one good time wit' my brother's baseball bat. This fool called herself coming to *our* house, to fight *me*, over *him*. I *whooped* her ass."

I listened but violence wasn't my style. Plus, I didn't even know who this girl was. "I'm not really much of a fighter." I admitted.

"Me neither. But sometimes these bum ass bitches only respect violence. If you fuck one of em' up, *real* good. The rest will get the message. I'm not saying you should, I'm just sayin'..." Nina didn't need to finish, I got the point. But I didn't feel the need to wanna fight over something that's supposed to be mines already. For some reason, I wasn't really mad at the prank caller. I was mad at Pharoah.

"I hear you." I said, and then I left it like that.

It was 9:30 when I was done. And, I did a damn good job too. Nia gave me $250. The extra hundred was for the cost of the materials, plus a small tip. I thanked her, and then let her out before locking up and putting on the alarm.

Upstairs, Phee was inside the spare bedroom we used for a closet. When he heard me come up, he stepped into the hallway half dressed. He looked like he was 'bout to get into the shower.

"Baby, I made reservations for 10:15 at Salvatore's. Can you be ready in time?"

"I don't feel like going anywhere. I'm going to bed." I walked into our bedroom to undress. All I wanted to do was take a long bath, shower then go to sleep.

Phee walked in behind me. "But I thought-"

I turned on my heels "What? What did you think, Phee?" I put my hand on my hip and glared at him with an attitude.

"You wanted me to take you out, right?" I looked at the stupid expression on his face, it irritated me even more.

"I told you that *earlier*, but did you hear what I told you just a second ago?" My temperature was up and I was steaming. See, this is just what the prank caller wanted to happen. I knew that by being angry with him I was stepping into her into the trap.

"Listen, Boo, I'm sorry. Whatever I did to make you angry, I apologize. Let's get in the shower, get dressed and go. I made reservations for us. We can talk about it over dinner." He called himself tryin' to reason with me.

"I'm not going *any*where!" I started raising my voice. "Call your little *girlfriend*, the one who keeps calling my fuckin' phone everyday. Take her out to eat wit you!" I yelled at him while I brushed past on my way to the bathroom.

Phee followed me. I tried to close the door on him but he forced it open. "I keep telling you, you're my one and only-"

"I don't believe you. And I don't care whether I am or not. But at least have some respect! Tell her to stop harassing me! I shouldn't have to deal with shit like this!"

My eyes started to water. It seemed like I'd been doing way too much crying these days. The fact that I couldn't control my emotions was starting to really aggravate me.

"Believe me, if I knew who she was I would."

"It's the bitch you was wit' earlier today!"

I could tell that he was doing everything in his power to stay calm and be patient with me. "Boo Boo, I been working all day. Do I gotta put your life in danger, by taking you with me everywhere I go? Just so you can know I'm not playing around?" He backed me up against the bathroom sink and grabbed me around my waist. I didn't answer. "Monday, I'm changing your phone number-"

"*No*, you're *not!*" I exclaimed.

"Yeah, I am. 'Cause I'm tired of hearing 'bout this shit."

"My phone number ain't the problem. *You*, and whatever you're doing behind my back is the problem, Pharaoh!" I accused him. "And just so you know, I'm pregnant! But, it's obvious that neither of us is ready to be parents. So if we gonna do *any*thing on Monday, its go to the damn clinic!" I shouted in his face.

Instantly, his whole facial expression and posture changed. The way he looked at me, scared the shit outta me. The love of my life had vanished, and the devil himself was standing in front of me. His jaws tightened, and a vein appeared on his neck. His arms began to spasm and twitch like he was fighting himself not to hit me.

"April, I'm only gonna tell you this *once*. If you *ever*, kill *any*thing, that has the same blood as me. You'd better kill yourself too." Phee blatantly threatened me through clenched teeth. "I love you more than anything, but don't make me hurt 'chu." He towered over me, with my back pinned against the sink. I didn't know what to say, I was so terrified by the way he was looking at me.

Well, ladies and gentleman, it's official. You just heard it first, I'm gonna have a baby!

I flinched a little when he pulled me close to him, but I didn't resist. "I need you, April. I promise, I'll be a good father. Just give me until the nine months is up and I'll stop hustling. I'll open up a business or something, and go to college like you want me too." That quick Pharaoh's whole demeanor switched back to the Phee that I loved. "We'll be a family, I'm serious."

I was so confused. I loved him, but my parents would kill me! But shit, if I got an abortion, he would *surely* kill me. There was no way I could tell him no. It was *his* baby too, he had every right to feel how he did. My parents would just have to understand.

"You'd better not leave me stranded." I said softly. "Don't make me look like a fool. You know how much shit I'll have to go through with my Daddy?" The thought made me cringe. I was equally scared of both these men, but I doubted that Daddy would actually murder me. Pharaoh on the other hand, I wasn't so sure.

Phee nodded. "Don't worry, I got you." Pharaoh bent down and picked me up, he threw me over his shoulder then carried me back to the bedroom. He dropped me on our bed and quickly pulled off my panties and bra. Within seconds, his face was between my thighs. A couple of minutes after that I almost passed out. I cried his name when the feeling hit me. Just that fast, my attitude and anger had evaporated. Phee had a way of making my pain go away, or at least numbing it.

When I recovered, I decided to return the favor. To my amazement, it tasted like it did when he left this morning. It tasted how it was supposed to! His manhood still had my scent all over it from the last time he'd been inside me, over twelve hours ago. The bitch on the phone was a liar! Pharaoh had been faithful to me today, just like he said. He must've read my mind cause he tugged at my ponytail and let me know that I'd been wrong.

"I told you I was working all day." I heard him say to me while I did my thing. I felt bad that I'd accused him. I didn't respond though, I just kept sucking. I used my mouth to apologize. I did it just the way he liked, the way he taught me. When it was time for him to finish, I didn't gag or cough. I handled my business like a grown ass woman. And he loved every second of it.

Trust me.

Hours later, I lay on top of him while he slept. We never did make it out the house we hadn't even made it out the bedroom. I put it on him good, so I wasn't surprised that he was able to rest so easy. But I couldn't. All the heavy burdens I was carrying kept me awake. Who would've thought that I'd be a mother at fifteen? In the past few months or so, my life had changed so much.

It seems that I only remember to pray when something drastic happens, and hopefully that doesn't offend God. Hopefully he understands. Tonight, I prayed that Pharaoh would keep his promise. I needed him now more than ever. I had a long eight or nine months ahead of me and this was only the beginning.

CHAPTER THIRTY-FIVE

Today was Saturday May 4th. I'd just gotten out the shower, and moisturized my baby soft skin. I put on a black and gold lace La Perla lingerie set and checked myself in the full-length mirror inside our closet. I was almost two months, but I hadn't yet start showing. Still, my body was continuously developing. My waist was now a tad bit wider, and my hips and ass at a whopping 42 inches. I'd been eating up everything in sight; all the food seemed to be going straight to my hips and ass. I'd even grown about an inch or so from the ground.

I took my time squeezing into the brand new $400 black denim jeans, then I admired myself quickly. Marc Jacobs had never looked better. The matching top was a double-breasted vest, made out of denim with gold stitching. Just imagine a tight fitting, double-breasted sleeveless jean jacket. I was rocking some gold Alexander McQueen open toe heels, made outta alligator skin with matching purse, the same kind that Nia had, and belt. When I was done dressing, I put on my lady Rolex and the rest of my jewelry. All together, a bitch was draped in over $15,000 worth of clothing and accessories. I was gonna be the baddest bitch in the spot tonight, Pharaoh went out his way to make sure.

Today was my baby's Birthday. We were on our way to his birthday party, well *our* birthday party. My birthday is the 14th, but he said we should celebrate them together. He said he'd share his birthday with me, if I shared mines with him. So, that's what we decided. We were going to do it big tonight, and then in a few days, do it big again for my birthday as well.

"You ready Mami? The Limo's here." Phee called from downstairs.

"One second, Bae!" I called out. I double-checked myself in the mirror to make sure everything was tight and right.   After a quick application of MAC lip-gloss, I cautiously walked down the stairs, careful not to trip in the 4" heels.   Pharaoh took my hand when I reached the bottom, then he twirled me around to look me over.

"Damn boo! I'm gonna marry you one day." He pulled me into his chest and held me tight. I smiled all over. "I love you forever." He added softly in my ear.

"Love you too."

Phee let me go and just stared. "Baby, you wearin' the shit outta those jeans."

"Thank you." I struck a little sexy pose for him. His tongue was damn near out his mouth as he gawked at the lower half of my body.   "Bae, what about my face?"   I grinned.

"You look like an angel." He smiled at me.

"That's better." I teased, and then scoped him out top to bottom. Pharaoh wore a pale yellow Ralph Lauren Polo Rugby shirt with a big black logo on the left chest. Black denim jeans, with crispy ass wheat colored Timberland construction boots. The 2-carat yellow diamond studs in his ears glistened. A 1-inch thick 30" Cuban link necklace dangled from his neck with a yellow diamond encrusted

Jesus piece pendant. His matching Rolex yacht master was on his left wrist, with a yellow diamond pinky ring, and Phee had his black Pittsburgh Pirates cap on lean. "Awww, you look so cute!" I smiled at him "Happy Birthday." I told him for the gazillionth time today.

"Thanks baby. C'mon, lets go." He grabbed me around the waist and ushered me out the back door. I double-checked my handbag to make sure I had everything while he locked up the door. Hand in hand, we walked down the long driveway of our duplex. The weather outside was beautiful, the news said 68 degrees. But it was almost 11pm, so it would be cooling down soon.

The limo driver opened the back door as we approached, then closed the door once we were seated. I immediately crawled into Pharaoh's lap sitting sideways across his legs.

"Where's my present at?" he asked quietly as the limousine pulled off.

I giggled. "You said not to get you nothing', right?"

"You thought I was serious?" He asked.

"Ummm, yeah I did. You said it a gazillion times. 'Baby, don't get me anything, the baby will be my present.'" I repeated, mimicking his deep voice. "You said that, right?"

"I changed my mind." We both laughed.

"I think it might be too late, Boo." I teased him.

"You really gonna do me like that?"

I gave him a wet kiss on the lips, and then made a loud smooching sound with my mouth. "How was that for a present? Good enough?"

With a big ass grin on his face, he shook his head no.

"I'm sorry to hear that. Maybe next year you won't be so shy to tell me what you want." I gave him another sloppy kiss.

"You know what I want." He tugged at my belt.

I cracked up laughing. "Well, you not gonna get it right now." I said grabbing his hands. "And you better behave yourself tonight, or you not gonna get none later neither." I stuck out my tongue and made a silly face.

"Blah, blah, blah!" He said 'cause he didn't believe me. We both knew he could get it *when*ever and *wherever* he wanted. I wrapped my arms around his neck and we rode the rest of the way in silence, just holding each other.

When we pulled up at Birchfields Bar & Grill, on Main and Glenwood Avenues, the intersection was packed with cars. The whole block looked like a car show. All the Cedar Springs dudes had pulled out their new whips for the spring. There was nothing but shiny, sleek, glistening automobiles with big chrome rims parked outside. The whole hood had come out to show him love for his birthday. There was a long ass line outside the front door. Most of them wouldn't get in, 'cause if you didn't know somebody who was in the circle, you weren't welcome.

I looked out the tinted windows as our black Lincoln Navigator stretch limousine double-parked right in front. Everybody stopped to look at our arrival.

Pharaoh had a big ass smile on his face. "Phee, don't get too gassed up. Most of these people came to get a glimpse of me, not you!" I told him playfully, Phee just laughed.

"You probably right." He kissed my cheek. "I can't wait to show you off. You ready?"

"Yup." I answered.

Phee gave me a look. I already knew what was coming next. "Boo, I know a couple of your girls is gonna be in there. But don't disappear on me, stay close. If you gotta go to the bathroom or sumthin', let me know, I'll send Rell wit' you..." his eyes were trained on mines, I nodded. "*And,* don't let me catch you drinking anything but soda."

I nodded in compliance. "I won't make you look bad." I reassured him.

Pharaoh had told me once before, that I was his weakness. He said that everybody knew I'm his soft spot, so I had to be careful. According to him, if someone wanted to hurt him, but couldn't, they would come after *me* instead. I guess it made sense. He also put me on point about how niggas would try to use me to be his downfall. I always kept this in the back of my mind at all times. Whenever a dude tried to talk to me, I always wondered if he was one of my boyfriend's enemies. Whenever I met a female, and she seemed *too* friendly, seemed to want an instant friendship, I wondered who her boyfriend was, or her brother and if there was some hidden agenda. Pharaoh had turned me just as paranoid as he was, but I guess it came with the territory.

"As far as these dudes go. If I don't introduce you to him, don't speak to him, at all. A nigga say sum thin' to you, ignore him. Somebody touch you, tell me immediately. If a fight breaks out, sit still and don't move. If shots are fired, get on the damn floor! You got it?"

I nodded. "Yes baby."

"Stay close where I can see you. Don't make me have to look for you." He gave me another kiss on the cheek.

"Okay." I answered softly. I hoped he was done. This boy made everything seem like a math quiz. He had rules and instructions for *every*thing. I could only imagine how he was gonna act a year from now when the baby came. Not to mention when I finally got my drivers license and was able to move around on my own. This crazy fool would probably give me a big ass rulebook! Luckily, the driver had come around to open up the back door for us.

"C'mon. Get up." Phee lifted me off his lap. He stepped out the limousine then extended his hand to help me down. I'm not gonna front, I took my time. Imagine me falling flat on my face and how embarrassing that would be.

"Hold this, Baby." I gave him my alligator bag so I had a free hand to hold the door. When I made it to the ground safely, he passed it back. "Thank you." I said as he held me around the middle of my back and walked me to the door. The bouncers greeted Phee with pounds and handshakes, dudes looked at me with quick glances not trying to stare. But I know they wanted to! As soon as Phee turned his head, niggas eyes would wander down to my lower regions, or drift to my chest. It was amusing to me just how bold they were to look my way, when they thought he wasn't paying attention. Then I'd watch then turn to cowards in his face.

"Ladies and Gentlemen! The Birthday boy is in the building! Make some noise, Happy Birthday King Pharaoh!" DJ Huk Her was shouting from the DJ booth. The joint was packed from wall to wall when we stepped inside. People was dancing, drinking and having a good time. Two of the bouncers walked in front of us and led the way to the back area, which was roped off and reserved for V.I.P guests. There were leather sofas and small tables scattered around. All the faces inside this section were familiar to me; only the people who were considered friends had access.

Pharaoh was bombarded when he stepped past the velvet rope with hugs and happy birthday wishes. He paused to kiss the side of my face. "Have fun," he nodded to the corner where I saw my sister Tiffany and everyone else who came here for me. Then he let go of my arm and we separated.

"Pooh, look at 'chu!" Tiffany squealed out to me over the loud music. "You look *sooo* pretty! You're glowing!" My big sister gave me a big bear hug. Everybody gathered around and I hugged them all. Let me tell you who all was there, of course Nica and Asia! Asia's sister Tionna, my other cousins, Tamara, Nikki, Shonika and Janet. Plus, Nia had come with Milk. I'd invited my girl Lauren from the beauty shop and Toccara was with her. Everybody had met each other before I arrived and seemed to get along, so the vibe was great. The food was excellent, and I just kicked it with my girls.

Pharaoh made his way over about twenty minutes later, Xavier was right behind him. He was polite and said hi to all guests and thanked them all for coming. Then, he snatched me up and pulled me over to the corner.

"You enjoying yourself?"

"Yeah."

"Everything good?"

"Yeah."

"Aight. I just wanted to check." He ran his palm under my denim vest and across my stomach where our baby was growing. Then, kissed my forehead. "I'll be back in a second, we bout to take a walk around." Phee said nodding to the other section of Birchfield's, where the regular people who weren't V.I.P were partying.

"Okay." I said watching as he took off. Xavier turned as they walked away and looked at me real stupid-like. I paid him no attention. A crew of them disappeared past the velvet rope, out our section to move through the crowded dance floor.

I was 'bout to go back to my tables when both Cam and Rell walked up to me. "What's up, brothers." I greeted them and gave them both a hug. Rell just gave me one of his silly ass grins, his eyes were glossy and I could tell he was faded.

Cam spoke up. "A, we gonna be over there..." he nodded a couple yards away. " If you need us, just yell or wave or sumthin'. Phee said, when you and your friends ready to go dance, let me know. Me and Rell gonna make

sure niggas don't act stupid, touching and grabbing 'n shit."
Cam said before going back across the room.

Time had started to fly; when I looked at my watch, it was nearly 1:30am. We had eaten up all the food in our section. Tiffany, Tionna, Lauren and Toccara were tipsy and wanted to go dance. So we all decided to go, we all held hands and moved towards the dance floor. I made eye contact with Phee; he winked at me so I knew it was okay. Then I saw him tap both Cam and Rell, they followed us.

As we moved through the crowd some faces I recognized from around town, but most I didn't. We formed a circle and set up shop on the dance floor, we shut it down. DJ Huk Her was playing all the new club joints and we were havin' a ball. A couple dudes must didn't get the memo that I was with Pharaoh, a few got too close. They found out fast. Rill had a big ass silver pistol on his hip, and he loved to see the looks on their faces when he pulled it out.

After an hour or so, we headed back to our section. As soon as I walked past the rope, I saw Phee with a drink in his hand, in front of him was a light skin chick with a tight ass mini-skirt on. She looked familiar, and it only took me a split second to remember. It was the same bitch from the nail salon a couple months back.

Royce.

I played it cool. It had been a good night so far and I didn't wanna ruin it. Plus, Phee wasn't sayin' anything. His mouth was closed, and his face was stone. He wasn't giving her any play, but her mouth kept running. I followed Tiffany back to our side, and everyone was chilling. When I turned around Pharaoh was walking towards me, the bitch Royce was on his heels. As soon as she saw my face, she stopped. Phee couldn't see her, 'cause his back was to her. But I scoped the whole thing. Me and her made eye contact, then she got lost.

A second later Pharaoh was all over me apologizing. "I didn't say nothing' to her-"

"It's okay." I said quickly holding up my hand to stop him. I smiled and kissed him to let him know I wasn't angry. For the next half hour he clung to me, everywhere I moved he was right there. He was going out his way to reassure me that he was all about me, it was cute. We were in the far corner cuddled up on one of the sofas when I got the urge to pee.

"Boo, take me to the bathroom." I said in his ear. We both got up from the sofa, he held my hand and pulled me towards the rope. I just happened to catch sight of the broad Royce standing with her back to me. She was talking to another chick that Phee told me was her sister. Xavier and Phee's other friend Ky was with them. The only reason she had been allowed into V.I.P was 'cause her sister and Ky were together. Suddenly, I got a funny feeling, call it female intuition. "Hold on baby, wait." I tagged at Phee's hand to stop him.

I left him standing there and quickly walked over to my sister, where she was talking to Nica. "Tiffany, do me a favor." I pulled out my phone and scrolled through my call log to find the number that I receive all the prank calls from. I gave her the phone number and some instructions, and then I went back to Phee. He walked me through the crowd, and then stood outside the restroom while I went inside.

I took my time. After I peed, I washed my hands and fixed my hair. My phone rang and I answered it. "Hello."

"That's her number. When I dialed it, she opened up her purse." Tiffany said over the phone.

"Thanks, Tiff."

"What'chu want me to do?" She asked.

"Nothing. I got it." I hung up immediately. I won't lie to you. I had butterflies flying all around my stomach. All along this bitch Royce had been playing on my damn phone,

I was furious. I dried my hands and walked out the bathroom. Phee was right there. Again, he took my hand and I followed him back to V.I.P.

Royce was still standing in the same spot. But Tiffany was right behind her leaning against the wall with Nica, they were talking, looking very nonchalant. If you didn't know any better, you'd think nothing of it. But, I knew better. And I knew Tiffany, and with *or* without me, Royce was about to get her ass whooped. So, I figured that since it was *my* beef, then *I* should set it off!

I let go of Phee's hand and darted in their direction; by the time he turned around, I was out of reach. I was a couple feet away and Royce still had her back to me. That's when I saw the empty Moet bottle on one of the small tables, and I grabbed it. Her sister tried to warn her but it was too late. I feel like the whole thing was happening in slow motion. I just remember aiming, and smashing the champagne bottle over the top of her head. Don't ask me where I got the courage, 'cause I really can't tell you. All I could think about was Nia's words to me, and I could hear her voice.

'Fuck one of 'em up real good, the rest will get the message'. Royce staggered, the bottle exploded against her head and blood splattered *every*where. Then her legs buckled. Next thing I knew, shit got crazy! All the girls that were with me came running, Royce and her sister ended up on the floor gettin' kicked and stomped by at least ten different sets of stiletto's. Things got even worst when security came and tried to pull us off these bitches. When the bouncers started grabbing my friends and me a little too rough, Phee's friends got mad and started pulling out all types of guns. You already know what happened next. Niggas started shootin'! Talk about a disaster?! You had to see this shit. Everyone was running and scurrying to get out the way of the gunfire. Suddenly, the music stopped.

All you could hear was people screaming. How was I supposed to know that what I did would start a damn riot?

Unbelievable.

I don't know *how* he found me. But he found me. Phee picked me up and carried me out the night spot to get away from the action. But that's when we realized that we'd been safer inside! From across the street, gunfire started to spray in the direction of the corner that Birchfield's was on. It sounded like a war zone, the type of shooting you only see on TV. Bullets were flying, bullets were shattering car windows and with my own eyes I saw people actually get shot. By now, I was screaming Phee's name. My heart was beating out my chest, terrified is an understatement.

Pharaoh pushed me down to the ground then fell on top of me. We were lying on the side of a parked car right in front of the nightclub, and I'll never forget the distinctive smell of all that gunpowder in the air. "Don't move baby. We gonna be okay." Phee said shielding me with his body while the gunfire continued. Finally, you could hear Police sirens in the distance. Then and only then did the shots cease. Next, the sounds of car tires squealing as the shooters hopped inside their cars and left the scene. When Phee stood that's when I saw the gun in his hand. I sat up and looked around, people were on the ground all over the place. Some were shot, but most were just ducking for cover. He pulled me to my feet, and pushed me in front of him down Main Street.

"Let's get the fuck outta here." He said pushing me away towards where the limousine was still parked. Everyone else obviously had the same idea, people was running to cars, as the police sirens got louder. I hoped that my sister, cousins and friends were all okay. But I wasn't bout to go back looking for anyone. We climbed into the back seat of the stretch Navigator and the driver pulled off.

Phee looked at me and shook his head, my eyes dropped down to the floor. I knew he was disappointed at me for doing what I did. When he didn't say anything, I just sat quietly. I didn't wanna be the first one to speak.

We rode in silence until the driver pulled over a couple blocks away. I didn't understand why we were stopping, until I turned around and saw the flashing lights of the BPD police cars behind us. Pharaoh saw them too. That's when I remembered that he had the gun. And he was still out on bail for the last gun charge. The look on his face said it all. The police surrounded our limousine; the bright beans from their flashlights penetrated the tinted windows. Our driver wasted no time hitting the power locks. Both doors flew open at the same time.

"Buffalo Police! Hands up, hands in the air. *Now!*"

CHAPTER THIRTY-SIX

You know what? I won't even drag this shit out. To make a long story short, Pharaoh's ass got locked up. *Again*. And as it turns out, the scuffle I started inside the club had *nothing* to do with the ambush shooting outside. Them Midtown boys figured there was no better night for revenge then my Boo's birthday party. The whole party was filled with dudes from the Cedar Springs neighborhood; they'd been waiting outside all night. Soon as Phee came out the club carrying me, they started shooting.

Three people were killed. Two outside the club, one inside. Coincidentally, the dead body inside, was the bouncer who decided it was okay to pull my hair while breaking up the fight. Go figure. And ironically, Phee's friend Ky was killed outside. Ky was the one who unknowingly allowed Royce and her sister Diamond into the V.I.P area. The other victim I didn't know personally, but he was well respected from Phee's block. His name was Toot, and unfortunately he was one of the people I saw get shot outside on the sidewalk. Besides the casualties, seven more people were wounded. The only good news was that all the females that I'd invited made it home safely.

This time Pharaoh had three charges. Felony weapons possession, misdemeanor reckless endangerment, and misdemeanor endangering the welfare of a minor. Guess who the minor is? Yes, yours truly. Imagine the look on Mommy's face when I called at 3:30 in the morning, from Central Booking. When she came to pick me up, she was angry, and then when she realized that I wasn't being charged with anything she relaxed a tad bit. She gave me a long ass lecture about being responsible. I listened intently and didn't doze off at all. I'd put her through so much lately, and she was still digesting the fact that she would be a grandmother before she even turned forty. It was a tough pill for her to swallow. But I had to admit; she'd handled it gracefully. My Daddy on the other hand still didn't know I was pregnant. He was still in bad condition and under heavy medication. He was pumped full of so many pain killers that he was unconscious to everything around him.

But that was an entirely different story. The matter at hand was getting my unborn baby's Daddy out of county jail. Right now, it was 9 o'clock on the dot the next Sunday morning. I'd been up all night since Mommy had picked me up. I sat in the first row of the spectator's section and watched as the two Sheriff Deputy's escorted Phee into the courtroom. His hands were cuffed in front of him, but there was no visible sign of worry on his face as he walked over to where Andrew Lotempio stood at the defense table. He turned around to search the crowd, when he saw me his face lit up. When I flashed him a smile and blew him a kiss, he gave me a wink. The confidence on his face told me that things would be okay. Somehow, some way.

The Judge had been looking down doing some paperwork, when he looked up and saw Phee he took off his reading glasses. "Well, if it isn't Pharaoh Green." He sneered in a sarcastic tone. The Judge turned to look at the district attorney "Let me guess, this is just some sort of misunderstanding, right?" He chuckled along with the prosecutor. I scrunched up my face, these two white men were laughing while my Boo's life was on the line.

"Not quite your Honor. It appears as though Mr. Green here was found in possession of yet *another* loaded, unregistered and defaced firearm. Also, there was a round inside the chamber of the weapon, and he was in the company of a minor under the age of seventeen." The prosecutor said smugly looking over at Phee.

I watched the Judge. I followed his eyes over to the defense table. "Seems that you've acquired some sort of fascination with guns Mr. Green,..." the judge said. Pharaoh leaned over and said something to Mr. Lotempio but he didn't answer the judge. His lawyer shook his head and whispered something back. "...I gave you and your attorney a break last time you were here. Actually, that wasn't too long ago. If I remember correctly, you pled guilty to one count of criminal possession of a firearm and in return, the court was lenient and agreed to 5 years probation. Isn't that correct, Mr. Lotempio?"

Pharaoh's lawyer cleared his throat. "That is correct Your Honor."

"And yet, here we are *again*. Your client hasn't even been sentenced yet on *that* plea agreement and already he's went and bought himself another gun." The judge smirked. "The previous agreement, is now *off* the table-"

"Excuse me your honor, you can't do that!" Andrew Lotempio exclaimed. I watched the Judge laugh like it was the funniest thing he's ever heard. "We had an understanding-"

"A *verbal* commitment. Nothing on paper." The judge snapped. I wasn't any type of legal genius, but this didn't sound too good at all. "How does your client wish to plead in this case?"

"Not guilty." Mr. Lotempio said reluctantly. The lawyer looked pissed.

The Judge shrugged his shoulders. "Fine with me. Bail is set at $50,000, property, bond or cash.

"I object!" Now the D.A. was on his feet. "Your Honor, the prosecution askes that Pharaoh Green be held without bail. He is a threat to society; he is the leader of an organized cocaine operation in this city! He comes from a well-known criminal family and is known for violence. *Please*, he needs to be off the streets." The prosecutor pretty much begged the Judge to keep Phee locked up indefinitely.

"Judge," Phee's lawyer spoke up. "The prosecution has no evidence to support *any* of these accusations, it's all lies! My client has *no* convictions to speak of on his record. He's innocent until proven guilty, and we think that the bail that you've set is quite fair. Thank you."

The Judge just rolled his eyes. "Mr. Green, I have no doubt that you'll make bail, your next court date will be within 90 days. If I were you, I'd stay out of trouble until then. You're already facing up to seven years if convicted...." The Judge kept talking but the rest of what he said was a blur. I didn't hear shit after seven years. These people was 'bout to try to take my baby away from me. Yeah, he had guns. But he wasn't looking to hurt anybody. Pharaoh only wanted to protect himself.

I snapped outta my daze when Phee turned around. "I love you baby." He was smiling like everything was straight. The sheriffs were trying to escort him back out the courtroom, but he was looking over his shoulder at me.

"I love you too." I whispered. I know he couldn't hear me, but I was sure he could read my lips. When he was gone, I gathered my purse and spinned off to contact the bail bondsman who was expecting my call. I was waiting for the elevator when Mr. Lotempio caught up to me in the hallway.

"Good Morning, April." The Lawyer said walking up behind me.

"Hi." I smiled trying to be polite. I really wasn't in the mood for another lecture like the one he'd given me twenty minutes ago when he'd first showed up. He stopped next to me, one hand in his pants pocket, the other holding an expensive looking briefcase.

"Tell Pharaoh to be in my office tomorrow morning. I just told him, but I need you to make sure he shows up. Can you do that for me?"

I nodded. "Sure. Do you want me to be there too?"

He shook his head. "That's not necessary. We need to talk man to man. He's in a lot of trouble. I know this judge. He won't hesitate to send Pharaoh away for 5 or 6 years. I've seen him do it. This is his second felony possession, and he's facing 3-7years, or anywhere in between."

My heart dropped down to my knees. My right hand instantly ran across my stomach. I didn't wanna be stuck raising a child alone. This was turning into a nightmare. Mr. Lotempio must have read my mind. He put his hand on my shoulder.

"I've got an idea that may save him. But, it'll be his decision whether or not he'll do the right thing to be there for you and the baby. Tell him 10 o'clock, my office I'll be waiting."

"Alright." I said as we stepped onto the elevator and rode down to the first floor of the court building. We said goodbye and went our separate ways. Immediately, I called Mr. Baker the bondsman and told him how much the bail was. I had the ten percent with me inside my purse. He said he'd be downtown in ten minutes. I walked outside to the black Lincoln town car that the car service had provided; I climbed into the back seat and waited patiently.

*   *   *   *   *

I was dead sleep when I heard the phone ring. I rolled over when I heard Phee answer it. "She sleep, Nica. I'll tell her to call you back when she wake up." He said sleepily. Whatever she said next I couldn't hear but Phee responded. "Alright, I'll let her know," then he put the phone down on the nightstand.

"Let me know what?" I yawned, then cheeked the clock. 3:26pm. We was both laying in the bed in mid afternoon, still exhausted from last night.

"Nica want you to go somewhere with her later. She said to call her back." Pharaoh lay back down behind me and kissed the back of my neck. "Let me see my birthday present one more time." He whispered.

"It's not your birthday anymore." I teased him.

Phee pulled back the blanket. We were both naked underneath. "Stop playing, let me see it." He used his strength to pull me up on top of him.

"I'ma start charging you." I giggled. I straddled him then climbed up his body until I was sitting on his upper chest looking down at him.

"I can afford it." He smiled looking up at me. I rose up on my knees and cocked my legs wide open above his face. He used his fingers to trace over the fresh tattoo on the skin between my thighs right above my peaches. It was his birthday present. I'd gotten his name spelled out in cursive, two hearts underneath, with a crown on top. Because he was my King. And our hearts were joined together. The artwork was official. The original design and tattoo itself had cost me almost $500. Pharaoh loved it!

"Glad to hear that." I whispered. "You can start paying right now." I smiled then squatted down right on top of his face. That's all he wanted anyway was to taste me. I enjoyed every second and treasured every Moment. Who knew how long this would last. One day I might look up and Phee would be gone. Then, all I would have is these memories. So, for the time being, while we were together, I'd make the best of it. At the top of my lungs I screamed, once I released all my tension I looked down at him and smiled. All the built up emotions I'd had inside me now covered his face, I'd left a puddle of stress behind.

The next couple of days, I took them as they came. Pharaoh hadn't appeared to be slowing down much at all. But he had promised me that he wasn't carrying a gun anymore. I didn't know whether to believe him or not. I wanted to believe that he was smart enough not to get jammed up a third time. But I also knew he didn't really feel safe without one, so eventually common sense told me he'd get comfortable and start carrying a pistol again. The only thing that would change his mentality was to get out the streets completely. This is why I kept reminding him of the promise that he made me. When the baby came, he was done! No more hustling, no more guns. Seven more months, I couldn't wait.

As far as I knew, Phee had gone to the meeting with Mr. Lotempio on Monday. But he was being very secretive about it, which made me very suspicious. Every time I asked him what happened, or what was going on with his cases, he just shrugged it off. He told me not to worry and that everything would be fine. He hasn't seemed too concerned at all, which made me relax. But then again, maybe that was his plan; he probably didn't want to scare me. So far it was working, I trusted him completely. Call me stupid, but I believed he had everything under control.

When Asia and me stepped out the side door of the high school at 2:20 dismissal, the black Lexus was parked in its usual spot. "Bye Asia, see you tomorrow." I gave my best friend a hug.

"Yup, call me later. I wanna know how my God baby is doing." Asia gave me a smile as I headed towards Phee's car.

"I will." I said walking to the curb. Once I was inside Pharaoh grabbed my ponytail and gave me a long wet kiss.

"I missed you." He said in between kisses.

"How much?" I pulled away and tossed my backpack onto the backseat.

"This much." He laughed and made a gesture with both hands. I sat back in the black leather bucket seat and crossed my legs.

"That's it?" I scrunched up my face playfully.

"Not enough?" He asked. I shook my head, no. "This much?" He made a bigger hand gesture.

"That's better." I leaned over to plant a kiss on his cheek. As the LS430 pulled off from the curb, I saw the envious stares. Through the tinted window, I peeped the looks from multiple jealous bitches as the Lexus glided past the bus stop. I rolled my eyes as one bitch tapped her friend and pointed to Phee's car, and then said something. As far as I was concerned, I'd done my job. I'd shown these young broads the blueprint to success. You can lead a horse to a pond, but you couldn't make it drink. I'd gone from a broke, Old Navy shopping freshman. To a paid, wife status bitch wearing Christian Dior and YSL. And, I didn't have to ruin my reputation to do it. That's why most these broads were mad. 'Cause I had no dirt on my name. No high school sex scandals to speak of. It wasn't one boy in *any* high school in the city who could *honestly* say he knew how it felt between these soft thighs. I'm a prize! My man could hold his head high when we were out in public together. That's where these bitches fuck up at. They give away so much butt for free, that when a good dude come along who can afford to pay for it... he don't want it! 'Cause everybody else already had it!

"You hungry?" he asked me while he drove past his block.

"I'll eat afterwards." I said. Phee nodded. He turned up Main St. then made a left into the parking lot of the gas station that sat on Glenwood Ave across from Birchfields. Birchfields was now closed indefinitely, probably because the building was littered with big ass bullet holes.

"Stay right here, I'll be back in a second." Phee parked the car at one of the gas pumps. I looked at the dashboard, the tank was already full. But I remained quiet, curiosity killing me.

Phee got out the car and headed into the gas station, slash convenient store. From where I sat, I could see the entrance. It was like nine or ten dudes posted up outside the front door of the mini-mart. They all acknowledged Phee with either a head nod or handshake when he walked past them. As soon as he disappeared from my vision I opened his glove compartment, it was a bad habit that I had. I wasn't looking for anything particular, just being nosy on some baby mama shit. Honestly, I was curious to see if there was a gun anywhere inside the Lex. Next, I checked the middle console, nothing. I kept one eye on the door of the store, so I wouldn't get caught snooping. I fished underneath both of the two front seats and came up empty. This was a good thing. Two months ago, I would've found at least one pistol, maybe two.

Pharaoh stepped outside the store. My Boo looked handsome in some air max 95's, dark blue denim and whit V-neck T-shirt. His necklace stopped traffic as the spring sunshine reflected off the yellow gold and canary diamonds. He had a big brown paper bag in his hand, he said something to the dudes outside then came to get into the car.

"What 'chu get me?" I grinned at him biting my bottom lip. I didn't really want anything, but I knew he'd probably got me something sweet to snack on. I didn't want a full course meal, but some candy would be nice.

He opened the bag. "Here." He handed me a grape soda. "I just asked you if you were hungry, you said no-"

"I didn't say no. I said I'd eat after the appointment." I corrected him. I took the grape soda then snatched the brown paper bag out his hands. I figured he was playing and there was something else for me inside the bag. I was wrong. The bag was filled with stacks of money. He took the bag from me, closed it up then pushed it under the drivers seat.

"You hungry or not?" He asked impatiently.

"Yes, I'm hungry. But, I'm not supposed to eat a full meal before my doctors appointment." I explained to him with a sad face.

"Then you gonna have to wait." Phee said. He took my face in his hands. "Don't *ever* snatch anything out my hands like that again." He said sternly.

"Sorry." I sat back as he pulled off heading towards my new doctors office. I wondered how much money was inside that bag, and where he'd gotten it. No one else had come out the store behind him, so to me it was a mystery.

Close to twenty minutes later, we both sat inside the waiting room of the doctor's office. There were a couple pregnant soon to be Moms waiting for their check-ups. Phee was the only man anywhere to be found.

"Told you men don't come here." Phee whispered.

"Their husbands are probably at work..." I whispered back to him. "Maybe you should get a damn job. Then *you'd* have an excuse not to be here too." I smiled.

"Oh so now you want a man with a job, huh?" Phee said quietly. "Be careful what you ask for, you just might get it." He smirked at me.

"What 'chu mean by that?" I asked him

Pharaoh started laughing. "Nothing. You'll see."

I shot him a look just as the receptionist called my name out over the intercom, "Ms. Showers, Dr. Rice is ready for you." The voice echoed. Phee and me got up, walked down the hall, and found the right examination room.

Dr. Rice was a middle aged black woman. She was pretty with a short haircut, about 5'6" and slender with smooth chocolate skin. She had one of those real genuine motherly smiles. The first time I'd met her was when I'd first told Mommy I was pregnant. Mommy had come with me to my first appointment.

"Hello April. How are you?" Dr. Rice smiled as we walked in.

"Fine. And yourself?" I asked politely.

"Good. I'm good." She looked past me at Pharaoh. "This must be your boyfriend..." Dr. Rice introduced herself to Phee and they shook hands. I was glad I'd made him put on his polo shirt and tuck in his necklace. Now he looked more presentable.

"Nice to meet you." Phee said quietly as he took a seat over in the corner.

"Well, Ms. April. Why don't you have a seat up here." Dr. Rice tapped the examination table. I used the mini step stool to get up into the surface. "How've you been? Any problems?" She asked me pulling out her stethoscope. She tucked the two earpieces in and put the device under my shirt.

"No. No problems."

"Take a deep breath for me, sweetie." She instructed.

I inhaled deeply, and then exhaled loudly. Out the corner of my eye, I could see Pharaoh watching intently. His eyes were glued on me.

"Unbutton the top of your jeans for me." She said. Once I complied, she placed the stethoscope on my lower belly and listened. After a minute or two, she took out the earpieces and let them fall around her neck. "Everything seems fine so far. You're approaching the end of the first trimester, so within the next couple of weeks you'll start showing. Its very important that you take care of yourself, physically and mentally..." Dr. Rice went into a long speech about prenatal care. What I should eat. What I shouldn't eat, etcetera, etcetera. Phee was listening too. But his ears really perked up when she talked about how having lots of sex was healthy during pregnancy. He's definitely gonna use that to his advantage, I'm almost sure of it. She gave me a couple pamphlets and brochures on maintaining healthy pregnancy. She made me promise to call her night or day whenever I had a question. Then we left the office.

"Where you wanna eat at baby?" Phee asked once we were inside the car. First I checked my watch, it was almost 5pm.

"It's too late. I gotta get to Mommy's house and make sure La ain't kill Cory or Lito yet." I told him.

Phee put the Lexus in drive and pulled out the parking lot, and then he turned to me. "How 'bout we *all* go eat. Then, I'll take y'all to the hospital to see your Dad." He knew this would make me happy.

"Okay." I responded with my face glowing. Pharaoh was very thoughtful like that. He always went out his way to make me smile, even if it wasn't convenient for him.

So, that's what we did. We went and picked up my sister and brothers then went to a buffet called the Golden Coral. The whole time I fell back and let Phee run the show. I was anxious to see how he'd deal with Cory and Carlito.

Those two were more than enough to give you a headache. La La and me kicked it, while Pharaoh handled my brothers.

At first Phee had taken the big brother approach with the boys. That was cool, but with Cory and Lito that would only get you so far. Once they saw that you were too nice, they turned into miniature Tasmanian devils!

La nudged me under the table "April, look!" She whispered nodding towards the ice cream dispenser. The entire buffet was self-serve; my brothers were definitely helping themselves. There was ice cream *every*where, broken cones and sprinkles all over the place. Pharaoh sat across from La, and me with his back to the rising disaster.

"Why would you let them go get ice cream by themselves? Look, they 'bout to get us kicked out this restaurant." I said to Pharaoh.

Phee turned around then shook his head. "What you want *me* to do?" he was oblivious. "They don't listen, they crazy!" He looked clueless.

"Baby... they're six and seven. Stop trying to be so nice. You gotta put a little fear in them-"

"Just slap one of them!" La La chipped in laughing. I couldn't help but laugh along with my sister, plus the look on Pharaoh's face was funny.

"Phee..." I wiped the smile off my face. "Would you let *our* kids act like that in public?" I asked seriously

He turned back around to look at the madness. "No."

"Then I think you should go do something, 'cause in a minute they gonna break that ice cream machine. And that shit look *expensive*! I'm broke, so guess who gonna end up paying for it?" I reasoned with him. Phee cut his eyes at me, and then he got up to go get the boys. La Reina and me were cracking up laughing while Phee went over and obviously tried to negotiate with the baby terrorist. My little brothers showed no respect. Now they were running around acting even *crazier*.

After me and my sister had enough laughs, I sent her to help. "La, go get them before these people call child services or something!!"

Then I sat back, watched her walk over, and snap her fingers two times. Cory and Lito were terrified of my sister; they both ran right to her. She pointed at our table and they scurried over and slid back into the booth across from me.

When everybody was back at the table, I looked at Phee. "You better hope it's a girl!" I told him. He didn't respond.

"Ooh! Mommy said y'all might have twins." La La looked at me "She said that Daddy and Aunt Tracey are twins. And, her brothers are twins too. Twins run on both sides of the family." My sister looked at Phee and laughed. "Look what 'chu got yourself into!" We all started laughing, but Pharaoh was rubbing his temples like he hoped it wasn't true.

"I'm not ready for two." He said looking at me.

I shrugged. Shit, I wasn't even ready for one. But I kept this to myself; we'd already had that conversation. I'd never thought about the whole twins thing. Wouldn't that be something? For some reason, the thought brought a smile to my face.

"I'll babysit for y'all whenever you want." La La volunteered with a real sinister smile.

This time Phee and me burst out laughing. "No thanks!" We both said at the same time. That bitch was crazy as hell if she thought I'd leave my baby with her unsupervised! Wasn't no way in hell.

After desert, we rode back across town to ECMC to see my Daddy. Can I be honest for a second? I missed my father like crazy, but I hated to see him like this. Whenever I was on the way to the hospital, I was excited. I'd have butterflies in my stomach. Then, soon as I saw him in that bed sedated by all the painkillers, I was ready to leave. I didn't understand how Mommy could sit there all day. I think La La and the boys all felt the same way. After 15 minutes inside the room, they started to get fidgety.

Mommy wasn't any fool. "Why don't you take them home so they can get ready for school tomorrow." Mom said to me.

I nodded. "La La go ahead. Tell Pharaoh I'll be outside in a second." I told my younger sister. The three of them kissed and hugged Mommy goodbye, then kissed Daddy glumly and left the room. Mom and me hadn't really had the chance to do too much talking over the past couple of months. With everything that was going on, we both were coming and going in opposite directions most of the time.

"What's the latest with Daddy?" I asked her once my siblings were gone.

"Every time he wakes up, he wakes up screaming in agony. So, they keep him under anesthesia for the pain. Hopefully it won't be too much longer before it goes away." She said.

I exhaled loudly. "I don't know how you can look at him like this all day. It's too depressing for me, Mom. I hope you not mad at me for not coming here more often but it's-"

"April." Mommy stopped me in mid sentence. "Its not your place to be here all day, everyday. That's my job. I took those vows, not you. Even though your Dad and me had separated, I still love him and he's still my husband. This is what being a wife is all about. You'll be someone's wife one day, hopefully Pharaohs..." Mommy smiled and patted my stomach. "So when that day comes, you'll have to be there for him. For better or worst. In sickness and in health. Remember that!"

I nodded. "I wont forget." I responded. What she said made sense. I wanted to ask her if she and Daddy were going to get back together once he got back to normal. But I decided to save that for another time. "We went to see Dr. Rice today, she said everything seems okay." I told Mommy with a bashful smile. I was still a little uneasy about discussing the pregnancy with her.

"Are you excited?" She asked me. Those eyes of hers were once again looking straight through to my heart and soul.

"I'm scared." I told her honestly. "I guess I'm excited too, but mostly I'm scared."

"What are you scared of?" Mommy put her arm around my shoulders.

I paused; I wanted to choose the right words. "Ma, I don't wanna end up a single mother. I don't wanna throw my life away. I'm scared that I made a *big* mistake, but it's too late. I'm confused. One minute I'm happy about it, the next minute I'm worried and depressed." I laid my head on her shoulder and confessed.

"All these things you should've thought about before you put yourself in this position. I did the only thing I could. I made sure you knew how to protect yourself. You and Pharaoh were irresponsible, now you have to live with the consequences. There's no other options, your pregnant, your going to have this baby! And regardless of whatever happens between you and Pharaoh, I'll always be there to help. If I'm able to go to college and still take care of you, La La and those two little devils. I know you can do it with one baby." Mommy stroked my hair. "Don't worry, everything will be fine." She added.

"That's what he keeps telling me."

Mommy chuckled. "I think Pharaoh's going be a wonderful Dad-"

I cracked up laughing, "Oooh Mommy! Let me tell you..." I told my Mom about how Cory and Carlito ran all over Phee earlier at the restaurant.

"April. Your brothers are a different story! You know they don't have any damn sense." Mommy was laughing at my play-by-play recap of earlier at the Golden Coral.

"I know. But I'm just sayin'. Phee got a gazillion rules that he makes *me* follow! He shoulda' gave Cory and Lito some rules to follow!" Mommy and me were rolling. "You should've seen his face, Mom."

"I wish I could've..." Mommy smiled. A couple seconds went by before she asked, "Is he going to have to go to jail?"

I shrugged and shook my head at the same time. "Don't ask me. All I know is what he said."

"What did he say?"

"He said, he's not going to jail. He told me his lawyer worked something out for him. But he won't tell me any details-"

"Did you ask him?"

I lifted my head and gave her a crazy look. "Mommy, are you serious? Who you know that asks more questions than me? Of course, I asked him. He told me not to worry." I said checking my watch. "Mom, let me get outta here, they waiting for me. I gotta get them ready for tomorrow, plus I got a lot of studying to do. Final exams are almost here, and Biology is killing me." I said giving Mommy a hug and kiss. I grabbed my purse, stood up and looked down at Daddy one last time. I kissed his cheek then left my Mom alone with him. If I didn't hurry, Cory and Carlito might tie Phee up and steal his Lexus. The thought cracked me up.

CHAPTER THIRTY-SEVEN

Tomorrow's my fifteenth birthday and Pharaoh is getting on my fucking nerves! He keeps playing with me. First, he promised to take me outta town for the weekend, now he cancelled at the last Moment. See, my b-day falls on a Thursday this year. Not too much, you can do on a Thursday, especially since I have school. Originally, he was gonna take me to New York City to go shopping. We were supposed to fly out Friday as soon as I got out of school and stay until Sunday. But now for whatever reason, it's not going to happen.

I was at home studying, not at my Mom's house. At *home*, me and Phee's house. Mommy was done with school so she'd readjusted her schedule. During the day, she was at the hospital, and then she'd pick up my sister and brothers and go home. I kinda drifted back and forth. Whenever Mommy needed my help, I went over to babysit the boys. Other than that, I was here keeping an eye on Pharaoh. I guess Mommy figured what harm could it do for me to move out. I was already pregnant, and the damage was done. So here I was, going on fifteen years old living in my own house. Cooking, cleaning, paying bills and fucking, like a grown ass woman.

I was sitting Indian style on our bed. My Biology textbook and all my notes were spread out around me. I had a quart of Fudge Brownie ice cream in my hand with a big ass spoon. There wasn't no shame in my game, I was goin' in. My tummy was starting to get a little pudgy, but you couldn't notice it, unless you really paid attention. The way I'd been eating for the past few weeks or so, I didn't know if the belly was from the baby or the food. My brain was working overtime; right now, I had my flashcards out working on some definitions. I had no intentions on letting my grades drop. I'd dug a hole for myself, but I was determined to stay on top of my schoolwork.

Before I knew it, I looked up and it was almost 8pm. Phee would probably be home soon. I put my books away and started to get ready. I freshened up, slid on a clean pair of panties, matching tank top and some tiny boy shorts. I filled the bathtub with hot water and added bubbles. Once the candles were lit, I went downstairs to the kitchen. Earlier I'd made barbeque chicken, broccoli with cheese, sweet potatoes and fried rice. I turned on the oven and put Pharaoh's plate inside to warm it up. Even when he got on my nerves, I still treated him like my King. Every night when he came home, I sat on his lap at the kitchen table and fed him. Then, I took him upstairs, undressed him, sucked him dry and took a bath with him. Afterwards we'd lay around, watch Television and talk about our day. The evenings were our alone time, we both looked forward to it. I did everything in my power to make my man wanna come home to me. Everything he needed was right here.

I dashed up the stairs when I heard my cell phone ringing. I didn't know who it was, but I knew who it wasn't. The bitch Royce hadn't called my phone since I smacked her upside the head with that gold bottle. I'd heard she needed quite a few stitches to close that shit up. I guess Nia had been right after all. Some people only respect violence.

"Hello." I grabbed my phone off the charger and sat on the bed.

"Hey bitch!" Nica yelled at me.

"*Queen* bitch!" I corrected her with a smile.

"*Slut* bitch is more like it! What 'chu doing? You busy?" She asked.

"Not right now. Why?"

"I just wanted to know what 'chu doing tomorrow."

"Don't know. Hopefully something special-"

"Special? Ho, ain't *nothing* special about turning fifteen! You still can't drink, can't drive, *or* buy cigarettes *and* you still jait bait!" Me and Nica cracked up laughing.

"You a *professional* hater!"

"I try my best." Nica joked. "Anyway, what's up wit Phee's friend Xavier, he fine as hell."

"And he's a slut." I thought that would end the conversation.

"So, what. They *all* dogs anyway." Nica guessed wrong.

"Trust me, you don't want *him-*"

"So *who* you gonna hook me up wit'?" Nica asked.

I rolled my eyes. "Hooker, I thought you didn't want no *street* dude. Aren't *you* the one who told me to stay away from the bad boys and the thugs?" I asked her.

"Maybe I was wrong." Nica replied.

See, Nica only knew what she *saw* on the outside. She saw my clothes, the money and how my life changed for the better. But she ain't see how it changed for the worst. Now she wanted to not necessarily be in my shoes, but wear a similar pair.

"No, you were right! Everything not always what it seems Nica-"

"Oh bitch don't be tryna get all deep and philosophical 'n shit with me. I'm tryin' to catch one of Pharaoh's friends. What's up?" She asked again.

My eyes rolled. "They having a party for Memorial Day weekend. I'll make sure you get invited, but you gonna have to hook yourself up. I'm not playin' matchmaker 'cause most of them niggas is good 'n crazy! That way you can't blame me if sumthin' goes wrong."

"Alright. Well I'ma let 'chu go. Happy Birthday! Just in case, I can't get ahold of your nasty ass tomorrow. You prolly gonna be somewhere doing all types of freaky shit!" We both laughed. I jumped as the house phone started ringing.

"Okay. Talk to you later." We hung up. I put the phone back on the charger then grabbed the cordless handset.

"Yeeeees?" I answered with a sweet voice like I was singing.

"How's my boo doing?" Phee asked, and I rolled my eyes again. The fact that he was calling wasn't a good sign. "Fiiiiine." I sang.

"Good. Listen, I'ma be late. *Real* late. I probably won't make it home until early tomorrow morning. I'm still in Cleveland."

"I thought you was already on your way back?" I questioned.   Cleveland Ohio was a three-hour drive. But three hours ago, he specifically told me he was on his way.

"I *was* but something came up. Tomorrow's your birthday so I gotta make sure everything is straight tonight. That way I can spend the day with you tomorrow with no interruptions." He explained. My blood started to get hot. Phee was full of shit.

I paused before I responded, and I chose my words carefully. "Phee, you're full of shit." I said softly.

He ignored my carefully chosen words. "I love you. Don't wait up for me-"

"You get on my damn nerves!" I snapped before I powered off the cordless phone. I sat on the edge of the bed for a Moment. I wasn't tired enough for bed, and I didn't feel like studying anymore. I went into the bathroom and blew out the candles, then went downstairs to turn off the oven. This boy was gonna drive me crazy. This was the shit I had to put up with in exchange for all the gifts. Don't ask me if its worth it, today I'd tell you no. Tomorrow, I'd probably tell you yes.

I grabbed the stack of bills off the refrigerator and went into the living room. I turned on the television, and then went to find my purse. A couple minutes later, I was sitting on the floor in front of the coffee table with our checkbook. I figured I might as well get it out the way. Phee had upgraded me, he'd taught me a lot of things. But, I'd brought some things to the table too. Can you believe that all the money he made, he didn't even have a checking account or savings. When I asked him why not, he said 'cause he couldn't put dirty money in the bank. So I gave him an idea, something I'd learned from Daddy a long time ago. These days, Pharoah got a paycheck every week. He paid a local business owner to cut him a payroll check that he could deposit into our account. It was because of *me* that we *actually* had some *legit* money. Credit cards, debit cards, things we didn't have before. Slowly, I was trying to turn Pharaoh into a tax-paying citizen. How else was he gonna explain being 19 with a Lexus and a Range Rover. They say behind every good man, is a good woman. I was more than a good woman; I was the brain of the operation!

Shit, we even had benefits through his "employer," I wasn't covered but at least the baby would be. My next step was to invest money into some mutual funds. That, and make Pharaoh buy some real estate.

"Beep! Beep! Beep!"

I jumped at the sound of the alarm. Someone had pulled into the driveway. I used the remote to switch the station to the closed circuit channel so I could watch the camera, but I didn't see a car. Sometimes, a cat or squirrel would trick the motion sensor and set off the alarm. I watched for like two minutes, I didn't see anything so I went back to writing this check for American Express. $1,682.77. I used the AMEX card to build up Phee's credit, but he of course still paid for everything with cash.

"HONK! HONK! HONK! HONK!"

This time, it was the car alarm that made me jump. The sound of the Lexus' horn going off made me cringe. Again, I checked the camera. I didn't see shit. Pharaoh had driven the Range Rover to Ohio. The Lexus was inside the garage, and the alarm was wailing. I skipped into the kitchen where the extra sets of keys were; I looked out the kitchen window into the backyard. I could see the garage and part of the driveway. Wasn't nothing moving back there. I hit the button on the key ring to silence the car alarm. The only thing I could think of was a squirrel or cat was trapped inside the garage again, and it wouldn't be the first time.

I stayed in the window. I half expected to see the garage door fly open and some crazy ass car thief speed down the driveway like that movie "Gone In Sixty Seconds." But it didn't happen. As soon as I put the keys back, the alarm went off again. I went back to the window. Nothing. I silenced the alarm again. Then ran up the steps to the bedroom, I threw on some sweats, sneakers and went back downstairs.

After I deactivated that ADT alarm system, I opened the back door. The backlight was on; it illuminated the whole backyard that we shared with the family next door. I walked down the back steps, down the short walkway, up the driveway to the garage. I prayed that it wasn't any damn pit bull or something that was trapped inside. I stood outside the door and listened. I didn't hear no barking or scratching, so I lifted up the garage door. It was dark inside, I looked at the Lexus. Wasn't anything wrong with it? No big furry animals came running out the garage either. Soon as I stepped inside, I found out what set off the alarm.

Two big niggas wearing ski masks over their heads, and they had two big ass guns pointed at my face. I opened my mouth to scream, but nothing came out. All I remembered was the instant pain I felt as something smashed me in the back of my head from behind. My body went limp, and the last thing I remember is my body crash to the pavement.

CHAPTER THIRTY-EIGHT

I woke up to a bucket of ice-cold water being splashed in my face. When I opened my eyes, there were three masked men standing in front of me. All black everything. I had a headache. I was laid across the living room sofa, hands bound together behind my back. You already know what came next, the tears. I started crying uncontrollably as I looked down to see if my clothes had been ripped off, but they weren't. They could have all the money in here, but I didn't wanna get raped. Soon as they saw I was awake, one of them kneeled down and put his gun right between my eyes.

"You better not scream. We not here to hurt you, but you will die today if your not careful." One of the dudes said in a real raspy voice. I heard him, but I was crying so hard that everything was blurred.

"When's Pharaoh coming home?" The same man asked me very calmly like he'd done this a gazillion times before. He still had the gun pushed against my forehead. A chill went through my spine when he mentioned Phee's name.

"He's out of town. I don't know when he's coming back." I whispered. The dude used his hand to smack me on the back of my head. That shit hurt like hell, but I somehow managed not to scream. I held it down, but I began to cry even harder.

"You a bad liar shorty. I'm not gonna keep asking you the same questions all night." The man warned me. "You see these two niggas behind me? You keep lying to me and I'm gonna give them a box of condoms and let 'em take turns with you." I looked at the two big goons pacing back 'n forth in my living room. Their eyes were all I could see behind the ski masks, and I could tell they were looking at my body.

I started running my mouth. "I don't know when he coming back, but I know where his money is. It's about $40,000 upstairs inside the safe, plus we got lots of jewelry. I'll give you *every*thing, just please don't hurt me. Take the money and leave." I was crying hysterically, I couldn't help it.

It didn't take raspy voice long to decide. "Bring her upstairs!" He ordered the other two, and it became clear to me who the boss was. The biggest one scooped me up off the couch like I was a twenty-pound dumbbell; he threw me over his shoulder and carried me up the stairs. You already know this nigga made sure to palm and grope my ass the entire way.

Inside the bedroom, the giant tossed me onto the bed. "Where the safe at?" raspy voice asked me. I took a deep breath. I had two options, I could tell him where the *real* safe was. Or I could tell him where the dummy safe was. The *real* safe had $75,000 inside plus all our jewelry. The dummy safe had about $10,000 inside, and a bunch of slum jewelry. The $10,000 was mostly in one-dollar bills, but it was inside two vacuum-sealed blocks. From the outside, it looked more like $100,000 'cause all you could see was hundred dollar bills. It was designed to look deceiving, and make you think it was *way* more than it actually was. But once you bust the plastic open, you'd be pissed because the rest of the bills, were George Washington's.

"Inside the closet, in the back on the floor." I directed him. The two goons went to investigate. Raspy voice stayed, he stood over me as I lay across the bed. I avoided eye contact 'cause I didn't wanna make him angry. All I could think about was what Phee would do to this fool if he ever found out who he was. They was probably some Midtown dudes, I was willing to bet.

"Found it..." one of the dudes yelled. "We need the combination!"

A light bulb went off in my head. I knew that voice. I hadn't heard it that many times, but I was a hundred percent sure that I knew who it belonged to. My heart sank as I vividly remembered the night Phee confided in me about not being able to trust anyone. At that Moment, I could hear his voice echoing in my head. And as silly as it may have seemed *then*, it was only now that I truly understood what his words meant.

If I focus on my enemies, who's gonna protect me from my friends?

"Five... fourteen... eighty seven." I told raspy voice the combo before he got a chance to ask. He repeated my answer to the two dudes inside the walk-in closet, and I prayed that these fools were too dumb to cut open the plastic and count the money.

A minute later, they came out carrying the two blocks of money and the fake jewelry from the dummy safe. I could tell they were smiling, even though I couldn't see their faces.

"Find a bag to put that shit in." Raspy voice told his goons. Once they put everything inside Pharaoh's big Jordan duffle bag, I expected them to leave. But they didn't. Raspy voice picked up the cordless phone from the nightstand. "Your gonna give me Pharaoh's phone number. I'm gonna dial it. Then your gonna tell him to come home. Tell him you miss him, or tell him whatever it takes. I know he'll hurry up to get home to your sexy lil' ass! I know *I* would." The raspy voice dude held the phone like he was waiting for me to call out the number.

"I gave you the money. What you need him to come home for? I'm not doing that." I told him through a series of sniffles.

He put the gun back to my forehead. "What's the number?" he asked.

I closed my eyes. I didn't know what to do. Well, let me rephrase that, I *did* know what to do and I knew what I *shouldn't* do. "I'm not gonna set him up for you. You have our money, just leave us alone!" I said through my tears.

"*Fuck* that money! We ain't come here for no fuckin' *money*! Either you going to tell Phee to come home, so we can kill *him*, or we gonna just kill *you*! But, one of y'all gonna die *tonight*!" At that Moment, the leader of the three goons made their intentions very clear.

All of a sudden, I felt like I was going to throw up. This was the end for me. This was how I was gonna die? Even if I called Pharaoh and begged him to come home 'cause I needed him, yup he'd eventually come, but these fools would probably kill us *both* anyway. Why would they leave me alive? I was a witness. I knew how many of them were here, their sizes and body structures and I knew one of their voices. Once Phee came home, we'd both be dead.

"Call him yourself," I finally said, while praying these wouldn't be my last words.

The dudes started laughing. "Okay, Shorty, I'ma stop being so nice to you. You think this shit is a game..." dude with the raspy voice pulled out one of those jumbo-sized freezer bags from his hoodie pocket, along with a long shoe lace. "All I'm asking you to do is get him here, and then we'll let you go. We don't have no problem with you, this a personal beef wit' Pharaoh." He stared at me.

When I didn't respond, he tried to put the freezer bag over my head. I started kicking and screaming, and that's when the dude pulled out this big ass crocodile Dundee knife and put it to my belly.

"I'll cut your fucking baby right out your stomach if you don't shut the *fuck* up!" He barked at me, with the eyes of a psycho killer. The look he was wearing scared the shit outta me, and I immediately closed my mouth. Once I was completely silent, one of the goons put some duct tape over my lips. Then the dude with the raspy voice pulled the clear plastic freezer bag over my head. "You   got about 10 minutes at the most before you suffocate inside this bag. Whenever you ready to cooperate, show me a sign." He smoothed the plastic over my face to make sure there was no air trapped inside, and then he used the shoestring to tie the bag tight and securely around my neck. And honestly, that's the Moment I realized that I was going to die.

Almost immediately, I started having trouble breathing. I had duct tape over my lips. Plus, the string was so tight around my neck that it was becoming nearly impossible. I opened my eyes, and saw that the freezer bag was starting to get real foggy. Dude was standing there holding the cordless phone. But, I couldn't betray Pharaoh like that, could you imagine the look in his eyes when he'd come home and see that I led him into a trap. I was starting to get light headed. Every time I tried to inhale through my nose, the plastic pressed against my nostrils limiting the oxygen.

"I'll take it off right now. But you better cooperate. Call Pharaoh, and tell him to come home. You ready?" The dude with the raspy voice asked me. I was getting *really* dizzy. I thought about Mommy, La La and the boys. Then, my Daddy crossed my mind. He would go crazy when he got better and Mommy had to tell him that I was dead. "This your last chance, April! Nod your head and let me know you ready to call Pharaoh! Or, you're gonna die right here, you *and* your baby." I heard him say.

I *thought* about it, trust me I did. But I couldn't see myself calling Phee and pretending to be okay. How could I call the love of my life and tell him I need him home to me, so that these dudes could kill him. I'm selfish, I'm materialistic, and the list goes on. But *this*, I wouldn't do!

As I started to pass out and lose consciousness, I shook my head. I shook my head so these niggas would know that it wouldn't be that easy. I displayed the ultimate defiance with my gesture. I hardly had any fight left in my body. I was extremely weak and emotionally drained, but with all the strength I could muster, I shook my head to show them that I was loyal to my man. If they wanted Phee dead, they would have to do it without me, because there no way I was going to help them. As my muscles relaxed, I began to feel myself drifting off. Involuntarily, I lost control of my bladder, I began to pee on myself and simultaneously I started choking at the same time on my own saliva.

The plastic was so foggy that I couldn't see shit, and my tears burned my eyes. I began to see flashes of my life; all the highlights and low points came together, edited together like a home movie. I cursed the day that I saw Phee standing outside. I cursed the day of Daddy's accident, knowing that if he were healthy he would've kept me sheltered from this lifestyle. *And*, I cursed God, for allowing it all to fall on my barely fifteen-year-old shoulders.

I stopped fighting. I just gave up. I made my peace, relaxed and prepared to let death take me over. I had wanted so badly to be a gangster's wife, but now it didn't look as though I'd ever get my ring. I just prayed the Phee would somehow know exactly what I'd ultimately sacrificed. Maybe I wasn't that selfish after all.

I smiled.

Xavier thought he was slick. But what he didn't know, was that Phee had paid a lot of money for the GPS device that was hidden inside the bundles of money that they were stealing. So, as the life slowly drained from my body, I found comfort in knowing that Phee would have the last laugh.

I took my last breath, and I let my eyes close for the last time.

Coming Soon...

THE COLDEST APRIL EVER

The Sequel to 'April Showers'.

TREY BRANSON

The Coldest "April" Ever

A...

The Sequel to "APRIL SHOWERS"

Trey Branson, is a 32-year-old Author and Freelance Journalist from Buffalo, New York. He is the author of eight books, including; No Justice No Peace: Trayvon's Revenge. Log onto www.TreyBranson.com or contact at treybranson360@gmail.com

Made in the USA
Middletown, DE
09 April 2016